THE
EMPEROR'S
SWORD

TURNER PUBLISHING COMPANY
Nashville, Tennessee
www.turnerpublishing.com

Cover design: Mark Swan
Text design: Karen Sheets de Gracia

LIBRARY OF CONGRESS CATALOGING-IN-PUBLICATION DATA
Names: Klavan, Andrew, author.
Title: The emperor's sword / Andrew Klavan.
Description: First edition. | Nashville, Tennessee : Turner Publishing Company, [2021] | Series: Another kingdom ; book 3 | Summary: "Having survived the Nightmare Feast, Austin Lively is living the dream. He has returned to Hollywood and his movie career is in full swing. His new script, Another Kingdom, has been unexpectedly purchased by a top producer at an enormous price. Beautiful women flock to his bed, movie stars court his attention, and the powers-that-be are predicting stardom. His only problems: a recurring vision of a magical landscape he can't quite remember, and a giant mouse who seems to be following him—a giant mouse with a woman's face. After his beloved Jane Janeway is accused of murder, Austin begins to realize that this dream he's living is a nightmare in disguise. He is caught in the coils of a terrible magic, and the only way he can save his soul is to give up his success, re-enter the Eleven Lands, and find the Emperor Anastasius so he can restore Queen Elinda to her throne. But when he arrives at the emperor's encampment, he is shocked to find Anastasius dead. With a weird hitman on his trail in Los Angeles, he must break Jane out of prison before a murder plot takes her life. In the Eleven Lands, he must follow the Emperor into hell itself where he will face the most shocking revelation of all"—Provided by publisher.
Identifiers: LCCN 2020053845 (print) | LCCN 2020053846 (ebook) | ISBN 9781684422708 (hardback) | ISBN 9781684422715 (epub)
Subjects: GSAFD: Fantasy fiction.
Classification: LCC PS3561.L334 E45 2021 (print) | LCC PS3561.L334 (ebook) | DDC 813/.54—dc23
LC record available at https://lccn.loc.gov/2020053845
LC ebook record available at https://lccn.loc.gov/2020053846

9781684422708 Hardcover
9781684422715 eBook

PRINTED IN THE UNITED STATES OF AMERICA

21 22 23 24 25   10 9 8 7 6 5 4 3 2 1

ANOTHER KINGDOM

THE EMPEROR'S SWORD

BOOK THREE

ANDREW KLAVAN

TURNER
PUBLISHING COMPANY

This book is dedicated to
Michael and Alissa Knowles,
in friendship.

"For we do not wrestle against flesh and blood, but against the rulers, against the authorities, against the cosmic powers over this present darkness, against the spiritual forces of evil in the heavenly places."

——Ephesians 6:12 esv

GALINIAN COUNTRYSI

NETHERDALE

RUINS OF GALIANA

SHADO

Southern Gate

Edgemond

Eastrim

Northern Gate

OOD

1

With a savage battle cry, the knight in silver armor plunges into the swirling snow. As he rushes from the darkness of the cave into the blizzard, he is nearly lost to sight in the vortex of white and wind. His weirdly flowing armor becomes one with the storm. His sword, clasped in both his mailed hands, raised to deliver a slashing strike from behind his right shoulder, is nearly invisible. Only his face, bared beneath his lifted visor, shows clearly through the wild weather. His dark eyes blaze with fury and fear. His mouth gapes wide on a ragged and murderous cry. He rushes toward the beast.

The white beast is part of the weather too—lost in the weather too: a hulking, hungry presence as it moves to reclaim its den. The knight can see the creature clearly through the tempest only because its eyes—its ravenous eyes—glow an unnatural red and shine out of the depths of the maelstrom. The knight can hear the thing as well. Even over his own hoarse shout, even through the hoarse and steady roar of the wind, he can hear the Yeti growling low. That growl—it's not a fierce sound. No. It's a growl of satisfaction. The beast can smell the knight. He can see him with his red eyes, see him charging. He's growling with anticipation of a fresh kill, a fresh feast, a new pile of bones to add to the others already scattered in the shadows of the cave.

As the knight draws back his sword for the attack, the Yeti flexes his massive paws so that the claws switchblade out of them with a whispered snap. The claws are curved and sharp and daggery and, like the knight's armor, nearly invisible in the snow.

Another split second of swirling white confusion, of shouting and growling and the roaring wind. Then the two opponents clash, the knight's sword swinging, the beast's claws slashing.

The whirling storm turns red.

2

"THE WHIRLING STORM TURNS RED."

Just there, on what I hoped was a dramatic note, I paused and lifted my eyes to the actors.

There were twelve of them seated around the long table, each with a script lying open before him or her. Most of them weren't looking at their scripts, though. Most of them had their eyes lifted toward me, their gazes trained on—locked on—me. Such yearning, eager gazes. One might even say desperate gazes, if one wanted to revel in one's own power over these people, and, oh, I so did. I wanted to swim naked in the dark pools of their sycophancy.

I could tell just by looking at their faces that they were awed by the genius of my writing. At least, I could tell they were pretending to be awed by the genius of my writing—and really, this was Hollywood, so what was the difference? In this town, to be admired and to be in a position where people had to pretend to admire you were pretty much the same thing. In fact, the latter might've been a little tastier than the former, when you came right down to it.

Most of these beauties, these artists, these thespians—from the sinewy old hack who was up for the role of the evil wizard to the dumpy-yet-sensual babe who looked right for the smart-mouthed waitress part—hadn't been signed yet. Indeed, most of them had agreed to participate in this table read in the hope of winning the favor of the writer/producer, namely me. So here we all were, in the first dark of a late spring evening, in one of the conference rooms at my agent's offices, with massive windows on the twinkly colored lights of Beverly Hills, seated around a table shaped like a deformed kidney and delivering the first-ever dramatic reading of my screenplay *Another Kingdom.*

The writer/producer—did I mention that was me?—was seated at what would have been the head of any ordinary, non-deformed table. It was my job to read the descriptions of the action out loud. The actor-hopefuls were there to deliver the dialogue of whatever character they'd been assigned. That way, I'd be able to hear what I'd written, be better able to judge whether the lines would work outside my imagination. My agent, Ted Wexler; my coproducer, Mel Hirscheim; and the director, Andy Brown—all seated against the wall to my left—would also listen and give me rewrite notes. It was an early stage in the process of making the film.

But for the actors, this was do or die. They were here to show their stuff, to impress me—and Ted and Mel and Andy too, but mostly me—so I would hire them, cast them in the parts they were reading. So again, who cared what they thought of my writing as long as they had to pretend to love it? They were only actors, after all. By nature, they were slaves to their ambitions, addicted to their need for the applause of strangers. For a part in a big-time production like this? Any one of them would have chopped up his grandmother and sold me her body parts for food if he thought it would increase his chances of getting a nod. So they were all chained to my approval like ragged captives dragged behind the chariots of a homecoming king. What choice did they have what to think of me? They could either call me a genius or toddle off in their jalopies to the next cattle call. Whichever. It certainly made no difference to me what they really thought.

With one exception. The girl at the end of the table, last seat on the right side. Jessica. Jennifer. Juniper. Something like that. I did care what she was thinking. Even as I was reading, that's all I was really wondering about.

See, Jennifer believed she was here to audition for the central role of Lady Katherine. But she was not here for that, not at all. Ted and I were desperately seeking a major movie star for that part. Jessica was here because her face was the face of an angel from some pornographic heaven, slender, smooth, and doe-eyed, framed by straight cascades of glistening golden hair. Her body, hidden now under a long, baggy sweatshirt, had (as I knew from our original meeting) a shape of impossible allure, tight and sleek at waist and leg but blossoming at breast and hip with breathless generosity.

My point is: Juniper or Julia or whatever-her-name-was was here because I wanted to have sex with her. It was my sincere belief that she would sleep with me in hopes of landing the Lady Katherine part. In return, I would find her some small part with a line or two, maybe as a diner in the restaurant scene at the beginning. So it would be a big break for both of us.

So yes, I cared what Joanna or whatever was thinking. So when I looked up from reading the blizzard set piece, the exciting storm-fight between our hero and the abominable snowman, I did a quick survey of the eager, not to say desperate, faces gazing my way. I pretended to gauge their opinions of my work, as if I gave a damn. But really, it was just my way of stealing an ever-so-casual glance at Josephine or Juliet or whoever she was, so I could get a sense of what was passing through her shapely mind.

For a second, our eyes met, hers and mine. And even from all the way down the long table, I saw her yield, the black pools of her pupils softening and expanding to allow my hard glance to penetrate her consciousness to the core. The edges of her red, rich, full, red, rich, red mouth trembled upward like the petals of a flower in a breeze.

I looked down at my script again.

"For a moment, we can see nothing of the battle," I read. "We can only hear the sting of the sword as it meets the first vicious swipe of the monster's claws."

That's what was on the page anyway, so I guess that's what I read. But I wasn't listening to myself anymore. I was listening instead to my own quiet, contented psalm of triumph:

Oh Jillian. Or Jennifer. Whoever you are. I am going to have you.

AND I DID have her, whoever she was. That very night, in the vast bed in the vast bedroom of my vast new apartment high in the Westwood sky above Wilshire Boulevard. And for my own sake, for the sake of my own dignity and sanity, I do want to record those last few moments with her before everything in my fantastic new life began to unravel.

Because she was, truly, beautiful. Jessica or Jennifer or Johanna or whatever. Naked, she was a sweet hymn to material creation. The rose and ivory of her skin. The flowing liquid shape of her, from her cuddly shoulders to her suckable little toes. The silk of her hair between my fingers and the honeyed cream of her breast against my palm. And every time I went into her, and every time my midriff slapped against the infinitely yielding curve of her perfect bottom, and every time her head reared back toward me till my lips could press into her reddening cheek, and every time she let out her own unique signature cry of animal pleasure—or the pretense, at least, of animal pleasure, and this was Hollywood, so what was the difference?—every time, I asked myself: What greater bliss on earth is there than the flesh of a woman? Really. What greater bliss than flesh on flesh, my flesh into her flesh, dream flesh becoming girl-flesh, girl-flesh becoming pleasure, pleasure becoming bliss, and what bliss greater?

It was, I mean to say, not for nothing that I had become the low and scurvy little dirtbag I had recently become. I had done it for this, this bliss, this pleasure that was everything.

I READ SOMEWHERE you're supposed to feel sadness after an orgasm. *Tristesse*, the French call it. But what do the French know? I felt terrific. The girl rolled over onto her back when I released her. Lounged there beneath me with a sly smile, her blue eyes misty, her cheeks still flushed nearly scarlet.

She was clearly thinking: *I have the part of Lady Katherine for sure!*

And I was thinking: *Wow! Look at that. What a wonder she is, and I just had her. Me! Austin Lively!* She was the seventh in just over a month and a half. The seventh spectacular beauty I had brought to this bed in the last six weeks alone. And I was thinking: *Wow! Good for me!* I mean, really, screw the French and their *tristesse*. I felt absolutely wonderful.

I lowered myself down on top of her and lavished kisses on her breasts and her neck and her cheek and her lips until she must have thought I loved her or at least knew her name.

But it wasn't her I loved. It was life. This life. This new life of mine as a guy with money and power and a movie getting made. A guy who was therefore able to bring girls like this to his bed.

I made my gentle excuses and left her lolling in the sheets as I padded naked into the bathroom, the vast bathroom with its rose marble walls. I washed at the sink. Brushed my teeth. Stood another second or so grinning at my own reflection. Who was this happy man? I wondered. This Austin whom I barely knew? How long ago was it—only six months?—that he was a nobody on the road to nowhere, a hobo shadow roving into the vanishing dark?

I had come to this town—oh, years ago now—right out of film school, aspiring to become a moviemaker. Well, I had failed at that. I had talked my famous brother into landing me a job at a production company as a reader of other writers' works. That had driven me half insane. Then, after my kid sister, Riley, went all-the-way insane, after she disappeared and hid herself away in the funhouse at a Walnut Creek amusement park (long story), after that, I had headed north to find her and bring her home. And when I had found her, and when I'd returned with her to LA, even my crappy, hanger-on reader job was gone. I was out of work completely in a town where only work matters. A non-person in a city that runs on personality. It felt as if the last shred of my identity had been torn from the obscure figure that had once been me, like clothes ripped off an invisible man.

I was nobody then. When I was at home, the place was empty. I was all washed up in the City of Angels.

That was six and a half months ago. Six and a half months—and one phone call. One phone call from Solomon Vine.

And that, my friends, had made all the difference.

I winked at my reflection. I tousled my own hair in affectionate congratulations. I turned to glance at the small bathroom window that looked out toward the Hollywood Hills.

And I screamed.

It was a real scream too—a real, half-hysterical high-pitched shriek. I staggered back across the tiled floor, my hands thrown up in the air.

"Oh my God!" I shouted.

Suddenly, a hand seized me by the elbow. I shrieked again in purest terror. I spun around.

But it was only Juniper, small and naked and afraid, grabbing hold of me.

"Jennifer!" I shouted wildly.

"Jessica!"

"What?"

"For God's sake, Austin, what's the matter?"

"The window! Look at the window, Jessica! Look!"

She looked. She looked harder. She narrowed her eyes.

"What?" she said. "I don't see anything. What is it? There's nothing there."

"Nothing . . ." I whispered.

I looked too. Stared at—gawped at—the windowpane. I took a slow step toward it, and then another, the floor tiles cold against my bare feet. I leaned, tremulous, closer to the glass, half-expecting the horror to jump-scare out of the darkness at me.

But no.

The window was at the height of my face. My flabbergasted image was reflected on it, transparent. Through my own features I saw the night city stretched out into the distance. A starless, sapphire sky. White lights and red lights and green lights strewn across a rolling sable plain like jewels scattered from a genie's hand. The blurry streaks of cars on the freeways. The spotlit Hollywood sign far away and the lighted spear of the cell tower behind it. The anonymous jags of the Santa Monica mountains finally, like a rising, falling stain on the horizon.

And—as Juliet said—nothing else. That was all.

Her voice came softly from behind me. "What? What was it?" she asked. "What did you see?"

I shook my head quickly. "Nothing. Nothing. A trick of the light. I thought someone was standing there. It must've just been my reflection."

After all, what else could I have told her? The truth? Forget it.

She would have thought I was crazy. She would have run from the apartment. She would've called the police.

But I was not crazy. I had seen it. It had been there. A thing that could not exist, standing in the night, standing on the ledge where nothing could be standing.

An enormous rodent with the face of a woman.

3

I COULDN'T GET TO SLEEP AFTER THAT, NOT FOR anything. I lay on my back awake, staring at the ceiling mostly, but also, from time to time, stealing wary glances at the bathroom doorway. Jessica was with me, softly snoring in my arms. I didn't send her home as I usually did with such one-offs. I needed her there, someone to cling to. I was afraid to be alone in my own apartment.

That thing—that thing I had seen. It absolutely terrified me. And you may say, Well, yeah, Austin, it was a gigantic rat with an eerily human female face grinning in at you through a window on the thirteenth floor; that *is* pretty spooky. But it wasn't that. It wasn't just that. There was something more, something even scarier.

I recognized it. Whatever it was. I knew it. I had seen it somewhere before.

But where? How could I ever have seen such a thing? And if I had, how on earth could I have possibly forgotten it?

The sleeping girl murmured against my chest. I looked again across the top of her golden head at the bathroom door. I racked my brains, trying to remember why that creature seemed so familiar. Was it an image from a movie? A dream? An idea I'd had for a story? After all, it wasn't possible it was real, was it?

Was it?

I searched my memory. I found myself thinking back—six and a half months back—to when I was on the road north, hunting for my sister, Riley. She had been hiding out. Her crazy videos had pissed off some even crazier thugs. Thugs and the police, both were after her. And they came after me, too, as I tried to find her. It had been a weird, dreamlike journey even at the time, but now . . . Now, I could only remember shreds and snatches of it. The details were gone. Just gone. Why was that?

Hours went by in meditations like these. Sleepless hours. I don't know how many. But finally, I couldn't stand it anymore. Gently, I worked my arm out from beneath the girl's shoulders. She gave a low complaint and rolled onto her side, still asleep. I sat up, gazing through the shadows at the bathroom door.

I slipped out of bed. I had to go look at that window again. I had to see for myself that the creature had not returned, that it wasn't sitting out there, peering in at me. I didn't want to look. But I had to. I couldn't stop myself.

Naked, I moved across the room. The bathroom door was half open. I held my breath. I pushed the door in the rest of the way. I peered into the darkness—darkness lit to gray by the city lights outside. I glanced back over my shoulder to make sure the girl was still sleeping. Then I stepped across the threshold.

And I fell—dropped—plummeted through nothing. The floor had vanished! I was falling down into darkness!

I cried out, stupefied. I flailed at invisible emptiness. I screamed and twisted. I fell down and down. The gray glow of the bathroom spiraled away into the distance above me. It grew small—a point of light. Then it was swallowed by the darkness, and the darkness turned black. I could not stop screaming, flailing, falling. My gut went hollow as I realized: I'd dropped too far, too long, to land safely. When I hit bottom, I was going to splatter and die.

Then—*whump*—I did hit bottom. But I didn't die. I dropped onto my back hard, like a cinderblock hurled from a height. My scream turned to dust as the breath was knocked out of me. I lay coughing and gagging with terror, gasping for breath. I felt dry, rotten leaves under me and cold, damp earth. I rolled over on them, groaning. I pushed up with one hand. I reached out into the darkness. I touched something. Stone. I grabbed the top of it. Hacking, fighting for breath, I pulled myself slowly to my feet. My whole body was trembling violently. I still couldn't fully grasp what had happened to me. I was too dazed and jarred to be as frightened as I should have been.

Then I looked around me—and I was frightened. Plenty frightened.

I was in a graveyard in a forest. Slanting stones and monuments dotted a clearing ringed with shadowy pines. Mist twirled among the graves. An eerie light that seemed to come from nowhere and everywhere at once gave a living aspect to the staring statues that marked some of the burial sites.

I looked down at myself. I wasn't naked anymore. I was dressed in a strange peasant outfit, breeches and a loose shirt made of some rough cloth like burlap.

Still shaking, still dazed, I massaged my aching head. What the hell? What was happening to me? This had to be a nightmare, right? I mean, I'd just dropped through the bathroom floor onto the set of a horror movie—what else but could it be a nightmare?

But I couldn't wake myself up. I pounded the heel of my palm against my brow, but I was still here. Bruised, shaking, surrounded by gravestones in the dead of night. Still here.

My breath came out of me in an unsteady stream as I turned my head to scan the scene. Beyond the field of graves was a deepening cluster of trees, bent, wintry, naked in the uncanny light. I kept turning. I saw more statues, statues everywhere. A faceless mourner in a heavy cloak of stone. A child staring sightless into the mist. An angel pointing toward the earth . . .

I paused on that last one, squinting to see it better. *Wait*, I thought. *Shouldn't angels point toward heaven?* And what was with that grin on its face? That was not an angelic expression at all . . .

My heart turned black inside me. This was a bad place. An evil place. And not a nightmare. Real.

I turned one more arc—and saw the mansion through the trees.

It should have been a church, I thought. This was a churchyard; there should've been a church nearby. But no. It was a large house, visible through the tangled branches of the thickening forest.

And I knew it. I recognized it.

A gibbering, nearly hysterical voice spoke in my head: *No! No! I escaped from there. I'm free from there! I got out, I got out!*

And as if in answer, a low, mocking chuckle echoed from the woods around me. I spun toward the noise, but the noise was everywhere. My eyes flashed from statue to statue, from face to stony face.

Then I saw him. Deep in the trees. A silhouette mingled with the silhouettes of the branches, almost invisible among them. A small figure in a starry cape of liquid night. Not a statue. A man. Laughing at me.

"Who's there?" I shouted, terrified. "Who are you?"

His laugh subsided only slowly, and still the mist continued echoing with the sound.

You know, Austin. You know who I am.

Had he spoken aloud? Or was I hearing the voice inside my head?

"I'm done with you," I shouted. "I escaped this place!"

But though the words came out of my mouth, I didn't understand them. I didn't understand what I was saying.

The shadow within the shadows smiled. His eyes burned red. In the eerie glow, I caught a glimpse of his face, as wrinkled as a raisin, as wicked as a secret sin, a tuft of hair on his forehead, a tuft on his chin.

You didn't escape, Austin. I let you go. Don't you remember? I offered you your freedom. I told you you'd never have to return. I told you you wouldn't even remember this place existed. I offered to give you back your life—and more than your life. A better life. The life you always wanted. Have I not kept my promises?

I shrank from him. I held up my hands. I couldn't get his voice out of my head.

"No!" I said through gritted teeth. "No! I didn't agree to that! I didn't agree to that! I didn't . . . I . . ."

And then—another voice. Not his voice. My own. Tolling in my mind like a hammer striking a great bell.

I didn't say no.

The caped figure in the woods started to laugh again, and the laugh echoed through the mist. The mist swirled with the laughter and glowed red so that the gravestones and the monuments and the grinning not-an-angel pointing toward the earth all glowed red as well.

I clutched my head in my two hands.

"Stop it! Stop!" I shouted.

And the voice in my head—was it his voice now or still mine?—I wasn't sure. But it spoke again with that same tolling clarity.

You didn't say no. And now you're mine. You belong to me.

Furious, I dropped my hands, ready to confront him face to face. But he was gone. There was nothing in the woods but the shadows of the trees, their dead branches stirring in the mist, the mist swirling around the graves and monuments.

Then—a noise.

I groaned with terror. Something was moving in the dark. The earth at the base of the gravestones was trembling, rumbling. The dead leaves were rattling. The wind was whispering in the high branches.

And figures—figures were rising out of the dirt into the mist. I strained to see them, but the mist thickened and I could make out only vague shapes, clawing their way free of the graves on every side of me.

I heard something large slither toward me over the leaves. That was off to my left. Off to my right, I heard something skittering— tiny footsteps rapidly approaching over the forest floor. Then another sound to the right of that: the thud and drag of a limp. A hungry grunt. All of the noises getting louder every second. All of them coming closer, converging on me.

In growing panic, I turned this way and that, my eyes passing over the graves, over the trees, over the mist. My heart seemed to seize in my chest as I picked out the shapes of the statues again—the angel, the child, the cowled mourner . . .

And then another shape, but this one not of stone. Not human either. A huge sinuous, serpentine shape uncoiling slowly from the ground, rising like a viper ready to strike.

I heard the sounds of beasts approaching from every side of me. I knew—or sensed—what they would do if they reached me. I could feel the heat of their yearning hunger for the glowing source of life within me.

I ran.

With a cry, I dashed into the mist. I raced around the graves, high-stepping like on an obstacle course. The grinning angel that was not an angel turned its marble head to follow me, still pointing down. I cried out again, throwing my hands up, afraid the angel would grab me, hold me so the slithering beasts could run me down and swarm over me. But the angel only watched me go and I stumbled on, leaping a smaller headstone as it became suddenly visible at my feet, crashing into the tree line, breaking through the clawing, scratching branches as I plunged into the forest.

I ran and ran some more. The night grew thicker as the woods closed in. I could hear nothing but the sound of my heavy breathing.

And then I did hear something. A throaty grunt. A thudding step. Right behind me. A thing—a creature—a Soul Leech—closing on me, drooling with eagerness.

I looked over my shoulder. That was a mistake. I saw it, the looming shadow of it, a hellish hulk, horned and scaly, its hands outreaching, webbed and clawed. Teeth—fangs—dripping—bared.

A womanish squeal forced its way out of my throat. I faced forward. Too late. A humped root smacked into my right ankle. I grunted in pain and went down, rolling over the spiky earth.

I began to scramble to my feet—and the beast grabbed me.

I felt its claws begin to sink into the flesh of my left leg just above my ankle. Like some computer screen in a lightning storm, my mind flickered green-white with an image of the creature so awful it scoured my mind of everything but fear. A surge of pure terror gave me strength and speed. I leapt to my feet before the Soul Leech could sink its claws into me. I felt the sharp tips of those claws scrape over my skin as I yanked my leg out of its grasp. A split second later and I was rocketing deeper into the forest. Bursting through branches and brush. Arms pumping. Teeth gritted. And this time, I knew better than to look back.

A movement in the corner of my vision caught my attention. I glanced to the side. Beyond the trees, I saw a rectangle of smoky light. A doorway in the atmosphere. A way out? Maybe.

Dimly, through the hanging branches and curling vines, I saw the figure of a woman standing by the light, visible in the outglow. I thought I saw her beckon me.

There was no time to consider. I turned and raced toward her, dodging around the trunks of trees—trees that were becoming sparser as the woods gave way to a clearing.

I heard another hungry grunt behind me. Slobbering gibbers all around me. Hisses. Hissing cries. But I didn't look. I just ran. And now, through the gloom, I caught a clearer glimpse of the light in front of me. What I saw made absolutely no sense, but then, what did make sense in this place?

I saw a doorway in the dark. A passage into a smoke-filled room. How nuts was this? It was some room out of an old movie. A little cubbyhole somewhere with four burly men sitting at a table, playing cards, smoking cigars. The woman by the door seemed to be drawing me toward them. I caught a clearer glimpse of her too. A gorgeous rose-and-ivory valentine of a face, framed by a tumble of raven hair. A name tried to rise into my consciousness but couldn't quite. And yet I knew her. Trusted her. And that room, that card game—there was hope in there. Not safety, but hope.

Something roared not yards away. The wild, hungry snickering all around me grew louder, and I felt something slither near my feet.

With a roar, I put on a final jolt of speed. I reached the lighted doorway. Smelled the cigar smoke. I dashed across the threshold and sat up in bed with a muffled shout, bringing Jennifer or Jessica or Julia bolt upright beside me.

"What! What! What is it?" she cried out.

I sat there, panting hoarsely, staring around me. I gave another groan and held my head.

"Oh God," I said. "Oh God. It's nothing. Nothing. A nightmare. I had a nightmare. I'm fine."

She touched my arm in an instinctive gesture of womanly care. "Take it easy. Take it easy."

"I'm fine," I said, gasping. "Just a nightmare. I'm fine."

I reached out for the lamp at my bedside. Switched it on. In superstitious fear, I looked down over my own body, naked to the cover-line. Naked, I thought. No burlap shirt and pants. Of course not. It had been a dream. A nightmare. The images were already dispersing, disappearing from my memory as the images from dreams will do.

I ran one hand down over one arm, then the other hand down the other. No scratches from the trees. No dirt from where I'd fallen. Of course not.

"A nightmare," I murmured again.

With a sigh of relief, I glanced over at the girl. Eyeing me warily, she removed her hand from my arm. She'd only come here to get the part, after all. Sex for a shot at fame was one thing. But actual womanly care for a stranger in distress—that was way too much to ask.

I steadied my breathing. Just so there'd be no doubt in my mind, I pushed the blankets down further to examine the naked rest of me. No leaves or dirt on my legs. My feet clean. Of course. Of course.

I sighed. The dream was almost entirely gone now. Only scattered images remained, and those were swiftly fading.

"What's that?" said the girl.

She reached down and gingerly touched my calf. I turned my leg until I could see what she saw.

"It looks like something clawed you," she said.

I stared. She was right. There were thin scratches on the flesh of my lower calf. They didn't hurt or anything. They weren't deep. They were already scabbed over. But when I tried to think where they had come from, I couldn't.

"How'd you get those?" the girl asked me.

Slowly, I shook my head.

"I don't know," I told her quietly. "I can't remember."

4

THAT NIGHT WAS THE START OF IT. NOTHING IN MY
perfect life was perfect after that. Nothing was even good, not even
the good parts. The whole world was haunted.

The next morning, for instance: I was driving my silver Mercedes
to the production office, peering gormlessly at the tinted windshield
through a mental fog of exhaustion. All in all, I hadn't slept more
than an hour, just that last fitful hour before dawn, you know, when
sleep is barely worth the trouble. And now my car was jerking and
stuttering forward with the jerking, stuttering vehicles all around
it. I kept trying to tell myself that this—my usual morning traffic
jam—this was the only real trouble I had. But my mind was filled
with the image of that creature I had seen at the window. That giant
rodent with a woman's face. And other images that seemed the shreds
of some forgotten nightmare. Creatures moving toward me through
a forest. Gravestones. A grinning angel. The caped silhouette of a
red-eyed man.

The scratches on my leg tingled and itched.

As my Mercedes approached the corner of Santa Monica
Boulevard, the light turned red. The traffic, barely moving, stopped.
I turned idly to glance out the passenger window—and my breath

caught in my throat.

There, just beyond the car, was a small tent city, one of those villages of the homeless poor that increasingly blemished the Angeleno landscape. Yellow, green, and blue canvas tents were clustered together in the long, narrow parking lot behind the coffee shop, right beside the street. Sad, mad, shuffling hoboes moved through the morning light: bent, gaunt, bearded figures in mismatched rags, warming themselves by trash fires, spraying their armpits with water bottles, relieving themselves in the bushes that bordered the pavement, conversing with the empty air.

But that's not what made me gasp. It was the woman there. Standing there amidst the miserable human carbuncles. Erect, tranquil, beautiful—and very like a queen. A fine, full, soft figure draped in a flowing dress of royal blue. A mesmerizing face with an expression of both feminine sweetness and regal authority.

And she was staring straight at me.

The light turned green. The cars inched forward. I went with them but kept turning to look back at the homeless camp—and yes, the woman's gaze followed after me.

I moaned softly—an awful sound. One hand went to my throat as if I expected to find something there. A necklace. A locket. What? I didn't know.

But that woman. There was something about her. An awful familiarity. Like the rodent at the window. Like the images from my dream. I knew her. But from where?

I couldn't remember.

THEN CAME THE email.

This was twenty minutes later. I was at my desk at the *Another Kingdom* production office. We'd rented the space left open by a furniture showroom that'd gone bust. It was a long, linear expanse behind a glass storefront on the second story of an elegant shopping mall. The white walls of the main room were decorated with half-finished drawings and charts, set designs and character designs, budgets and schedules, and whiteboards full of scribblings. The offices were elegant little work spaces with leather furniture and glass desks. Mine was the first one you came to after passing the inscrutable beauty at the reception desk: my old friend Wren Yen, a sometime fashion model and living Eurasian stereotype who rarely cracked a smile or spoke a word.

So there I was, just settling in behind my desk, just gratefully grasping the mug of black coffee Wren had brought me, just scrolling through the morning emails on my computer. And there—there was one email that set off that uncanny sense of déjà vu again, a chill of eerie familiarity that felt as if I'd been stabbed in the balls with an electric icicle.

Cambitus@Cambitus.com—that was the return address. And I knew it. I knew that name. But how? And why did it make me shudder?

The coffee mug half lifted to my lips, I clicked on the email and read it.

Let wisdom reign and each man go his way—wisdom, which is to love the good, the greater good more than the lesser.

But what is the good, Austin? What is the good? You must find the answer.

Cambitus.

I sat there, still, my mug hand frozen in air. I stared open-mouthed at the monitor like some drooling idiot, my stomach churning.

Anger and frustration geysered up through me. *What is the good?* I thought furiously. *What is the good? What sort of question is that? Who even gives a shit? My script is being produced! I had sex with Jennifer last night! I drive a freaking S-Class Mercedes! Do you not understand the words that I'm saying to you? Am I not speaking English here? Cambitus! Whoever you are. What kind of name even is that?*

My hand trembling, my breath trembling too, I lowered the coffee mug until I heard it clank down dangerously hard on the glass desktop. My fingers went to my throat again. Then down to my leg to scratch the itchy scratches there. I swallowed thickly.

What is happening here? What is happening?

But before I could think anymore about it, a movement caught my eye. I looked up through the glass wall of my office to the glass door near the reception desk.

God had just walked in.

BY GOD, OF course, I mean Solomon Vine. Who was the closest thing to God we had here in Los Angeles. He was even better than God, come to think of it. God could only speak the universe into being. Solomon Vine could green-light a picture.

He was richer than God too. Did God own an enormous beachfront property in Malibu as well as an entire skyscraper in downtown Manhattan? I didn't think so. Was there a God wing of the UCLA hospital or a God Theater in the Los Angeles music center? No, there was not. There were buildings named after Solomon Vine all over the place, not just in California and New York but even in some of those empty places in between with names from way back in Indian days like Minnesota or Kansas or something. There were superstars in music, movies, and television who owed their careers to the studio he had owned or the agency he had owned or the record companies he had owned. These were A-List celebrities who would answer his phone calls in a heartbeat. You think they would answer phone calls from God? I wouldn't count on it.

I didn't know how old Vine was. I wasn't sure people that rich actually had ages. But I guessed he was seventy or so since he looked about fifty. Tall, slim, fit, elegant in a V-neck sweater and jeans. Bald except for the faintest shadow of silver hair around the fringes. A surprisingly ready and approachable smile below surprisingly magnanimous pale brown eyes.

He strode through the office door—he strode everywhere, never simply walked. He greeted Wren Yen with such a bright, friendly grin she nearly grinned back at him. Even Wren, I think, might have made the effort for Vine if there'd been a percentage in it. But of course this was Hollywood: he was gay. Who wasn't?

Vine headed straight for my door. Right behind him was my agent, Ted Wexler, scurrying and bent over like Igor trailing Dr. Frankenstein. That was Ted for you. He may have had the soul of a soulless asshole, but he was a slavish hunchback in his heart.

I leapt to my feet to greet my benefactor. For so he was. From Solomon Vine all my blessings flowed. After I had returned from finding my sister, after I had lost my reader's job at Mythos, I had hidden myself away in a hot fever of semi-madness and depression. I barely remembered the weeks that followed. All I knew was that the next time I stumbled out of my crappy North Hollywood apartment, I had completed the screenplay *Another Kingdom*, a gripping fantasy-suspense story that had come quite suddenly into my fractured mind from I know not where. When I heard the news that Ted Wexler had finally lied enough and cheated enough and broken enough promises to get promoted from assistant to full-time agent, I begged him to take a look at my work with an eye toward representing me. The next thing I knew: that phone call. Solomon Vine. AKA God. *Let there be success.* He bought the script and put it into production almost overnight.

"Austin!" Vine said as he strode through my office door—spreading his arms as if we were old college buddies reunited after way too long.

I came rushing around the desk into his embrace. He hugged me. Hugged me! Solomon Vine! Then he stepped back. Smiled proudly down at me from his greater height. Gripped my shoulders.

"Great news," he said. "We got her. I'll let Ted tell it, since he made it happen."

Wexler didn't exactly stoop and giggle and rub his hands together like a slavering toady, but he somehow managed to project the image of a slavering toady into my mind as he said, "Alexis Merriwether! She's committed to play Lady Katherine."

It took no effort for me to display the appropriate wonder and delight. This was wonderful and I was delighted. Even after her last humiliating flop and the likewise humiliating divorce that was still the talk of celebrity media, even with the rumors she had taken to drugs and become unemployable, Alexis remained a genuine star. She was a name people knew. She would bring in investment from overseas and garner publicity and reviews stateside. With Alexis as the female lead, *Another Kingdom* would be a big picture, the kind of picture that made news.

Solomon Vine patted my shoulders. "Congratulations, Austin," he said. And then he added, "Ah, here she is now."

Startled, I followed his gesture toward the front door and saw, to my amazement, the great woman herself. Everyone in the long showroom stopped to stare at her as she entered. All the hip, young designers and programmers, the po-faced line producer, the semi-autistic social media geek—all the boys and girls together froze in place and brazenly gazed.

She was swathed in the hyperreality of her stardom. She was spotlit from within. Her face, with its arch eyebrows and lofty cheekbones, with its naughty lips and infinitely vulnerable blue eyes, was so familiar from the screen it seemed to break through the veil of the ordinary into a new level of pure presence. As for her body: How often had I scoured the internet for freeze-frames from her few precious nude scenes? And now here that body was before me, real and somehow more naked than naked in a white blouse unbuttoned to her glorious cleavage and jeans that clung so tight around her lower half I wished that I were they.

And as I—as we all—stood watching her, awestruck, she swiveled with military swiftness on the toes of her high-heeled boots and proceeded to unleash one of the cruelest, most devastating, most demeaning, most lacerating tirades of pure invective I or anyone had ever heard: a brutal tongue-lashing, smacking full force into the face of the cringing assistant who had trailed in behind her.

Jane Janeway, the only woman I had ever loved.

IT WAS AWFUL, as dreadful a scene as I'd ever witnessed, as sadistic as a human interchange could be without actual physical violence.

"Do you think I pay you to be a drooling fool?" Alexis shouted. "Do you?" My office door was open, but I'd have heard her through the thick glass wall. I'd have heard her through cement. "Can you do absolutely nothing right? Don't you hide your face from me! It's bad enough you drag behind me looking like you look, like some suppurating boil on my ass that's as disgusting as it is useless. But your incompetence is beyond tolerable! I'm not even asking you to think for yourself, God forbid, just to do the simple things I tell you to do the way I tell you to do them. Is that so hard? Is it? Just to do what you're paid your overblown salary for? You should be ashamed to take my money and display that level of complete and utter stupidity . . ."

On and on. And even that's a translation. I've removed all the obscenities, not out of delicacy—although she was calling Jane names no civilized human being should even whisper to another—but just to save space, because each savage phrase was tied to the next by such a spate of foul language that the entire harangue seemed to run on forever like a sort of freight train of abasement: insult linked to profanity linked to brutal interrogation like so many boxcars chugging endlessly along the encircling horizon of humiliation.

Jane, meanwhile . . . well, what can I tell you about Jane? She was the sweetest creature I had ever known, the most tender, the most feminine girly girl ever fashioned in the Girly Girl Workshops of highest heaven. That's why I loved her so, why every man who knew her, and most women, too, instantly respected her and obeyed her quietest request as if it were an imperious command. She was pure, gentle yin, and it was hypnotic, radiant, magical. Her whispered word of praise could turn your ego to iron; her kindest reproach could make your conscience rear before you like Judgment Day. If her touch could not literally heal wounds it could, so help me, make them feel all better. She was the wife men secretly dreamed of, the mother little children pretended they had. I had forgotten how much, how instinctively, I adored her—how she lived in my fantasies as the Eve of my future generations.

It had been a long time since I'd seen her last. She'd been overseas with Alexis when I left town to search for Riley. By the time she came back, I was immersed in making *Another Kingdom*, which is to say I was in such a blind ecstasy of leasing my new car and renting my new apartment and bedding starlet after starlet in my new bed that I would have been ashamed to have her look at me and see what I'd become.

Now, though—now when I saw her there—my darling Jane—I wished I had died before I'd ever forsaken her. She stood patient as the saints of old under the movie star's tirade. Her head was unbowed.

Her expression was calm. Yes, silent tears ran down her cheeks, but—as I suspected even then and as I learned for sure later—she was not crying for herself but for the inner pain and degradation of the woman who was abusing her. Oh, my plain little Jane, with her face absent makeup, her hair absent style, with her fine figure hidden beneath the baggy sweatshirt and baggy jeans she nearly always wore because she did not want to outshine her narcissistic mistress with her own lovely looks—those looks that were magnified to beauty by her womanly sweetness. So help me, I wished I had died.

The merciless harangue went on and on. I couldn't take it anymore. I had to stop it.

Without thinking, I took a step forward, ready on instinct to do what a man ought to do, to charge to the defense of his lady-love. I had it in my mind to stride out of my office into the main room. I was going to plant myself right smack between the two women. I was going to tell Alexis then and there that she could shut the hell up or get the hell out of my offices. I was going to take Jane in my arms and tell her she need never suffer such abuse again. I would take care of her. I would protect her. Not just now, forever.

But before I could move any farther, Solomon Vine touched my arm with the tip of his index finger. "Oh, you don't want to get in the middle of *that*, Austin," he said with an ironic quirk of his lips. "I know Allie. Believe me. Let it go. It'll blow over."

Our eyes met. I hesitated. I had forgotten. He did know Alexis. They had been married once, briefly, back in the day, before the rumors about his secret orgies surfaced.

And that was all it took—that hesitation, that touch of his, those words—all it took to liquefy my high resolve.

Because now, I also remembered everything else I had forgotten in my one moment of courage. This was my movie. My big chance. My big break. This was Alexis Merriwether, my big star. This was Solomon Vine standing here, my patron. It was he who had convinced Alexis to sign on to the production. If I offended her, I offended him. If I lost her, I lost him. He could—he would—shut this whole enterprise down. He could make it vanish into nothing with a finger snap. My car, my apartment, my women, my wealth, and my new status—it would all be gone, just like that.

Oh sure, go ahead. Tell yourself in my place, you would have been a hero. You lie. You would have done what I did. I stood there. I turned back to the open door. I watched the scene out there. I listened to it. And I was silent.

Somehow, I think Jane sensed that terrible moment. As Alexis continued to immolate her, she—Jane—lifted her eyes like a martyr in the flames. She looked past her tormenter. She looked at me. Her face was full of sorrow. And it was not sorrow for herself. It was sorrow for me. Pity for me. Me, who was standing there, gutted. Empty of courage. Empty of integrity. Empty of even the semblance of manhood.

My eyes met hers. Oh God, it was awful. Seeing her like that. Standing there, useless. It was an unbearable death to die and go on living.

Finally, the movie star's onslaught ended. Alexis swept her hand dismissively across Jane's face as if to slap her, but only her words slapped her, one brutally brusque command:

"Now get me my coffee the way I like it this time!"

Then Jane, still silently crying, and yet with some impossible dignity of feminine forbearance, turned and walked out—walked out and took with her my pride, my self-respect . . . well, everything worthwhile about my life except the one thing: my success.

I watched her go, thinking: *What is the good, Austin? What is the good? You must find the answer.*

Jane pushed the front door open. And what did I see there? I blinked and stared as she stepped out into an impossible snowstorm. Right there, right beyond the threshold, there was a whirling blizzard.

And as Jane vanished into the whiteness, I spied the dim silhouette in there of some great beast, some hulking bear of a creature with burning red eyes.

It was that scene—that scene in my movie script—the battle between the knight and the abominable snowman . . .

I squeezed my eyes shut. Shook my head. I heard my own voice shouting a command in my head—*No!* I felt a violent motion of my will. And when I looked again, the storm outside had vanished. There was just sad, slovenly Jane, visible for another moment through the glass as she slumped off to fetch a better cup of coffee.

That blizzard—that vision—it must have been my imagination. That's what I told myself.

But there was no time to think about it. Because now, Alexis Merriwether—still, amazingly enough, surrounded by that aura of stardom and that inner light of fame—now she came marching through my office door, snarling "Idiot bitch!" Then in a single second, she transformed herself. She brightened at the sight of me, threw open her arms, and cried happily, "Here's the man of the hour!"

She clasped my shoulders and kissed me. Alexis Merriwether kissed me! On the cheek, but so close to the edge, her lips touched mine. Alexis Merriwether's lips touched mine. Her scent surrounded me, and her starry halo too. "Your script is genius!" she said. "Really. No exaggeration. Genius."

"That's such a compliment coming from you," I weaseled. "I'm such a fan," I simpered. "I've seen all your films," I sniveled, before I could stop the cliché from coming out of my mouth. "I can't tell you what an honor this is," I gushed.

"Oh, stop," said Alexis Merriwether. "It'll go to my head. I'm already impossible to work with! I'll be worse."

I laughed—loudly.

I was a disgrace to my own testicles.

This sort of thing went on for the next little eternity or so. All of us—me, Solomon, Alexis, and Ted—stood together in my office grinning and flattering and laughing and being totally disgusting. As if the Immolation of St. Jane had never happened. As if she didn't really exist at all.

Finally, after I'd explored every possible variation on the themes of oily flattery and self-abasement, Solomon Vine clapped his hands together and said, "Well! I think Alexis should sit down with her director and discuss their vision for the part."

We all made our fulsome and contemptible farewells. Solomon took his ex-wife by the elbow and began to lead her out of the office for her meeting with Andy Brown.

But before they reached the door, he paused. He turned. He pointed one well-manicured fingernail at my chest. He said, "Oh, I'm having a little bash at the house Friday night. I'll have my assistant email you the address."

This would have seemed nothing, a casual remark, to the uninitiated. But not to someone in the show biz know. An invitation to one of Solomon Vine's Malibu house parties was to Hollywood what St. Peter's nod was to heaven: benediction through the gates of paradise.

In that moment, with that invitation, I became one of the Hollywood Elite. And all it had cost me was everything.

A small price to pay.

5

FRIDAY CAME: THE NIGHT OF THE PARTY AT SOLOMON
Vine's.

That afternoon, I went to visit Riley in the madhouse.

I was a wreck by then. Thick-headed, lackluster, cloudy-eyed.
Barely sentient as I guided the Mercedes along the whiplashing
curves of the road through the Santa Monica Mountains. At my
windows was the eerily forsaken wilderness between the hustling
city and the Arabian vastness of the Mojave. It was the living image
of my desolate inner world.

I could not remember the last full hour of sleep I'd had, or the
last moment free of shame or free of fear. The shame was a constant,
a burgeoning fungus clogging all the wellsprings of my vitality. Try
as I might—and I tried and tried—I could not rationalize away
my failure to stand up for Jane. Weren't we past the days of white
knights? I would ask myself. Wasn't Jane a modern woman who
could fend for herself? Yeah, I tried selling myself all that crap, but
my conscience was buying none of it. When I was awake, the scene
in my offices haunted me. In those rare moments when I dozed, I
dreamed about it.

In one dream, I stood in a misty forest graveyard. I watched, frozen in place, as Alexis Merriwether savagely berated Jane. In the eerie distance, a caped figure observed me with red eyes, grinning. I tried to move, to go to Jane's defense, but those red eyes held me fast. And all the while, a gigantic rat-like creature with the face of a woman perched Cheshire-like on a branch and repeated over and over in a bizarre, high-pitched, nasal voice: *Be a man! Be a man! Be a man!* When I woke up, I was shuddering uncontrollably.

So much for the shame. As for the fear: it sprung up at odd moments. I would look at a window half-expecting to see that nightmare squirrel thing staring back at me. I would hesitate to go to the bathroom at night, worried the floor would disappear beneath me. And more than once, I paused at a threshold, afraid to step over lest I find myself in a blinding blizzard where a yeti waited for me with razor-sharp claws . . .

I was constantly on the watch for impossible dangers. It was exhausting.

Blinking off sleep, I drove on. The Mercedes wound through a narrow mountain pass, around a long bend, the final bend. Then the scenery opened. On my right was red and rocky wasteland. On my left, up on the ridge against the afternoon sky, I saw the asylum.

The Orosgo Retreat—that was the official name of it. It was a private facility, named after its main benefactor, Serge Orosgo. He was a gazillionaire media mogul whom my family knew well. He sponsored the Orosgo Chair in Psychology, which my father held at UC Berkeley. He funded the sociology research my mother did there. He ran the think tank where my brother, Richard, had become his famous Richard self writing famous Big Books of Big Ideas on how to solve the Big Problems of the day. He even owned the studio where I used to work as a reader. It was only with Orosgo pulling strings that we could afford for Riley to stay in this place as long as she had.

Six and a half months. Ever since I'd brought her home from the funhouse in Walnut Creek. My sister had been locked away in this place for six and a half months.

She had entered the facility of her own free will. That's what I kept telling myself anyway. I didn't like to remember that it was I who had talked her into signing the papers. It had to be me, as my family kept insisting. I was the only one she trusted.

My spit turned sour in my mouth when I saw the place hove into view above me. The fearfully looming main building was a complex black shadow against the passing clouds. It was red brick with white trim that should have looked bright and cheerful but didn't. There was gloomy gray slate on the dominating mansard roof above the central tower and more gloomy slate on the pitched roofs that jutted off in several directions. All the roofs had gabled windows. All the windows stared like dead men's eyes. Even the great bays on the ground floor seemed to reveal a perpetual darkness within.

Six and a half months. While I prepped my movie and drove my Mercedes and drew pretty women to my luxurious bed, Riley had been imprisoned here all that time.

HILLARY BAINE, THE program director, met me at the front door as she did every week. She was a small, squat, cheery woman in her forties, her skin caramel colored, her curly hair dyed an unnatural red. She had apple cheeks and a kindly voice, thin and high like the voice of a cartoon character. Her eyes were so big and white I sometimes imagined they would keep glowing brighter and brighter until they burst into two circles of white-hot flame.

She always treated me with respect, did Hillary Baine, even deference. Like I was a visiting dignitary on an inspection tour. I guess this was because of my family association with Orosgo. She was kind and attentive, and she never spoke a wrong word that I noticed. All the same, the woman scared the shit out of me. There was just something deeply sinister about her. I always had the feeling she was waiting for me to say some untoward thing so she could have me dragged off and locked up in here with my sister.

She led me down an endless, empty corridor, the heights of its ceiling lost in shadowed vaults above.

"She's doing very, very well," she said, in that chirpy cartoon voice of hers. "I think Doctor has her medications just right now. She's so much calmer, and it's helping her get so much more out of the group sessions. I'm sure we're going to start seeing some real progress in her individual therapy as well."

She smiled up at me. My guts curdled.

"Here we are!" sang Hillary Baine.

She pushed open the door of what was called the Family Room, and there was poor, crazy Riley.

Dressed in a child's jeans and striped top, my sister was sitting on a brown leather sofa—just sitting there, just staring into space. The room around her was as bright and pleasant as any bottomless pit of despair could be. The shiny wooden floors were decorated with Native American throw rugs. The high windows looked out on rolling lawns. There were pictures on the wall and flowers on the shelves. In the center of that broad, bland institutional space, Riley, who was a tiny little creature anyway, looked especially small and vulnerable.

Plus she looked dead. To my brotherly eyes anyway. Her cute little pigtails were gone. Her straw-yellow hair was cut short and ragged like a fringed cap. Her round face was at once slack and jittery as if the drugs had both tranquilized her and given her subtle spasms. Her eyes were so deep and hollow they seemed completely vacant. Nobody home.

"Look who's here!" sang Hillary Baine.

Riley slowly raised those corpse eyes and saw me. Her faraway gaze focused slightly as if she almost remembered who I was but not quite.

The shame-fungus grew inside me. It stopped up my life force and ate at me. I made myself smile so I wouldn't burst into tears. *Oh, Riley*, I thought, *what have I done to you?*

"Aus?" she said softly, as if calling from far away.

"Well, I'll leave you two alone," said Hillary Baine cheerfully. And she left the room. Thank God. What a nasty creature.

"Aus?" said Riley again.

I hurried to the sofa and sat down next to her. The leather squeaked as it sank under my weight. I lifted Riley's slack hand off her lap and clasped it in both of mine. I could practically feel the fungus of shame creeping inch by inch over my interior landscape.

I said, "Hey, Ri. How you doing?" I kept my voice as upbeat as I could. Cheerful and calm. Like the dutiful brother of a mentally ill kid sister.

Riley slowly licked her pale lips. "Fine . . ." she said, gaping at me. "I'm . . . fine . . ." She blinked dully.

I tried to speak again. I tried to say, *That's great, Ri. That's great.* But my eyes filled and the words wouldn't come. In my exhaustion, in my shame-filled, fear-filled state of mind, I could no longer pretend I wasn't seeing what I was seeing. She was worse. Every week, every time I came here, she was worse than the time before. The drug haze was thicker. Her mind was duller, her eyes emptier. It's for the best, my parents kept telling me. It's for the best, my brother, Richard, said. But how could this be for the best? I mean, look at her! How could it be?

"Damn it, Riley!" I said softly. "What the hell are they doing to you here?"

Well, I was sorry the moment I said it. Exactly the sort of thing I was not supposed to say. Don't get her excited, my parents told me.

Don't get her started on her crazy conspiracy theories, my brother said.

But it was as if the shame—the growing fungus of shame—forced the truth up out of the depths of me and onto my lips.

And it was too late to take it back. Almost instantly, my words seemed to rouse Riley from her stupor. Her fingers fumbled to find my wrist. She clutched it with both hands. She peered at me with her hollow eyes. "They're killing me, Austin."

I tried to slip back into calm big brother mode. "No, no . . ."

But she wouldn't let go. "They've drugged me all up so I can't think, so I won't tell."

I choked out the words, "Riley, don't . . ."

She leaned toward me, and her voice dropped to a conspiratorial whisper. "Look at me, Austin. You know. You know about Orosgo. Orosgo and the Illuminati." Oh, this was bad. This was the stuff she wasn't supposed to talk about. The loony theories from the *Ouroboros* videos she used to post online. Her dreamy, childlike rants about a conspiracy of space aliens and elites who had joined forces to take over the world. This was the very crap that had gotten her stuck in this place to begin with.

I began to shake my head at her. I was about to try to talk her back to reality. But the look in her eyes: the yearning, the urgency, the desperation. I couldn't bring myself to say what I was supposed to say.

And so Riley went on. "You have to remember, Aus! Why don't you remember? They're all in it. Orosgo. Mom. Dad. Richard . . . They're killing people, Aus. You know this. For years and years. They've been killing them and blackmailing them and . . . and ruining them with scandals. Heads of countries, heads of TV stations and newspapers, universities, movie studios. Killing them and destroying them and replacing them with Orosgo's followers. Please, Aus. Please remember. They make laws and write articles and make movies and teach students to believe that Orosgo and his people should run everything, the whole world. You have to remember. The book—remember the book you read? *Another Kingdom*. Please, Aus. You have to."

This was also part of her delusion. She kept insisting there was some magic book that I had read and somehow forgotten. A book with the same title as my screenplay. It was all confused in her mind.

For another moment, she went on gazing at me urgently, desperately—with such painful hope. I didn't know how to answer her. I patted her hand weakly.

She gave up. Her shoulders slumped. She turned away from me and gazed longingly out the high window at the lawn and the hills beyond. "The mad girls know," she murmured gently, as if to console herself. "It's not just me. The mad girls hear their voices."

I didn't want to encourage her, but this was new. I hadn't heard this part before. Curiosity got the better of me, and I said, "What mad girls?"

"The girls in the Common Room," said Riley.

"You mean the other patients here?"

"Yes."

"They hear voices."

"Yes. They hear voices from another kingdom."

I shook my head. "From the book? I don't understand. What do you mean, Riley?"

My questions seemed to reinvigorate her. When she swung around to face me again, her eyes were very bright, eerily bright. There was a small smile on her lips as if she were about to reveal a secret to me. She leaned close. She whispered: "Sometimes they don't swallow their meds. Then they hear voices."

"Well, yeah, Riley. Because they're crazy!"

"Yes. That's why they can hear them. They can hear them calling."

"I still don't get you. Calling what?"

"Calling *you*, Aus."

The way she said it—and the eerie glow in her eyes—sent a chill of fear through me. I straightened in my seat, the leather cushion creaking under me. "Look, Ri, you've got to stop. That's enough, all right? You're starting to creep me out."

"Tauratanio is calling for you, Austin."

"Taura . . ." My throat had suddenly gone dry. That name— where had I heard that name before?

"And sometimes the queen. Elinda," said Riley.

I had to try three times before I could swallow and whisper back at her: "Elinda . . ."

"She's waiting for you, Aus. She's waiting for you to remember. We all are. We need you to remember."

I drew my hand away from hers so she wouldn't feel me shaking. "Really, Riley. Stop. You know it upsets me when you talk crazy like this. It's not good for you." And then—before I could stop myself—I heard myself ask: "What does she say? The queen. What does she say to the mad girls?"

Riley leaned even closer, whispered even more softly: "Let wisdom reign. And each man go his way."

I must have looked like a fish on dry land the way my mouth kept opening and closing. Those words. They were the words from the email—that bizarre email from someone who called himself Cambitus.

Wisdom is to love the good . . . but what is the good, Austin? You must find the answer.

"She's hiding," Riley went on. "The queen. She's hiding with the homeless people. No one would think to look for her there. A queen hiding in their tents, you know. No one would think of it."

That did it. That broke me. I stood up quickly, the leather sofa letting out a squeal, or maybe it was me. How could Riley know about that woman I'd seen, the serene and regal woman I'd seen standing among the homeless in the tent city? How could she know?

Riley lifted her wild gaze to me. "The queen. Tauratanio. The mouse lady too," she said. "They're all calling to you, Austin. They're trying to break through. They're all waiting for you to remember."

I felt the blood drain out of my face, out of my fingertips and my feet. All my extremities went weak and cold. *She's crazy*, I thought. *Remember she's crazy.*

But then what was I? I saw the queen too. I saw the mouse lady. Was I crazy? Did it run in the family?

Riley went on staring up at me with those wide, bright, mystic eyes. She smiled her eerie mad-girl smile. "They *need* you to remember, Austin. I need you to."

My mouth twisted. I shook my head at her fiercely. I snarled and averted my glance from her. *I don't remember*, I thought. *I don't. I'm not crazy like you, Riley. I'm happy. I'm successful now. I'm happy. I don't remember . . .*

I opened my mouth to speak, but before I could, there was a shocking *crack*. I spun around. The door to the room had swung open so fast it hit the wall.

And there stood Hillary Baine. The cheery, apple-cheeked demoness was looming at the threshold with one hand on the doorknob. She grinned at us with her flaming white eyes. Two large male aides hunkered in the hallway behind her.

"Time for your session, Riley, dear!" she sang out in her cartoon voice. Then she looked straight at me, still grinning. "You should go now, Austin," she said.

RILEY WAS SILENT and dull-eyed again as the two aides led her away—to her "session," whatever that was. I was silent, too, as I walked beside Hillary Baine along the endless corridor toward the mansion's exit. I felt dazed and dizzy, as if my mind were caught in a vortex, whirling, swirling down to drown in my own confusion. I couldn't make it stop.

"She's getting better every day, isn't she?" Hillary Baine gabbled away beside me as we walked. "Better and better every day. Although I must say: I have noticed she suffers an occasional relapse. Just a little setback from time to time. Don't you think? I may have to speak to Doctor about adjusting her medications again . . ."

My senses were still reeling as she ushered me out into the evening air. Disoriented, I paused on the front path and watched as Hillary Baine retreated back into the endless hallway within. The door swung slowly shut, and she was gone.

Alone, I lifted my gaze to the towers and rooftops of the mansion looming over me in the deepening dark.

The day was ending. The night was coming. Friday night. The night of Solomon Vine's party.

It was a night that would be filled with madness and murder—not just here in Los Angeles, but there too.

There, I mean, in another kingdom.

6

SOLOMON VINE'S HOME—HIS COMPOUND—WAS ON A grassy cliff above the ocean in Malibu. It was a moonless night that night, but the main mansion—a faux English country house—was lit so bright it glittered like the moon on the water, and like the moon, it washed the stars from the sky above. The traffic on the Pacific Coast Highway soughed beyond the screen of cypresses at the rear of the house. The waves of the ocean soughed out in front. But we—we chosen few within—we could only hear the cars and the waves in those moments when the music segued, in the quiet before one fading instrumental blended into a freshly thundering bass. After that, a new song surrounded us, and everything was music and light.

Inside the compound—all over the broad lawn above the night-dark water, in the lounge chairs around the swimming pool under the whitewashed sky, at lighted window after window in the stately manse—men and women of such glamour gathered that a golden glow seemed to rise and hover over them, making the ambience celestial.

Exhausted and crazed as I was, I was enthralled all the same by the scene. I drifted among the fabulously famous faces, my obscurity covering me like a pallid shroud. I felt transparent, insubstantial, a gray shadow among creatures of numinous reality. It was a strangely glorious sensation. It was like floating invisible among the constellations, among the heroes and the gods. I passed from pool to lawn like a voyeur ghost among women so beautiful they were famous merely for their beauty and men so wealthy they were famous merely for their wealth.

I was dazzled. My shame was forgotten. My fear was held at bay. I put the squirrel woman out of my mind. I forgot Jane's humiliation and my cowardice. The queen among the homeless. The email from Cambitus. That weird conversation with my kook of a sister. All of it was buried, smothered, silenced beneath this starry blanket of celebrity.

Then this happened.

Solomon Vine spotted me wandering on the grass. He came to me, greeted me, took me by the arm, and introduced me to a small cluster of incredibly famous people standing under an oak tree decked with fairy lights.

He said, "This is Austin Lively. A major, major talent. I'm making his script, and I'm telling you: this time next year, he's going to be a star."

He left me there and for the next—oh, I don't know—twenty minutes or so, I was living inside one of my own daydreams. I was the focus of a group that included two of the most popular actors in the country and three of the most beautiful women in the world. I won't tell you their names but, yes, your first guesses—that's who they were. They asked me questions about my project. They laughed at my self-effacing jokes. One of the women put her hand on my forearm and said, "Oh, you're really charming, aren't you? You're going to do great." All of them so friendly and natural that I melded with the group and felt I was one of them.

I thought: *Is this not heaven? Is this not the life I wanted? It is. It truly is.*

After a while, the cluster of luminaries dispersed. I floated away in a serene ecstasy of self-fulfillment. No one would ever be able to take that moment away from me. It was screwed into the face of time like a ruby in the forehead of an idol.

I ambled into the house. The house was sort of a celebrity in itself. It had been featured in news stories about expensive homes and big-money real estate deals. I wanted to get a closer look at it so I could describe it to my envious friends.

I meandered through a main room crowded with famous faces. I examined the art on the walls. They were all just framed slashes and blotches of muddy color to my untrained eyes, but I was sure they were future museum pieces. I snagged a glass of wine from a serving girl's tray and sipped at it as I studied the Oscars and Emmys and Grammys in the trophy case.

I don't quite remember how it happened, but at some point, I found myself on the far side of the massive kitchen. I was strolling down a hallway toward the rear of the mansion, a quieter corridor away from the main crowd. I kept wandering along, glancing out windows at various views of the estate. The music and the jabber of conversation grew distant and dim. It was a relief to take a break from the intensity of the party experience.

Then I turned a corner—and that's when my night of glamour ended and the night of madness began.

I was in another hallway, suddenly alone. I had a sense that I was not supposed to be here, that I ought to go back. But I didn't go back. As if drawn on an invisible tide, I drifted down the hall a bit farther. Turning another corner, I came into a secluded alcove. There was an armchair there, an elegant Queen Anne with floral upholstery. There was a window on the wall above it, just to the right. I sipped my wine and looked with satisfaction at my own reflection on the glass.

Why, isn't that Austin Lively over there? I thought. *I hear he's a major, major talent. By this time next year, mark my words, he'll be a star.*

Then my focus shifted. I looked through myself into the darkness beyond. And as I began to comprehend what I was seeing, the world seemed to drain away from me in a vertiginous rush.

I was looking at an angle across an empty strip of grass. I could see over a wall into a little garden on a lower tier of land. There was a separate house down there, a guest cottage, I imagined, but big enough for a full family to live in and as brightly lit as the mansion itself. A tall oak spread its branches between me and the scene outside. The branches partially blocked the view, but only partially.

I saw another party going on down there. A little private party in the little private yard around a little private swimming pool outside the guesthouse. And of course I had heard about such parties. I had heard all the rumors about Solomon Vine. Everyone in Hollywood had heard them during his divorce from Alexis Merriwether years back. From time to time since then, the stories had resurfaced on the internet as one former child actor or another told his sad tale on some podcast or some blog. But the scandal would never quite break out, never make the mainstream news or even the trades. It would fade away, and the former child actor would go silent—bought off or maybe scared off; who knew?

But my point is: I understood right away what I was looking at. I understood right away how appalling it was, how unforgivable. The men so powerful, the children so young. Two media moguls were there, a director everyone has heard of, the owner of a cable news outlet, a superstar actor, some sort of diplomat I'd seen on TV once or twice—and of course Solomon Vine himself. As for the children: they were little creatures of ethereal beauty, most of them in the business somehow. The boy from that kiddie sitcom. The girl who did those influencer videos online. The eleven-year-old actress who had stunned the festival viewers at Cannes with her sensual performance in an indie feature. And a dozen other lovely hopefuls

I did not yet recognize.

I stood there, staring at them. Staring at the children's faces. Their eyes were glazed, as if their souls were hiding in some inner recess from the bleak reality around them, this moral moonscape of wealth and power in which they'd been abandoned and betrayed.

But why should I have felt so shocked? So deflated? So sickened—not just physically sickened, but sickened down deep in the invisible spaces where the real me lived? Why, when, as I say, I had heard all the rumors about Solomon? We all had. It was not that I hadn't believed them either. It was not exactly that. It was that I hadn't imagined what it was like. I hadn't let the truth of it become real to me. The eyes of the children. The flesh of their little bodies. The men in their serpentine confidence, with their hands draped lightly over the tiny shoulders. I hadn't thought about any of that.

And now it was there—right there in front of me. Not even hidden. Just down a little hallway, in plain sight, a few yards away from the big party in the main room.

My throat closed. My gaze misted. My focus shifted. I saw my reflection on the glass again. And I saw something else too. I saw a figure standing behind me. A caped shadow with red eyes—the same dark figure who had spoken to me in the forest graveyard in my only half-forgotten dream.

I gave you back your life. And more than your life. A better life. The life you always wanted.

This life.

I knew what I had to do. I had to turn around. I had to walk away. I had to go back to the party and forget what I had seen. Why not? Everyone else at this party knew what I knew. Everyone else had forgotten it. Why not me too? I had to do it or all was lost. My movie. My money. My women. My life. All of it. I had to go back and join the glittering celebrities. I had to forget and become one of them. I had to be happy and successful and forget.

Maybe I would have. I'll never know. Because before I could do anything at all, the phone buzzed in my jacket pocket.

I drew it out. I read the readout. Jane Janeway.

I answered quickly.

"Hello?" I said. "Jane?"

There was a long silence. Static. Rapid breathing. I blinked, trying to get my thoughts in order.

"Hello?" I said again.

Then came a voice—Jane's voice, but as ghostly as a whisper.

She said, "Austin. I need you. Help me."

Then the line went dead.

7

THE MERCEDES SPED EAST THROUGH THE DARKNESS. I clutched the wheel, staring through the windshield with lantern eyes.

I had run out of the party without a second thought. Jane was in trouble—that's all I knew, and suddenly nothing else mattered. I hurried away from the window, back through the house. Past the vacuous famous faces and their empty, white grins. Past the crappy, overpriced works of art on the walls. Through the haze of glamour and the headache of music. Across the too-bright lawn and down the darkening driveway to the valet stand. In a growing fever of panic, I flashed a big bill to get my car fast.

Now, on the road, my mind was a rushing blur of half-formed thoughts and half-seen images. The hallway window at Solomon Vine's. The children I'd seen there. The squirrel girl at my bathroom window. The half-remembered graveyard in the woods. Jane humiliated by Alexis while I stood watching. Riley in the asylum with her drugged eyes . . .

And more. New images. Strange ideas. A locked room in a tower with a dead woman on the floor. A dungeon with an ogre chained to the wall. A mansion in the woods. A dragon in a hellish pit of bodies.

What *were* these things? I couldn't make any sense of them. I was too desperate to reach Jane—so worried and desperate I couldn't think straight. And yet—and yet I had a feeling all these images mattered. These scenes flashing through my mind—I had the sense they were all plot points in a single story: my story, a story careening toward its end now, wild, like a movie monster rampaging down Broadway, crushing every obstacle in its path.

I sped on. The traffic wasn't bad on the freeway, but once I reached Franklin Avenue I hit clusters of congestion outside the clubs. I plowed through it like a crazy man, darting into every opening I could find, no matter how narrow. I cursed and honked my horn and careened in and out of the oncoming lane, dodging the swerving fenders. I ran the light at Western and took a hard left, jamming the gas to head north at full speed.

A night mist was rising here. It drifted over me out of the dark reaches of the park. It thickened as I joined the rushing traffic on Los Feliz. It became a white fog. It pressed against the car's windows. It clung to the shafts of the headlight beams.

By the time I turned off the boulevard, I was barreling half blind through white obscurity. I nearly missed the bend in the road and just avoided sideswiping the parked cars by inches. I knew I ought to slow down, but I kept remembering Jane's voice, the strange, whispery, frightened sound of it.

Help me.

I almost went right past her house—one of Alexis Merriwether's houses, the house she let Jane use. I recognized the driveway only as I was racing by it. My tires screeched like the last girl in a horror movie as I swung the wheel and shot up the drive toward the garage. The car shut down as I tumbled out the door into the fog.

For another few moments, the Mercedes's headlights went on shining. The beams cut through the whirling white so I could see the front walk. I could make out the elaborate shape of the Spanish

Colonial house with its towers and chimneys rising out of its red tile roof, the oak trees looming over it, the branches hanging down.

Then the headlights went out and there was only darkness, only fog.

I banged my foot on the front step. It hurt. I stumbled. Grimacing, I climbed to the door. I pressed the bell. No answer. I tried the knob. It was locked. I pounded on the door with my fist.

"Jane!" I shouted.

Again, no answer.

Moving swiftly, I made my way back down the path and started pushing through the gathered mist on the sloping lawn. I tried to look in the windows, but the curtains were drawn and no lights were on inside. I couldn't even see my own reflection on the glass. With the fog clinging close around me, I was invisible.

I came around the side of the house. It was even darker here, even mistier. Shrubs tugged at my jacket sleeve. The grass dampened my socks.

Stepping into the backyard was like stepping into some kind of hallucination, fog and liquid night twining together like white and black snakes in a basket. The shrouded house was gigantic to my left. The trees were like looming specters all around me. Their branches creaked in the soft breeze. An owl hooted.

I stumbled forward by slow steps, my hands out in front of me.

Then a branch snapped in the darkness to my right. My gut ached as I held my breath and swiveled toward the sound. The fog churned. The night spiraled. And did I see a ghostly figure drifting toward me? I stood and stared, uncertain.

The owl hooted again. And yes, there it was: the figure grew more distinct, a white form mingling with the mist, moving toward me through the mist.

"Who's there?" I whispered.

And with a psycho shriek, the figure rushed at me.

I saw a white phantom. I saw bright, frightened eyes. I saw a butcher knife raised high above me, gripped in a hand stained red with blood.

Her crazed scream enveloped everything as the knife came plunging down toward my neck.

"Jane!" I shouted.

I was fast—faster than I would have expected. As the knife came down, I turned sideways and swung my forearm, knocking the blade aside and pushing Jane away from me. I caught her from behind, grabbed her wrist with my right hand, and wrapped my left arm around her chest, pulling her close against me. I could feel her naked form through the white cotton of her nightgown.

"It's me, Jane! It's Austin! Drop the knife, angel! Drop it!"

For another second, she fought me, but there wasn't much to her and I held her tight. I shook the hand that gripped the butcher knife.

"Drop it, sweetheart!" I shouted again.

Finally, I felt her whole body shudder. She let out a trembling little cry and slumped in my grasp. I felt her arm go slack. The knife fell into the grass at her feet. I sighed with relief. Turned her to face me and wrapped my arms around her.

"It's all right, Jane," I said. "I'm here. It's me. It's all right."

I held her head against my chest. For a long moment, she rested there, trembling.

"It's all right," I murmured again.

Then she drew back. She looked up at me. Even in the mist, even in the dark, I could see her eyes were swimming in hazy, crazed confusion.

She smiled—smiled insanely. "It's not, you know," she whispered. "It's not all right at all."

8

HER KNEES BUCKLED. I CAUGHT HER AS SHE FELL.

"Jane!"

Her eyes fluttered as she fought to keep them open. "In the house," she gasped. "We have to help her."

"Help who?"

But her mouth dropped open, her eyes fell shut, her head lolled on her shoulders. She answered nothing.

I worked her to her feet. Half dragged her, half carried her through the fog and darkness toward the house. Her chin was on her chest. She was mumbling and muttering incoherently.

"How do we get inside?" I asked her.

But her answer was incomprehensible, a slurred jumble of half-formed words. Her head fell forward, then snapped up as she fought to regain consciousness. I groped for the back door.

Then suddenly, she went taut in my arms. She reached up and gripped the front of my shirt. Her desperate face was close to mine; her blurry eyes were bright with terror.

"What if he's still in there?" she whispered.

"Who?" I whispered back.

But she was gone again. She looked into the distance and mumbled something I couldn't understand.

I swallowed and eyed the house. I didn't know what to do. Someone needed help inside—but was there someone else in there too, someone dangerous, waiting for us?

And what about Jane? I turned to stare stupidly at her. What was wrong with her? Was she drunk? Had she taken some drug or something? And the way she looked—her cheek, her hand, the front of her nightgown—they were all stained with blood . . .

I should call the police, I thought. But something stopped me. Some fresh awareness of danger and mystery. Something I'd forgotten.

They're all in it.

Another set of images flashed through my mind. Police lights flashing. Sirens screaming. Headlights chasing after me. A gun pointed at me.

Somehow, by rushing out of that party, by hurrying here to Jane, I had weakened some barrier in my mind. The memories were leaking through the cracks. Dribbling, streaming, faster and faster.

You have to remember, Austin. We need you to remember.

Jane's legs went limp again. She became a dead weight in my arms. I had to set her down somewhere. I found the back door. Reached for the knob. But the door was ajar, and the moment I touched it, it swung in, opening onto shadows.

I hesitated, looking into the dark, afraid. *What the hell am I doing here? I'm just a guy, just a moviemaker. Call the police!*

But there was another voice speaking to me at the same time. A strange, high, buzzy voice I couldn't quite place. It was saying to me: *No. No. Be a man.*

And I thought, *What the hell? Here I go.*

I helped Jane into the dark house. She was still muttering. I shushed her. She fell quiet. I listened. Not a sound inside. The house sounded empty. I sure hoped it was.

I managed to find a light switch. As the light came on, I had a momentary vision: the Soul Leech who had grabbed me in my dream—I saw him there, hulking right in front of me, about to pounce.

I nearly cried out at the sight of him. But he vanished in an instant. Just my imagination, that's all. Still, the shock made those scratches on my leg start to tingle again.

I puffed my cheeks and blew out a breath. More images. More memories. But I had to fight them off. I had to keep my mind straight. I had to.

We were in the kitchen now. It was a pleasant little space with red-tiled floors and yellow walls, very homey. I set Jane down on one of the chairs at the kitchen table.

"Who needs help?" I asked her. "Is there someone here?"

She didn't answer. She swayed in her seat, her eyes rolling, her mouth open, drool on her chin. She groaned and murmured.

What now? I thought. Who else could be here? Jane used to share the place with our mutual friend, the crazed comedienne Schuyler Cohen. But I'd heard that Schuyler had finally gotten over her unrequited crush on Jane and moved in with some more available woman. So then who needed help?

I had to search the place.

I settled Jane in her chair and straightened. A crawling sense of foreboding rose inside me, like roaches swarming up my inner walls. I eyed the blood that stained Jane's nightgown. I remembered the butcher knife she'd been clutching outside. Why had she had it? What was threatening her? What the hell was I going to find inside this house?

"Stay here, sweetheart," I said.

She made a noise of reluctance. She grabbed clumsily at my shirtfront. "Don't go."

"Ssh," I whispered. "Stay here. I'll be right back."

I had left the butcher knife out in the grass. I grabbed another big blade, a cook's knife, out of the rack on the kitchen counter.

What if he's still in there?

Gripping the knife for protection, I headed out of the kitchen, down the hall.

I lit the place up as I went along. Each time I passed a doorway, I reached in and flicked the light switch so I could check the room. All the rooms were empty, all silent. There was a workroom first with a computer on the table. Then a small bedroom with the small bed unmade, an overturned glass on the floor and a reading device lying next to it. Must have been Jane's room: I could see her shlumpy clothes hanging in the closet.

I went on, down the hall, gripping the knife, my palm sweaty, my guts crawling.

I was nearing the end of the hall. I remembered the layout. The front door was up ahead of me, but before that there was a large living room, with sherbet-colored stuffed furniture and a big wagon wheel chandelier. I reached the entryway. I put my hand on the wall, on the light switch. And I stopped.

I could already smell the death in here. I could already smell the blood.

I flicked the switch. The lights in the chandelier glowed brightly.

I saw Alexis Merriwether.

The body of the movie star lay sprawled on her back along the length of the red sofa. Her head and one arm dangled down over the side. She and all the cushions and the rug and the floor were soaked in gore. The walls were spattered with it. Through the shreds of her nightshirt, I could see her flesh had been ripped to pieces with savage strokes of a blade. The famous and beautiful face was mangled. The blue eyes stared at me through a mask of blood.

I had only a moment to register my horror at the sight—an upward-spinning horror as my mind flashed back to the scene outside my office—Jane humiliated by her cruel movie star boss . . . And now Jane here, drugged out of her mind . . . covered in blood . . . a butcher knife in her hand and Alexis murdered . . .

The police will think she did it, I thought.

And right then—fresh horror—sudden sirens skirled loudly just outside. The edges of the window curtains flashed red and blue with the lights of patrol cars. What seemed only a second later, there was pounding on the door. A man shouting.

"LAPD! Open up!"

I hurried out of the room. Headed breathless down the hall to the front door, turning on the foyer lights as I went. Only at the last moment did it occur to me to ditch the cook's knife in the nearby coat closet. Then, quickly, I pulled the front door open.

I stared, aghast.

Two detectives were standing on the front step—and here was the thing that rocked me: I knew them. The second I saw them, their names leapt into my head as if out of nowhere: Graciano and Lord.

He, Graciano, was a smallish white guy who looked like he was made entirely of rectangles. She, Lord, was a large black woman with features fixed in a permanently bored and suspicious expression. They were both wearing trench coats against the chill of the mist.

As I gaped at them, I heard Riley's sleepy whisper inside my brain: *They're all in on it, Aus.*

And yes, I suddenly remembered: these cops, Graciano and Lord, they were both wholly owned and operated by Serge Orosgo.

I stood confused and staring as the two detectives stepped over the threshold into the foyer, Graciano first, then Lord. I was about to say something to them, to try to explain. But what could I say? And anyway, they were gazing right past me.

I looked over my shoulder, following their stares.

There was Jane—blood-drenched Jane. She was standing in the hall behind me. Swaying on her feet. Open-mouthed. Dazed. Drugged.

Graciano and Lord shoved me aside and went to her. As they passed the open entryway, they glanced over into the living room where Alexis lay dead. That was it. Just a glance. They didn't even look surprised to see her there. They didn't react at all.

"Jane Janeway," said Lord in a flat, ironic tone. "You're under arrest for the murder of Alexis Merriwether."

Just like that. And just like that, she maneuvered Jane's arms behind her and began to snap a pair of handcuffs on her wrists. Jane stood woozy and unresisting.

I finally broke out of my stupor. I moved toward them. I said, "Hold on a second! How did you—"

Graciano turned and put his hand flat against my chest, not a blow, but a jolt that brought me up short. His eyes met mine, hard.

"You were never here," he said.

I stood stunned.

The two detectives pushed past me again and hustled Jane out of the house.

9

IT WAS LONG AFTER MIDNIGHT WHEN I MADE IT BACK
to my apartment. I went to the police station first to try to see Jane,
to try to help her, but there was no chance of it. By the time I got
there, the station house was surrounded by reporters, besieged by
a giant, pulsing mass of them like some kind of immense single-
cell organism with cameras and microphones instead of pods. They
blocked the doors. I couldn't get around them. And as I retreated,
the veil between me and my memory finally began to shred and
dissipate like mist at morning. I began to understand dimly what
was happening. To sense how bad this was. How bad it was, I mean,
for Jane.

They're all in on it, Aus. Heads of TV stations and newspapers . . .
They make movies and write articles.

Yes. Yes, Riley was right. That was exactly how it would be. A
movie star had been murdered. It was a big story. A huge story.
It would be the headline everywhere for weeks, maybe months—
maybe years in this city. With a nauseating inner rush, I understood:
these men and women gathered there—these journalists with their
mikes and their cameras—they would be the instruments of Jane's
destruction. That's what they were here for. That was their purpose.

They would convict her on their sites and screens and pages before she was tried, before she was even arraigned. *Put-upon Underling Cracks and Stabs Downspiraling Movie Star . . .* That would be the way they told it. In the news. In books. In movies. Documentaries. TV shows. Everywhere. For years. And people would believe them too. Who wouldn't? When every reporter, every moviemaker, every professor and writer and sage is saying the same thing, only a wild-eyed conspiracy theorist would doubt them. Only a kook. Like my sister, Riley.

But now I was beginning to remember: Riley was right. I couldn't quite call up the reason I knew it, but I did know it, down deep. Crazy Riley was right, and all the sane world was wrong: They were all in on it.

And I was in on it too.

You were never here.

That was what Graciano had said to me. Because the detectives hadn't expected to find me there with Jane, had they? I was supposed to be at Solomon Vine's party. And when they did find me there, they just assumed I would be willing to disappear without making trouble, without leaving a trace.

This also I began to dimly comprehend. They thought I was one of them now. They were sure of it.

I offered you your life. More than your life. I offered you the life you always wanted. You didn't say no. And now you belong to me.

Yes. Yes. I was beginning to remember. I was beginning to understand. Finally.

With a leaden burden on my heart, I went home—drove home in my sweet, soft, comfortable Mercedes. With the leather seats like a pool of velvet and the heated steering wheel warm against my hands and the sweet music on the state-of-the-art sound system. I went home to my luxurious apartment high above Wilshire. I walked through my apartment door and headed straight to the bar in the corner.

I poured myself a single malt. Very expensive whiskey, very smooth, very fine. I could afford that now. I could afford just about anything I wanted. I was a major, major talent. Celebrities spoke to me under oak trees decked with fairy lights. Beautiful women touched my arm. *You're really charming, aren't you?* I so was. I was going to be a star.

I sat on the sofa and sipped my whiskey. I looked through the bedroom door into the shadows.

There was a box in there. I remembered now. There was a box hidden in the bottom drawer of the bureau. If I opened that box, if I took out what was inside, there would be no going back, no returning to my wonderful new life. If I opened that box, I would remember everything.

After a while, I looked down at my glass. It was empty. The malt was gone. There was still time, I thought. I could go to bed, go to sleep, forget, forget what I did not want to remember.

I stood up, still undecided. I stood still, leaning neither left nor right. I tried to think of nothing. I thought: *Jane. Jane. Jane.*

I need you, Austin. Help me.

I remembered how she had nursed my head wound when I had shown up nearly dead at her house. I remembered the gentleness of her touch. The tenderness of her voice.

I loved her. I had always loved her.

I remembered her silent tears falling as Alexis screamed at her and I stood and did nothing.

And I remembered the rodent with the woman's face. I remembered the queen in the homeless camp. Riley in the asylum and the men at Solomon Vine's party. The children there. Their faces, dull, distant, withdrawn from the agony of their abuse.

It was all one story.

Like a marionette moved by some invisible hand on its strings, I walked step by jerky, hesitant step into the bedroom.

I flicked the light on. There was the bureau against one wall. I took a brief glance at myself in the mirror on top of it, but the sight of that corrupt asshole was intolerable. So I knelt down and opened the bottom drawer.

I pushed aside the sweatshirts and T-shirts. I reached into the drawer's far rear corner. I wrapped my hand around the little jewelry box I had hidden there. It had been there since I sold my script, since I'd moved to this apartment. I took it out now. I carried it back into the living room.

I set the box on the glass coffee table. I sat on one of the stuffed chairs. I sat and looked at the box a long time. Even then—even then—I did not want to open it. I did not want to make the choice I had to make.

I opened the box. I looked down at the locket inside. A golden locket on a golden chain. I lifted it out and held it in my hand.

I whispered a name.

"Betheray."

It had been her locket once. Lady Betheray, that great and beautiful and courageous lady. I remembered. She was wearing this very locket when she died in my arms, murdered by her husband, Lord Iron, for trying to restore the wisest queen in all the world to the throne he had stolen from her. I remembered.

I pressed the button on the locket's side, and the locket sprang open. There was the queen's portrait inside. Queen Elinda, also known as Ellen Evermore, the author of the book *Another Kingdom*. There was no doubt about it. It was the same woman I had seen outside the tents of the homeless.

She's waiting for you, Aus. I could hear Riley's voice as if she were sitting beside me. *She's calling you. She's waiting for you to remember. We all are.*

My eyes shifted from the queen's portrait to the locket's facing side. There was an emblem engraved there: a sword across an open hand. Those words again:

Let wisdom reign and each man go his way.

I could hardly read them through the tears in my eyes. Let wisdom reign. Wisdom, which is to love the good; the greater good more than the lesser.

But what is the good?

You must find the answer.

My mouth twisted with self-disgust. I snapped the locket shut. I raised my damp eyes to the apartment door.

Gritting my teeth, I stood. I went to the door. I opened it. I looked out at the hall. Just a hall in a luxury apartment building. My building, where I finally lived. Where I was a success. A Hollywood success, just like I'd always wanted.

I sneered. I nodded. I lifted the locket chain and slipped it over my head.

And I caught my breath. With a flash like sheet lightning, the whole contents of Ellen Evermore's book came back to me. *Another Kingdom.* That magic volume that I had read sitting in the car next to Riley. Those mysterious words that somehow shifted the very nature of my consciousness.

I remembered . . . I saw . . . Galiana. The Eleven Lands. The story of that other world and this story—they were one story, all one story, and somehow I had to bring them together again. I had lost my way in those distant kingdoms. It was there I would have to find my way again. It was there I would have to confront the evil that underlay the evil here. If I did not go back, I would not be able to do what I needed to do to help Jane.

I didn't understand all this. Not yet. But I knew it suddenly. Suddenly I remembered.

And I remembered something else too. The book—reading the book—had given me a new power. I could control the passageways now from one world into another. Before, I had had to find a door, but now . . . now, I *was* the door. My mind was the door. And I could choose if and when to open it.

I slid the locket inside my shirt. I shut my eyes. I bowed my head. I went down deep into myself. I called up the power of my will.

I was the door.

And I thought: *Yes! Do it! Yes!*

Instantly, the wild, whirling wind of the blizzard blew into my face so hard I gasped. I opened my eyes and saw the cyclone of snow where the hallway had been. I heard the beast growl within the depths of the storm. I saw the hulking blur of the creature's shape waiting for me, waiting to slaughter me, his red eyes burning.

As I began to move forward, I felt the liquid metal of Elinda's magic armor spring out of my flesh. I felt her sleek, silver, deadly sword sprouting from my hands. I felt the heavy fur I had been wearing grow up around me.

I had forgotten how disorienting it was to make the transition, to step from the ordinary world into the Eleven Lands. The turbulence and confusion of the storm seemed only a projection of the turbulence and confusion inside me as I confronted once again, after all these months, how real this mad illusion was, how quickly reality faded to a dream as I moved across the threshold.

Still . . . there was one second—one last second—when I hesitated . . . when I wished . . . Oh, I don't know. I wished . . . Not that I could stay in LA. Not that I could stay and make my movie and screw more starlets and be rich and famous and have people say what a major, major talent I was at fine, high-status parties on the Malibu coast. Not that exactly. I just wished . . . I wished the world were different. You know? I wished that Hollywood was different, a place where good things might happen and no harm done. I wished that Solomon Vine was not depraved. I wished that Serge Orosgo was not Orosgo. I wished my father and mother and brother weren't in league with them, with all of them. I wished that men had honor and women had virtue and the powerful didn't want all the power for themselves.

I wished I lived in a golden age of golden people in a golden land.

I wished that wisdom reigned so that each man could go his way.

Well . . . wish away, dude.

I charged through the door into the blizzard.

10

WITH A SAVAGE BATTLE CRY, I PLUNGED INTO THE
swirling snow. After the familiar and luxurious peace of my
apartment, the vortex of white and wind was pure chaos, blinding.
I felt suddenly weighted by the liquid armor flowing beneath the
heavy fur I wore. I felt my face, bared under my lifted visor, pelted
hard by the wild blizzard. Confused and afraid, I discovered that my
sword, clasped in both my mailed hands, was already raised to deliver
a slashing strike. Half insane with the unfathomable transition, I
rushed at the beast, my mouth jacked wide on a ragged cry. My
heart was ablaze with fury and with fear.

With his white fur, the creature seemed part of the weather—
hard to make out—just a hulking, hungry presence lumbering
toward me. Only its eyes—its ravenous eyes—showed clearly,
glowing an unnatural red that burned brightly out of the depths of
the maelstrom.

But I could hear the thing well enough. Even over my own
hoarse shout, even through the hoarse and steady roar of the wind,
I could hear the Yeti growling low. It was an unnerving sound. Not
fierce. No. It sounded to me more like a growl of satisfaction. The
beast could smell me—that was the thought that ran through my

mind in the seconds before we came together. He could smell me, and he could see me charging at him with his red eyes, and he was growling in anticipation of a fresh kill, a fresh feast, a new pile of bones to add to the others I had seen scattered in the shadows of the cave behind me.

Why oh why had I ever left LA?

We drew close to one another. The Yeti loomed out of the blizzard, rearing. As I drew back my sword for the strike, the creature flexed one massive paw so that his claws sprung out like switchblades with a whispered snap. The claws were curved and sharp and daggery. They flashed and vanished and flashed again out of the tempest.

One more split second of swirling white confusion, of shouting and growling and the roaring wind. Then—long before my mind could adjust to the staggering supernatural impossibility of the moment—the fight began.

My sword swung down. The beast's claws slashed swiftly from the side. I saw the angle of the attack just in time. Swiveled my hands and turned my weapon to block it. My blade and his claws struck each other with a steely sting, lighting the snow with red sparks. The beast's strength was shocking. The force of his blow not only threw my blade easily to the side, it sent me lurching over the icy ground. And the Yeti's speed was as awesome as his strength. Before I could recover my balance, he was on me. He swung again, a swipe of those long claws that was clearly meant to take my head off.

I ducked. The claws swept over the top of my helmet. As the force of the swing turned the beast to the side, I stepped left, lifted my leg, and kicked him as hard as I could in the kidney.

The kick had exactly zero effect on the gigantic creature, but it did send me stumbling off in the opposite direction, away from him. And good thing, too, because now the Yeti let out a gonad-chilling shriek of rage and swung a vicious backhand at my face. But because I'd fallen back, the razor-sharp claws missed my nose by half an inch.

Then, for a second, the beast's center was open to me. I was leaning away to dodge the backhand, but I changed direction as fast as I could and lunged straight at him, thrusting my blade at his guts.

My swordpoint never touched him. The Yeti continued to come around with the force of his last swipe, and before I could plunge the sword into him, he hit me on the shoulder with his other paw. Luckily the claws weren't extended, or if they were they missed me. But I took a full hard shot with the pad, and the creature was so strong, the blow sent me reeling.

I stumbled to the side, then fell to the ground, then rolled over and over again through clouds of wet whiteness. For what seemed like forever, the snow swirled and the wind swirled and I swirled within them, my fur coat drenched, my face cut raw by the ice covering the frozen earth, my roar of frustration lost in the roar of the wind.

I leapt to my feet, but I was totally disoriented. I stared wide-eyed, and for a second—two—all I could see was the white cyclone everywhere. Where was the beast? From which way would he come at me?

Then—a roar. Red eyes, gleaming. The creature was still there, just to my right.

I squared up to take him on, my sword held before me in my right hand, my left hand stuck out into the hurricane wind for balance. I thought the beast would charge again, but he stayed where he was, growling low, that deep, eager growl I could hear even through the storm.

I hesitated too, my lungs pumping, my face cold and dripping, my fur heavy with damp. My whole body was still vibrating with the force of that blow. And my mind—my mind was as wild as the weather. What the hell was I doing here? Was this even happening? I was supposed to be making this film, not starring in it. I was supposed to be in Hollywood having the time of my life. Casting the leads. Budgeting the scenes. Offering pretty girls bit parts in exchange for sex.

But insanely, I was here instead, lost in a blizzard, in a fight for my life. My real life. Because I knew this was no dream. And if I died here, I'd be just as dead in California.

My heart pounded. My eyes scanned the whirlwind. I braced myself, trying to ready my mind for the force of the beast's attack.

But nothing could have prepared me for what happened next.

For a second, the wind subsided. The snow stopped whirling and slanted down hard, pummeling my face like hail. And in that quieter moment, I could hear my own harsh breathing.

And I could hear other sounds—sounds that turned my bowels to acid.

There was no longer just one growl rumbling from the creature in front of me. There was another growl further to my right—and another—and then a roar to the left of me and another growl in front of me and more and more on every side.

My eyes flicked this way and that. I saw a second pair of red eyes shining through the snow, then a third, a fourth, then more and still more pairs of red eyes moving out of the invisible white distances, closing in on every side.

A whole army of abominable snowmen was surrounding me, and there was no way to escape them.

Like a black shroud drifting down over my head came the realization that—just like that—my life was over. Any way I played this scene, I was a dead man. The knowledge made me afraid, yes, but also sad. Wasn't it just seconds ago that I was thirteen snazzy stories above Wilshire Boulevard? Wasn't the real world—the real, safe, beautiful, modern American world—only a mere few steps behind me, just through the entrance to the cave? How I wished in my sorrow I were there again, making my picture with Solomon Vine, driving my Mercedes, living my paltry dream, oblivious to this idiot nobility. The hard snow battered me, and the wind chilled me, and the beasts closed in all around me. In that final moment, I did not remember the corruption I'd left behind or Jane or Orosgo anything. I just remembered the weather. There are no blizzards in Hollywood, only sunny days.

But wait! I had forgotten something. The book! I had the read the book. *Another Kingdom*. It had changed the structure of my brain somehow. I was the doorway now. My mind was the portal in and out of the Eleven Lands. All I had to do was reach a threshold—the cave entrance behind me, for instance. Then I could will the door to open there. I could step through and I'd be in my apartment again, my wonderful, luxurious apartment.

I didn't know how I'd ever be able to return. Time didn't pass here while I was gone, so the yeti band would just be waiting for me in this place forever. But I couldn't think about that now. I was surrounded. If I wanted to live, I had to get the hell back to Hollywood.

I spun around to dash back toward the cave entrance.

And there, towering over me like the shadow of death itself, was an abominable snowman so huge he made the others look like cubs.

He growled—growled so loud and deep my whole body vibrated with the sound. His red eyes flashed down at me like two scarlet klieg lights, pinning me where I stood. My jaw dropped in awe at the sheer size of him.

I only saw his enormous paw sweeping toward my head the second before it hit me.

I had a sense then of flying through darkness, tumbling through a darkness studded with colored stars that sprinkled down around me like confetti. There was silence inside my head, but it was a throbbing silence, like phantom bells tolling silently. I did not lose consciousness. My consciousness simply went far, far away.

I felt my body slam into the ground as if it were happening to someone else, as if it were someone else's breath being knocked out of him, someone else's bones being jarred and rattled painfully. Even the blizzard seemed distant. The snow, the wind, the cold—they had nothing to do with me.

I lay on the iced-over earth staring up helplessly at the broad indigo sky dimly visible through the downpouring snow. Only vaguely—and without any real emotion—did I understand that the animals all around me were now going to tear me apart and devour my pieces. The horror of what was about to happen was present to my imagination, but obscure. I couldn't do anything to stop it. I didn't have the will or the strength to move. It was as if I were present at my own destruction and absent from it at the same time.

The sky went out as the Great Yeti came to stand over me. He looked down at me with those red kleig-light eyes. Other smaller—smaller but still huge—yetis also gathered closer, also looking down.

Then the Great Yeti's mouth opened and I saw his teeth. They were the size of scimitars.

And the gigantic beast said, "Bring this idiot back to Center Base. Unfortunately, we're not supposed to eat him."

11

I WAS STILL BARELY CONSCIOUS WHEN ONE OF THE creatures grabbed me by the ankles and began dragging me unceremoniously through the snow, *bumpety-bump-bump*, on my back. With drifty dimwittedness, I watched the blizzard dropping on me and the distant darkness of the sky. I felt the whole platoon of beasts marching along all around me. I heard the frozen snow crunching under their large feet.

After a while, I was jarred back to some level of sentience by the pain and irritation of being thumped along the rough mountain ground. With the fight over, my liquid armor melted back into me, and there was nothing but my furs to protect me from the rocky terrain up here above the tree line. I wondered vaguely about my sword. I must have lost it when the Great Yeti sent me flying. But it was a magic sword, after all, so maybe it would be there in my invisible scabbard when I reached for it next time. I didn't know.

But that thought, and all my thoughts, were put on hold as fuller consciousness returned to me and I became aware of voices in the storm. They were just audible beneath the continual whooshing of the wind.

The yetis were chatting as they marched along. They were chatting about me.

"How was I supposed to know?" said one of them. "He sure looked like food." He had a deep growly voice, like a bear talking.

"No fear. It was a mistake anyone could make." That must've been the Great Yeti. A voice like thunder. The sound was unmistakable.

"You might at least have asked, Yek." This voice was a bit higher but still low and growly. "You don't have to attack everything that moves right away."

"You make a good point, Neg," Yek answered. "How would it be if I bit the front of your face off?"

"How would it be if I disemboweled you and let you watch me feast on your intestines while you died?"

Yek answered with a deep, threatening growl, and Neg answered with a less deep but just-as-threatening growl.

And the Great Yeti said, "How would it be if I picked up both of you in my two paws and ground you together into a single wad of beef, then swallowed you whole?"

The growling stopped at that. The beasts dragged me on in a disgruntled silence for a few moments, *bumpety-bump-bump.*

"I could walk, you know," I tried to say. But my words were soft and slurred. Even I couldn't understand them. And no one paid me any mind anyway. They continued to drag me along, my legs lifted in the air. I bumped over the rocks, trying to remember under what quixotic delusion I had left Los Angeles to come back here.

"You're not to blame," the Great Yeti thundered then—speaking to Yek, I guess, who was, I guess, the beast who had first attacked me. "I only found out because Cambitus sent one of those falcon messengers a few hours ago. You know, the ones he speaks to and then they repeat his words when they arrive."

"It's amazing they can do that," said Neg. "I mean, a talking bird. Whoever heard of such a thing?"

I grunted as the back of my head went over a sharp rock. The blow made my eyeballs roll in their sockets. But even so, I remembered Cambitus now. The guy who had somehow sent me the email about wisdom and the good. He was, I recalled, Queen Elinda's father, the Not Altogether Wise King of Menaria. In his royal city of Vagos, his people turned to stone by day due to one of the wizard Curtin's curses. I remembered Curtin too. He was that caped figure with red eyes. The one I had seen in the forest graveyard . . . It was all coming back to me.

"The falcon told me to watch out for this one," the Great Yeti went on. Meaning me, I guess. "He said he'd be taking the shortcut over the White Mountains to reach Anastasius so the emperor can bring his armies to restore the queen of Galiana. He asked for safe passage for him through our territory."

"Eh," said Yek. "What is the queen of Galiana to us? What is Cambitus to us, when it comes to that? I'd eat them both. And this one too. He looks very tasty."

"Quiet, before I rip off your right arm and devour it," the Great Yeti replied. "Before Anastasius won these mountains for himself, we could no more speak than a bird could. Do you want to return to that life? This morning, at Center Base, I smelled a blood-red darkness coming from the east. Curtin's power is spreading from Edgimond and Galiana. Once the Eleven Lands are his, we will be beasts again and slaves again as beasts must be. Do you think only of your belly, Yek? Can you not skip one afternoon snack to keep your freedom and your mind?"

"Yek thinks only of his belly because he has no penis to think about," said Neg.

"How would it be if I had your penis for a snack instead of this man here," said Yek.

"How would it be—"

"Hey!" I shouted in a thick voice. "Hey!"

I tried to lift my head off the ground to stop it from bumping over the rocks. But the blow from the Great Yeti was still sending throbs of pain through me, and I lay back again, groaning.

"The food is talking," said Neg. "First birds, now food. It's a world of wonders."

"Isn't it enough we haven't eaten him?" said Yek. "What more could he want?"

"Let me up," I groaned at the snow and the sky. "I keep hitting my head on these rocks. They're killing me."

They continued dragging me along for another few seconds, my head bouncing up and dropping down as it hit each new jag and outcropping.

Then I heard the Great Yeti rumble, "All right."

I stopped moving. My ankles were released and my legs dropped to the earth, sending another shock of pain all through me.

"Get up then, food," growled the Great Yeti. "Walk on your own and save us the trouble of dragging you."

With many more groans and a few curses, with many spasms and aches in my head and shoulder and lower back, I rolled half over and pushed myself off the ground, fighting to stand. One of the beasts—Neg, I think—grabbed me under the arm. He hauled me upright so sharply, my feet left the earth for a second before I came back down upright. That hurt too.

"Thanks a lot," I grumbled.

I looked around—and I felt my innards go cold at what I saw. Beast upon beast stood in the blizzard all about me, huge shadowy hulks nearly lost in the snowstorm, their red eyes burning like beacons. And when I faced front, there was the Great One. He seemed to me about the size of a brownstone.

"If you wanted me to go with you, you could have just asked," I told him.

"I could also have bitten your head off, swallowed your brains, and spit your face down the stump of your neck," he explained.

"Right," I grunted. I rubbed the spot where he'd hit me. It was lumping up. "I appreciate your restraint."

In case the information should ever prove useful to you, I can testify that abominable snowmen have a tin ear when it comes to sarcasm. The Great Yeti's only response to my remark was to tilt his head toward the horizon and rumble, "Come, food. They are sending an escort for you."

"Who is?" I asked.

But he turned away without answering. He lumbered on.

The other beasts followed him. All but Yek, who stood still another moment, gazing balefully at me with his red eyes. I could tell he was itching to finish our interrupted fight. He wanted to prove how easily he could have ripped me to pieces. My hand wandered toward my invisible scabbard, and I wondered again whether my sword would be there when I needed it. But Yek didn't make a move. I was under the Great Yeti's protection.

After a second or two, Yek slowly, deliberately licked his chops with a thick tongue, showing me his dripping fangs as he did it. I nodded to let him know I got the message. He huffed, mist swirling out of his mouth. Then he turned his back on me and thumped away.

I trailed behind him, stumbling through the storm. It was hard going, up the side of the mountain. We climbed into the clouds. They rolled over us, cold and damp and blotting out everything. I pulled the hood of my fur tight around my head, but my face was unprotected. The skin of my cheeks stung for a while and then went numb. My shoes were damp too. Soon my feet were as frozen as my face.

But on we tramped, the beasts and I. My head ached from the Great Yeti's blow, and my shoulder ached from the fall to the ground, and my back ached from being dragged over rocks, and the climb through the thin air made me increasingly breathless. But after what seemed a long time, we emerged from the clouds. All at once, as if magically, there was clear night sky above us, dusted with stars. The blizzard was left below. The Great Yeti changed direction and moved along the side of the mountain. The climb became more gradual, the hike easier.

At last, through light mist and darkness, I saw a huge rock formation rise up in front of me, a great rectangle of white stone, limestone maybe, dotted with cave openings, one next to another. It looked like some sort of primitive apartment building. There was a line of campfires lighting the night outside and the wavering red glow of other fires lighting the shadows within the caves. There were creatures—deer-like animals with single antlers like unicorns—in fenced pens at the bottom of the formation.

Clearly, we had reached Center Base.

The return home of the yeti army was a crazy sight to see. Their families came out of the caves to greet them. The abominable snowwomen were smaller than the snowmen but plenty abominable for all that. The abominable cubs were actually kind of cute, especially the really little ones clinging to their mothers' fur. And as the yeti men arrived at the camp—so help me, I'm not making this up—some of them casually grabbed their women, turned them around and took them right then and there, the children dancing about them, oblivious. Other men went straight to the deer pen, reached in, and with a single swipe tore the head off one of the poor creatures there, held it by its horn and chomped away at it like it was a candied apple while the body gouted blood and thrashed and died.

The scene did not instill confidence in someone like myself who had been mistaken for a meal only a couple of hours earlier and who was still being casually referred to as "food."

All I could think was: *These people are animals!*

I stood unnoticed as the reunion went on. Only when the enormous Great Yeti finished rape-greeting his likewise enormous wife did he bother to glance over at me. Then, with his enormous dingus receding into his fur, he made a gesture with his also enormous head. He was ordering me to enter the nearest cave mouth. Seeing the light of a fire within, I obeyed eagerly, desperate for the warmth.

And it was warm inside, thank heaven. A high fire of grass and sticks was snickering merrily just over the threshold. Other than that, the place was a dump. Bones of half-eaten creatures lay everywhere amidst piles of other organic junk, I hate to think what. There was a thick stench that seemed to mingle the smells of wet fur, shit, and urine. There were stone bowls and utensils piled haphazardly against the wall, and a charred wooden spit with maggots swarming over the bits of cooked meat still stuck to it.

It seemed odd to me: the savage scene outside, the traces of semi-domesticity within. Clearly the yeti womenfolk were engaged in the age-old female enterprise of civilizing their men. Just as clearly, they hadn't gotten very far with the project.

I heard a huff and turned and saw some yetis come in after me: a female with two cubs toddling and tumbling around her. When she looked at me, I noticed for the first time that the female's eyes weren't red like the men's but large and dark and almost gentle.

"I am Ga," she said. She had a grumbly voice but softer than a male's. "Sit and eat now."

It had been hours since I'd snacked on hors d'oeuvres at the party in Malibu, and I was hungry after our long trek. I hoped there was something to eat here besides deer head covered with maggots.

Still—when in Yeti-land, you do like the yetis do. So I sat down as ordered, glad to be near the fire, stinky as it was. I held out my hands toward the flames and shivered as my palms began to warm.

To my relief, the abominable snowwoman turned out to be a pretty good housewife or cave wife or whatever she was. She went about setting up a little stove of rocks on the fire. She then used the stove to heat up some broth in a stone bowl. Finally, she handed the bowl to me.

"Thank you, ma'am," I said, nodding up gratefully at her great, fanged, monstery face.

Her eyes softened even more. "I am glad you are here," she told me. "You are welcome."

There was a large roaring cry from outside where the rowdy reunion was growing rowdier by the minute. There was loud, roaring laughter.

Ga glanced at the cave entrance, then at me. She seemed embarrassed by the orgy. "Anastasius taught us how to live when he conquered these mountains," she told me. "But we do not yet know the whole of it. Our men are not yet really men. They think of nothing but their stomachs and their . . . their things."

"Yeah, well, men are pretty much like that where I come from too." I sipped the broth she had given me. It was dreadful shit, but at least it was warm. "It's good," I managed to gasp at her. She seemed gratified by the compliment.

While I sat hunched and shivering, sipping the brew, Ga moved away into the shadows. I heard pottery rattling as she dug amidst a seemingly random pile of objects against one wall. She lifted something out of the mess and carried it over to me, holding it carefully in both of her big white paws, as if it were a great treasure, delicate and precious.

"One of the emperor's soldiers gave this to me, when the armies passed through."

I looked at her prize. It was a piece of a painting, a piece of canvas cut roughly out of the whole, threads dangling from its jagged edges. It was very good work, very detailed, very sophisticated. It reminded me of pictures I'd seen in museums.

The fragment showed the head and shoulders of a man. He seemed to be wearing armor and a cape, so maybe he was a soldier or a knight. He was looking down as if at a defeated enemy, his face very stern, very determined, very manly. The scene was dark, but the knight's face glowed. And there was a portion of stormy sky above him, to his right. The heavy clouds were parted to reveal an area of golden radiance from which several cherubs looked down upon the action. I guess this was meant to suggest there was another level of meaning to what was going on below, like it was the work of heaven being done on earth or something. I don't know.

"The soldier who gave it to me said I should hang it on the wall, but Neg doesn't like it," said Ga. "He says he feels it's watching him all the time. It makes him nervous."

I glanced up at the oddly gentle eyes in her furry snow-monster face. It was clear this thing was very important to her, but I wasn't sure why. I wasn't sure what I was supposed to say.

"It's very beautiful," was what I finally came up with.

She nodded proudly. "I think it may be the Emperor Anastasius himself," she said in a tone of awe. "Do you think that's possible?"

After a moment, I nodded. I pretended to study the picture carefully, just to please her. "Maybe," I said. "Maybe so. I don't know."

"This is what I think our men will look like when they are truly men," she said. And then, shyly, in a low voice, she added, "Like you."

I started to laugh but then stopped because I saw she was serious and that it meant something to her. As I looked up into Ga's yearning eyes, I thought of my life back in LA. The party at Solomon Vine's. How could I tell this poor beast that if she and the yeti women worked very hard and managed truly to civilize the yeti men, the yeti men might one day build them a civilization so great, so rich and safe and powerful, that they would all be free to become savages again, as we had.

"I guess it does look a little like me," I told her with a smile. "I can sort of see the resemblance."

She drew the fragment back toward herself and studied it tenderly, smiling kindly, if monsters can be said to smile. Then she said, "I will make you a place to lie for the night. I am told someone is coming to get you."

She moved back to her little stash of objects and gently replaced the painting among them.

"Yes," I said. "That's what your leader said. Someone is coming for me. Who is it? Do you know?"

She shook her head. "I am only a female. I am not told these things."

Shooing the cubs who wrestled and tumbled around her, she fetched a rolled deer skin from the wall and spread it out beside the fire. She then shepherded the little ones into a deeper part of the cave, away from the firelight.

Left alone, I sipped the horrible broth and eyed the skin on the floor. Apparently, I was supposed to spend the night in this place. I turned my head and cast a wistful glance toward the cave entrance and the night outside. I could hear the celebration out there getting even louder. I caught glimpses of yetis passing by, gulping drinks from skins. They staggered, roaring, as the drink took hold. I heard a masculine shout and a blow and a female cry of pain.

As I looked at the cave mouth, I decided to try an experiment to test my new skill at creating portals. I reached mentally into my core and made a motion of my willpower toward the opening. A dim, hazy light appeared there, like a veil dangling over the entranceway. Through that veil, I could make out the hallway of my apartment building in Westwood. My pulse quickened. All I had to do, I realized, was stand up and walk through the veil and I'd be out of this craziness. I'd be home.

I relaxed and released my will. The veil disappeared and so did the scene beyond it. I couldn't leave yet. I had work to do here. Find Anastasius. Send his armies to restore the queen. I still felt this instinctive certainty that if I was going to help Jane get out of prison, I was going to have to accomplish my quest here first.

I finished the broth and lay down on the skin. I listened to the rowdy noise of the party outside. For comfort, I reached into my fur to touch Lady Betheray's locket where it hung around my throat. But the locket had changed shape. Oh yes, I remembered: here, in the Eleven Lands, the locket became the talisman, the bolt-shaped symbol I had found in the castle at Eastrim. This was what I had to bring to Anastasius. This was Elinda's signal to him that she needed his help.

My fingers closed around the jagged shape of the bolt. I felt a shock of power surge through me. A vision came into my mind, so clear it was almost real. I seemed to be high in the air. Laid out below me was a long grassland bordered by cliffs above a roiling sea. A vast army of various creatures was camped along the plain down there. These, I understood, were the forces of Anastasius. I had no idea how far away they were, but, somehow, I had to cross the rest of these lands and reach them.

My hand released the talisman. The energy surge ended. The vision faded away. I lay where I was, filled with anxiety. Would I be able to do what I had to do? Could I reach the emperor? Could I free Jane? Could I get Riley out of that damned madhouse?

I closed my eyes. The noise of the party continued outside. Woefully, I told myself I would never be able to sleep under these conditions.

I was asleep in seconds.

WHEN MY EYES next fluttered open, there was daylight at the mouth of the cave. The fire beside me had gone out. My body was stiff and chilled from a night on the cold ground. I drew a deep breath and sat up, shivering. I looked around.

In the gray dawn, I could see the whole cave. I could make out the shapes of Ga and her yeti family, way back in the shadowy rear, asleep against the wall. The furry wannabe housewife was curled up in a ball. Her man, Neg—at least I think it was Neg; all these monsters looked pretty much alike to me—was sprawled out beside her. Her head lay on his belly and rose and fell with his snores. The children were curled up in the crux between the two adults, nestled in their parents' fur.

I worked my aching body to its feet. I rubbed my shoulders for warmth. I stretched and yawned. I wandered out of the cave.

A mist had fallen on the mountainside. Through the drifting haze I saw the shapes of yetis who had passed out on the ground. They lay amidst wine sacks and piles of crap and vomit and the bodies of dead unicorns. Some of the abominable snowmen were beginning to stir where they lay. One or two were already on their feet, their hulking shapes moving slowly through the fog.

I turned my back on them and relieved myself against the base of the rocks. When I was done, I turned around again—and let out a curse as I suddenly found myself staring smack at the navel of the Great Yeti himself.

I had to crank my head way back to look up at the enormous fanged face hovering over me. I realized it would only take him a second to bite my head clean off. By the look in his red eyes, I suspect he was thinking the same thing.

But he didn't attack me. He merely growled, "Your escort has arrived, food."

He stepped aside. Beyond him, through the mist, I saw a form approaching. At first, in the drifting tendrils rolling through the hazy light, it looked like a fearsome thing, an incomprehensible shape that seemed to float above the ground like an alien spaceship. But as the thing came nearer, I began to understand what it was I was seeing.

A faint hope—and then a stronger hope—rose like a second dawn from the dark inside me. For the first time in what seemed like forever, I laughed out loud with pure, untrammeled gladness.

It was my horse. My old friend, the black stallion. He had abandoned me at the foot of this mountain the day before. He had left me to go on alone as he returned to his master, King Tauratanio, in Shadow Wood far away. After all our adventures together, all the times he'd saved me, I thought I would never see him again. It was uncanny, in fact—even miraculous—that he could have found his way here so quickly.

He plodded forward a few more steps. He broke out of the mist. And I saw the shape of the creature perched on the pummel of his saddle.

The giant rodent with the woman's face! And now, at last, I remembered her.

"Maud!" I cried out.

In all seriousness, I don't think I was ever as happy to see anyone in my life as I was to see that mutant squirrel girl. Not exactly what you would call a friendly face, but a familiar face and a friend all the same. I ran toward her and the stallion. All around us, the waking yetis gathered to watch our meeting. I could hear their growly voices murmuring to one another.

"That looks tasty."

"Yes, I've had horse. It's quite good."

"I meant the rodent. Her face alone looks like a delicacy."

Meanwhile, I reached my two old companions. I nuzzled the stallion's nose with genuine affection. Then I looked up at the rodent girl riding him.

"You're here," I said gratefully.

She gave a dismissive snort. "Oh, now you recognize me," she said in her high, buzzy voice. "When I looked in your bathroom window, all you did was screech like a little girl."

"That *was* you! In LA!"

"How many people do you know who look like this?"

"But how did you get there?"

"You called me."

"I called you?"

"Well, some part of you called me anyway. The vanishingly little piece of you that still retains some sense of manhood, decency, and honor."

I laughed. "I've missed you too."

"And since you're the doorway now, I was able to come through you and find you. Until you closed the door and sent me hurtling back again."

I nodded. I understood. Sort of. "Cambitus sent me an email too."

"What's an email?"

"It doesn't matter. But I guess that came through me too. But how did you get here, then?"

"One of King Tauratanio's falcons saw your stallion returning to the forest. The king put me on another of his birds and sent me to meet him."

"But then . . . how did you get here so fast? It took us forever to climb the mountain."

"That's because you traveled over land," said Maud.

And with that, she reached out her small rodent forelegs, seized some strands of the stallion's mane in her rodent claws, and gave them two sharp tugs.

I stumbled back as the horse whinnied once and reared on its hind legs above me. With a loud fluttering sound, two vast appendages sprung from the beast's flanks, one on each side. The appendages spread in the air, dark and wavery and huge—so huge they blocked the misty dawn from view.

Wings! The black stallion had grown a pair of wings!

"Saddle up," said Maud as I stood gaping, flabbergasted. "Our time is short. We have to reach Anastasius before Curtin does or the Eleven Lands are lost forever."

12

MY FAREWELL TO THE YETIS WAS SHORT AND MORE OR less sweet.

The stallion settled to the earth, his wings folding so neatly into his flanks they became virtually invisible. I took hold of the saddle, put my foot in one stirrup, and swung up gracefully into the seat, right behind Maud.

The Great Yeti lumbered toward us. He was so large, he towered over me even when I was mounted. The other snowmen gathered around us in the morning mist. They continued to gaze hungrily at the horse and the squirrel girl, their fanged mouths watering.

"Goodbye, food," the Great Yeti grumbled to me. "I wish we could have eaten you."

I had no idea what the polite response to this was. I said: "Well . . . maybe next time."

The Great One turned to Maud: "Tell the emperor we let this food live though he looked tasty."

Maud nodded solemnly. "I'll make sure he knows." Then she glanced over her rodent shoulder at me with her ever-so-eerily human face. "Ride," she said.

I nodded. I lifted my eyes to gaze through the mist at the rock formation with its tiers of caves. At the entrance to one of the lower caves, the cave where I had slept, I saw Ga. She was standing and watching me. Her cubs clutched at her legs. Neg hulked sullenly in the shadows behind her. She lifted one paw to me in a wistful farewell—and I saw she was holding her little scrap of a painting, her picture of what a man might be.

I felt a twinge of pity for her. She would live her whole life here, yearning for humanity in a world of savage beasts. Poor thing. It would be just like living in Hollywood.

I snapped the stallion's reins and shouted: "Ha!"

Then—what a sensation! The black horse ran, and as he ran, he spread his wings again with another great flutter. He pressed his nose into the wind and bolted forward with such sudden speed, I rocked back in the saddle and had to hold on hard. The horse raced beneath the rock formation. Its wings began to rise and fall in majestic undulations.

And suddenly, the bump and rumble of hoofbeats on stone ceased, and we were airborne.

"Yah!" I shouted in wild exhilaration.

The stallion banked to the right, away from the caves. I gripped the reins tight and leaned forward. We rose, the mist washing over us with increasing speed until we broke into the clear blue skies, where mist and caves and all the many monsters grew small and smaller and then faded away into the vanishing landscape below us.

Ahead stretched range on jagged range of snow-capped mountains. They were white up close, then blue in the distance, then little more than the suggestion of shadows against the far horizon. The horse's wings kept heaving toward the sky and wafting toward the ground in a great, graceful cadence, their loud flutters beating the air with a symphonic rhythm.

On we went and up we rose, the wind in our faces, the sun behind us and all the wide world before.

Soon, the stallion stretched out its wings and left them still. We glided, and there was a mystical stillness around us full of the rushing wind. The mountains tilted and straightened below. I gazed at them over Maud's sloped rat shoulders, awestruck.

"Could he always fly like this, and I just didn't know it?" I asked her.

"Don't be an idiot," said Maud—and I could tell by the dreamy tone of her voice that even she was struck by the breathtaking beauty of the scene around us. "The wings are a gift from Tauratanio. But the stallion couldn't receive them until he had earned them in his journeys with you."

I nodded as if I understood. And I sort of understood, but not really. The rules of this bizarre kingdom—like the very fact of its existence—remained a strange yet familiar mystery to me. I felt I understood them in my heart, but I could never quite explain them to myself in words. As always when I was in Galiana and the Eleven Lands, I felt I was a character in a story that was already written but which I had not yet read.

The stallion swooped and banked and flapped his giant wings again, and we rose into the daylight toward the unseen stars. We passed over the White Mountains until smaller, greener hills slanted away beneath us. With shocking suddenness, the horse dove toward them. The wind rushed up over us, and soon we were twisting through narrow gaps and banking around elaborate rock formations past vast and lovely waterfalls that tumbled into rushing rivers and filled the air around us with sparkling haze and rainbows.

After a while, the land beneath us leveled. I began to become accustomed to the wonder of flying and the majesty of the view. At the same time, something began to trouble me. I couldn't place it at first. It was just a vague sense of foreboding, like that minor chord of music in a movie that alerts you things are about to take a turn for the worse.

I scanned the horizon—and that's when I noticed it: a darkness gathering at the furthest edge of the sky. It was like a line of smog. It had an unhealthy rust color, like a thing gone rotten. And now and then, when the wind shifted, I thought I caught a whiff of something sour and unholy: bad eggs, burning tires.

"Look there," I said to Maud. "What is that, do you think?"

She turned the woman-face on her rodent body and glanced toward the distant murk.

"Curtin," she said bluntly. "That's his new army."

"What do you mean?"

She gave me one of her patented Maud looks—like: *If there were no rocks, you'd be the stupidest thing on earth.* "He read the book too."

It took a moment before I understood this. Then I did. I felt a twist of nausea, like a corkscrew in my gut. "*Another Kingdom*? He read *Another Kingdom*? But how?"

She turned away, silent. I was growing unhappier by the second.

"Maud?" I said.

She muttered something into the wind. I couldn't make it out.

"Maud . . .? Is this . . . is this my fault somehow?" I already knew the answer. I could feel the answer. It was like a lead-heavy toad squatting on my stomach. "Come on," I said. "Tell me. What happened? Did the wizard get his hands on the book while I was . . ."

My voice trailed off, but Maud was only too happy to finish the sentence for me. "While you were busy transforming yourself into a depraved, twisted, sick, destructive, soulless, demonic maggot of a human being? It's possible."

The wind kept washing over me, but my face grew hot and sweaty all the same. I smelled the sulfur and burning rubber again and tasted it on my tongue. I had to swallow hard before I could answer her.

"Okay, so you saw that."

"Oh, we all saw it. Tauratanio opened a portal, and we watched the whole show. Nice vehicle, by the way."

"Thanks. It's a Mercedes."

"Lovely."

"Look, I sold a screenplay. I was making a movie. There's nothing wrong with that. It was a lifelong dream of mine."

"Which part? Manipulating the women or toadying up to the child molester? Or was it putting your manhood in a jar so you could stand by doing nothing while that sweet woman you should already be married to was abused right in front of you?"

A flair of annoyance went through me. There is nothing more irritating than a moralistic rodent woman. It's like talking to Jiminy Cricket, only as a rat. "Look, I got wrapped up in what I was doing and I forgot about the book, all right? I forgot about all of this. I had some kind of amnesia or something. Curtin must've put a curse on me somehow."

"Somehow, yes."

I flinched as if she'd slapped me. I knew she was right. I couldn't lie to myself about this anymore, as much as I would have liked to. I remembered too much now. I remembered the mansion in the woods. That mansion I had seen in my nightmare about the cemetery—if a nightmare is what it was. I had been lost inside that mansion, caught in the wizard's maze. I knew if I did not find the exit by sunrise, I would be stuck there forever, trapped forever in a repeating scene of unimaginable horror. I would be one of hundreds of prisoners devoured by a great beast again and again, day after day, without end, without hope of release.

I was terrified, desperate to get out. Who wouldn't be, right? So somehow I fought my way to the heart of the house, to a place of deep darkness and confusion. And there, I had confronted the wizard himself, face to face.

An arrangement might be made, Curtin had said to me. *I can make it so you never have to return here ever again. You wouldn't even remember. I can give you your life—and more than your life. A better life. The life you've always wanted.*

A sound escaped me as the flying stallion rose and fell on the gentle thermals.

"Yes," said Maud.

I tried to defend myself. "Well, I didn't agree to it," I said—but it sounded like wheedling even to me. "I mean, he made that offer, but I didn't say yes. I damned him. I remember. I damned him right to his face. And I . . . I pushed past him. And I escaped the maze and found my sister and . . ."

I stopped, overwhelmed by full comprehension and remorse. Maud said nothing. She just waited for me to understand it all.

I did understand. I cried out, "Oh! Oh! Oh!" I tilted my face up at the sky. "Shit! Oh shit! I'm such a piece of shit!" I pounded on my forehead with one fist. "I didn't say no. I didn't tell Curtin no. That's why he let me out of the mansion. That's why he let me find Riley. Why he let me find the book. He knew if I didn't say no . . . Oh! Oh! Oh!"

Maud still didn't answer.

"It was all about the book," I went on. "I was going to burn it. That was my plan. I was going to burn it after I finished reading it and then return here and set everything right. But, just as I reached the last page, the phone rang . . ."

"Ah," said Maud.

"And it was Solomon Vine and he . . . and I . . ."

"Yes?"

"Well, he offered me this deal and . . . I got distracted, that's all. I got distracted. And then, the amnesia . . ."

I fell silent. It was all clear to me now. It was all one story. We rode on for a long time without speaking.

Finally, when Maud figured I had wallowed in my own guilt long enough, she said quietly, "Curtin is very expert at what he does.

His only power is in the minds of men, and he knows how to use it. When you didn't say no, he knew you would ultimately belong to him. *No is your whole power, Austin. No* is the one magic that could have defeated him. Wisdom is to love the good, and to everything lovable that is not good, you must say no. Again and again. Every day. The minute Curtin heard your silence, he only had to bide his time. He only had to wait until you had the book, then make his move. What did he offer you? A little gold. A few women. A—what did you call it?—a movie? Nothing really. He bought you for nothing, Austin. When you didn't say no, he knew he could."

I felt something collapse inside me. It was my ego. It went down like a house of cards burning. Each flaming card bore a moving image on it. Riley in the asylum. Jane humiliated by Alexis. The party at Solomon Vine's with its perversion and abuse hiding in plain sight. And me, all the while, with my memory gone and my movie greenlit and Curtin stealing the book *Another Kingdom* right out from under my nose.

"He read the book," I muttered. "And now what? Now he can open doorways too."

"He opened the doorway into the dark realm where Anastasius imprisoned his demon army after the rebellion failed."

"Crap!" I glanced off toward the ugly red cloud on the far horizon. "And that's them. He let them out. The army. He freed them and now . . ."

"Now they're heading right where we're heading—toward the camp of the emperor."

The black stallion flapped its wings once to keep us moving forward. The lovely land raced by beneath us, but all its charms were lost on me.

"But how could things have changed like that while I was gone?" I asked. "Time doesn't pass here when I'm in LA. I always come back to the exact moment when I left."

Maud's usual tone of sardonic nastiness was gone now. She just sounded grim. "The dark realm Curtin opened doesn't operate on our time anymore than your realm does. His army entered where he had been, just as you entered where you were."

I nodded. Again, I didn't understand completely, but instinctively I understood. As I eyed that red darkness on the horizon, as the ashes of my ego smoldered within me, I could feel the needle on my Self-Esteem Meter falling from Corrupt Asshole to Apocalyptic Shithead. "How big an army is it?" I asked. "Can it defeat the forces of the emperor?"

And Maud answered, "I suppose we're going to find out."

As if this were his cue, the black stallion flapped his great wings again and kept them flapping this time. He stretched his neck out like a racer. I followed suit and flattened myself in the saddle like a jockey.

We put on speed. When I looked again, the stinking red haze had grown even fainter, even more distant than before. The air around us seemed to freshen. The day seemed to brighten. Curtin's rebel army fell away behind us.

We can still beat them, I told myself desperately. *It's not too late. There's still time.*

We sped on across the sky.

WE FLEW LIKE that for hours. The land continued to grow flatter and greener. The stallion dropped lower, and soon I could see cottages and small farms and even a little village nestled in the hills here and there.

"What is this country?" I asked Maud.

"Kore," she said. "The tenth of the Eleven Lands." She raised one squirrely paw. "But there—look up ahead. That's where we're headed. That's Aona."

I followed her gesture and caught my breath. What a sight! What a wonder! I stared and went on staring as we grew closer to this last and most marvelous country of all.

I saw, among rocks and above a valley, a city rising. It was unlike any city I had seen outside of video games and dreams. Crystal palaces and temples and towers sprung half formed from the hillsides as if they were growing there organically. They seemed to be made of mirrors and glass, so that the entire town was bathed in prismatic colors, and a nimbus of gold hung over the whole. Construction engines and workmen moved among the unfinished streets and climbed on scaffolding around the soaring pinnacles and domes.

But as awesome as the city was, it was what I saw beyond that most amazed me. As the stallion soared over the sprawling mansions of the suburbs and on out over the open valley, I realized, with a fine blast of wonder and satisfaction: this was the country I had seen in my vision. This was the long, blue-green grassy plain I had seen in my mind last night when I touched the talisman. And now, when I lifted my eyes to the far horizon, I could make out the spot where the scenery melted into blue nothingness. I understood: We were approaching the cliffs and the sea.

"Maud . . ." I said—but so softly that the word was carried off by the wind. I tried again, louder. "Maud, have we reached . . .?"

"Yes," she said. "There they are."

My hand went to touch the shape of the talisman beneath my clothes. My throat grew tight with emotion. Over a ridge, on the open plain before me, the aqua grass grew dark. A vast crowd of living creatures spread across the valley to the sea.

The emperor's army.

Well, this was something at least. This was something to cool the smoldering remnants of my ego. I mean, I had done it, hadn't I? For all the time spent lost in the maze of the wizard, for all the delay and error caused by the corruption of my heart, after the crime and tragedy of Betheray's murder, after my battle with the forces of Lord Iron in Galiana, the dragon fights in Edgimond, the yeti fights in the White Mountains, after the fights in California with Orosgo's agents and assassins, I had finally made it across the Eleven Lands. I had reached the armies of Anastasius. I was within sight of the emperor and the end of my quest.

The realization spread over me like the radiance of dawn, like bright water hosing the red cinders of my self-disgust.

The stallion began to descend toward the armies on the plain.

A towering cylinder of rock rose to our left. The stallion banked and we curled around it. As we did, I spied, far off, at the edge of the army encampment, on an open patch of ground right near the cliffs, an array of gaily colored pavilions, large, elaborate tents of rainbow-striped canvas, with crested pennants fluttering on their impressive peaks.

Headquarters, I thought, excited. The pavilions of the emperor himself.

We headed toward them, sinking lower and lower, the earth rising up to meet us. Soon, I could make out a small crowd of creatures gathered outside one of the tents. Other flying horses were circling above them. No one even noticed us as we joined their ranks.

We continued to descend. At first, I thought we were going to land in the open grassland right beside the tents. But in another moment, as the scene below grew clearer, I saw Maud stiffen where she sat on the pommel. She leaned forward quickly to whisper in the stallion's ear.

At once, the horse veered to the left, toward a large outcropping of white rock a small distance away from the pavilions. There was a flat patch of dusty ground behind the rocks. That was where we landed, hidden from the army and the creatures outside the tents.

We reached the earth. The stallion's hooves clopped swiftly

across the dirt as he slowed. A brown dust cloud flew up around us.

I coughed.

"Ssh!" said Maud. "Be quiet!"

I swallowed the next cough, and blew the next one into my fist. The stallion came to rest. His wings folded with stately grace until they vanished into his flanks.

"What?" I whispered to Maud. I was breathless from the ride. "What's the matter? Why are we hiding? What's happening here?"

"Ssh!" she said again. And then she gestured with her head: *Follow me!*

With that, she leapt off the pommel, hit the ground, and scrambled squirrel-like up over the rocks. I swung out of the saddle behind her. The rocks were easy to climb, and as Maud leapt nimbly from jag to jag, I went up nimbly after her.

I followed her into a narrow gap between one outcrop and another. Maud perched on a little shelf there, and I crawled up until I could prop myself just behind her. From there, through the gap, we could spy on what was happening around the pavilions.

There were about two dozen creatures gathered in a little crowd here at the furthest edge of the great army. The crowd was standing outside the main tent where a wooden platform had been erected, with stairs leading up to a stage: the sort of thing you might see at a local parade, where the mayor was going to give a speech. The crowd beneath the platform was composed of magical people and fairy-tale beasts, many of kinds I had seen before in the court of Tauratanio, the king of Shadow Wood. There were centaurs with the muscular torsos of warlike men and the haunches of battle stallions. There were pointy-eared elves with round, bright eyes, and there were peak-capped gnomes like lawn decorations. There were fauns— horned men with the legs and tails of goats—and great, hulking ogres with clubs in their hairy mitts and a single eye in the middle of their bouldery foreheads. There were all these and human men, too, and all of them, I noticed now, were arrayed in black clothing. Even the ogres wore black loincloths on bodies covered otherwise only by rough hair.

We watched from our hiding place. The flaps at the entrance of the large tent moved, and three more figures emerged. One by one, they climbed up the steps of the platform and stood on the stage above the crowd.

These were not fairy creatures but men, noble, knight-like men, all three, though each was very different from the others in appearance. The first to step onto the stage was tall and broad-shouldered, muscular and virile, with a face so handsome under its loose blond hair and short blond beard that he could have been a movie star. He, too, was dressed in black, though his black clothes glittered as if they were sprinkled with silver.

"That's Sir Littleman," Maud whispered to me.

I couldn't help but smile. If ever a knight were poorly named!

The next man up onstage was very strange looking. Small as a boy of ten but fully adult and not misshapen. He had white hair and angelic features, sweet and almost feminine in their beauty. He wore black too.

"Sir Goodchild," Maud whispered.

I nodded. A more appropriate name, no question.

"And here's Sir Hammer," Maud said. "These are the Emperor Anastasius's most trusted knights. His closest advisors."

The last guy to step up onstage was the most appropriately named of all. Sir Hammer looked like a hammer, with a long, lean body like a hammer's handle and a narrow head that seemed to stick out bluntly in front and curl back sharply behind. All the knights wore serious expressions, but Sir Hammer's expression was so serious it was nearly no expression at all.

The three knights, dressed in black, stood onstage in a wedge before the gathering. Sir Littleman was out in front. Sir Goodchild and Sir Hammer flanked him to his left and right.

The handsome Sir Littleman lifted one hand and pointed to a smaller pavilion off to his left, near the cliffs.

"Bearers, come out!" he called. He had a deep, booming voice that seemed intended to reach the entire army where it stretched out over the plain. I could hear a low murmur among that vast company, as if they were passing Sir Littleman's words from one to another.

The cloth of the side tent rippled, and through the flaps emerged two centaurs, draped in black. They carried between them what at first I thought was a stretcher. But then I realized, no, it was a pall—a coffin, draped in a black cloth with a golden insignia on it.

I heard Maud give a low, moaning sigh, a sound I'd never heard from her before.

"What?" I whispered. "What is it?"

But she didn't answer me. She went on staring through the cleft in the rock at the gathering. So I stared too.

The centaurs carried the coffin to a spot directly in front of the stage.

And in the same stentorian tones as before, Sir Littleman said, "The time has come! The time of sorrow! According to our rites and customs, the funeral will begin." He made a ceremonial gesture, unfolding one arm until his hand pointed down at the coffin below him. "It is time for us to lay to rest the body of our emperor: Anastasius."

"Wait—what?" I said.

And with that, everyone began weeping.

13

THE SOUND OF MOURNING ROSE FROM THE VAST ARMY like the sound of a roaring wind. Individual cries, wild shrieks of grief, pierced the general clamor.

"No, really, Maud—what did he just say?" I asked again.

I looked at her. She was facing away from me. Still, she did not answer. I heard her make a noise, a terrible noise like a tomb door groaning open.

"Maud?" I said, horrified.

I climbed forward a little on the rocks until I could see her profile. Only then, in that moment, did the situation become real to me.

Because Maud was weeping too. Crystal tears streamed out of her woman's eyes, dripping down her fur to fall and stain the rocks she clung to with her squirrel-like claws.

"No," I whispered harshly. "No. No, Maud. This can't be happening. Right? There's gotta be some kind of mistake."

She turned her head and gazed at me with an expression of mingled despair and scorn, a look that told me both that her heart was broken and that I was the biggest fool she'd ever met in her life.

"Maud!" I insisted, whispering louder. "The emperor can't be dead. Can he? He's the whole reason we came here. He's the only one who can defeat Curtin's armies. The only one who can restore the queen to her throne. He's the whole point and purpose of everything—everything that's happened. He can't be dead. It makes no sense!"

Still weeping, she sneered at me and turned back to the funeral.

And I turned back. The centaurs and the gnomes, the ogres and the elves and fauns and the men, too, had all bowed their heads, and all were grieving. The sounds of their laments flooded over me relentlessly.

In that flood, I felt something being washed away inside me, something I hadn't even realized was there until that moment: my faith—my inner conviction that everything would eventually turn out all right. I mean, all this time, fighting, surviving, lost, alone, desperately striving—all this time, I had been to myself like the hero of a story. It was a story about finding the emperor. Alerting the emperor. Bringing the emperor and his armies into the fight for the throne of Galiana. I never knew whether I would survive at any given moment, but deep down, I had believed that, in the end, the story would tell itself the way it was supposed to, would work its way through to the most fulfilling conclusion, the way stories do.

I hadn't even known I held that conviction until now, when it left me, but suddenly I was aware it was gone. And without it, I was utterly gray and empty inside. Hopeless.

There was no emperor. The emperor was dead. All at once, the story was over. There was not going to be, there could not be, a happy ending.

My eyes filled. The scene blurred. I blinked as the out-of-focus centaurs gave a great heave of their muscular arms and lifted the coffin high into the air above their heads. The sounds of mourning grew louder and more awful. I peeked around the edge of the rocks at the army. I saw the array of rough-faced fighting men and their sturdy wives and their vital children—all of them sobbing out their heartbreak without restraint.

Sir Littleman lifted the hand that had been pointing down at the coffin. He held it up, asking for silence. But there was no silence, only quieter sobs. The knight's movie star face was grim, and the faces of the knights on either side of him, the angel face and the hammer face, seemed more than grim, seemed dark with fury.

Sir Littleman nodded at the centaurs below him. They lowered the coffin again and began to carry it in a slow march toward an open cave behind the pavilions at the edge of the cliffs. I now noticed an ogre standing there at the cave entrance. He had a gigantic drum strapped over his gigantic shoulder. He banged the drum with his huge ogre club. The slow, hollow beat was added to the general lamentation.

I watched—everyone watched—as the centaurs carried the coffin to the cave mouth and then into the cave, where they disappeared from sight in the shadows. The drum went on beating. The crowd went on weeping. And a small wedge of cowled figures stood chanting outside one of the pavilions. Priests, I guessed, singing a dirge.

I could not deny it to myself anymore, hard as I tried. This was all real. It was all really happening. They were burying the Emperor Anastasius. My whole quest, my whole adventure, my whole story had been useless. Meaningless.

A few moments later, the centaurs emerged again, empty-handed. The ogre continued beating his drum. The priests continued their wordless threnody. Two more centaurs moved to join the others, and all four lifted a huge slab of rock from where it lay on the edge of the cliff. With a great effort, they set the slab in position and sealed the cave's entrance to transform it into a tomb for the emperor.

And that was it. That was the end of the funeral. The chanting stopped. The weeping quieted. The drum fell silent.

A moment passed. Then, Sir Littleman's voice boomed out to the crowd again.

"And now, we must finish this grim business," he told them. "Nothing can heal our hearts but time. But even as we grieve, we must have justice."

A new noise arose from the army. Like a wave, starting with those nearest to me and moving toward the rear as Sir Littleman's words were passed among them, a growl of anger sounded, pierced by harsh shouts.

"Justice!" I heard the people cry. "We want justice!"

"I do not need to tell you," said Sir Littleman, "what happened to our emperor was not a tragedy but a crime. Just as we completed the conquest of the Eleven Lands, just as we finished driving the savage armies into the sea, just as we began to build the Crystal City which the emperor promised us, and just as we prepared to begin the new lives of peace and freedom, wisdom and love which he told us would be our reward for following him—just then, our great leader was struck down by a hand empowered by treachery and a heart befouled with corruption and greed. Just as he was about to lead us into Paradise, the emperor's life was ended—by murder."

"Murder! Murder!" the people cried. "Justice! Justice!"

And over those cries, Sir Littleman's mighty voice roared out: "Bring the guilty forth!"

There was a tumult from within another of the pavilions. A moment later, three people—a man, a woman, and a little boy—were shoved through the flaps into the open air. They were followed at once by two enormous ogre guards, each with his single eye glaring. The male prisoner was in his late thirties. He was dressed in a ragged brown robe, his beard unkempt, his forehead bruised, his wrists and ankles shackled. The woman's robe was dirty white. She was shackled too, and her hair was in tangles. Her sweet, round face was grimy with tears.

The boy—the boy was so pitiful it was hard to look at him. Such a little guy. No more than four or five years old. With no clear idea of what was happening to him or why. His little wrists were tied in front of him with a small cord. His face was contorted with confusion and terror as he bawled miserably for his mother, who could not move her chained arms to comfort him.

"Favian!" Sir Littleman thundered down at them from the stage. "Brother to Anastasius! You once earned glory among us by leading the forces that put down the wizard Curtin's rebellion. But your envy of your brother and your lust for power led you to poison our great leader just as his triumph was to become complete. For that, you and your family must die the death!"

I wasn't sure what to make of the vast crowd's answer. There were individual shouts from among them.

"Burn them!"

"Justice!"

"Let the sentence be carried out!"

But overall, I thought their reaction was muted and uncertain.

Nonetheless, at another gesture from Sir Littleman, the crowd at the base of the stage stepped back and made a clearing. Quickly, the centaurs and their ogre helpers brought three large poles to the open place. The ogres, lifting the stakes over their heads, drove them down into the earth with a single mighty stroke. The centaurs, meanwhile, brought armloads of wood to lay around the stakes as kindling. With mind-boggling rapidity, they built a place of execution.

The centaurs lit torches and held them high, ready to set the blaze. They were standing right beneath me, and I could feel the heat of the flames wash over me among the rocks where I hid.

The reality of the thing struck me like a blow: they were going to burn these three, this man, this woman, this child. Burn them!

The little boy let out a high scream of inconsolable terror: "Mommy! I don't want the fire! I don't want the fire! Mommy!"

His mother cried out to him, "It will be all right, my darling!" But the ogre held her back so she couldn't reach him, and she wept uncontrollably in the knowledge of what was about to take place.

The man—Favian—the emperor's brother—managed to stagger forward in his chains. He fell to his knees, his ravaged face turned upward toward the three knights.

"Sir Littleman! Sir Goodchild! Sir Hammer!" he cried to them in a breaking voice. "I am innocent! You know I am! But if you need my sacrifice to keep the peace among the people, let me burn and join my brother in the palaces of the dead. But my wife, Beltan, has done nothing! My child, Rory, is only five years old! What harm could he be guilty of? Spare them! In the name of Anastasius, who loved you. Littleman! Goodchild! Hammer! Spare my wife and child!"

These words—the prisoner's words—seemed to be passed on among the vast army, mouth to ear. Their general murmuring quieted. One voice shouted, "Burn them all!" But only one. The rest, I think, were waiting for Sir Littleman's verdict before they decided what to think.

The ever-so-handsome knight turned and bent for a moment to consult with the small angel-faced knight and the knight with the hammery head standing beside him.

He then straightened and announced, "It is a hard truth but a truth nonetheless that the family of an executed prince will be a threat to the future peace of the empire. This cannot be allowed. They all must die!"

This was greeted by a long, solemn murmur from the crowd. I couldn't tell the meaning of it. Some, I thought, agreed with the decision. Some seemed unconvinced.

But Sir Littleman, apparently unmoved, turned to the ogre guards and nodded down at them. Loudly and clearly, he pronounced the words, "Put them to the flame."

Until that moment, I had been staring—gaping agog—at the drama, my heart filled with pity and with horror. I didn't know what to think of any of it. These were Anastasius's people. The followers of the great emperor, who was known throughout the Eleven Lands as a mighty warrior for all that was good.

And yet—there was no denying it: they were about to carry out what seemed to me an atrocity.

On instinct, I turned to Maud for her reaction—and I was shocked to find that her weeping had ceased and she was staring right at me, her hard eyes dry.

"Well?" she said, in her buzzy rodent voice.

"What?" I said. "Well what?"

"Well, are you just going to stand there and let them burn an innocent child to death? What are you?"

Startled by the words, I straightened so quickly my back hit the side of a boulder. "Me?" I said, my voice breaking out of its whisper. "What the hell am I supposed to do?"

"Well, something!" said Maud. "Anything! Stop them! You're Elinda's knight. You're her chosen hero! Do you think she would have stood by and let this happen in her fiancé's name? Do you think she would see a child burned in the name of the Emperor Anastasius?"

My mouth fell open. All at once, my horror at the events unfolding before me was transformed into . . . well, into horror at the idea that I was supposed to do something about it. There was an entire army out there. Elinda's knight or no, I was only one man. What could I do?

But when I turned back to the scene before us—when I saw one of the ogre guards grab Favian and his wife by their arms, one arm in each of his massive hairy hands—when I saw the other ogre pick up the crying child in order to carry him to the stake where he'd be tied along with his parents—when I heard the boy screaming,

"Mommy! Mommy! I don't want to! I don't want to!"—when I saw the shackled woman reach for him, shrieking, "My boy! Have mercy! For the love of God! Have mercy on my boy!"—I realized Maud was right: I actually *couldn't* just stand by and let this happen. I actually did have to do something!

"Hold on!" I shouted before I could stop myself, before I could think of a better plan or think of any plan at all. Even as my inner voice was shouting at me, *What the hell do you think you're doing, you asshole?* I was at the same time leaping from the rocks to land on a slope of raised ground above the shocked crowd and beneath the glares of the three noble knights on the stage.

"Stop right there!" I shouted in my best imitation of a hero— which was not all that great, I'm sorry to tell you, especially since I slid and stumbled on the slope before I got my footing. Only then did it occur to me to add, "Stop—in the name of Queen Elinda!"

No one was more surprised than I was when they all actually stopped what they were doing. The ogre dragging Favian and his wife toward the pyre stopped and so did the ogre with the shrieking child squirming in his arms. The centaurs and fauns and gnomes all turned to stare at me, and even the vast army went utterly silent. In the gasps between the child's exhausted sobs, the whicker of the flames from the torches was loud in the air, and the whisper of the ocean waves way, way down at the bottom of the high cliffs could be heard even where I was standing.

"Who are you?" shouted Sir Littleman. "How dare you stand between these criminals and justice?"

I opened my mouth to respond, but what was I supposed to say? It was a good question. Who was I? What right did I have to interfere?

"You're Queen Elinda's knight!" Maud whispered urgently from where she clung to the rocks behind my head. "You're her chosen hero."

"Right! Exactly. I am Queen Elinda's knight," I shouted. "I'm her chosen hero!" I wanted as many people to hear me as possible in case there were some Queen Elinda fans in the crowd who might come to my defense.

"She would have been their empress," Maud prompted.

I hadn't thought of that. It was a good point. I shouted, "If Anastasius hadn't died, he would have married her, and she would have been your empress!" I turned to address the vast crowd head-on. "You know her! Even if her husband had been murdered, would she have burned an innocent child?"

My heart leapt up with hope as a murmur of support passed over the seemingly endless crowd. I could hear voices nearby:

"He's right. She would never have done it."

"It can't be imagined."

"She was the gentlest of ladies and the most righteous queen."

"I loved Queen Elinda."

Beneath all that, I heard Maud whisper again, "The emperor called her 'his wisdom.'"

I glanced at her. "He did? That's really sweet."

"Use it, you jackass!"

"Oh! Oh, right!" I raised my voice again. "The emperor called the queen 'his wisdom.'"

"That's true," I heard someone say. "He always did."

I faced the knights on their stage but spoke as loudly as I could so as many people as possible would hear me. "If the emperor's wisdom would not have done this deed, then how can you permit it in the emperor's name?"

Even as I said the words, I was surprised to realize: this was actually a pretty good argument. Which made me wonder: if Littleman, Goodchild, and Hammer were Anastasius's most trusted knights, why were they looking to do this terrible thing in the first place?

Well, there was no time to figure that out now.

The crowd was growing restive. Someone dared to shout out loudly, "It's true! The emperor's wisdom would not have allowed this to happen."

And someone else added, "Whether it was expedient or not, whether it was necessary for the future peace or not, she would not have allowed it."

Other lower voices seemed to mutter their assent.

I saw Sir Littleman scan the vast array of faces before him from under lowered brows. He glanced sternly to his right, down at the angelic Sir Goodchild. Sir Goodchild glanced across him in turn at the hammer-headed Sir Hammer. Then all three looked at me.

Sir Goodchild spoke. His voice rang like windchimes. "How do we know you are who you say you are? How do we know you are Elinda's chosen knight?"

My mouth went dry. Another good question. How could I prove it?

But Maud whispered: "Your sword, you fool. Your armor."

Of course. I remembered how the soldiers of King Cambitus in Vagos of Menaria had stopped in the process of cutting me to pieces when they saw I carried the sword and wore the magic armor of the queen. It was her gift to her hero.

My hand began to reach to the place where my invisible scabbard was. But I hesitated. Would the sword be there? Hadn't I lost it when the Great Yeti sent me flying? Well, I had to try . . .

I reached and—yay, magic!—the sword was suddenly in my hand. The armor flowed out of my skin and covered me.

The crowd gave a very gratifying gasp of surprise and wonderment as I stood before them clothed in flowing metal and armed with the gleaming blade. They could all see now: I was who I said I was, a knight and the queen's chosen.

All three of the knights on the stage above me drew a deep breath. All three nodded.

With a thrill, I thought, *I've done it! I've stopped them!*

Then Sir Littleman said, "Sir Knight. I see you are who you say you are. Well and good!" He turned to the people and raised his voice again. "We know that the Aona of Anastasius was to be a land of perfect justice. We know that in such a land, the outcome of contested questions will always be what it is meant to be. Therefore, to decide this dispute, this knight and I will meet in a joust on the field of battle. And whoever survives this trial by combat shall give the final verdict on the murderer Favian and his clan."

I was still trying to parse the sense and logic of all that verbiage when the crowd let out a cheer so loud it drowned out every thought.

The ogre who had been holding the squirming, crying child now put the boy down. The child's mother swooned to the earth in relief. Her husband gazed at me with an expression of the deepest gratitude.

I faced them, then faced the crowd. I raised my sword to my brow to salute them all—and right about then, the meaning of Sir Littleman's words made their way into my frazzled brain.

We were going to have a trial by combat. That's how we were going to decide the outcome: we were going to joust with each other to the death.

My sword sank to my side.

"Shit," I whispered softly.

14

ALL THIS HAPPENED IN SUCH A CONFUSION OF HIGH
emotion that I was mounted on my stallion on the field of battle
before I fully understood how completely and utterly screwed I was.

The crowd had shifted to watch the joust. Some had climbed
rocks or hills for a better view. Some sat in the branches of the few
nearby trees. Even in the distant Crystal City, I could make out
workmen perched on the high shelves of scaffolding, ready to enjoy
the contest from afar.

A long, narrow lane had been roped off right beside the cliffs.
From where I sat on my horse, I could look over the land's edge,
down, down, down to the wild sea far below. The whitecaps leapt
and broke on fantastical rock formations. Pillars and jags and rings
of stone caught the brunt of the tide. Water splashed through narrow
gaps, and the spray rose so high that some of the droplets, glistening
silver in the sun, nearly reached the land above.

At the far end of the field near the pavilion, Sir Littleman was
finishing his preparations. Attendant fauns, still in their black
mourning robes, were fastening his armor about him as he pulled
his gauntlets on over his hands. He seemed confident and calm.
Beside him was a white warhorse, a charger thick as a garbage truck,

who looked as ready for the fight as he was.

I, meanwhile, had been relegated to a dusty spot about a hundred yards away where a yellow pennant had been hastily stuck into the ground to mark the end of the lane. There I sat, clothed in my mercurial magic armor, trying to control my unsteady stallion. Much sleeker and weaker than Littleman's humongous mount, the horse danced under me, huffing and tugging nervously against his reins.

An ogre handed me my lance, slung it up at me as lightly as if it were a baton. But when I caught the thing, the weight of it nearly pulled me off the horse and sent me over the cliff down into the rocks and sea. The lance was as heavy as a steel girder. Fight with it? I had no idea how I was even going to hold on to it.

Next, the ogre handed me a shield, which was comical in its uselessness. It was about the size of a postage stamp and curved at the top and bottom, which made it seem smaller still. I figured if I used it just right, I might be able to defend approximately one nipple with it, not much more.

"Maud," I said breathlessly. "How do you joust?"

The mutant rodent sat perched atop one of the poles that held the rope bordering the field. "How should I know?" she answered. "Look at me. I'm a giant squirrel. And before that, I was a girl. Jousting is not the sort of thing we do."

I looked down the field at Sir Littleman. "He looks like freaking Thor," I said. "He's going to kill me. And then they'll burn the family anyway. So what was the point of my stepping in?"

"What do you mean, what was the point?" she said. "You're a knight. Elinda's knight. This was an injustice. You had to do something to stop it."

"That's crazy! If he kills me, I'm no good to anyone!"

"It's the principle of the thing!"

"The principle?" I cried, as the horse fidgeted beneath me. "Are you out of your—"

But now, Sir Hammer spoke from where he stood beside little Sir Goodchild on the stage. Even his voice was like a hammer blow, curt and hollow.

"Sir Littleman. And Sir Lively. Will now meet. Upon the field," he announced. "And who survives. Decides the fate. Of Favian and his kin."

The crowd cheered like it was a football game. What had happened to all the solemn mourning for their dead emperor? Well, never mind. I took some hope—a faint, thin, sickly hope—from the fact that a few voices were raised in my favor. There was even an attempt to start a chant for me.

Lively! Lively! Stay Alive!

But it didn't last long.

Neither would I.

"When the flag is lowered. Let the joust begin!" Sir Hammer said.

And with that—so help me, I'm not making this up—a cute medieval chick with cascading raven hair slipped under the rope and took up a place at the midpoint of the field between me and Sir Littleman. She was holding an emerald scarf to use as a starting flag. It was exactly as if we were in a drag race or a game of chicken on the streets of Compton. You know, where the prettiest babe waves the cloth before you hit the gas of your juiced-up Civic and shoot down Broadway Avenue? This girl wasn't wearing cutoff shorts and a halter top, but her snug thigh-length tunic with its top cut low enough to show her remarkable cleavage served the same purpose. I guess some essential rituals are universal, even in Fantasy Land.

I rounded my stallion to face Sir Littleman's charger. I pressed the butt of my lance against my side with my arm as hard as I could, trying to secure it. But the point kept swinging back and forth and up and down, too heavy for me to control.

Meanwhile, I couldn't help but notice that Littleman's lance was as steady as the Empire State Building and pointed straight at me. I shifted my shield, but the damn thing was so tiny I couldn't figure out which three inches of my body to defend.

The cute medieval hot-rod chick lifted her green scarf high above her head. I think I stopped breathing. This was it. Jousting time. The scarf fluttered in the breeze from the ocean. The babe looked at Sir Littleman. She looked at me.

She let the flag drop.

I spurred the stallion and charged.

If the next few seconds were not the scariest and most suspenseful seconds of my life, it was only because my life had been so unrelentingly scary and suspenseful ever since I'd first stepped through the magic door into this crazy other world. Sir Littleman's warhorse thundered at me like some great machine. My stallion raced toward him, swift and light. My lance point swung everywhere except in the direction I was trying to aim it. His lance point trained itself on my chest and never wavered. My heart was in my throat as my whole life seemed to narrow down to the single onrushing instant of our meeting.

Our two horses rushed together until I could see the blue of Sir Littleman's eyes through his visor. I could see the murder in his eyes too: my own sure and certain death hurtling toward me. We were mere yards from the fatal collision when it came on me like a revelation: this was nuts. I had no chance here. None. I was about to be skewered like a roast suckling pig.

And I thought: *Well, bullshit on that!*

I pulled the reins up hard and dug my armored heels into the stallion's flank. The horse knew what I wanted. In fact, I suspect he had been thinking the same thing. In any case, just before Sir Littleman and I collided, the stallion spread his lofty wings with a fluttering *pop*, and we lifted into the air.

Up we flew—and the crowd said, "O-o-oh!" as Sir Littleman charged by underneath me, his lance point skewering nothing but the air between my horse's flailing hooves. The stallion's great wings, meanwhile, pumped and rose, and we kept climbing higher and higher toward the infinite blue before me. My first instinct was to just keep going until I reached some semi-enlightened place, like Chicago maybe, where people killed each other with guns like civilized human beings.

But the roar of the spectators washed up beneath me, some jeering in rage, some cheering with enthusiasm. The sound reminded me that the contest wasn't settled. If I ran away now, I would be leaving Favian and his wife and child to burn.

I sighed. *Damn it*, I thought. Disgruntled, I pulled the reins to turn the stallion. His wings beat the high ocean air once again as he came swinging around in a long arc to return to the battlefield.

And as we turned, I saw—right there in the air in front of me— Sir Littleman.

His charger had wings too. His charger, too, had left the ground. His charger was also turning in an arc above the ocean just as I was turning. He was lower than I was, down beneath me. But we were both high, high above the ground as we completed our turns and faced each other.

So the joust wasn't over, not by a long shot. It had simply taken to the sky.

Once again, we charged each other. The black stallion's black wings rose and fell gracefully, tracing a majestic parabola in the air. The white charger's white wings flapped bat-rapidly, as if drumming a martial tattoo.

My higher position in the sky gave me some small advantage this time. I was rocketing down at Sir Littleman, picking up speed. Now, the stallion folded his wings behind him, and we went into a dive-bomb glide. But still, I could not get control of that massive lance.

I could not make it point the way I wanted it to. And Littleman, climbing slowly toward me on his powerful flying destrier, had his lance pinned right on me again, unwavering.

This was no good. I was going to die. The two horses flew closer and closer. I fought to control my lance point to no avail. His lance point moved ever nearer to my heart.

In the final second before the clash, I lost my nerve. I tried to make the stallion bank to the right to get out of the way of Littleman's weapon. Sir Littleman expertly shifted the lance and kept the point trained on me. Crying out in fear, I tried desperately to put the tiny shield in position to catch the blow.

And then, with a shattering crash, we came together in midair.

I have no idea where my lance point went. It was skewing off somewhere in space by then. Littleman's point smashed right into my chest, high on the left side, above my heart. The edge of my shield took some of the blow, and the liquid metal of my magic armor gathered at the spot in a last-ditch effort to keep me from being pierced clean through.

But the shot was a beauty all the same. Sir Littleman's lance exploded against me in a spray of splinters. I was knocked clean out of the saddle, my legs flying wide. I felt my brain rattle in my skull. The lump on the side of my head where the yeti had slugged me tolled like a ding-dong bell.

And I fell.

Through my helmet's visor, I caught a glimpse of the earth far below, far enough so the impact would surely kill me. I had lost my grip on my lance and could see it spinning down and down through the air toward the cliffs. Only the fact that I managed to hold on to the flying stallion's reins with my left hand kept me from plummeting straight to my death.

I dropped to the length of the reins, yanking the stallion onto his side. He let out a frightened whinny as we tumbled together toward oblivion. His whole body thrashed as he tried to right himself. I dangled helplessly, watching the ground speed toward me.

The stallion fought his way upright. He spread his wings again. One wing slapped me hard in the face and knocked me against the horse's flank. I clung to the reins with one hand and frantically reached up with the other to grab the saddle. I lifted my legs to try to keep them clear of the ground.

With only a few yards left before impact, the stallion went into a rapid glide, slowing our descent a little. Nonetheless, he hit the earth hard, running at a gallop. The jolt loosed my grip. I was thrown free and went flying through the air. The crowd gasped. I smacked into the ground.

"Oof!" I said as the breath was knocked out of me.

But I kept rolling, trying to absorb the blow. I went tumbling over and over in the dirt, catching glimpses of the edge of the cliff as I headed straight for it.

Dazed and coughing, I clutched at the earth with my mailed fingertips, cutting parallel furrows in the dirt. I got purchase— and stopped my roll just at the place where the earth ended. My head went over the side and I saw the great waves hitting the jags and rings of rock way, way down below. There, at the very limit of the world, I came to rest.

With the speed of panic, I rolled back the other way, putting some distance between me and the fatal drop. I lay on my back and groaned with pain, a sound lost under the crowd's cheering and the tumult of the distant sea. With a grunt of agony and effort, I turned onto one shoulder, my armor rippling around me. My vision doubled and undoubled as I searched for Sir Littleman.

There he was. His charger was just landing in a smooth trot. Even as the horse was still running over the field, the knight dismounted with a graceful, flowing motion, walking swiftly to keep his balance after he touched down. I lay dazed, watching, as he tossed the butt of his shattered lance aside. Still striding away from me, he drew his sword with a metallic swish.

Then he turned. Trained his eyes on me. Started walking toward me, ready to finish me off.

I felt hollowed out by the fall. Every part of me ached. My head was still buzzing from the shock of the lance. But Sir Littleman and his sword were coming at me relentlessly. I had to move. I had to stand.

I let out a ragged growl as I pushed myself to one knee. I braced one hand on my thigh, the other on the earth, and pushed myself up until I was on my feet, stumbling and swaying this way and that.

Sir Littleman threw up his visor. I could see his teeth bared with determination. I could see his eyes blazing with battle rage. He picked up his pace as he got closer, almost running at me now. He began to lift his sword to deliver the fatal blow.

I reached across my body for my own sword. My hand closed on the hilt. My bruised muscles sent pulses of pain through me as I used all my effort to draw the blade free. Somehow, I managed to lift the sword up in front of me just as Sir Littleman swung with his. Our two blades clashed together. The blow sent me reeling backward—which saved my life as Sir Littleman swung again at once, trying to cut me in half, and the edge of his sword whisked through the spot where I had just been standing.

Without a pause, he charged again. I braced myself, my sword up in front of me. I sensed the brink of the cliff right behind me, but there was no time to look and see where it was.

Sir Littleman gave a war cry and unleashed a backhanded swing at my throat. I turned my blade to meet it and blocked the blow. Our swords locked together for a single second. Our eyes locked together, our faces inches apart.

Then Sir Littleman lifted his foot high and kicked me in the belly.

I went staggering backward and tumbled off the edge of the world.

I went off the cliff and plummeted. It was a long way down, a long, long way. I fell and fell and fell toward the sea. My sword and armor vanished. My body revolved in air. I saw the crashing whitecaps and the rocks spiraling up at me from below. I saw jags and mounds and circles of stone and a seething turmoil of water. It didn't matter where I struck, whether I hit the rock or the ocean. Dropping from this height, even the sea would be hard as concrete.

The last waves withdrew. A shelf of ridged rock was revealed right below me. That was the place I would probably strike. There was a hole in the center of the shelf, a hole clean through. I could see the dark water beneath it, churning in a burbling, hellish blackness.

Like a doorway into death, I remember thinking.

And then I thought: *Doorway.*

With maybe a second left before I hit, I made a motion of my will toward the opening in the rock.

An instant later, I plummeted straight through the hole and was lying on the floor of the hall outside my apartment.

I made a childlike noise of terror and confusion. I looked around, open-mouthed, clutching at the hallway carpet with my fingers, my mind reeling. My eyes felt as large as two serving plates. They filled with tears. I felt a kind of madness of unknowing blow my thoughts away like feathers in the wind. I could not make sense of anything. I thought I would just go insane right then and there. I thought I *was* insane.

But I was alive!

Panting and coughing, I began to sit up. I groaned. My bruised body ached, and my bones seemed to rattle. I reached up to touch the throbbing place on my head where the yeti had hit me and felt a sharp pang from the throbbing place on my chest where the lance had struck.

Then I let out a high screech of shock and surprise as something made my body vibrate.

"What is it? What is it?" I grunted aloud.

It was my phone. The phone in my pants. Wasn't it after one a.m. here? Who the hell could be calling me now?

I dug into my pocket and drew the phone out. I read the readout. *Caller ID Blocked*, it said.

I answered: "Hello?"

A man's voice: "Is this Austin Lively?"

"Yeah. Yes. Who is this?"

"Jane Janeway. Is she your girl?"

"Yes. What about her?"

"You've got to get her out of lockup," the man said. "They're going to murder her in there."

"Murder her? Murder Jane? Who? How? When?"

"They're going to hang her in her cell. Make it look like suicide. Tonight. Around midnight. You've got about twenty hours to get to her. By day's end, she'll be dead."

15

WORST NIGHT EVER. SLEEPLESS. GUILT-RIDDEN. SCARED
out of my wits. My brain was like a zombie apocalypse movie,
crowded with images of ruin, death, and disaster.

And all of it my fault. Mine.

Jane was in prison, charged with murder. Would that be true if
I hadn't abandoned her? If she was guilty—if she had cracked under
her abusive boss's tirades—wasn't I to blame? If I hadn't stood there
and watched while Alexis humiliated her in front of my entire office,
I might have changed everything. I might have saved her before she
did what she did.

But she couldn't be guilty. She would never commit murder,
not Jane. The whole deal had to be some kind of setup. How else
had Orosgo's cops turned up like they had, all unbidden? Why else
would they have covered up my presence on the scene? *You were
never here.* And why else were they planning to hang her in her cell
and make it look like a suicide? They wanted to shut us up so they
could use their journalists and moviemakers and professors to tell
the story the way they wanted it told.

And wouldn't that be my fault too? Hadn't I forgotten about my
attempts to expose Orosgo and his people when I became distracted

by Solomon Vine and my movie? No wonder Orosgo's cops thought they could count on my silence. I'd joined their corrupt crew of propagandists when I signed that movie contract. I had become one of them.

And while I was mucking about making movies and bedding starlets and driving my fancy car, Curtin had gotten hold of the book *Another Kingdom*. That's how he'd opened up a doorway to release his army on the Eleven Lands. So that was my fault too.

And I was as helpless to stop the wizard as I was helpless to save Jane. The Emperor Anastasius was dead, so my quest had come to nothing. And anyway, if I went back to Aona now, I'd hit the sea at terminal velocity. A split second after I crossed the threshold, I'd be gone in a bloody flash.

I tossed. I turned. I brooded like a gargoyle over the landscape of my catastrophe. Every few minutes, some new anxiety occurred to me, some new guilt fed on me, some new mystery plagued me.

Who had called me with the warning about Jane? Was he telling the truth? Could I trust him? I thought the voice had sounded vaguely familiar, but maybe not; maybe it was just my imagination. If he was a friend, how did he know about the planned murder? Was he on the inside of the plot? Could he help me get to Jane?

And another puzzle. Why had Solomon Vine bought my screenplay in the first place?

This really was mysterious. Orosgo and I had had a deal. I remembered this too now. Orosgo had made some sort of pact with Curtin, back in his youth, back in Russia. Curtin had offered Orosgo power and influence—an entire age of history that would bear his name. And in return Orosgo had promised Curtin . . . something. Something that came due at the hour of Orosgo's death. His empire? His soul? I didn't know. It didn't matter. The point was: as the hour of his death drew inevitably near, Orosgo was growing terrified. He wanted me to recover the book *Another Kingdom* and use my power to defeat Curtin before Curtin could claim his prize.

So then why did he let Solomon Vine distract me by buying my script? Why help Curtin get his hands on the book? Did Orosgo think he could buy his way out of the deal by giving the wizard the power he wanted? Or was Vine a renegade, acting out some plot of his own?

I lay in bed, awake, exhausted, my body in pain, my mind in turmoil.

Only as the slow gray dawn ate its way through the night darkness—only then did I begin to formulate what could almost be called a plan.

WHEN SOMETHING LIKE morning finally came, I fired up my handheld and streamed the news. Alexis's murder and Jane's arrest were the lead stories everywhere. I lay in bed and watched the video from last night: a dazed and terrified Jane being led into the police station. Then came an early morning press conference led by the chief of police, with Graciano and Lord standing behind him. No one mentioned me. No one said I had been present at the scene of the crime. They really expected me to vanish. *You were never here.*

For the next hour or so, there was little new information. The news shows filled in the gaps with gossip. There were endless interviews with "associates" and "close friends" of Alexis. Stagehands and makeup girls and one minor costar eager to get her face onscreen. They talked about Alexis's divorce from David Thune, her movie star husband. They talked about the subsequent drug use that many said had left Alexis "unemployable." Thune's agent released a statement saying his client was "devastated" by the news of his ex-wife's death. And there was a statement from Alexis's first husband, Solomon Vine, too. Vine said he had been in negotiations with Alexis to "find her a major part" in his new picture *Another Kingdom*. *Find her a major part*. He made it sound like he was doing her a favor, an act of charity to help her get back on her feet.

Some time after ten a.m., Jane was brought to the courthouse for her arraignment. I lay in bed and watched the video images. The police forced a pathway for her through the globular mass of jostling reporters. Jane looked as scared and confused as she had when they arrested her, plus exhausted now too. Her eyes, narrowed against the merciless morning light, flicked this way and that as the reporters shouted her name.

I had often noticed how when I returned to LA from Galiana and the Eleven Lands, that other kingdom lost its reality for me. I came home with scars, bruises, life-threatening wounds—but somehow it made no difference. The monsters who'd attacked me, the villains I'd dueled with, the whole far-off country became dreamlike once I was back in the so-called real world.

Now, though—now as I watched my terrified Jane hustled through the crowd—the real world lost its reality too. I could barely bring myself to believe that what was happening was happening.

Jane was arraigned and sent back to jail without bail. Her lawyer came out alone onto the courthouse steps and gave a brief statement to the press. Roland Feltz, his name was. Young, tall, and gangly with receding red hair and blinky eyes behind big glasses. He looked as dazed and confused as his client was.

"I am still in the process of interviewing my client to get a fuller understanding of what happened last night. Then we'll determine what course of action to take," he said.

Right. In other words, Roland Feltz thought Jane was guilty and was trying to convince her to make a deal and cop a plea.

Still, he was my only point of contact, my one chance to reach Jane. She would have told him I was on the scene last night, and he would want to talk to me. So that's what I would do. If Vine or Orosgo or whoever was behind this mayhem—if any of them thought I was going to keep my mouth shut to preserve my greenlighted picture? They could greenlight my ass.

My memory was back. My soul was back. I was back. Those days were done.

I reached for the phone to call Roland Feltz.

But before I could grab it, the phone buzzed. I answered.

It was Roland Feltz.

JANE WAS BEING held in the Blackwood Women's Detention Center downtown. The Tower—that's what they called it. It was easy to see why. The jail looked like the crumbling ruin of some forbidden castle in a cheap horror movie. It loomed darkly at the center of a government compound, which otherwise consisted of a collection of low barracks-style buildings. There was a fence around the compound, a diamond-link fence topped with razor wire. There were guard towers and giant spotlights positioned at the corners.

The Tower itself was a strange pile of a place—really strange. Half of it was twenty stories tall and half was shorter, maybe fifteen, so that it looked lopsided, like it was rotten, sloping over, about to fall. The stone of the walls was basalt gray, a strange non-color that blended in with the cloudy sky behind it, so that portions of the structure seemed to vanish at times, giving the whole thing a weird, shifting, and sinister aspect. The place seemed at once vital and moribund: a hungry monster and a dying beast. I could imagine Jane looking out of the prison bus as she first arrived here, her heart sinking. I felt pretty much the same way as I met Feltz in the parking lot and he led me inside.

I had agreed to speak with the lawyer on the condition I could talk to his client first. The thing was: I didn't think my testimony would help Jane much. I had found her covered in blood and carrying a butcher knife while drugged out of her mind. If anything, I'd make a better witness for the prosecution than for the defense. Plus, I wasn't sure whether to trust the lawyer. If the guy who warned me about the attack on Jane was on the up-and-up, why hadn't he called Feltz instead of me?

Anyway, Feltz guided me through the security rigmarole in the jail lobby. Then, once I got through the metal detector, an enormous female corrections officer who looked, so help me, like the female corrections officer balloon in the Thanksgiving parade, took me to the row of visitor windows.

I sat on my little stool in my little booth and waited. After a few minutes, another balloon-like C.O. brought Jane in. "You have fifteen minutes," she told us.

Jane had always dressed in shlumpy clothes so as not to excite her boss's envy. But the sight of her in her county outfit—her papery yellow shirt and blue sweatpants—made my heart hurt as if a giant fist were squeezing it. The expression on her face told me she was still in shock, still stunned into passivity and despair. The thought went through my head: *It will be easy for them to kill her. She won't even put up a fight.*

She settled onto the stool on her side of the glass. We both picked up our intercom phones. We did that thing that jail visitors do in movies, where we put our hands on the small square window as if we could touch each other. It turns out that's just something you do.

A smile flickered at the corner of Jane's mouth.

"I knew you'd come," she said.

It was pitiful. That was all she'd counted on. I'd come. My eyes filled. "I'm so sorry, Jane."

"Oh, no. No . . ."

"What I did when Alexis yelled at you like that. How I just stood there."

"No, no, sweetheart, that's all right, really."

That word—that *sweetheart* on her lips—the fact that she was comforting me like I was a child who'd made an innocent mistake—it was like the drop of water that breaks the dam: emotion surged over my resistance and flooded through me.

"Listen to me," I said. "Here's the thing. The thing is: I love you. You have to know. I've always loved you. I've been afraid because . . . because I knew there was no loving you halfway. I knew it meant marriage and children and then more children and adulthood and a whole life together till death do us part and I . . ." I shook my head.

Jane gazed at me through the glass for an endless moment—and then she flushed and smiled and put her hand over her mouth. She said, "Oh! That makes me so happy!" And she burst into tears—tears of joy. No, really! She was in jail. She was charged with murder. And she was crying tears of joy because I loved her.

Which, of course, only made me feel worse. Even more guilty for how I'd failed her. "Ah, Jane," I said. "I'm so sorry."

And she said: "No. No. It's all right now. I'm happy now. I am. You know I love you too. You know I've always loved you. Always."

I put my hand over my eyes. I stifled a groan. I wished I'd never heard of Solomon Vine. I wished I could flash back to Aona right then and there and smash into the sea and be particlized on impact. Anything would be less excruciating than this.

Finally, I took a breath—a trembling breath—and got myself under control. Time was short. There was so much to say. I raised my eyes and looked through the window at her. She was still beaming, her cheeks still streaming with tears.

My gaze went up and around the little booth, checking for microphones or cameras. I didn't see any, but I figured they had to be there.

"They probably record these calls," I told her.

"Yes."

"Tell me what you can."

Her narrow shoulders lifted and fell under the papery yellow shirt. "I was working. I think I fell asleep at my desk. I woke up, and there was someone standing there in the doorway. A man, I think. But he was very dark, just a shadow. And that's all. After that, I don't remember anything. I remember you. I remember you carrying me into the house. But it's all confused."

"You must have been drugged, then. The man must have drugged you."

She hurriedly swiped the tears off her face. "I don't know. Yes. Maybe. I don't know, but . . . I would never have hurt her, Austin."

"Of course not."

"I wasn't even angry at her. At Alexis, I mean. Not really. She'd always been very good to me. She really was. I mean, she was a movie star and had her ego and all, but . . . she gave me extra money when my mother got ill. She let Schuyler live with me when she had nowhere to go. She was a kind person. It was just the divorce that made her . . . you know, what she turned into. The divorce and then the drugs. They ruined her. That's why I stayed with her. To take care of her until she was well. Because she took care of me when I needed it. It didn't seem right to just leave her. My plan was to wait until she was working again. That was her medicine. Work. She was desperate for work. But the stories about the drugs got around, and no one would hire her. Except Mr. Vine. She kept saying Mr. Vine would hire her. She was sure of it. And then, when he did hire her, well, I just thought, okay, she'll be all right now. I just wanted to make sure they signed the contracts, and then I was going to leave. And in the meantime . . . those rages of hers . . . the things she said to me . . . they didn't hurt me, Austin, because I knew she was in pain and I was helping her."

I smiled sorrowfully into her blue-green eyes, eyes glassy with weariness and with crying. What jury in the world would believe in Jane? I wondered. Who would believe in her kindness and her patience, her willingness to tolerate Alexis's abuse in order to do what she thought was right? The jurors would never buy it. They would just think it was weakness and passivity. They would think she had stored up her anger and finally struck back. They wouldn't understand Jane.

"Your lawyer," I said. "Can you trust him?"

She nodded. "He's an old friend from college."

"Is he in love with you?"

She rolled her eyes. "Don't be silly."

I nodded. So that meant yes, he was in love with her. Every man who met Jane fell in love with her. It was an occupational hazard of being the single most feminine human being on the planet. But it probably meant he was trustworthy.

"All right," I said. "All right. Listen." Then I said again: "Listen. Listen." Because I wasn't talking to her, not just to her. I was talking to the jail, to the people who ran the jail. "There are people who want to hurt you," I said.

Jane breathed deep. She nodded. She knew—or she'd guessed. Whoever had set her up couldn't let her live to testify.

"They want to make it look like suicide," I said. "But it won't be suicide. And I'll know it wasn't. Do you understand?"

"Austin, don't . . ."

"If anyone hurts you, if anyone touches you, they'll pay. I'll make them pay. And if they think I'm going to keep my mouth shut about it—"

"Austin, please. There's something going on. I don't know what. But it's dangerous. You have to be careful. I couldn't stand it if you were hurt."

"Listen to me. Look at me, Jane."

Her whole body shook as she peered through her tears and through the window.

"Marry me," I said. "Live with me forever. Have children with me. Lots and lots of children. A whole country's worth."

She sobbed and started crying again. "I always wanted to."

"You will. We will. I swear it."

She smiled even as she went on crying. It made that big invisible fist squeeze my heart all the tighter. And sure, I knew how hopeless this was. It was impossible for me to save her, impossible for me to get her out of this place before midnight, before the killers came.

But I would. Somehow I would.

I leaned forward. I pressed my nose to the cold glass. She leaned forward and pressed her face to mine. I clutched the phone in my trembling hand.

"So help me," I whispered. "So help me God, I'll come for you."

16

THE LAWYER, FELTZ, WAS WAITING FOR ME IN THE
Tower foyer, sitting empty-eyed on a bench near the metal detectors.
He stood up as I returned from the visitors' room, and we walked
together out into the parking lot.

Up close and in person, Feltz did not inspire confidence. He had
the look of a kid who'd prepared for the essay test in English Lit and
suddenly found he was taking the short-answer quiz in Calculus.
His gangly body waved like a stalk of wheat above me. He blinked
down at me gormlessly through his big glasses.

"You know she didn't do it, right?" I asked him.

"Well, she says her recollection is confused . . ."

"Yeah, that's the wrong answer, Feltz. Jane would never kill
anybody. You have to know that."

He did know it somewhere deep down. But that sort of
knowledge had been lawyered out of him at lawyer school.

"She saw a man in her workroom doorway," I went on. "After
that, she can't remember anything. The guy obviously drugged her."

Feltz swayed back and forth up there. "It's a hard sell to a jury.
The way she was. The way you found her. It looks bad."

I nodded, glancing off across the barren complex. Faceless barracks. Heartless barbed wire. He had a point.

"I have a source who says they're going to try and kill her tonight."

Surprised, Feltz let out a laugh. "Who is?" he asked.

"I don't know. The same people who set her up, I imagine. They're going to hang her in her cell. Try to make it look like a suicide."

For a lawyer, Feltz had a lousy deadpan. I could practically read his thoughts. He was thinking: *This guy is crazy*. "Well, she's in jail, remember. I don't think we have to worry too much."

I sighed. "Feltz. Feltz, look at me. Look in my eyes. Do I look like some lunatic conspiracy theorist?"

"Yes. Almost exactly."

"Okay. Maybe that was the wrong question. My point is, you have to take some precautions. Get her on twenty-four-hour watch. Tell the press there've been threats against her. Tell them she's not suicidal. You see what I'm saying? Maybe if they know we know they're coming, they'll think twice before they come."

Here, Feltz actually paused long enough to study me. His manner changed a little. He became thoughtful. "The press all seem to be against her. They've already convicted her."

I decided not to respond to that. How could I tell him: Orosgo had been taking over the press for decades; they were his people, in on the setup? It would only make me sound more paranoid.

"Listen. Feltz," I said. "This is Jane we're talking about. You know what she is, right? What she's like?"

His long body went up and down as he drew a deep, wistful breath and blew it out again. He knew, all right. He knew Jane. He loved her. They hadn't lawyered that out of him.

"So take care of her," I said. "And I'll be in touch." I started to move away toward my car.

He seemed to wake up at that. "What do you mean?" he called after me. "What are you going to do?"

"I'm going to see if I can find out what really happened."

"How? Wait. Maybe I can help. Where are you going? Who are you going to talk to?"

I kept on walking. If I couldn't tell him about Orosgo, how was I going to explain that I needed to talk to the queen of Galiana? *She's from this other kingdom, Feltz. She was exiled here to Los Angeles for her own safety by the king* of *Shadow Wood. Long story.* Hell, even I found that hard to believe.

But going to see the queen was the only thing I could think of. If Orosgo had framed Jane—and if Orosgo was in league with the wizard Curtin—then the wisest queen in all the world might be the one person who could help me make the connections and figure out what to do.

Moving under the shadow of the guard towers, I wove through the parked cars to my Mercedes. I was preoccupied, my mind as jammed up as a rush-hour freeway with images, anxieties, and ideas. Nothing made any sense to me. Why had Jane been set up? How had the emperor been murdered? Why did Orosgo let Curtin get the book? How could I get Jane out of the Tower before midnight?

I opened the car door and lowered myself inside. I pulled the door shut as I slid behind the wheel. I started the car and glanced up into the rearview mirror.

You know that scene in every thriller movie ever made where the guy gets into his car, looks in the mirror, and finds the evil assassin sitting in the back seat? Every time I've seen that scene, I've always told myself that could never happen to me. I told myself: If ever I were in some dangerous situation, I would never get into a car without checking the back seat first. Of course I wouldn't. What was I, some kind of idiot?

Well, yes, it turned out, some kind of idiot was exactly what I was. Because I looked up into the rearview mirror and, sure enough, there was an evil assassin sitting right behind me.

The guy looked like a veritable priest of the Cult of Death. Lean as a skeleton, dressed all in black, his skullish face topped with a black beret, his eyes hidden behind sunglasses with black lenses in their round frames.

He held up a gun so I could see it in the mirror: a boxy automatic. A Glock, I think. For at least one full second, I was absolutely certain he was about to blow my brains out.

But he didn't even point the weapon at me. He just held it there. Turned it this way and that. Showed it off to me.

Then he said, "Orosgo wants to see you."

17

I HAD TAKEN THIS DRIVE ONCE BEFORE. UP INTO THE hills to where the city disappeared, where there was nothing along the winding road except trees and wild grasses. Coincidentally enough, the last time I'd driven here, there'd also been an assassin in the back seat. Sera, his name was. Kitten-Face, I called him. A few days after we met, I'd smacked Kitten-Face in his kitten face with a piece of rebar and sent him falling off a girder to his death.

With that thought in mind, I glanced up at the guy in the Mercedes's rearview.

"One day it'd be nice to come here without a gun pointed at the back of my head," I told him.

Sera had been chatty. I'd gotten some info out of him. This fellow not so much. The black-clad Priest of Death just smirked and looked out the window at the scenery.

We passed through a gate onto the home stretch. The long driveway was lined, as it had been before, with armed guards, stony-faced ex-military men, each one holding a rifle on his hip.

Orosgo's mansion came into view above us: a flowing, modern ranch house that seemed to grow organically out of the hillside.

There were a lot of cars parked up here, nice cars, fancy cars, Mercedes, Beamers, even a Bentley, all bunched together in the cul-de-sac at the end of the drive. I pulled to the side of the road just where the cul-de-sac began. I killed the engine.

One of the stony riflemen held the door open for me. Like a typical LA valet but with more fire power. I got out of the car, and the Priest got out behind me. The Priest and the gunman exchanged looks but no words. I could tell by their expressions though: something big was happening here, something serious.

I walked up the flagstone path to the house. The Priest strolled behind me, his hands in his black slacks, his eyes hidden behind his black glasses, his gun hidden under his black jacket.

A butler opened the front door. I recognized him: it was the same killer I'd met at Orosgo's other mansion up north in Hope Ranch six months ago. We nodded at each other. Then I stepped past him into the house.

I went through the foyer into the expansive rustic living room. The gathering here reminded me of the scene at the cliffs back in Aona, the emperor's funeral. Everyone was wearing black here too. They were mostly men, but a few women mixed in. Some of them I knew by sight. Jonathan Broughton—he ran a movie studio here in LA, Apex Pictures. Gerald Hannity—he ran the big cable news station. The motherly little blonde, Susan Roth—she was the CEO of a giant tech company with search engines and all that.

Broughton and Hannity had been at the party at Solomon Vine's. I mean, they'd been at the party within the party, the one in the back by the guesthouse, the one with the children. I had recognized them then, but it was only now I remembered why I knew them, and why I knew Susan Roth as well. I'd looked them up online after I'd seen their names on the wall of Orosgo's forest retreat in Oregon. They were part of his 730 Club: movers and shakers he'd put in place over the decades after removing their predecessors through murder and scandal and extortion. They were the ones who would be shaping the narrative—the news stories and the feature articles and the books and the movies—about Jane and Alexis: how Alexis abused Jane, how Jane killed her and then hanged herself in her cell.

And here they all were, gathered together in the big room with its towering stone fireplace ablaze, with its columned wall open on the misty spring morning, and with a majestic view over the patio onto the sprawling city far below. Here they all were, dressed in mourning. Murmuring to one another in somber tones. Lifting bone china coffee cups with gold inlay to their grim lips.

When I entered the room, the conversation paused for a moment. Every gaze turned my way. The Priest of Death didn't give me much time to gaze back. He kept moving behind me, shepherding me along like he was a herding dog and I was his flock. But before I was forced clean out of the room, I did see one thing—the main thing—the shocking thing.

I saw a cluster of worthies gathered in one corner. I could tell at a glance this was the room's power center; this was the place where the really important people were. And as the really important people turned to look at me, the cluster opened to reveal the focus of their attention: the VIP of VIPs, the king of the room, the godfather *di tutti* godfathers. And who do you think that was? Sitting there in a thick leather armchair like a man enthroned?

That's right. My big brother. Richard.

He lifted his bone china cup from its bone china saucer. He sipped from it. Gazing at me over the rim with death-cold eyes.

I actually gasped at the sight of him—and at the sight of the crowd around him, that crowd of worshipful attendants. There was the narrow arrangement of sharp edges I called my mother. There was the blinky, distracted, professorial fascist I called Dad. And Solomon Vine—he was also there, paying homage to Richard. Vine turned to gaze at me with a baleful expression that made me suspect the green light for my movie had just turned red forever.

All this I saw in a single stomach-churning, mind-melting, soul-crushing moment, just long enough for me to realize—or to realize again—or to realize with grim finality—that I came from a family of very nasty people—that all my childhood memories were lies—that my whole life had led me to this present darkness.

Then the Assassin Priest hurried me on. We passed out of the living room. We headed down a shadowy hall. There was a double doorway at the end. Both doors were open wide. There was a rifleman standing to the left of the entrance and a rifleman standing to the right. With the Priest behind me, I walked between them, full of dread.

I crossed the threshold and saw Orosgo.

The old man was dying. There couldn't be any doubt about that. He was a mere remnant of what he'd been just months ago, a shriveled worm of a former man. He lay on a four-poster bed the size of Sacramento. He seemed a tiny figure there, propped on a mountain of pillows, floating in a sea of tangled sheets littered with notebook pages. It would have been amazing to me that so powerful a figure could sink so near to death without making the news, except for the fact that most of the people who ran the news business were in his living room sipping coffee from bone china cups.

There was no one else in the room but a nurse, a reedy young blond man of girlish beauty dressed in hospital white. He was seated in a chair against the wall to my left. He was slouched in the seat, watching Serge with what seemed to me a languorous hunger. He seemed to be waiting for the old man to melt to pure fluid so he could gulp the remains of him down in a milkshake glass. He looked like a figure out of allegory: Oblivion Personified.

With the Priest of Death pressuring me from behind, I moved closer to Orosgo until I was standing beside one of the posters at the foot of his big bed. I looked down from there at the ruins of the man.

His body, clothed in a scarlet bathrobe, had shrunk to nothing. His head seemed enormous, a great gray square. The last time I'd seen him, his face—made papery smooth by plastic surgery—had had the wide-eyed expression of a startled baby. Now it looked to me like melted wax, his eyes just two huge, viscous orbs floating in the sagging mess of what had been his features.

Those giant eyes stared up at me. There was no expression left in them but sheer terror—terror of the death that had finally come for him.

"You," he said, in a hoarse, harsh whisper.

"How you doing, Serge?" I said.

"How am I . . .?" he rasped. "Look at me."

I nodded. "Sorry."

"You . . ." he whispered again.

I made a helpless gesture to indicate his condition. "Not me, Serge. It is what it is. You know that."

He moved a trembling hand toward one of the pages that lay spread out on the sheets around him. "You said . . . you said you would destroy him . . ."

I followed his gesture.

Until that moment, I had thought the pages scattered on the bed were documents of some kind, graphs or spreadsheets, business stuff. But now I looked closer at the page he indicated. The faint lines scrawled there weren't graph lines after all. They were a pencil sketch of a figure, a man. All the pages were pictures, and all the same, the same man.

The man in the pictures wore a dark, flowing robe. He had a cowl pulled up over his head. Under the cowl I could make out his face, his raisiny wrinkles, the tuft of hair on his chin, his burning, beady little eyes. It was a face I knew, the face I had met in the dark of the forest mansion, the face I had seen in the graveyard in the woods. It was the face that had tempted me into amnesia: the face of Curtin, the wizard.

Orosgo heaved a gasping breath. "I see him all the time now," he croaked. "Every hour of the day. In the shadows. Hidden in the glare of the sun when it comes through the window in the morning. In the mirror, standing behind me. Floating over me when I wake up in the night. He's waiting. Waiting for the end. Where does he come from, Austin? How does he come?"

I gazed down at the old man dolefully. It's funny about death. It can make you feel sorry for almost anyone. "I don't know how exactly," I told him. "Remember you said something about, I don't know, quantum mechanics and metaphor minds and how subatomic particles get arranged so we can pass between realms. Whatever. It's something like that. We become doorways. That's all I know. We become doorways into another kingdom. The people there pass through us into this world and sometimes vice versa. That's all I know."

"Doorways," Orosgo repeated dully, staring at me with the giant eyes in his melted-wax face. Those terrible, terrified eyes grew misty. And he whispered again, "You promised . . ."

I didn't know what to say. The mystery that had plagued my sleepless night returned to me. If Orosgo wanted me to go back to the Eleven Lands and destroy Curtin, why had he allowed Solomon Vine to keep me here? Wasn't Vine Orosgo's protégé? Why had he arranged to distract me while Curtin got hold of Elinda's magic manuscript with all its doorway-making powers?

I was about to speak, but I stopped with my mouth open. I drew a sharp breath as the answer came to me. I glanced over my shoulder toward the bedroom's double doors. My lips moved silently, shaping a single word—a single name.

Richard. My brother.

Orosgo made an awful noise. A long, rattling sigh, like a man dying. But he wasn't dying yet. He was crying out to me, crying out in anguish with all the breath he had left, "Don't let him, Austin. Don't let him take me . . ."

I turned back to face him. I looked into those puddling eyes, those fallen features. How could I explain to him that there was nothing left for me to do? The emperor was dead. My quest had failed. And even if I returned through the doorway into Aona, I would plunge into the ocean and die myself. Curtin had already won.

With his desperate cry, Orosgo had knocked one of his sketches off the bedcovers. It had floated to the floor facedown, near my feet. I stooped to pick it up. As I lifted it, I saw that this sketch—this one alone—was different from the others. Not a picture of Curtin. It was a still life. A flower. A rose, maybe. Something like a rose. There was a scrawl underneath it. Letters? Numbers? I wasn't sure. I put it back on the bed. He clutched at it, crumpling it in his withered hands.

"I'm sorry, Serge," I said softly. "There's nothing I can do for you anymore."

His answer was a stuttered gasp of horror and despair. His shoulders shook. He was crying, I think, but his substance was so drained and dry, there were no tears left for him to shed.

I looked at the others. The beautiful, hungry nurse, waiting. The Priest of Death, his eyes hidden behind his black glasses. A room without pity.

I started moving to the door. I had to go see my brother.

I WALKED QUICKLY back into the living room. To my surprise, it was empty now. Nothing moving here but the fire in the great stone fireplace. No sound but the crackling blaze. It was like some sort of magic trick: in the little space of time I'd been gone, all the black-clad VIPs had vanished.

No, wait, there they were. They were out on the patio. All except three.

Richard and my mom and dad were still here, still in the room, still in their power corner. My brother was still enthroned on his leather chair, his blue eyes bright beneath his swept-back golden hair, his lips tight behind his golden beard. My parents still stood around him, my mother ramrod straight, her angular body clothed in a taut black dress, her patrician face haughty beneath her brittle curls, my willowy father fidgeting and muttering beside her.

My family.

I strolled over to them, casual as I could. My hands in my pockets, I lifted my chin to them. I gave my brother a half smile, a cynical smile.

"Your man is dying," I said quietly.

Richard gazed up at me. It was hard to meet his eyes. There had been some feeling between us once, not that long ago. Used to be I could catch a glimpse of some tremulous candle flame of remorse in him, some tremulous flicker of humanity.

But no more. Because Orosgo was dying. And now all that power was about to fall into his successor's hands—into Richard's hands. My brother's eyes were a viper's eyes now, dead and deadly.

"Everyone dies," he told me.

My father, like some muddled Greek chorus, murmured to himself, "That's true. You can't deny that. That's perfectly true."

"Yeah. Everyone dies," I agreed. "But not everyone dies like this."

Richard snorted. "Like what? Death is death."

"Is it? Because I don't think it's death he's afraid of. Not just death anyway."

"Serge has lost his nerve," Richard answered cooly. "He has some fantasy of damnation. Who knows what goes through a man's mind at the end? The point is just: he's lost his nerve for the job at hand."

"The job of making the world a better place," I said.

"That's right."

"The Orosgo Age."

He made a gesture.

"Or the Richard Lively Age now, huh," I said.

"It doesn't matter what you call it."

"Doesn't it? No. I guess it doesn't. As long as you're the one in charge of things, right?"

He didn't answer.

"You or the man in the cowl," I said. For a moment, Richard averted his eyes. His lips tightened. I said: "So you've seen him, too, huh. The man in Serge's drawings. The little wizardy man with the wrinkled face . . ."

"I've seen his drawings," Richard said. "Those drawings would give anyone nightmares."

"Yeah," I said. "Nightmares. That must be what they are."

He gazed up at me coldly again. "Like I said: Serge has lost his nerve. That's all. Once a man loses his nerve, he's useless."

"What Richard is saying is: we can't let Serge scuttle his life's work just because of some deathbed conversion or other." This was my mother, speaking with a tone of great authority—and yet speaking neither to me nor Richard nor anyone else unless it was some unseen phantom in the shadowy air between us. She was lecturing the empty space around her.

"It's true," Richard added. "He would have thrown it all away to save himself."

"And from what?" said my mother, as if there could be no reasonable answer. "Save himself from what?"

My father was pretending to study the arm of the armchair, squinting down at it, picking at the brass buttons. "Exactly," he said. "Save himself from what?"

I wasn't sure what they were talking about. What had Orosgo

been planning to do? Was he going to confess his sins to the world? Spread the word that he'd murdered and blackmailed and finagled people out of their jobs until every news source, every source of entertainment, every university and high school in the country was brainwashing people to accept their own enslavement at his hands?

And here's another thing I didn't know: what had Richard done to stop that confession? Serge was old, really old. He was going to melt into the bedsheets eventually. But had Richard decided to help him along to keep him quiet? Was that why everyone was dressed in black—because they already knew how the day would end?

I didn't suppose I'd ever learn the answer to that. But there was something I did want to understand.

"Was it you who told Solomon Vine to buy my screenplay?" I asked him. "You, not Orosgo?"

Richard answered with a smug little smile. "I told you, Austin. Didn't I? Didn't I tell you you could choose a good life or a bad life, a happy, successful life with achievements and rewards, or you could choose a hunted life, a bad life, a despised life. A short life. I just made good things available to you so you would choose wisely, that's all."

I laughed mirthlessly. "A short life, huh," I echoed him. "Are you threatening me now, big brother? The good life or the short life. Is that the choice you're giving me?"

"No one is threatening anyone," said my mother.

"Who's threatening?" my father muttered.

But Richard—he answered nary a word. He just looked at me. And I looked back. And we exchanged those silent looks, the two of us, for a long, long time. I was thinking about how my big brother taught me to swing a baseball bat when I was little. How he stood behind me, holding my shoulders, adjusting my stance. He taught me how to choke up and shorten my swing after the second strike. I was always a good singles hitter because of him.

I indicated the crowd of black-clad power players out on the patio. "So that's it, huh?" I said. "The work goes on. All these pooh-bahs are in *your* pocket now. Now they'll spread *your* news and tell *your* stories and push *your* philosophy and elect *your* followers to run *your* world. Is that how it works?"

After another long moment, Richard finally answered me. "Don't trouble your mind, little brother. Make your movie. Serge is not long for this world. Whatever deal you made with him, it's done. Make your movie, Austin. Make your money. Enjoy your women. Enjoy your fame. Forget about all this. It's just the world. The world belongs to those who want it most. Do you think anyone cares who runs it, who makes the decisions for them? As long as we give them their daily bread, our will be done. Make your movie with Solomon, Austin. Why are you fighting us? To win what? Are you so fond of the burden of battle? Set it down, bro. Make your movie."

"Well, that's the whole point," my mother said. "What *can* you win but the burden?"

"That is, that is," my father agreed. "That's the whole point."

I looked at my brother, then my mother, then my father, then my brother again. It was odd. Standing there with them, I thought I could smell the house I grew up in.

I suppose I could have gone all moralistic on them then. I could have brought up Solomon Vine's party. The cable news guy and the studio guy out by the guesthouse. Those children with their empty stares of despair and betrayal: those helpless slaves of men's desire.

But no, Richard was right. Make your movie. That's what all the most beautiful people did. All those beautiful people at Solomon Vine's party. They were making their movies while the little shindig at the guesthouse went on in plain sight.

And while Richard took over everything.

Well, screw it. What could one man do against all this power? A schmo like me. A nobody like me. If big brother wanted the world so badly, he could have it.

"Okay," I said. "I'll make my movie."

"Good man," said Richard.

"On one condition."

He lifted one corner of his mouth. "What can I do for you, bro?"

"Jane," I said.

Richard's brows lowered. He was puzzled. "Jane?"

"Jane Janeway. The girl who was arrested for killing Alexis Merriwether."

"Oh, right. What about her?"

"I love her. She didn't do it. Let her go."

My brother made a noise of dismissal: *pffft*. He wrinkled his nose and screwed up his lips. "Come on, Aus. I can't do that."

"Sure you can. Look at you. You're the head honcho, the capo de cappuccino, the tutti de tutti fruttis. Just say the frigging word."

He lifted his shoulder again. "Sorry, man. It's complicated. I can't explain the whole thing to you. You're just gonna have to trust me on this."

"Oh, for goodness' sake, Austin," my mother scolded. "There are plenty of other women in the world. Of all the things to get hung up on."

"Plenty of women," my father echoed dreamily.

I would have laughed in their faces if I could have laughed at all. These people, I thought. People like these. These people who want everything—they always want too much. You know? If they'd just let you breathe a little, let you speak your piece, let you have your loves and hates and be your human self, if they could just step back and let you think what you think and choose this over that and have a say in how your life goes day to day, well, you might just shrug them off. Let them have their governments and their news outlets and their social media and their movies. Let them run the whole shebang, who would care, if they'd just leave you alone, just a little.

But they can't do it. That's not who they are. They have to control everything. The mere idea that somewhere someone might be thinking a thought that's not their thought—might secretly in their heart of hearts disagree with them or condemn them—they can't abide it. So you either have to live on your knees forever or take your free soul in your fist and cram it down their throats until they choke on it and die. There's no third way.

I looked down at my big brother in his leather throne with his golden hair and his golden godlike beard. The guy who had taught me to play baseball when we were kids. I looked at him and I thought: *I have to stop you.*

And he looked up at me and he thought: *I have to kill you.*

We didn't have to speak. We were brothers, after all.

We heard each other, loud and clear.

18

DEATH WAS WAITING FOR ME AT THE FRONT DOOR. The Priest of Death, I mean. The small, skeletal assassin all dressed in black with his black beret and his round black sunglasses. He was not Orosgo's assassin, like I thought at first. He was Richard's. He was my big brother's boy. And as I came out of the living room and walked toward him where he blocked the door, he grinned a savage grin at me, a grin so bright and shiny and ravenous he might have been a crocodile in human form.

I thought to myself: *He might do it right now. Richard might give the order, and he might kill me right here and now.*

I reached the man. We stood confronting each other, nearly toe to toe. He grinned and grinned, his glasses reflecting my frightened face back at me.

Then he said, "See you soon."

And, still grinning, he stepped aside.

I pulled the door open and walked out of the house.

I DROVE TO find Elinda.

With the emperor dead, with Jane in jail, with my homicidal brother waiting for Serge to die so he could seize the reins of his organization's power, with nothing waiting for me in Aona but a plunge into the seething sea, where else could I go? I had no other ally but Ellen Evermore, the queen hiding among the homeless. I had no wisdom of my own. I needed hers.

It wasn't a long drive, but it also was. My encounter with Richard had left me weak, shaking. I could feel death trailing me: an invisible assassin always in my wake.

Meanwhile, Southern California in the springtime was so aggressively alive it seemed to mock my rapidly dwindling life expectancy. The cloudy morning had cleared. The sky through the windshield was bluer than blue. The hills at the windows were green as green could be. Bougainvillea bloomed on the bushes by the roadside, riotous colors, purple and red and orange and white and gold. The silent tick-tock of time filled the car.

I descended into town. I found a parking space on a Century City side street and walked over to the coffee shop at the Wilshire juncture. I went down the narrow alley to the lot in back where the tent city stood.

It was past rush hour now, but there was still plenty of traffic on the streets everywhere, cars weaving around each other in a swift stop-and-go dance. In the parking lot, though, it was oddly quiet, oddly empty. The minute I stepped into the homeless camp, I felt uncannily alone. There was not a human being in sight. The tents rose up on every side of me, yellow, khaki, white, and blue. They blocked the view from the street so that the drivers in their cars could not see me. Even the traffic noise seemed to be muffled and distant. Mostly I heard the plastic tents fluttering in the spring breeze.

Where were they? I wondered. Where were all the drunks and schizophrenics and hoboes who had been here before?

I moved deeper into the silent encampment. My body still ached from the joust in Aona. My head ached too. I felt uncomfortable and self-alienated, like a stranger in my own skin.

I came to rest in the middle of the tent cluster. I panned my eyes across the eerily empty scene. Abandoned sleeping bags. Piles of clothes. A shopping cart stuffed with junk. A half-eaten burger here. An empty whiskey bottle there. Cold french fries.

A soda can went rolling over the asphalt with a metallic rattle. Fast-food wrappers flapped and shuddered and tumbled past me, pushed by the breeze. I felt like a ghost amid the ghostly pavilions.

I was about to leave—to give up and walk away. I drew a long breath. Sighed.

There was a cough close behind me. Startled, I spun around.

A man in rags was suddenly standing there, inches from me. The stench of him poisoned the spring weather. He was a white man. Grimy. With copious red and silver hair springing from his head and face. His whacked-out eyes seemed to peer at me from the copper depths, like a tiger's eyes through the leaves of a red jungle.

"Where you from?" he barked at me. And before I could answer, he barked: "What planet?"

His breath smelled like a rotting body. I caught a movement at his thigh and glanced down. He was gripping a stake in his right hand, a piece of a chair leg sharpened to a point. His left hand was clenching and unclenching with tension and excitement.

Shit, I thought.

"I'm here to see Ellen Evermore," I told him. "Elinda. Queen Elinda."

A great animal snort came from behind me. I spun—and there was another man, a black man this one, draped in the remnants of an old dark trench coat. He was big—tall and thick—unshaven—with exhausted, yellow eyes.

"No one would see it if you died in here, little man," he grumbled.

As he spoke, more men emerged from behind him, from his left and right, fanning out like a deck of cards. They encircled me. Their stench closed over me. Their animal eyes stared at me hungrily. Where had they all been hiding?

"Lots of people die in here," the red-haired stake guy said. "No one ever sees."

"No one," said a woman—a five-foot monster girl, crew cut, tattooed, shaped like a wrecking ball. Enormous breasts under her stained black T-shirt, wobbling with every move she took. "This is our city. No one comes in here unless we let them."

"No one leaves here unless we say," said the black giant.

I licked my dry lips. I looked at each staring, psychopathic face in turn. And all the while, my glance kept flashing back to the red-haired guy and that sharpened stake. His free fist opening and closing. He was all pumped up with energy and suspense. Ready to lunge, ready to plunge that shaft into me at any moment.

I swallowed hard, afraid. I passed one more circle of glances over the mob surrounding me. My eyes came to rest on the eyes of the stake guy. His wild, white stare met mine from the depths of his hairy tangle. He seemed to be the leader.

I had an idea. "Let wisdom reign," I said to him.

The words had no effect. Or wait—maybe they did. Maybe a small measure of uncertainty entered that lunatic gaze. I glanced around at the rest of them. They all seemed uncertain now.

I raised my voice. "Let wisdom reign!"

Finally, the big black guy nodded. I looked from him to the redhead. The redhead nodded too.

"And each man go his way," he answered.

There was a movement. I turned toward it. It was the black guy. He'd stepped aside. They all stepped aside, the circle parting to my left and right.

And there, suddenly, she stood. The woman I had seen through my car window. The woman Riley had told me was hiding here. The author of *Another Kingdom*. The queen of Galiana. My queen—the woman who had made a knight of me. Right there in front of me. Right here in LA. Ellen Evermore. Elinda.

I'd found her.

She was standing just at the entrance of a large yellow tent. Her back was straight. Her hands were folded in front of her. She was dressed in a long tan skirt ending just above her ankles and a crisp white blouse that gave an aura of purity to her full figure. Her golden hair was in a tight bun. Her eyes were majestically gentle and feminine. She looked regal, beautiful, serene.

And I—I with my motherless heart—I smiled at the sight of her. She was the one who had started all this. She had called me to another kingdom. She had written the book that gave me the power to pass between her world and mine. She was the reason I was hunted and haunted, the reason I had turned away from the life of my dreams. She was—she had always been—the source and purpose of my quest.

"Austin," she said, and she smiled sweetly back at me. "I'm glad you've come."

WE WENT TOGETHER into her yellow tent. I was relieved to be there, away from the homeless crazies and their awful smell. I could hear them milling around protectively in the parking lot beyond the tent flaps. I could hear them muttering and snarling at one another.

But in here, in the tent, it was quiet, even peaceful.

That said, there was nothing particularly queenly about the place. It was a homeless tent like any other. A sleeping bag unrolled against one wall. A paper shopping bag full of clothes and baubles: her wardrobe, I guess. There was a book with a cracked brown fake-plastic cover, the binding stripped to its glue so I couldn't read the title. The only luxury here, if you could call it that, was a rectangle of felt-covered rubber—a piece of padding, like you might put under a rug. It gave an extra layer of softness to the tent floor. We sat on it, cross-legged, she on one end, me on the other.

Despite the shabby surroundings, though, there was no doubt in my mind that I was in the presence of a queen. Elinda radiated royalty and command. I felt at once that I was there to serve her, that I should serve her, that it was only right.

She inclined her head to me, as if to give me leave to speak. She said, "What do you have to tell me?"

I drew a breath and tried to organize my thoughts. It was only then I realized what I would have to tell her. My heart sickened inside me. "I have bad news, Your Highness," I said. "The worst news. Your fiancé—the Emperor Anastasius—he's dead."

Her reaction surprised me. A quiet nod. A straightening of her spine. Deep sorrow in her eyes, infinite sorrow. But when she spoke, she spoke very calmly. And what she said was: "It's all right. Death is not always death in the Eleven Lands."

I thought she was trying to comfort me. I said, "It's my fault."

"No, Austin."

"I didn't protect the book."

"It's true. You didn't."

"I got lost."

"You did. I was told."

"Now Curtin has an army."

"Yes."

"And Anastasius—I don't know what happened. They say someone poisoned him. Murdered him. His three knights—they tried to blame his brother, Favian . . ."

"Oh!" She shook her head. "Littleman, Goodchild, and Hammer."

"Yes."

"I tried to warn him about those three, but he sees the good in everyone. He believes anyone can be redeemed."

"They were going to burn Favian. They were going to burn him and his wife and son."

This was the first piece of news that seemed to disturb her deep serenity. She leaned toward me, concerned. "Favian and Beltan? Little Rory? They were going to burn the child too?"

"Yes."

"In Anastasius's name?"

"Yes."

Now came the first trace of anger in her eyes, not anger like fire, anger like ice: hard and clear. "They will pay for that."

"They haven't done it yet. I stopped them—for now anyway."

Her icy anger melted. "Did you? Stop them?"

"We had a trial by combat. A joust. I jousted with Littleman."

She reached across the length of the padding and touched my knee. "Oh, well done, Austin! Well done!"

I felt my cheeks flush. It was embarrassing how much her praise meant to me: as much as praise means to a child. I shook my head. "It didn't go so well. I lost. Littleman knocked me over the cliff. Now I'm stuck. If I go back there, I'll fall into the ocean and die."

She nodded quietly. "And you're afraid."

"Yes."

"Don't be. Death is not always death in the Eleven Lands."

I tried to smile hopefully in response, but I failed miserably. I knew that whatever happened to my body in another kingdom happened here as well. I had the bumps and bruises and scars to prove it. And while death might not always be death in the Eleven Lands, it was always death in this town, every single time. No matter what the queen said, I doubted I'd survive in any recognizable form if I plunged into the sea of Aona at terminal velocity.

But the queen seemed unperturbed. Her deep eyes sparkled kindly at me. Her expression remained lofty and serene. Looking at her, I had the feeling that I—I and my fear and my guilt and my anguish—seemed silly to her—or not silly, maybe, but childish, small, as if I didn't understand what really mattered in life.

And when I saw that—when I saw the way she looked at me—a great ball of emotion seemed to well up inside me all at once like the bubble of an underwater atomic blast. Before I could even form the thought, I heard a question burst from my lips, my voice cracking. "Is this all some kind of dream?" I asked her. "Is this just, like, a brain tumor I have or something? Have I gone crazy? Am I dead? Am I in a coma somewhere, and this is all some elaborate hallucination? Is that it?"

Elinda smiled. She had a beautiful, gentle smile. It lifted my heart. "Is it all in your imagination, you mean."

"Yeah. Yes. Is it?"

"The imagination is an organ of perception, like the eye. The eye doesn't create the light, it sees the light—it sees the light as the eye sees."

Oh great. What the hell did that mean? I threw up my hands.

"You don't believe me," she said.

I rolled my eyes. "I don't know what I believe. Ever since I walked into Galiana, I don't understand anything about anything." I gave her a helpless look. "Why did you pick me for this, Your Highness? Why me? I mean, look at me. What the hell?"

"My book chose you," she said. "*Another Kingdom*. I made it as a sort of test. Anyone can read the story, but not everyone can live it. It takes a certain kind of person to become what he reads there, to change accordingly. He is the one who can pass through the door. I searched among the writings of your people and found your work . . ."

"My screenplay. *Three Days in Forever.*"

"Yes. I read it, and I suspected you were a man after my own heart. So I sent the book to you."

Under the force of her kind—her gentle—I would even say her *loving*—gaze, I had to look away.

"But I didn't even understand it," I said. "The book. *Another Kingdom.* It was just . . . It was just about me. It was just me telling my own story."

She gave a gentle laugh. "That's always where it begins. With you telling your own story."

"And then, after I finished it . . . I didn't live it. I didn't change. I just . . . I forgot. I forgot everything. I let Curtin get inside my head . . ." My voice trailed off. Then on a trembling breath, I said, "I ran away."

"Yes. It's a common reaction."

"Reaction to what?"

"To hearing your own story told."

When I tried to speak again, my voice was little more than a whisper. "I failed you," I said.

She laughed. It was a laugh like a harp playing. "Where I come from, there is nothing behind you. Everything is before. Where I come from, you have *not* failed me, not finally, not yet. That's the only thing that matters."

My own laugh was miserable, dejected. It sounded like a baby dropped down a well. "But everything is falling apart, Your Highness. My brother is trying to take over the world. He's going to kill the girl I love, and if I try to stop him, he's going to kill me. If I return to Aona, I fall into the ocean and die. You may be right there's nothing

behind me, but what's ahead of me isn't looking so great either."
Now our gazes met again, and I felt a yearning for her I could not
explain or express. "Tell me what to do, Queen," I said.

"What to do about what?"

"About everything. About Jane, first of all. They're going to kill
her tonight. In, like, twelve hours. What do I do?"

For a moment, she seemed to ponder this, then she spoke very
slowly, very carefully. "Your realm is not my realm," she said. "You
must listen to those who hear the voices of my kingdom but can
speak in the voices of your world."

I made a helpless, hopeless noise. "I don't know what that
means."

"Yes, you do."

I was about to protest, but then I realized: she was right. I did.
So instead I said: "What about Aona? What do I do in Aona?"

"You know your quest: Let wisdom reign."

"Wisdom, which is to love the good," I said.

"The greater good more than the lesser, yes."

I kept my eyes trained on her beautiful face now. I had this
strange feeling that as long as I was looking at her, everything would
be all right. "Then tell me," I said to her. "What is the good, Your
Highness? Tell me: What is the good?"

She answered quickly, simply, as if I had asked her for the time
of day. "The good is the direction you travel to become the man you
were made to be."

I started to reply, but my throat closed. My eyes filled. I had to
force the words out: "I don't know what that is. I don't know what
that is."

She gave me another smile, another marvelous smile, and she
touched my knee again, and again my heart lifted.

"You know what you need to know," she told me. "Now do as I
tell you. Go. The time is short."

When we stepped out of the tent, the bums and crazies stopped what they were doing. The ranting, the boozing, the picking at foot sores—it all stopped. They drifted toward us, closed around us slowly, like a gathering mist. The smell of them was ripe and awful. The sight of her, the sight of the queen, and such a queen, surrounded by them, surrounded by their poverty and madness and misery and addiction, caused me pain.

I stood among them and faced Elinda. "I'm sorry you're homeless here," I said.

She inclined her head, a royal gesture. "It's the way of your world."

She held her hand out to me. I clasped it in both of mine. In another sudden overflow of feeling, I raised it to my lips and kissed it. I started to sink to my knees in front of her.

"No, no," she said quickly. "If someone sees you, they might guess who I am. Then they would come for me, and all would be lost."

I straightened, but I went on clasping her hand. "I'm kneeling to you on the inside," I said. "You are my queen."

She smiled. "That's all that's needed. Now go your way."

I forced myself to release her. I turned. The homeless men and women drifted apart to make a path for me. I walked among them. The black giant lifted his fist as I went by. I touched his knuckles with mine. The red-haired nutjob raised an open hand. I high-fived him.

I went on to the edge of the tent city, where the alley opened to the street. I wanted to stop there, to look back, to set eyes on her one more time, but I was afraid she might have vanished. I was afraid if I saw she was gone, I would lose my courage.

So I kept walking.

I headed for the madhouse.

That's when Death came for me.

19

I DROVE TOWARD THE OCEAN. MY CONVERSATION WITH
the queen had strengthened me. I felt strangely hot and light. Full
of energy and purpose.

*You must listen to those who hear the voices of my kingdom but can
speak in the voices of your world.*

That's why I was heading back toward Riley's asylum.

Some of the mad girls hear voices, my sister had told me. *Voices
from another kingdom.*

I had to go back there and hear what the mad girls had to say.

I traveled quickly. All the noontime traffic was heading in from
the ocean toward the center of town. The way west was nearly clear.

Nervously, I kept checking the rearview mirror, trying to make
sure I wasn't being followed. I didn't want Richard to figure out
what I was up to. Powerful as he was, my brother did not yet fully
understand or believe what was happening here. He thought Curtin
was just a dream or a fantasy. He thought Orosgo was deranged and
hallucinating and losing his nerve. He didn't fully understand about
the other kingdom and its connection to our world.

But he knew enough. He knew tremendous power was about
to fall into his hands, and I was out to stop him. And whatever

family feeling he had left, if he realized Riley wasn't truly insane, if he found out she had some information that could help me, he would kill her just as coldly as he would kill me.

I reached the coastal highway. Headed north. The sun had cleared the mountains to my right, and the ocean leapt and sparkled outside the window to my left. I was still reviewing the conversation I'd had with Elinda, still relishing the warmth of being in her presence, going over her words again and again and going over my words too.

Is this all some kind of dream? Is this just, like, a brain tumor I have or something? Have I gone crazy? Am I dead? Am I in a coma somewhere, and this is all some elaborate hallucination? Is that it?

The closer I got to the asylum, the more these questions dogged me. What if even my conversation with Elinda was imaginary? Was that possible? After all, here I was, going to talk to some schizophrenic women about what the voices in their heads were telling them. As if the voices in their heads might be imparting some urgent piece of information I could use. What sort of crazy idea was that? You couldn't get any crazier.

The imagination is an organ of perception, like the eye, the queen had told me.

But that's exactly what she *would* say if she were a figment of my imagination.

Nuts, I thought. *I must be nuts.*

But that didn't stop me. I drove on. If talking to crazy women was the only way I could find out how to save Jane, then crazy women it would be.

I reached the turnoff and headed away from the sea, up into the mountains. Once again, I was struck by how quickly the city fell away behind me as I rose into the wilderness of red sand and green, scrawny trees. In only a few minutes, all the traffic vanished, and I and my Mercedes were alone on the road.

Now the ground sloped up and away to one side of me, rising to peaks of white rock. On the other side, there stretched a bleak expanse of dirt and scrub brush dotted here and there with pale yellow flowers. Ahead, through the windshield, the pavement snaked and switchbacked. I handled the sharp curves without thinking, my mind far away, lost in thoughts and doubts and hopeful daydreams. In that lonely place, I forgot to keep an eye on the rearview mirror.

That's why I never saw Death coming. All at once, I just glanced up into the mirror and he was there. The Priest of Death with his grin and his black glasses. Following close behind me in a black Ford pickup, a formidable monster of a vehicle, quick as a rocket, blunt as a battering ram.

My heart began to hammer in my chest at the sight of him. A thousand fearful thoughts ran through my head like a crowd in a panicked stampede. How long had he been following me? Had he seen me with Elinda? Did he know where I was heading and why? No, I told myself, trying to stay calm. Orosgo's organization had the power to track me anywhere. He could have easily followed my phone or the GPS in my car. For all Death knew, I was simply going to visit my sister as always. He may have just figured this was a good place to take me alone, that's all.

But there could be no doubt about his purpose here. There was no staying calm about that. The truck was barreling toward me at top speed. As the road swung sharply around and back, the high sun hit the truck's windshield. Death's face vanished behind a starburst of yellow light. The moment we turned again, the moment the starburst vanished, I saw him clearly, behind and above me in the Ford's high cab. I saw the bright, murderous grin on his lips. I didn't need to see the eyes behind the glasses. I could well imagine the malevolence there.

The truck loomed like black night in my rearview, larger and larger and darker and darker.

I cursed—and jammed my foot down on the gas.

The Mercedes flowed forward, a sleek and silver bullet. The truck dropped away behind me, but the curve ahead came barreling toward me way too fast. I twisted the wheel and my face twisted. The tires screamed and gripped the asphalt as I centrifuged around the bend.

For a second, the truck went out of sight, obscured by the scrubby hill behind me. A short straightaway appeared in the windshield. Encouraged, I pressed the gas pedal even farther toward the floor.

The car accelerated smoothly, but my heartbeat leapt in a ragged instant to a machine-gun rattle. I was really racing now. The scenery blurred on both sides of me. The next curve was coming toward me in an impossible rush.

I took one quick glance up at the mirror. What the hell? There was the black Ford again, swinging around the bend behind and charging after me. What kind of engine did he have in that thing? My Mercedes could not outrace it.

The truck sliced through my wake, its massive black grill growing larger in my rearview. As fast as I was going, Death was catching up with me.

What now? Only an instant to choose. If I slowed, he'd ram me. If I hit the curve at this velocity, I might fly off the road completely.

I bared my gritted teeth and kept the pedal down as I flew into the turn full speed.

I had no chance. As the Mercedes reached the apex of the curve, the unbalanced forces overwhelmed it. The car lost its hold on the pavement. The rear tires swung out behind me. The car flew into a skid, then a spin. The world went into slow motion as the Mercedes rotated around the axis of the centerline.

I fought for control. Took my foot off the gas. Wrenched the steering wheel hard in the direction of the skid. The car kept turning, sliding, spinning. A wall of rock went by the windshield. I came around the full one-eighty and saw the Ford screaming around the bend like a predator rushing to pounce. The Mercedes kept turning.

My car was lengthwise on the road when Death's Ford struck it broadside in the tail.

There was a tremendous crunching smash. A jolt like a punch in the head. The airbag exploded from the wheel, smacked me in the face, and knocked me silly. In a dreamy daze, I felt the car continue spinning until it hurled itself off the road, tilted over onto its edge and dropped upside down. I heard crunching metal. I heard shattering glass. I threw my arms up as the airbag sagged and the car turned over again and came to rest upright.

The engine died with a rattling hiss like a man dying. Steam rose up in front of me. I smelled gasoline. I smelled fire. A trail of blood ran from the corner of my mouth down my chin.

Staring stupidly into the drifting mist, I understood—in a dazed and distant way—that the car was going to explode. Any second, I might be engulfed in flames.

That thought, like a cry of warning from far off, jerked me out of my fugue state. I fought my way toward the light of consciousness. In a fit of fear, I scrabbled wildly for the seat belt release. I turned and looked out the window.

Up at the top of a little slope, the great black Ford had stopped at the edge of the road. As the bright morning sunlight broke through the rising steam and smoke, I saw the dim silhouette of the Priest of Death come around the front of the truck.

Slowly, casually, he started walking toward me, down the hill.

A fresh line of blood trickled from my forehead into my eye. Quickly, I wiped it away with my palm. Blinking, squinting, I saw the pistol in Death's right hand.

I had to get out of this damn car and run for it. I had to try anyway. I finally found the seat belt button. Popped the belt off. Grabbed the door handle. Yanked it. Shoved the door.

It wouldn't move. It was stuck. The roof of the car had caved in over it.

I roared out in frustration. I rammed my shoulder into the door, hard. It hurt, but the door budged a little.

The Priest of Death kept striding down the desert slope toward me.

"Come on!" I shouted, in a blurry voice like a drunk's.

I shoved the door again. Again. The latch gave a painful cough. The hinges gave an agonized screech. The door broke the grip of the crumpled roof and swung open.

But it was too late. The Priest of Death was too near. Still approaching steadily, he lifted his pistol and trained it on my face.

I knew what I had to do. I had no choice. I could only hope that Elinda was right and death was not always death in the Eleven Lands, because here, there was no escape from what was about to happen to me.

I focused on the open door and willed the veil of transition into being.

A white haze of light appeared. Through it, I could see the black tunnel of the rock formation beneath the cliffs of Aona. I could see the roiling black ocean at the bottom, spitting foam.

In this world, the Priest of Death came toward me, his gun upraised.

I tumbled through the open door of the Mercedes and back to Aona, where I plummeted through the hole in the rock and smashed full force into the sea.

20

IT WAS A TERRIBLE THING TO DIE. A SAD THING, VERY sad and lonely. It was like losing a wife you were never grateful for, a familiar old wife who kept your house, who brought you coffee in the morning, who set your dinner on the table every night, all unnoticed after so many years. Then suddenly she's gone—she's gone and you realize: it was all love, all of it, the kept house, the coffee, the meals, every little thing she did was an act of fathomless love, and only now can you see it, only now with the incomprehensible loss of it, only now can you understand the vast black loneliness her silent sweetness filled.

Yes, that's what it was like to lose my life. Black loneliness where love had been, all unknown.

Elinda was right, of course: Death wasn't quite death here, not quite the utter end of things I had expected. But it also was. That is, my body was smashed to a ragdoll corpse on impact with the concrete sea, and I knew whatever I had been before that moment, I would never be again.

And oh, man, I missed myself! The moment I passed away, it broke my heart to be severed from even the aches and annoyances of flesh and anxiety. I wished I had the moment back. I wished it was that instant again before I struck the surface. I would have lived even that, even that one instant, over and over forever, anything in order to stave off the completeness of my destruction.

I was dimly aware of my corpse sinking into the wavery depths of the water. I couldn't see it exactly, but I sensed it all the same: my body, broken and limp and drifting down, while the flickering reef fish nosed the still shape of it and darted away.

But that dead body was no longer me. I was gone—gone into a lonely blackness so lonely and so black that words like *loneliness* and *blackness* could only suggest the absolute lightlessness and solitude.

As my cadaver descended through the medium of water, I—this lifeless but still imagined I—sank through this other medium, this lonesomeness, this blackness, into an expanse without end or sensation, a country of nowhere and nothing, no borders, no horizon.

I'm not sure how long I fell, how far I went, how deep I sank. I'm not sure any of those words had meaning where I was. But after a time—or after all time—after all my time anyway—I began to imagine myself as I had been before: as a form, a body; Austin. It was just an illusion. I knew that even then. It was a trick of my shocked imagination, which couldn't bear to face the loss of myself. I told myself I was still a body and I saw myself as a body. And I came to rest on what I imagined as a shelf of rough anthracite—black, jagged, faceted coal—the surface flickering in and out of imagined sight as if lit by some distant flame.

I climbed slowly to my feet. This is how I described it to myself. I knew my body was gone, but I had to think of it somehow, and this was how. I climbed to my feet. I found myself on a narrow ledge above an infinite descent into weeping nothingness. Every fiber of me was in a panic to climb up out of there, away from the tortured, crying voices I heard rising from the depthless depths below.

But there was no up. The narrow path didn't lead that way. I couldn't even make myself imagine *up*. There was only the winding pathway down. Down and down.

I did not want to begin the journey. I so did not. But I had to. Like in a nightmare, my will fought what was happening at the same time my mind relentlessly created it. I had to go down.

I went, step by step. I hoped this wouldn't be like hell, but of course it was. It was just like hell, because that was the only way I knew how to think of it. As the anthracite path wound downward over the anthracite walls, the smell of sulfur thickened. Yellow gas twined up out of the deep and swirled around me. I felt the first heat of flames. I heard the flames crackle. I saw the flamelight flicker. The crying and the screaming of the voices in the hideous world below grew louder.

But I had to go down.

Even worse than what I knew was waiting for me was what I felt was happening to me as I went. I was decaying. Even this imagined me, this dreamed-up Austin, this illusion of physical being that I was forced to perceive because my nothingness was intolerable: even this was rotting away. I could feel myself becoming soft and curdy, empty of inner life. I could smell it too. The smell of my flesh going bad like week-old meat: it mingled with the suffocating aroma of sulfur.

The scarlet flames grew brighter on the sable rock. *Don't look at yourself*, I thought. But I had to. I raised my hand before my eyes. It was crawling with maggots. The flesh was beginning to melt and drop away from the bloody sinew. The stench was awful.

I wanted to weep. I wanted to wilt to the ground and lament for my poor dead self.

But I had to go down.

I neared the end of the descent. The ledge began to level out. I saw a burbling lake of fire that was the shape my mind gave to its own molten anguish. The air was full of drowning cries of agony, deafening. The imagination is an organ of perception like the eye, and with my imagination, which was the only living organ I had left, I saw the coal-black ledge diverge from the infinite cave walls around me. It stretched out in a narrow bridge over the immensity of embodied torment that looked like lava to me. Now and then, a smoking, rotten hand reached out of the liquid flames and desperately seized the rock, then slipped back down again. Now and then a face appeared—unspeakable.

Helplessly, I headed for the bridge.

I came to a stop where the bridge began, at the shore of the sea of fire. I knew I would have to go on eventually, but somehow, for the moment, I was allowed to pause. In the flamelight, I looked down at my hand, my arm, my body. I won't describe what I saw. It was too horrible, too disgusting. Even in imagination now, I could not hold my shape together. I was a long-dead corpse. I sobbed with self-pity to see what I was becoming.

But then, even then, as I stood, as I mourned, I began to notice an unexpected sweetness in the air. Was it real? Had I conjured it in denial? No. No, it was there. Beneath the heat of the fire, beneath the screeching cries of the impotent damned, beneath the stench of my own rotting body, there was the faint fragrance of a woman: a wild, yearning scent like night-blooming jasmine.

I whispered her name—and she answered:

Don't turn around.

She didn't speak the words. They just appeared in my mind: a soft but urgent command that cut through the shrieks of agony bubbling up from the bubbling lava.

Betheray? My eyes filled with tears of grief and frustration.

Don't. Turn. Around, she repeated—like that: a full stop after every word.

I managed to keep myself from looking at her. It wasn't easy. Try as I might, I could not remember her face, and I would have given anything—anything—to see it again, to comfort myself with the sight of her in this chill, merciless underworld.

But from the tone of her voice, I understood I had to obey her. Something dreadful would happen if I confronted her beauty with my rotted, flesh-dripping horror movie of a skull. So I stood there, my back to her, taking deep, helpless breaths of the hot sulfuric clouds.

Can you help me? I tried not to ask, but the thought came into my head and she heard it.

No one can help you, Austin. You're over. You're not there to help anymore.

I would have wept like a child then, howled like a hysterical child, but even here, I couldn't bear to have Beth see me so unmanned.

What do I do then? Just die? Just burn?

While there's time, do what you came to do, she said.

I couldn't imagine what she meant. *Do what?*

The emperor, said Betheray urgently. *Find the emperor. The emperor is here. The emperor is among the dead.*

Somehow these words put some spirit back in me. I felt myself straighten a little. Straighten and grow strong. Everything was not yet done. I still had a purpose. Find the emperor.

What then? I asked her. *When I find him. What can I do? Look at me, Beth! I'm dead. I'm becoming nothing. What can I do?*

There was no answer. Just silence. I was afraid—I was terrified— that she was already gone, that I was alone again, that I had to live out the rest of this death by myself.

But then—then the scent of jasmine grew subtly stronger beneath the choking sulfur, beneath the anguished flames, beneath the gurgled shrieks from under the lava and the smell of my own rotting flesh. I felt her spirit on my neck like breath, and she slipped something cool and solid into my hand.

I stood very still, waiting, hoping I'd feel her flesh touch the crawling ruin of mine. But there was only this cool metallic cylinder against my palm. I closed my fingers around it—and I recognized the shape.

I lifted my hand—my skeletal hand with the crawling flesh dangling from it.

I was holding my sword. The shining blade reflected the furious red from the lake of fire.

I heard Betheray sigh. The next moment, I knew she had left me.

I stood there, solitary, beyond the edge of life on the very shores of torment. I stood there, the very image of death, and raised my sword.

I wanted to weep for myself. But instead I thought: *Find the emperor. The emperor is among the dead.*

I started across the coal-black bridge.

It was a long way. The path was very narrow—narrow and slippery and uneven. The slightest loss of balance and I would pitch off the side of the faceted rock and plunge into the fire. What's more—to make things even worse—as soon as I started to edge away from the black shore, the pitiful creatures trapped in the flaming sea began to reach up out of that seething molten lake of pain to try to grab me, to try to use me to pull themselves up onto the bridge.

They were horrible things. Damned things. A screaming corpse of a woman with the corpses of infants sucking at every inch of her like burning leeches. A headless man shrieking for help from a gaping wound just beneath his waistline. A pudgy child fighting uselessly to tear away the reptile biting his face, its snakelike tail whipping back and forth with hungry glee. A man and a woman locked together, struggling to disengage their insect-riddled loins from the disgusting ruins of each other. And those were the ones I can describe. The rest were nightmares beyond words, beyond imagining. They mainlined into what was left of my mind without any imagery whatsoever. Pure horror, two hundred proof, injected straight into the soul of me.

All of them, all these things, reached up from the fire. Their fingers clawed at the gleaming black stone. Their eyes searched for me. Their hands tried to get hold of me. They fought to crawl up my body out of the bottomless lake.

And what could I do? Each time one lunged up out of the lava, I nearly toppled off the bridge and joined them in their hell. Pity for them would have killed me. I had to fight them off, slash at them with my sword, kick at them, send them spilling back into their damnation. What could I do but cut away at them, a corpse swinging his blade at corpses, a skeleton fighting skeletons as I inched forward over the black stone?

At first, I couldn't see the far side—just the seething red lake extending forever into yellow smoke, the anthracite walls rising on every side of me forever. The fumes choked me. The flames choked me. A babbling zombie of an old lady suddenly leapt up at me, wildly flailing. I kicked her and she went down, but I trembled there, off-kilter, fighting not to fall in after her. Only with the greatest effort did I regain my balance. Then—a rotting skeleton with a sword in my bony hand—I inched on.

Slowly, through the yellow tendrils of mist, the far shore came dimly into view. I paused. I took a cautious glance back over my shoulder and saw I was halfway across. The knowledge filled my rotting guts with panic. There could be no quick retreat now. It was just as far to the end as it was back to the beginning. I tried to steady myself, but my muscles were turning to mush. I had no strength. I was trembling all over. I had to hurry before there was nothing left of me. I started moving again, took another step, another.

And with that, something enormous sprang up at me on a roaring wave of fire.

It was a shrieking forest of personalities, all of them ablaze. It was one man, a monstrous man, but with a dozen bodies of every kind squirming in the core of him. In the split second I saw him before he struck, I understood each person within him was savaging the others in a murderous frenzy and all were simultaneously hurling themselves at me.

I screamed once in pure terror. Then the flaming beast washed over the crawling mess that I'd become. My skeleton was suddenly drowning in gibbering flame-faces. On every side of me hung entrails gripped in gory hands. Scorching pain entered my dissolving bones like acid. And I could feel my feet losing purchase on the anthracite as the many-headed Wave Man began to carry me away.

With all that was left of my strength, I planted myself on the bridge. I struck upward, hard, with the point of my sword. The blade plunged deep into the babbling forest fire of self-murdering humanity. I ripped at it, tore at it, all in a second, fighting the tide that tried to drag me down with it into the fire.

A black hole opened at the core of the thing. I grabbed the edge of it with one skeletal hand. I worked the sword with the other, sawing at the red-hot substance of it.

The creature tore open like a canvas sack. Black bats with human faces flew out of it, flew up into the high shadows, cackling as they went.

The burning monster dissolved into lava around me. The lava splashed down at my feet, then seeped over the rims of the bridge and dribbled back into the greater sea of flame.

But the jolt of it had made me stumble. I was heading toward the edge of the bridge, tipping over the edge. I threw my arms out to either side of me for balance, the bony fingers of my right hand still wrapped around the hilt of the sword. I was on one foot, on tiptoe, teetering on the last inch of anthracite.

I steadied. Got my other foot down. Stayed on the bridge—just barely—just.

I remained where I was a moment, trying to recover. It seemed the wave of fire—of fire and anguish and pain—had cleansed me somehow. The stench of the sulfur was still thick around me, but my own stench was gone. I no longer felt the carrion insects crawling over me. They'd been burned away. I was now just white bones dressed in the rags of flesh.

I went on, exhausted. More creatures leapt up out of the lava at me. I fought them off, but I was weary, and I was growing wearier with each step.

Luckily, as I neared the far shore, the attacks grew less frequent. The damned grew paler, weaker. Their hands would begin to reach up but then sink again before they even touched the bridge. One skullish face grinned at me from just below the fire's surface, then the flames engulfed it and it was gone.

Stepping gingerly heel to toe, I hurried across the narrow path as quickly as I could.

Finally—finally—I reached the far shore and collapsed onto the hard coal.

For a long moment—maybe an endless moment, who could tell?—I remained there on my hands and knees, flickering in and out of existence as my mind recoiled from the abomination I'd become and the emptiness I was rapidly becoming.

I tried to inspire myself to stand. I looked at the sword in my bony white fingers, the bright silver blade laid out across the black anthracite. Where had I gotten it? Who had given it to me? I could not remember. I had a vague sense there had been some comforting presence near me. I remembered the scent of jasmine. But the face of that presence was gone, its name forgotten.

All that was left inside me was the one thought: *Find the emperor. He is here among the dead.*

I wasn't sure whether I had eyes anymore. I suspected all that was left of my eyes was the jelly I felt dripping slowly down the front of my skull. All the same, by will and imagination, I lifted the line of my vision. I saw a narrow corridor threading between two walls of black rock. I can't convey how forbidding the passage seemed to me. How dark. I knew somehow it led to the final place, that once I entered, there would be no returning. I did not want to go.

But what was behind me? The lake of fire? The bridge? I glanced back. No. The bubbling red expanse was gone. It had faded away, and there was nothing left but thick yellow smoke and echoing cries of endless misery. I could no longer remember what it had been like to cross the bridge or what the lava had looked like. There was so much now I could not remember. I was reluctant even to wonder who I was, afraid that, too, was already gone, that I no longer had even my identity.

I was just death now, just this death or else nothing.

I rose. I moved—moved without walking—drifted like a lazy daydream, like the fading memory of a man. I went down the dark corridor, my whole soul sobbing because I already knew what would happen next.

There was a deep rumble, like the growl of a waking beast. The anthracite walls shifted—began to move—suddenly snapped shut behind me—*bang*—the crash echoing.

Any possibility of retreat was now cut off. I drifted on toward the end of the corridor. The rock growled again. The walls trembled. Any second, they would quake—slam shut—crush me.

I emerged from the corridor seconds before the quake hit. Then the walls smashed together, and there I was on the other side, trapped.

This—this last place of all—was more awful even than the lake of fire, more awful even than the creatures I had seen tortured in its liquid flames.

There was nothing—neither space nor blackness—merely an infinite emptiness beyond imagination and meaning, beyond language and thought. It was corrosive. The very fact of it was eating into me. All that was left of me was dissolving into atoms of nonexistence and becoming part of the nothingness everywhere. Only that—only the fact that the void was devouring me—gave it any quality at all, gave it any aspect that could be described.

It was as if there was a great serpent twining all around me, slithering over me, ingesting and digesting me. Cool and enormous, its writhing length caressed me, coaxed my being from itself so that bit by bit I became part of its vast non-body. The slow deconstruction of my self was like a whisper—a whisper that said, *There is nothing left of you, no flesh, no meaning, no hope, no joy, no life, no desire, no tomorrow nor yesterday, no memories, no dreams, you are already dead, you are already dead . . .*

How weird was it—how wonderful and weird—that it was that whisper that saved me? That whisper, which was nothing more than the way my imagination perceived this Serpent of Nonexistence, this quality of black destruction, this acid of despair that was dissolving me within itself. That whisper was the Worst Thing of all Things— and yet—and yet, whatever was left of my mind caught hold of it. It gave me one faint half-sparkle of hope.

Fading, dying, dissolving there, somehow, in that evil hour, some everlasting logic occurred to me, some fabric of reason that had supported the world before even the world existed: a riddle that had stood forever at the time before time.

The serpent whispered: *You are already dead.*

And I thought: *Who? Who's dead? Who are you talking to, Snake of Death?*

That was it. That was what saved me. That was how I found myself—what was left of myself, this dying, dissolving former thing in the belly of emptiness. The voice of utter destruction spoke to me out of total blackness, and I followed the voice and located myself and realized at some level I must still have being, some flickering spark of the eternal flame of life and love.

With all my soul, I set my being against the dark. I used the power I'd gotten from Elinda's book. I willed a doorway in the black core of nothingness. I willed that door to open.

There was then a wrenching tremor in the bowels of hell. A quaking fissure in the absolute night. Blinding whiteness appeared. Life—life like light—poured in through the opening—washed over me like a reviving tide.

I gasped. Sweet breath. I roared with effort. I fought my way into the brightness. I forced my way through the blinding white. Every brutal step through infinite distance, I felt my being coming back to me, my body reconstituting, unrotting, reforming.

I forced my self out to the other side.

And I tumbled from the crumpled, smoking ruin of my silver Mercedes. I fell on my side in the red desert dirt. I rolled away just as the car exploded into flames.

Bleeding, aching, I clutched my chest—my living, pulsing chest—in my two hands. I raised my eyes to heaven. My eyes! I had my eyes again! And my body: it felt good. It felt purged. It felt healed.

I climbed up onto my knees. I cried out, sobbing: "I'm alive! I'm alive!"

Then I saw: the Priest of Death was there, standing over me, his pistol pointed at my face. With a movement like a whiplash, he smacked the barrel hard against the side of my head.

A rocket of pain shot through me ear to ear. I pitched forward face-first, into the dust, and lost consciousness.

21

WELL, THIS WAS A BIG DISAPPOINTMENT, I DON'T MIND telling you. Here, I had crossed the fires of hell. I had outwitted the Serpent of Cosmic Destruction. I had solved the riddle of life and fought my way back from the very heart of deathly death—and what did I get for it?

The next thing I knew I woke up stuffed onto the floor of the black truck's cab with my knees jammed up under my chin and my wrists bound tightly behind me. The pain in my head was like a shrieking madwoman trapped behind my eyes. Plus, the Priest of Death, that little shit, was sitting above me, behind the Ford's wheel, driving along jaunty jolly, without a care in the world, even humming a happy tune beneath his breath. Every so often, the bastard would sneer down at me, his eyes invisible behind his round black glasses.

So all in all, yes, this whole thing was a tremendous anticlimax. If I was a lesser man, I would have felt sorry for myself. And I was. And I did.

I groaned at the pain in my head.

"Shut up," said the assassin. "I'm tired of listening to you."

"My head," I groaned.

"I said, 'Shut up.' It won't last long. I'll put you out of your misery soon enough."

I glared at him balefully, and I really hoped it hurt his feelings too. "What are you going to do if I don't shut up, asshole? Kill me?" The effort of talking made my head throb all the more. I groaned again.

He grinned his skullish grin. "If you don't shut up, I'm going to bury you in an unmarked grave. If you do shut up, I'll do you a favor and blow your brains out first." He had amused himself with this apparently. He laughed a quiet laugh—*heh, heh, heh*—his head bobbing up and down.

The truck went over a bump in the road. I cried out as the jolt made the ache in my head flare through my entire body. That amused the assassin too. He laughed again. *Heh, heh, heh.*

The whole situation was incredibly aggravating—and that's an understatement, believe me. I mean, really, you'd think after you conquered Death itself, you'd level up somehow, you know? Like in a video game, you'd get some new superpower or something, the ability to move objects with your mind, something like that. As it was, I couldn't even string two thoughts together because the ache in my head was reverberating like a gong. So there I lay on the floor of the truck. Uncomfortable. Undignified. The whole event just one massive humiliation. And it probably wasn't going to end well either. More death—and this time, I had the feeling it would stick. Death was not always death in the Eleven Lands. But here in LA, you couldn't even come back from a flop picture, let alone a bullet to the head.

The car jounced again. I cried out again.

"Shut up," the killer said again.

And I snapped back angrily: "If you're going to shoot me, why don't you just shoot me? What do we have to drive around for?"

He grinned down at me. "I always prefer it when people

disappear. You know? Once there's a body, it's a murder. Anyone might investigate. The police, the press. We own a lot of those bastards, but there's plenty of rogues out there still. One of them might go off the reservation and look around and come up with something. But when a guy just goes missing—who the hell knows what it is? Right? Maybe he ran off. Maybe he has amnesia. Maybe he faked his death for insurance purposes. If there's no body, even if someone does investigate, he'll just be making up stories, that's all. Conspiracy theories and whatnot."

I shuddered. Obviously, he'd given this a lot of thought. And why shouldn't he? It was his profession. Executions like this were a regular occurrence to him. How many people had Orosgo sent to their deaths this way? How many people had Richard sent to their deaths this way—and with our mom and dad's approval?

"If they'd done it my way the last time, there wouldn't be all this hoo-ha," he muttered, more to himself than to me. "Now . . . all this hoo-ha."

It took me a moment to understand what he was saying, but then I did. "Alexis, you mean. You mean if they'd done it your way with Alexis Merriwether? If they'd just made *her* disappear like you're going to do to me?"

He glanced at me, as if surprised I had heard him. Then he turned back to the road. "Now there's all this hoo-ha," he muttered again.

"You're the one, then," I said. "You killed her. You're the black figure Jane saw in the doorway. You drugged her and killed Alexis and then had the cops set Jane up for it. And now you're going to kill Jane, too, and make it look like suicide."

He shook his head bitterly. "Big fancy plan. That was supposed to take care of it. Close the case. But with all this hoo-ha, anyone might take a closer look. Anyone might investigate and come up with some crazy conspiracy theory."

"The truth, you mean."

"I told them. She should just disappear. They wouldn't listen. All those big brains. Too smart for a working stiff like me."

"Why did they do it?" I asked him. "Why did Alexis have to die? What did she know?" The answer occurred to me even as I asked. "She was blackmailing Solomon Vine, wasn't she? Is that it? That's how she got him to hire her for the movie. She knew something, and she was threatening to tell. What was it: the kids? The way he uses those children and peddles them around town?"

This time Death gave me a longer look before returning his gaze to the windshield.

I went on, talking more to myself than to him: "No one wants to know. Everyone knows, so no one wants to. So once Jane dies, the whole story will be forgotten. Simple as that."

"Didn't I tell you to shut up?" the Priest of Death answered. "So then shut up."

I stared up at his profile, framed and darkened against the bright blue sky at the window. I tried to focus hard on his head. I willed his head to explode—on the off chance, you know, that I really had leveled up after overcoming Death in Aona and now had acquired some new power like making assassins' heads explode.

But no such luck. His head remained intact. He just kept driving along, humming to himself, not a care in the world.

We traveled on another half hour or so. I could feel the truck turn. I could feel it begin to ascend a steep hill. After a while, we left the paved road. We traveled over rough dirt, *bumpety-bumpety-bumpety*. It was worse than being dragged over the rocks by the yeti. Every *bumpety* was like a kick in my temple with a steel-toed boot. I started to worry I was going to be sick. That would be just perfect, I thought. I had defeated Death in the ultimate triumph of knightly courage, and not only did I not level up and get new powers but I was going to cover myself in vomit and give my assassin a big old laugh before he killed me.

Before that could happen, though, the truck came to rest. The Priest killed the engine.

"Last stop, dead meat," he said to me. He glanced my way. "Don't bother begging for your life. It only turns me on."

"I'm not begging for my life."

"Why not? Don't you like me?"

Heh, heh, heh.

The last guy Orosgo sent to murder me was a philosopher. This one was a comedian. Whatever happened to quiet professionalism?

He pushed the truck's door open and jumped down out of the cab. He walked around to the back, and I heard him rooting around in the bed. I used the time to struggle against my bonds. It felt like some sort of plastic tie around my wrist. I made a few attempts at snapping it. Each try sent another stab of pain through my head. None of it got me anywhere.

The passenger door came open then and there he was, natty and evil in his black suit, black beret, black glasses. He was holding a shovel in one hand now. He reached down with the other and grabbed me under the arm. He was surprisingly strong for such a skinny guy—very strong, in fact. He dragged me over the seat and right out the door. Then he planted me on the ground. I had to scramble to get my feet under me before I fell. By the time I regained my balance, he had shut the door and drawn his gun out from under his jacket. He stood in front of me with his shovel in one hand and his pistol in the other. Behind him, I saw a dirt road winding down out of sight into nowhere, empty hills in the distance beyond.

He jabbed me in the gut with the gun barrel.

"Oof!" I said.

"Walk, dead meat."

I started walking. The scene before me was shockingly beautiful. We were at the bottom of a slope of green grass. At the top of the slope was a deep stand of aspen trees. Their bark was snowy white. Their leaves were pastel green and yellow. The spring breeze moved through the branches with a mellow whisper. A mourning dove sang his doleful song.

As we climbed the slope toward the little wood, I felt more sorrow than fear, but it was a deep sorrow. I didn't want to die—not again. The descent into the hell beneath Aona seemed like a dream to me now, as my journeys to Galiana and the Eleven Lands so often seemed like dreams when I returned. But I remembered well enough the helpless grief of my body rotting, my substance dissolving. It made me want to weep with frustration to be marched toward that fate once again with no hope of escape.

We entered the woods. Despite my aching head, I could see full well that the light here was lovely, pale and strangely golden. The leaves fluttered in the wind like butterfly wings. Goldfinches fluttered in the branches, cheep-cheeping happily like young girls in conversation. I could feel my heart clinging to the beauty of the place, to every last second of life. I knew this was the end of everything.

Soon—too soon—the forest surrounded us, hid us. We were alone. No one would see me die here. No one would hear my body fall. The whisper of the wind and the chatter of the goldfinches and the mourning dove's *haroo-hoo-hoo* were all the sounds there were.

Then something dropped behind me with a clang: the shovel.

"Here," said the Priest of Death. "This is the place."

I stopped. I looked around me at the golden light and the trembling leaves against the bright blue sky. I drank it all in. My burial place. Would he shoot me now? Would I hear the bang or just go out like a candle?

But it didn't happen—not yet. Instead, in the next second, I felt a tug at my wrists. The Priest cut my hands free. Then, before I could react, he shoved his gun into my back, hard, so that I stumbled forward a few paces.

"Turn around, dead meat," he said.

Rubbing my wrists to get the blood flowing into my sleeping fingers, I turned to face my assassin. He swooped down and plucked the shovel up off the ground and tossed it at me. I caught it in a reflex.

"Dig your grave," he said. He pointed to a spot in the grass. "Right there."

I cursed. I shook my head. I was disgusted by the indignity of it. I, who had fought my way across the lake of fire, forced by this skeevy putz to dig my own grave in the middle of nowhere.

The Priest of Death read my mind. "This is where you say, 'What if I refuse?'" he said. "And I say, 'If you make me dig the grave myself, I'll cut you to slow pieces.' Then I see you thinking about hitting me with that shovel, and I tell you I'll bury you alive if you try. Finally, you realize you have no choice and start digging the grave. Then when you're done, I kill you and bury you in it."

"Gee, you could at least give me a spoiler alert before you tell me the ending," I said.

He gestured at me with the gun. "Dig, dead meat."

I did it. I dug my own grave. How did it feel? It felt pretty much the same as when I saw my own flesh rotting away in hell. Miserable. Helpless. I was strangling on useless rage and self-pity. I watched the shovel go *chuck* into the dirt. I watched the dirt go *shush* out of the shovel and pile up by the side of the hole. I watched the hole get bigger around me, longer, wider, big enough to hold my dead body—all as if someone else were doing it. It was me, but I could not make it stop.

The breeze whispered in the aspens above me. The goldfinches cheeped and chattered. The mourning dove sang.

"All right," the Priest of Death said finally. "That's enough."

I stopped digging. I was standing in a shallow grave, my grave, knee deep. I was sick with grief and anger. I looked up at the assassin above me. He was a dark shape against the green-yellow aspen leaves. He looked relaxed, almost bored. He pointed his gun at me. He sniffed.

"Toss up the shovel," he said.

I thought about throwing it at him, but what would have been the use? There was no way I could climb up out of my grave fast enough to reach him before he killed me. I threw the shovel out of the grave.

The Priest of Death took a step closer. He stood right at the grave's edge. He pointed the gun directly at my head, the barrel not twelve inches away. His dark glasses reflected me looking up at him stupidly. I wondered if I would see myself die.

"So long, dead meat," the Priest said.

I drew my sword and cut his hand off.

I know: it surprised me too! What the hell, right? But apparently, I actually *had* leveled up. After outwitting the Serpent of Infinite Nothingness, after willing my way out of the endless dark, I actually had acquired a new power. I just hadn't realized until this moment what that power was.

But now, on a surge of anger, with some new instinct I never had before, I reached across myself for my old weapon. And suddenly, for the first time ever in this world, right here in LA, Elinda's blade was in my hand.

I sent the edge of it arcing up backhand through the air. The sword chucked into the Priest's wrist with the full force of my terror, rage, and despair. The Priest pulled the trigger as the razor-sharp blade cut straight through flesh and bone without stopping. The gunshot went awry. The bullet hit the side of my shoulder and glanced harmlessly off the magic liquid armor that was swiftly flowing out of my core to cover me. The priest's hand, still gripping the gun, did a little flip and plopped into the shallow grave beside my foot. Arterial blood started spurting from the Priest's stump. In the quiet wood, I could hear it pattering down onto the flesh of the severed hand in the grave.

The Priest stared at the place on his arm where his hand had been. He was silent, at first. In shock, I guess. He looked from his stump to me—suddenly a knight in armor climbing out of his own shallow grave. How was he supposed to make sense of that? Who could?

Just as I came to stand beside him, he started screaming. One four-letter word, in a high-pitched shriek, again and again.

I killed him.

With deliberate movements, I drew my sword back and then plunged it straight into the center of him with all my strength. That shut him up, all right. His scream was cut off mid-syllable by a gurgling gasp. His body bent over my blade so that I could see the point come out of his back, spitting gore. As he jerked forward, his sunglasses popped off and dropped to the ground with a plastic clatter. I held his shoulder with one hand and yanked the sword out of him with the other. He gasped again and straightened. His eyes looked right into mine.

I had seen that look before, that dying look: the sudden knowledge that every dream of life is over. It's a horrible thing to see. It could make you pity the devil himself. No one deserves to die. That's how bad death is: worse than the worst of us.

And maybe the time would come when I would pity the Priest. Maybe I'd regret what I'd done and figure I should have let him alone, seeing as he was unarmed. No joke intended. Well, a little intended. Anyway, there might come a time when I felt sorry for him, but this wasn't it. Right now, all I thought was: *You tried to kill me, you piece of shit, and now you're dead. Too bad.*

The Priest of Death toppled sideways and fell into the shallow grave. Only his feet and ankles stuck up over the edge of the hole.

His stump spurted blood, then stopped. He let out a long, rattling breath, his last.

I sheathed my bloody sword and it vanished. The armor vanished, too, the liquid metal seeping back into my body.

Cool new power, I thought. *Almost worth dying for.*

I stood still for a moment in the aspen grove, listening to the breeze whisper. I raised my face to the sweetness of the spring. I watched the yellow-green leaves tremble and flutter against the so-blue sky. One of these days, I thought, I really had to learn to appreciate the beauty of every moment without having a gun stuck in my face.

But who had time for that now? I had to get to Riley.

I sighed. First, I had to get rid of the body. I picked the Priest's sunglasses out of the dirt and tossed them into the grave next to his corpse. Then I climbed in after them. I searched the dead man's clothes to recover my phone and wallet and keys. That was nasty. Even nastier, I pried his severed hand off the pistol. I wanted that pistol. Not the hand—I left that in the grave with the rest of him.

Then, with all that done, I climbed out of the hole and picked up the shovel.

Reader, I buried him.

22

I BORROWED THE PRIEST'S TRUCK. I FIGURED HE wouldn't mind, being dead and all. I drove back to the road and started to make my way to the Orosgo Retreat, to Riley.

I got about ten miles before the reaction hit me. All at once, I started shaking so badly I couldn't drive. I had to pull over. I killed the engine and sat staring out through the windshield at nothing.

It was like there was a thunderstorm inside me, thunder and lightning. Noise and energy making my entire body jump and quiver. I saw the lake of fire as if it were right there in front of me. I saw the blackness of death with the Serpent of Nothingness slithering through it. I saw the Priest standing over me with his gun and saw him again at the moment the sword cut his hand off. I felt like I was going crazy, sinking away from the steadfast world and into the feral territories of my own consciousness.

I had to do something. I had to move. I climbed down out of the cab and walked a little way into the desert. I bent over with my hands on my knees. I felt dizzy. I was gasping for breath. My chest hurt as if I was going to have a heart attack.

When I finally got control of myself, I slowly straightened up. I stared out over the desert, red sand and green brush and white rocks to a blue horizon streaked with a scud of gray clouds. I felt far away from everything, far away even from myself.

Who was I? I wondered. Who was I anymore?

Once upon a time, I was just Austin Lively. Just another guy who had come to Los Angeles to try to make it in the movie business. Just another guy who had tried and failed. There had to be a million people like me in Hollywood. A million wannabes who just don't have what it takes to win the world's approval. A million little hopeful stars winking out at the dawn of reality. I was nobody then. Just another nobody like everybody.

But the wisest queen in all the world had come looking for me. She'd come looking for someone like me, anyway, and I was the one she found. So who was I now? What had she made me? I had traveled between worlds. I had seen magic. I had flown above the earth and gone down below it. I had killed people. I had killed monsters. I had been killed myself. I had died and journeyed into hell and rotted away and become almost nothing. And I had come back somehow. And now I had this power, and I was not like anyone else on earth.

So who was Austin Lively now?

I drew a deep breath of the desert air. I realized with complete certainty that the life I had lived till this day was over. My dreams of Hollywood: over. Everything I used to value gone—left behind so I could pursue the queen's quest in that brain-tumor fantasy world that meant more to me at this point than the world itself, this world I'd always known.

Because I saw it now, this world. I saw the truth of it, and I would not be able to unsee it, not ever. This world—our world—it was all Orosgo. Him and his lies. And who was Orosgo? He was Curtin, wasn't he? He was a servant of that evil wizard whose purpose was to conquer and enslave. His mind was a door through which Curtin could come from the other kingdom into this. And when he died . . .? Well, then, my brother, Richard, would take over for him, and he would be that door. And then he would die and someone else would take his place, on and on, but really it would always be Curtin, in the end. Because it was his world. This world: it was all Curtin.

So who was I, then, in a world like that? What was I supposed to do?

I didn't know the answers. I didn't know any of the answers. But I did know this: I knew what I had to do next. That was it. And that was everything.

So I caught my breath. I calmed myself down. I walked back to the truck of Death.

And I headed back to the madhouse.

I USED THE big Ford's GPS to find my way to the right road. I figured no one would be tracking me for a while. It would take time for Richard to realize it was I, not the Priest of Death, who had walked out of the aspen grove alive.

When I rejoined the winding desert two-lane, I spotted my Mercedes a quarter mile in the distance: a sad, small, smoking wreck, its marred surface glinting silver in the sunlight. Too bad, I thought. It had been a hell of a nice car.

I drove on to the asylum. Once again, the forbidding red-brick mansion rose up before me with its central tower and its gables and its mansard roofs. I felt sick to think I had let Riley get put in there. Poor little Riley trying her crazy best to tell the only version of the truth she knew. I would have to set her free, and soon. But not today.

There was no Hillary Baine to meet me at the front door this time. I hadn't called ahead. I went to the reception desk inside the front entrance, told the security guard who I was. Then I waited. Then she came. Her squat little figure scurried toward me down the endless corridor. I thought I saw a too-bright light of panic in her eyes. The cheery grin on her apple-cheeked face seemed feverish. Her curly red hair had the aspect of a flame. My unannounced visit had caught her off guard.

Yet there was never a wrong word from our Hillary. Always that deferential tone in that squeaky voice like the voice of a cartoon. And always that terrifying undertone of threat, as if at any minute she would call her aides and have me locked up in a padded cell.

When she got closer, she pulled up short, open-mouthed. It would not have surprised me to see an exclamation point appear above her head like in the comics.

"Mr. Lively! Are you all right? Your face. You've been injured."

Oh, right. I must have looked like a bloody mess. I had forgotten. Ever since I'd climbed out of my shallow grave, I hadn't given much thought to my appearance.

"I was in a car accident on the way over," I told her. "I'm fine." I figured I'd leave out the part about getting pistol-whipped and shot at. Not to mention the joust on the flying horses and the journey into hell.

"Well!" Hillary Baine went on, edging toward me. "What can I do for you? We weren't expecting you. It's not visiting hours, you know."

I tried to sound as authoritative as I could. This wasn't a prison, after all. It wasn't even a hospital. Legally, Riley could walk out of here any time she wanted. And if I insisted on seeing her, they couldn't keep me away.

"I didn't have time to call," I said brusquely. "I have to leave town very suddenly, and I want to make sure Riley knows about it. I want to tell her I'll be back, face to face. I'll just need a moment with her."

"Oh! Oh! All right," she squeaked. There was a pitch of hysteria in her voice. "I'll . . . I'll take you to the Family Room, and fetch her."

"No," I said. "Take me to where she is right now. I only need a second with her." She hesitated. I could see her looking for an excuse to refuse me. But I stared her down and said, "Please. Right now. I'm in a hurry."

And really, what could she do?

"Well . . . She'd be in the Common Room at this hour," she chirped. And after a moment's hesitation, she led the way.

Down the haunted halls we went together. All the while, Hillary Baine kept babbling in that cartoon voice of hers. About Riley's doses and how well she was doing and how they were making great progress and she should be able to leave soon. The usual crap. I wanted to draw my magic sword and swipe her blithering head off. I restrained myself.

We came to double doors, and she pushed one door open and held it for me. I stepped through.

The Common Room was very large. Very anonymous and institutional. Its only point of grace was the huge picture window looking out on a spectacular view of the mountains and the sky. Otherwise, there were the usual institutional tables and chairs set about. A nurse's station, where two women in white surveyed the scene through the open top half of a heavy Dutch door. There was a TV playing a game show on one wall, and books and board games strewn here and there. And there were about twenty people sitting around. And all of them looked like they were dead inside.

This, I thought, was what the patients of the Orosgo Retreat looked like when you didn't warn Hillary Baine you were coming. Drugged to zombiedom. Slumped, staring, drooly faced. Some were muttering in slurred and dreamy conversations. A couple were playing Parcheesi in a grim sort of way. One young man was standing at the window, obsessively picking at his fingernails. Most of them, though, sat eerily still—they looked like some evil child magician had turned them into bizarre human plush toys.

One of these was Riley. She was seated on a stuffed chair with her legs tucked up under her. There were three other girls about the same age sitting near her in a sort of loose circle, two on a sofa, one on another chair. At first glance, it looked like a typical girl session, girls sitting around together, chatting. Only no one was chatting; they were just sitting there, no expressions on their faces. Plush toys. Doped-up girl-things positioned to look like a tea party.

But that was fine. In fact, it was a perfect setup for me. Because I hadn't really come here to talk to Riley. It was the mad girls I wanted.

The girls in the Common Room hear voices from another kingdom, Riley had told me.

And Queen Elinda had said, *You must listen to those who hear the voices of my kingdom but can speak in the voices of your world.*

So here I was.

"Look who's come to see you, Riley!" chirped Hillary Baine chirpily. Once again, I imagined drawing my magic sword. I imagined splitting her in half with it. The woman brought out the worst in me.

I turned and gave her a look. "Thank you," I said—meaning get the hell away from us.

She nodded and wandered off to the nurse's station across the room.

I stepped into the circle of girls. It felt eerie having those life-sized, button-eyed living dolls all around me. I knelt on one knee in front of Riley. She looked down at me and narrowed her eyes as if trying to remember who I was. Since our last conversation, these villains had obviously dosed the hell out of her—probably trying to quiet all her talk about another kingdom.

"Riley," I said, my voice low, almost a whisper. "It's me. I need you. I know you're in there. Fight your way to the surface, baby. Talk to me."

For a moment, there was no response. Then she drew a deep, deep breath. She gave a long, long, wistful sigh. "Aus," she said. But she barely moved. I wasn't sure whether she really knew I was there or not.

"All right. All right, listen," I said. "I know the truth now. Okay? I remember now. I remember everything."

She sighed again. Like the wind in the aspens. "Aus."

"You said the girls here—the mad girls in the Common Room— you said they can hear voices when they don't take their meds."

I glanced over my shoulder at the others. One was a pudgy brunette with a plain, hard face. One was a willowy ghost of a creature, a blonde, barely there. Those were the two on the sofa. The third, on the other chair, was a delicate beauty with honey-colored curls on her snow-white forehead. My heart went dark in my chest when I examined them. They didn't look like they'd been hiding their meds. They looked like their meds had turned them into dolls; staring plush toys.

I turned back to Riley, still kneeling in front of her. She kept looking down at me with a thin, stitched-on smile. Sighing: "Aus."

"The queen sent me here, Riley. Queen Elinda. You said she was waiting for me to remember her? Well, I did. I do. I remember. I went and saw her . . ." On instinct, I glanced toward the nurse's station. Hillary Baine had stepped through the Dutch door. I could see her back there, behind the nurses, talking on her phone. Who was she calling? Richard? Probably. I probably didn't have much time before some new killer came to get me. "I saw Elinda in the homeless camp," I told Riley. No answer. "She said the girls here would tell me what to do." No response. I glanced again at Hillary Baine. She was stealing looks at me now, still talking furtively into the phone. My voice became more urgent. "My friend Jane Janeway is in trouble, Ri. I don't know what to do, and the queen said the girls here could help me."

But Riley just went on staring at me with those button eyes and that stitched-on smile. Her head tilted. Her body slumped. "Aus," she whispered. A plush toy. I was losing hope.

"Riley, I can't stay long. Someone has to . . ."

"The forest is all one tree."

I started. Turned, my heart racing. The voice had come from over my right shoulder. A low, drifting, toneless voice—from the plump brunette on the sofa, or so I thought at least. But she hadn't moved. She was still slumped there, limp-lipped, staring at nothing.

"What?" I asked her.

"Plant the carnation in the earth beneath."

Quickly, I turned again. This mournful drawl seemed to have come from the girl in the chair, the delicate beauty. Or had it? She hadn't moved either.

"Go through the door."

I quick-turned to the willowy blonde—and this was really spooky because I hadn't seen her move either but she had: now she was staring right at me with glassy blue eyes. For a moment, she remained like that, motionless, seemingly inanimate.

Then she spoke again, her voice hollow like a ghost's voice, her eyes still empty.

"Go through the door where there's no darkness at all," she said.

"The blood-red shadow is falling," said the brunette. "It's the only way." She was staring at me too now, though I'd never seen her move.

"The forest is all one tree," said the beauty.

"Plant the carnation in the earth beneath," said the willowy blonde.

"Go through the door where there's no darkness at all," said the brunette.

And then all together in a chilling chant: "The blood-red shadow is falling. Go through the door. It's the only way."

I turned from one to the other as each spoke. They started the routine again.

"The forest is all one tree."

"Plant the carnation . . ."

Then suddenly, they stopped. They sank back into living death, plush toys. I was about to urge them to speak again when I sensed there was some reason they'd gone silent, some approaching danger.

I turned. And there was Hillary Baine. She had crept up on me. She was looming over me where I knelt, staring down at me with her cheery smile and her hair like curling flame.

"Well!" she chirped. "I'm afraid I have to ask you to leave now. It's time for Riley's session."

We exchanged hard stares as if they were threats and curses.

My stare said: *Screw you, bitch. You can't make me go.*

And her stare and her self-certain smile said: *Go on and stay then and see what happens, buster.*

She had received her orders from on high: *Get him out of there now. We'll take care of him later.*

It would have been crazy for me to hang around long enough to find out who was coming to get me. I had to go.

I glanced at the girls. They were all silent, stuffed girl-things again. They had said what they had to say. There was nothing more for me here.

I faced Riley. I took hold of the strengthless hand that was resting on her knee. My little sister's little hand. I leaned forward and pressed my lips to her ear. "Hang on, Ri. I'll be back for you."

She sighed—like a death rattle. "Aus," she whispered.

THEN ONCE AGAIN, I was walking with Hillary Baine down a corridor, another one of these corridors in the main mansion of the Orosgo Retreat that seemed like a corridor in an optical illusion, that seemed to go on and on endlessly with the doors and alcoves repeating themselves endlessly along the way.

Also endless was her squeaky monologue: her self-justifications, her excuses for the things they did to the patients here. She sounded like a cartoon mouse on trial for war crimes.

"It's not an exact science yet, but what a leap forward it is to have these medications . . ."

How good it would have felt to draw my sword and cut pieces off her. I would have left the essential bits for last.

We approached the main entrance, the huge doors with their glass panels looking out on the rolling front lawn. As we drew near, Hillary Baine's high-pitched babbling sank into the background of my attention. In its place, I heard the voices of the mad girls in the Common Room.

Go through the door.

It's the only way.

The blood-red shadow is falling.

Go through the door where there's no darkness at all.

This? I thought. This door?

As we walked, my hand slipped into my shirt. My fingers wrapped around Betheray's locket. The heat of inspiration came off the metal and flowed through me.

And all at once, like a picture coming suddenly into focus, the mad girls' seemingly mystic chant began to make sense to me.

Go through the door where there's no darkness at all.

I had escaped from the Serpent of Nothingness into a blinding brightness that wasn't light but was simply the absence of all darkness. That was the last thing I had seen in that other kingdom—that other kingdom where my quest was still unfinished—where I had never found Anastasius—where I had never brought him the talisman so he would lead his armies to restore Elinda to the throne of Galiana.

The blood-red shadow is falling.

I remembered the red cloud I had seen as I flew on my stallion toward Aona: Curtin's armies—the armies I had helped unleash—moving in to destroy the leaderless forces of the emperor. Was that the blood-red shadow the mad girls were talking about? Did I have to stop that cloud somehow to keep Curtin from becoming all-powerful there and here?

I didn't know. I wasn't sure. I just somehow understood that I had to go back. Back into the darkless light that brought me here. I had to pass through that light and . . . what? Something. Somehow finish my quest.

The blood-red shadow is falling.

Go through the door.

I let the locket go. I licked my dry lips. I nodded.

As we reached the end of the endless corridor, as the door grew closer, as Hillary Baine's irritating words of self-rationalization began to infest my brain like squeaking vermin, my steps slowed. I was becoming afraid. Really afraid. Deep-down afraid. If I walked through that brightness, what would become of me? Would it be worse than death had been? More than death? I sensed it might. I sensed that if I went into that light it would be the end of me in ways I could neither imagine nor comprehend.

Who would Austin Lively be then?

We reached the doors. I came to a stop, staring through the glass panels at the blue sky.

"In the end, believe me, we'll find just the right medicine to make all the sadness go away," said Hillary Baine. She smiled at me complacently: a cartoon-mouse-slash-cartoon-monster, the queen of the madhouse. "That's why we're here."

She pushed the door open and held it for me. I looked out on the California springtime. The green lawn. The green mountains. The air smelled like some sweet memory. I did not want to leave this world ever again.

But Jane's time was running out. The killers were coming for her at midnight. I wasn't powerful enough to save her from the Tower yet. I needed more than just a sword and armor. I needed to level up even further.

Go through the door. It's the only way.

I made an effort of will—and all the world beyond the entrance gave way to a lightless bright in which there was no darkness at all. In which there was nothing. Nothing.

I steeled myself.

I went through the door.

ALL IN A MOMENT, THE WORLD WAS GONE. EVERYTHING
was gone except the White Forever. Everything that had happened
up till now suddenly seemed unreal to me. Jane in the Tower. Riley
in the Orosgo Retreat. The Priest of Death above the shallow grave.
The joust above the cliffside. Even the absolute darkness of hell
and the Serpent of Nothingness twining around me, digesting me,
turning me into itself. All that and all the rest was gone like dreams
are gone. Only half-remembered images remained, and those were
swiftly fading.

Suddenly, life was forgotten, and all that had ever been real was
this bright, bright eternity.

Then I broke through—and I was swallowed in the depths of
the ocean.

The water heaved over my head. The violent current dragged me
down, then heaved again and hurled me upward. I burst up through
the surface into a chaos of foamy waves. I gasped for air, dazed and
bewildered. Then almost at once, I was sucked down again by the
undertow.

Caught in the ocean's grip, I sank fast. I couldn't fight it. I could
only watch the watery beam of sunlight above me grow dimmer and

farther away as I went down into the green dark. My lungs began pumping, fighting to take in air. Any second I would surrender to them, and the saltwater would rush in and suffocate me.

Then the ocean heaved once again, changing direction, lifting me. This was my chance. I kicked my legs and stroked my arms to speed my way to the surface.

I broke into the air again, gasping again. The raging waves roared and crashed. The blue sky swayed and rolled above me, this way and that. I was tossed back and forth like a cork atop the rough water. I caught glimpses of the rugged, black cliffs looming over me.

My confusion cleared. I understood. I had come out of the country of the dead, out of the flaming blackness of hell, and through the white of eternity. I had returned to the land of the living, and I was in the sea beneath the Aona cliffs where Sir Littleman had dropped me after our joust.

Well, I wasn't going to be here long if I didn't reach dry land soon. I was already breathless. My limbs were going cold, losing strength. If another undertow took me down, I'd be finished—and probably for good this time.

A wave lifted me up and up, then dropped me with sickening swiftness from the crest to the trough. Spitting saltwater, I bobbed amidst the rock formations. The high wind howled. The wave rolled on to crash into the cliff face. Through the foam, I caught sight of a darkness in the rock—a hole—a cave entrance.

I thought: if I could swim in there, maybe I could survive. If I missed, the waves would crush me against the rocks.

But I had to try it. My strength was failing fast. The ocean turmoil battered and tore at me. Another half minute and I'd be carried off and drowned.

A low rolling wave came at me. I timed it. Leapt out in front of it. It caught me, carried me rocket fast toward the looming cliffs. My stomach lurched with fear as the wall of black rock raced at me.

The water lifted me. Too high. I fought my way down beneath the surface, striving toward the cave entrance. I saw the stony wall coming at me at breakneck speed.

Then, the next moment, by some sweet chance, the water dipped, and I hit the hole like a bulls-eye. I was hurled tumbling into a narrow tunnel.

My back struck the rock a glancing blow. The rushing water threw me from one side of the tunnel to the other. Then the wave began to recede, dragging me with it, back toward the seething ocean outside.

I clutched in wild desperation at the stone. My fingers caught a knob of rock. I held on as the wave tried to pull me out, tried to sweep me back out into the main. Then the water was gone. I was dropped down onto the rugged cave floor.

Terrified of the next blow, I scrambled like a lizard to get deeper into the cave, away from the water. Finally, exhausted, I collapsed onto the floor. I rolled onto my back, wheezing. I lay there, overcome with fatigue, battered, dressed in nothing but rags. I didn't have the energy to move. I felt as if my innards were pulverized, as if no bones remained to hold me together, no muscles to give me strength.

But the waves kept coming. The next one lapped the soles of my feet. A few more and the water reached my ankles. A few more and it touched my shins.

Oh shit, I thought wearily.

The tide was coming in.

With a groan, I forced myself to roll over. I began to crawl deeper into the cave, the rocks scraping my knees through my shredded trousers. I had to find a way out of here or the tunnel would fill and I'd be trapped. It'd be a terrible way to die.

I crawled on, grunting with effort and with pain as the rough stone tore my naked flesh. Outside, the ocean roared. The waves smashed into the rock. The water seethed into the tunnel behind me, spraying the backs of my legs. As I neared the end of the passage, I saw a narrow opening in the ceiling: a crevice. I reached the bottom of it and twisted my body around until I could peer up.

I felt some hope. Some. The crevice rose high—so high it vanished into the shadows above me. I thought: maybe I could climb to another level and escape the waves.

Breathing hard, I tried to gather my strength. I was chilled and battered to the bone, the energy bleeding out of me. But the waves kept coming in, kept coming closer. I had to go.

Hacking, gasping, I repositioned myself. I drew up my legs until I was crouched at the bottom of the crevice.

I began to climb.

I braced my hands against the crevice's walls. I searched out fingerholds and footholds in the rough rock. I hoisted myself, braced myself, found the next foothold and pushed up again and went on. Soon, a dim glow appeared above me. Was that sunlight? Light from the surface? It seemed about another hundred yards away. I thought I could make it.

That's when my strength gave out. Suddenly, my arms seemed to turn to jelly. My feet and my legs seemed to dissolve. I couldn't catch my breath. I started trembling violently with cold. I could neither go on climbing nor make a steady descent. I looked down. I was too high. A fall would kill me.

I did my best to wedge myself in the narrow space. I hung there, resting, hoping my strength would return. I could hear the muffled rumble of the ocean crashing.

Then the rumble subsided, and I heard something else, something above me: a woman's horrified scream.

Beltan, I thought. Favian's wife. No time had passed while I was in hell. It was mere minutes since Sir Littleman had defeated me in the trial by combat. Now he and Sir Goodchild and Sir Hammer were going to go through with the execution as scheduled. They were going to burn the emperor's brother and his wife and his little boy.

In the queen's name, I had to stop them.

I willed myself to climb again. Crying out with the effort, I hauled my aching body up a few more yards, then a few more. Weakness overcame me. My senses swam. My hands trembled. My heart hammered. Sweat poured down my forehead into my eyes. When I blinked it away, I thought I saw a narrow opening above me, maybe thirty yards away. I didn't think I could make it. I looked down, then up again. Too high to climb. Too far to fall. Too weak to go on. Panic began building in me, like a fire rising.

I cleared my mind. I summoned my will. I went on climbing. I refused to let my arms give out. I refused to let my legs go wobbly. My breath came in great gulping sobs. My frozen limbs quivered violently. As the sea sounds grew fainter below me, I heard another noise from above: a large crowd cheering.

They were going to do it.

The break in the stone was now only twenty feet away. I could make that. I had to make it. I gave a savage growl and fought my way upward, scrambling over the walls like some sort of mad, enormous spider. My strength was utterly gone, my muscles like water. My eyes were burning in my head with desperation. There was nothing left of me, nothing but my will and my devotion to the emperor's wisdom.

A final stretch. The fingers of my right hand slid into the crack in the stone, then the fingers of my left. I gripped the rim. My feet scrabbled against the rock, searching for a toehold. I found one. Planted my foot. Pushed with the last of my strength. And up I rose, over the edge of the rock, into the narrow opening.

I spilled into another small cave. I lay splayed out on the floor of it, retching with exhaustion. I was lying in a narrow space, the rock roof just inches above me. But a few yards away, the ceiling of the cave lifted. There was a passage there.

Groaning, I slithered forward. The scrape of the rocks against my raw flesh made my face twist with pain. But I made it—out of the cramped hole and into an open chamber. And there before me, I saw what looked for all the world like an underground road ascending toward a dim, distant glow.

I took hold of the stone wall, pulled myself to my bleeding knees, got one foot under me, pushed upward. Stood.

What a mess I was. What was left of my clothes hung off me in shreds. Elinda's talisman, hanging around my neck, swung freely through the rags. My teeth were chattering. My naked body was shuddering uncontrollably. Pain and weakness and cold made it hard to move. I walked forward stiffly like a man made all of metal. I kept close to the cave wall, my hand braced against it. Step by step I went up the passage.

I could hear voices clearly now, not far away. I could hear what sounded like a man making a speech and a crowd sometimes cheering. I stumbled up the passage. The voices grew louder. I was getting close to the surface.

The path turned and there was more light: a pale glow, full of shadows. I hobbled toward it, step after slow, stiff step. I was half crazy with weariness now. One minute, I was giggling like a lunatic, the next minute, I was crying a lunatic's tears. The light grew brighter. The voices grew louder. I took another stiff step, and another. I could feel blood trickling down my legs. I could feel my heart straining in my chest. The passage continued rising. It made another shallow turn. I followed it.

And I came to a sudden standstill, stunned by what I saw.

I was on the threshold of a round rock chamber. The chamber was bathed in ghostly light. The walls were hung with banners—twelve banners, each bearing a crest. In the center of the room, there was a raised flat stone, about as long as a bed.

On top of the stone, there was a coffin.

Even in my addled state, I knew where I was. This was the tomb of the Emperor Anastasius. This was the cave where the centaurs had laid him to rest. The entrance was sealed with a large slab of rock, and the light—that white ghostly light—was coming in around the edges of it. The light filled the room with an eerie glow.

And in that glow, I saw: the coffin was open. The stone lid lay at the base of the platform, broken in two. Freezing, palsied, bleeding, weak, I shuffled into the sepulchre. I approached the box. I stood above it and looked inside.

It was empty. The body was gone. Nothing was left but the emperor's burial garments down at the bottom: a long white outfit adorned with the image of a haloed sword, a black undervest, black leggings, a scarlet mantle.

I was so cold, so incredibly cold. All I could think was: *I need those clothes.* I extended my trembling hand down into the coffin, gripped them, drew them out.

With feverish eagerness, I tore off the last of my rags until only the talisman remained, dangling above my chest. I pulled on the emperor's leggings and his undervest. I pulled the skirted white outfit over my head. I wrapped myself in the heavy red mantle. I clutched the cape closed around me.

With amazement and relief, I realized: there was magic in the uniform. As soon as I put it on, I felt heat coming out of the cloth, a wonderful, vital warmth spreading through my body. New strength infused my limbs. My aches and pains eased as if I'd spread some soothing balm over myself. Another moment, and my trembling subsided. I stood up straighter. My mind grew sharper. The madness of exhaustion started to pass away.

I raised my eyes to the entrance and the slab of stone that sealed the tomb. I heard the voices outside, the speechifying and the shouting. A child crying. A woman sobbing with grief and fear.

I heard the chime-like voice of Sir Goodchild raised in oration. "There cannot be mercy without justice!" he cried. "We cannot learn to forgive unless we first learn to condemn."

The crowd cheered its agreement. They were working themselves up to the atrocity.

"Mercy! Mercy for my child!" the woman cried.

The little boy howled in hysterical terror.

The crowd angrily shouted them down.

I walked around the coffin and approached the sepulchre entrance. With the magic outfit on me, I was growing stronger with every step. I did not know what I could do, but I knew I had to do something. I approached the slab that sealed the tomb. It was huge. Heavy. I remembered it had taken four strong centaurs to set it in place. I stepped up to the slab. I leaned close to listen.

I heard Sir Littleman now, his great voice booming. "The trial by combat is over," he said. "The verdict is confirmed. Justice must be done. Favian and his wife and child must die."

The crowd answered with a throaty cheer.

Listening, I pressed my palms against the stone. Shockingly, even at that light touch, the slab shifted.

Startled, I wondered: *How strong am I? How powerful is this outfit I'm wearing?*

I pressed the slab harder. It made a loud scraping noise, and it began to move.

I braced my feet. I gave the stone a full shove.

The slab tilted forward slowly—then swiftly fell.

A blast of light washed over me like a mighty wave. The stone dropped flat against the earth with a tremendous thud that made the ground shudder beneath my feet. Dirt flew up and filled the air with a moted haze. I heard a loud collective gasp of amazement.

I stepped out of the tomb.

The crowd went suddenly silent. There was no sound but the white noise of the breeze and the far-off ocean. I squinted through the dust into the blinding sun. Slowly, the vast army of the emperor came into view before me, face after face pressed close together, so many faces going so far back that they faded into foggy obscurity— and all of them gaping and staring with wonder, gaping and staring at me.

I glanced to my left. There, on the parade stand, stood the three knights: Littleman, Goodchild, and Hammer. Beneath the stand, in front of them, stood the three stakes driven into the ground, surrounded by piled kindling. There were the centaurs with torches, ready to set the kindling ablaze. And there again were the three victims, shackled, grimy, and unkempt, held captive by their ogre guards: Favian; his sobbing wife, Beltan; the little boy, Rory, crying for his mother, all three condemned once again to the fire.

But no one moved. They all just stood there. Every one of them. They all just went on staring—staring at me. Gaping at me. Shocked. Awestruck. Terrified.

Then, as my dazzled vision grew fully clear, I saw a single, great movement. I watched, astonished, as every man, every woman, even the children—everyone in that whole vast crowd—dropped to their knees before me.

And all their voices shouted as one voice, loud enough to reach the halls of heaven.

"Hail! Hail to the emperor! Hail!"

And one woman shouted in wild hysteria: "He has returned from death itself!"

And I thought: *Oh, come on! You have got to be kidding!*

24

I HAD SO TOTALLY NOT SEEN THIS COMING.

My first instinct, of course, was to correct their error. Better to tell the truth right away than have them find me out and get all pissed off at me for trying to fool them. So I stepped further out of the tomb to give them a good look at who I really was.

I raised my hand. I was about to say something like: *No, sorry, folks. Silly mix-up here. It's just me, Austin Lively. I just put the emperor's clothes on because I was cold. Sorry about the confusion.*

But before I could say anything, a woman rushed out of the crowd. A peasant woman, she looked like, plump and coarse-faced, wearing a worn canvas shift. I started back. I figured she was about to denounce me now that she'd had a closer look at my face.

But she dropped to her knees. She seized my left hand. She kissed it again and again. Dampened it with her tears.

"My Emperor!" she sobbed in a high, hoarse voice. "Forgive me for doubting you. I was afraid. I should have known that even death could not defeat you!"

I stared down at her. I looked up at all the others. Many of them had begun crying. "No, no, listen, there's been a mistake here . . ." I started to say.

But now the three knights were coming down the stairs from the parade stand. The handsome Littleman, the boy-sized and angelic Goodchild, the hammer-faced Hammer—all three were coming toward me with expressions of wide-eyed awe.

Even then, I thought they were going to accuse me. Even then, I was preparing to unleash my most ingratiating smile, to try to apologize for the unintentional deception. I mean, after all, they were looking right at me. Couldn't they see who I was?

No. They couldn't. The three knights—they dropped to their knees too, same as the woman, same as the crowd.

"My Emperor," said Sir Littleman, staring in abashed bewilderment at the ground. "We . . . We didn't . . . My Emperor . . ." he said. "Hail. We didn't realize . . . hail . . ."

"My Emperor," said Sir Goodchild in a trembling whisper. "Hail."

Sir Hammer mouthed the words, but no sound came out of him.

Well, at this point, I was completely confused. These guys were the emperor's knights, his closest advisers. If anyone would know him on sight, they'd be the ones.

And if all that wasn't enough, guess who else came out to greet me. Maud. That's right. She came squirreling out of nowhere in swift, bright leaps. She planted herself on the field in front of me. That eerily human face of hers gazed up at me—and not with its usual expression of disdain, but instead with an elevated look of elation and wonder.

"My Emperor!" she screaked in her buzzy voice. "Hail!" And she prostrated herself, belly to the ground.

Maud. No kidding. Prostrate before me.

My mouth opened and closed several times. Finally, I managed to say, "Maud? Maud, it's me. Don't you recognize me?"

She raised her black rat's eyes to me. "I recognize you," she said.

"My Emperor. Hail."

My mouth stopped opening and closing and just remained open. I stood in silence for a long, uncomfortable moment. I had to think before I spoke. Was Maud sending me a message here? Was she telling me I should try and pull off this hoax so we could escape with our lives? That didn't make sense, did it? The knights— Sir Hammerface, Sir Weirdchild, and Sir Cutiepie—they were all kneeling to me too. They weren't looking at me like, *Wait, that's Austin Lively; let's kill him.* They were looking me like, *Oh shit, that's the emperor, back from the dead.*

And when I thought about it, I didn't actually feel all that much like I *was* Austin Lively. That is, I was still me, but I was also not me somehow. I was something else too. Something more.

For one thing, I suddenly felt completely fine. I felt great, really. My aches were gone. The scrapes on my legs weren't screaming pain into my brain. They didn't even feel like they were bleeding anymore. I had thought this was because of some healing property in the emperor's outfit, but now I wondered if it might not be . . . well, something else. Something more.

Because here was another thing: it wasn't just me who was changed. Everyone else looked different to me too. Their faces. Their whole beings.

For instance, the three knights. When I had first seen them, they had looked like heroes. Noble, confident, brave. But now— now, their features seemed pale and gray and sickly. I saw shadows squirming over them like snakes. So help me, I could *feel* shadows squirming inside them too. I could almost hear their inner voices whispering with guilt and fear.

I looked from them to the prisoners, to Favian and his wife and his child, where they had fallen to their knees in front of their ogre guards—ogre guards who were also kneeling. I could see—feel— hear a tortured sweetness in them that was more than themselves.

It seemed to me the very Angel of their Innocence was standing behind them. I could actually see her there—her arms extended to embrace them, to comfort them through their coming martyrdom in the fire.

The vision overwhelmed me. "Holy smokes," I whispered to myself.

Then I looked at Maud.

"Holy smokes," I said again.

Because she was changed too. She was changed completely. Still a beast, still a rodent, but her face, that woman's face, had lost its weirdness. It had always seemed eerie and even disgusting to me: a human face on a rodent's body. But now I saw that she was beautiful. Really, truly beautiful. It was the spell that was disgusting, the disjunction between her misshapen ugliness and the fabulous beauty that was only now apparent to me.

I looked from her to the crowd—the army and their followers. Their faces too were crawling with shadows. While there was no sound around me but the wind and the sea, I felt I could hear the conscience of the people, as if the voices of their hearts were speaking straight into my soul, crying out for forgiveness.

This wasn't just the magic of the emperor's clothes. It couldn't be. This was me. This was happening inside my mind—still *my* mind but also now the mind of another. Still Austin, but somehow inhabited and informed by that far greater man than myself.

It was the emperor. He was inside me. Somehow, Anastasius had taken command of my soul.

The whole massive army—and the three knights and the three martyrs and the peasant woman at my feet and the people sitting on the scaffolding of the Crystal City in the distance—all of them knelt where they were, waiting for me to respond to them.

And all at once, with a kind of certainty I'd never known before— more certainty than I had ever felt about anything, including what to have for lunch—I knew exactly what I had to do and say.

I took my hand out of the grasp of the peasant woman. I touched her head, her rough, dirty hair.

"Go on. Go back to your family," I told her. "It's all right now."

Weeping, she beamed. She rose and returned to her place in the crowd.

Then I looked to the three kneeling knights. I could see—see, hear, and feel—their minds working out how to escape what they knew was coming.

My brows lowered. I frowned an angry frown. I spoke—and the sound of my own voice shocked me, an echoing stentorian boom that must have reached even the people in the city far away, the voice of command.

"Sir Littleman! Sir Goodchild! Sir Hammer! Rise!" I said.

They climbed to their feet unsteadily. They stood, trembling. Sir Littleman's hand was cheating across his belt toward the hilt of his sword. None of them could meet my furious gaze.

I continued. The sentences came out of my mouth before they had even formed themselves in my mind. It was the emperor: he was speaking through me.

"Was it not I who brought you to Aona and the Crystal City?" I asked.

Immediately, Sir Goodchild's face collapsed, streaked with tears of remorse. Sir Littleman started to give some answer, some excuse, but I cut him off.

"Did I not offer you lives of mercy, justice, peace, and joy here in Aona? What kingdoms did Curtin offer you that were greater than those? What blessings did I deny you that you would murder me and accuse my brother in order to steal his natural inheritance?"

What happened next defied imagination—even my imagination, which was pretty expansive by now.

First there was a collective gasp from the crowd, louder than the wind from the ocean. Glancing at the people, I could see—I could feel and hear—their anguish of regret and anger. They were ashamed of themselves for having followed the three knights. And they were furious at the three knights for having deceived them. The worst of it was, they had known all along they were being deceived, but they hadn't had the courage to speak out about it. That made them even more ashamed of themselves, and that made them even angrier at the knights.

At the same time, I saw Favian, the emperor's brother—my brother now, I guess—leap from his knees to his feet with a stifled cry of joy. In a glittering flash, his shackles fell from him, just magically dropped to the ground and dissolved. He rushed to his wife. Her shackles also fell away. She turned on her knees to seize hold of her little boy, who was also suddenly free. The sobbing child buried his face in her breasts. She turned and clung to her husband and, also sobbing, buried her face against his loins. And as the three embraced, I could see—I alone could see—the invisible Angel of their Innocence soar skyward in an open-armed hallelujah, celebrating that justice—justice like a rolling river—had returned to the broken land in the person of . . . well, me. Well, sort of me.

But I had no time to take it all in, because at the same moment all this was happening, the three knights went for their swords and rushed at me.

I laughed out loud. Strangely, when you see things clearly, as clearly as I could suddenly see, when you can see everything, including the inner hearts of men, it all becomes hilarious—tragically hilarious, yes—woefully absurd—but it's funny all the same how people destroy themselves in the very midst of their blessings.

Because here's the craziest thing of all. The three knights attacked me just as I was about to forgive them. No, really. Those were going to be the next words out of my mouth: a pardon for all their sins, including my own murder. I thought it would humble them and reform them to know I had set them free to start again.

But before I could speak, they drew their swords against me.

I didn't draw mine. I didn't have to.

This was the part that boggled the imagination. The moment the three knights drew on me, the moment their blades cleared their scabbards, the ground around them erupted. The earth rumbled. The dust flew.

And the people screamed in terror as the flaming dead rocketed shrieking out of the earth beneath their feet.

I knew them: the dead. I had seen them on the bridge in hell, seen them rising in their agony and anguish, trying to pull me down into the lava of their torment. I had fought them off and made my journey into the dark and into the light and back up the cliff face to life itself.

But Sir Littleman, Sir Goodchild, and Sir Hammer—they never stood a chance.

The flaming, shrieking skeletons seized them with hands that were dripping fiery, rotten shreds of flesh. The women in the crowd shrieked, the men shouted out in horror, the children looked on in wide-eyed amazement as the damned creatures swarmed the three knights, taking hold of their legs, hanging from their arms, crawling up their bodies to grab them by the throats and throttle them.

Sir Littleman tried to swing his sword, but a two-headed creature, half female and half male, coiled its flaming arms around his wrist, and the bright blade fell. The other two men—Goodchild and Hammer—were overcome instantly, engulfed in the blaze of the burning, rotting damned.

And as the rest of us stood—as even I stood—in gobsmacked revulsion, the creatures began to drag the knights down into the broken earth. It must've taken mere seconds, but it seemed to go on a lifetime, that's how dreadful it was to watch. As the knights struggled and shouted, the flaming corpses pinioned their limbs and held them helpless and pulled them inch by inch into the dirt. The knights' feet and legs went down so they were half-buried, trapped, unable to escape. Then their struggling torsos were hauled under to their necks so that only their heads remained in the free air. That was the worst of it. As they realized there was no hope for them, all three began to let out pitiable, high-pitched shrieks—shrieks that almost instantly were smothered and muffled as they were drawn down even further and the dirt poured into their mouths. At last, only their staring, pleading eyes remained—and then these also were gone.

There was nothing left but a cloud of dust and the lingering stench of death and damnation.

FOR A SECOND or two, I could only stand and gaze at the spot where the nightmare had taken place. Strangely, even though they had murdered the emperor—murdered me, I mean—I pitied them. It hurt my heart to know where they had gone and to know there was no time there, so their pain would never pass away.

Then after a while, I noticed the silence surrounding me, silence punctuated by whimpering and tremulous sobs. I raised my eyes.

The people had fallen on their faces. All the creatures had. Even the ogres were prostrate, their fat bodies quivering as they buried their noses in the dirt. Even the brave centaurs were groveling, their horse forelegs crossed over their human heads as if to protect themselves from a coming blow.

Only Favian—my brother—remained on his feet, clutching his kneeling wife to him as she clutched her child. Our eyes met, his and mine. He nodded at me and smiled a grim smile.

I turned to the frightened masses. I thought to myself: *Woof. This is a lot of power here. I better not screw this up.* But that was

Austin speaking. The emperor in command of my soul was not at all afraid.

I raised my voice again so that the whole crowd could hear me, the crowd and the city and, for all I knew, the entire world.

"Be of good cheer!" I told them. But then that didn't seem strong enough, and so, louder, I added: "Rejoice! Rejoice! All is forgiven! All is well!"

The people's transformation was instantaneous. In a second, their palpable fear turned to celebration. All across the vast field even to the scaffolding of the Crystal City, the people were on their feet again, raising their fists to heaven, cheering, embracing one another, weeping with joy.

It made me smile to see it.

AND NOW I turned to Maud.

My old friend had risen from the dust. She sat there, rodent-like but erect. Her expression was one I'd never seen on her face before: elevated, serene, and proud.

I wanted to ask her if she knew I was here—if she knew I, Austin, was sharing this body with the emperor. But I was not in control of what I said, and the words that came out of me were his, not mine.

"You, squirrel-girl," I said. I spoke to her softly, but my voice carried above the cheering all around us. "You have done well. By imperial decree, I remove the spell from you."

She blinked her black eyes, surprised. "But . . . but it was Natani who put this spell on me. Doesn't he have to remove it?"

"Damn it, girl. Who's the emperor here, you or me?"

She actually hesitated before she answered. Which made me laugh and shake my head. Ah, Maud.

"You are," she finally said. "You are the emperor."

"Good answer."

I reached out my hand and touched her eerie head. Then I stepped back to watch what happened.

Her transformation was as beautiful to see as the end of the knights had been horrific. Something in the air around her seemed to shatter—some dark and crawly barrier that had held her in her twisted shape—it cracked to pieces like black glass. A golden glow surrounded her instead, a sparkling glow that took the shape of a woman. She rose into that shape like coming home and, in a moment that seemed filled with silent music, she stood before me: a lithe, lovely, sprite-like young lady, with a look of such mischief and intelligence in her suddenly blue eyes it made me laugh again.

For a moment, she was naked, her skin all pink and pale. The shape of her was so slender and perfect that the sight of it filled me like some sort of wine. A moment later, and the remains of the golden glow sprinkled down over her blond hair and clothed her in a blindingly white shift that followed the gentle curves of her form.

"If I'd known you were that good-looking," I said, "I'd've been nicer to you when you were a rat."

She rolled her eyes but smiled.

I turned from her to the vast, celebrating crowd. Some were dancing now. Some sat on the ground and wept. Some clung to the people they loved. Some stood and cheered.

My heart was full—full of joy and sorrow, confusion and a grim purpose.

I glanced at the new, improved Maud. She was looking down at herself, turning this way and that, admiring her own beauty.

"Yo," I said. She looked up, startled. She blushed. "This way." I looked to Favian. "Come, brother," I said. He disentangled himself from his wife.

I walked toward the grand pavilion. These two followed me, Favian and Maud. I paused at the tent door. They gathered with me there.

I took one last glance at the enormous revel.

"Let them rejoice tonight," I said to my companions. "In the morning, we go to war."

I stepped through the tent door, and, like that, I was on the front path of the Orosgo Retreat, the mountains before me, the rearing pile of the madhouse at my back.

25

WHAT A SHOCK THAT WAS, THAT SUDDEN CHANGE, NOT just from Aona to LA but from emperor to Austin. I stood and reeled, unsteady with surprise. Ever since I'd read the queen's book, *Another Kingdom*, I had been in control of my transitions. I could change a door into a passageway from one world to the other, or I could will the passage closed and stay where I was. But not this time. This—this fingersnap of a metamorphosis from one world to another, from one being to another—had been completely without will and without warning. I was there, I was him, and suddenly I was just here, just me, the way it used to happen when all this started.

My mind swam, but I thought I understood. It was because of the emperor. It was because Anastasius was taking over my life. In that sense at least, I was right back where I had been when I first walked through the door in the Edison Building on the Global Pictures lot: I was completely out of my own control.

Which is not to say things were the same as they were then. Oh no. They definitely weren't. I found that out when, in my stunned state, in an effort to reorient myself, I looked back over my shoulder at the madhouse door where Hillary Baine was standing.

I let out a high shout of disgust and fear. There was a thing clinging to her. A reddish squirming creature. I saw it with a sort of double vision so that, at one level, the woman was still as she was—a squat, apple-cheeked bureaucrat with a curly red 'do and a thin, forced smile—but at another level, which I could also see, she had this slimy pinkish reptile wrapped around her, its claws sunk in her bosom and its teeth buried in the side of her neck. Its fat body pulsed and glowed as it sucked the substance out of her. And she gaped at me as if pleading for relief, her face a mask of torment and dread. Revolted, I adjusted my consciousness so that the awful vision faded away. But I could still sense its reality. I could not unknow that it was there.

I turned away, my gorge rising. I had to swallow hard to keep from puking on my own shoes. My legs were wobbly under me as I continued walking away from the asylum. I headed for the Priest of Death's black truck. My truck now.

I climbed into the cab and drove the hell out of there, tires screaming and kicking up dust.

I knew where I had to go. It had come to me like a deduction, but to be honest, I couldn't tell if it was my own brilliant reasoning that worked it out or the emperor whispering into my mind. All through the drive, I felt that confusion. What part of me was him now? What part of me was still me? I wasn't sure anymore.

But when I came down out of the desert, back into the city, when I saw people on the sidewalk near the shops in Malibu, I realized with a sickening sense of vertigo that what I had seen when I looked at Hillary Baine was not a one-time deal. He, Anastasius, was inhabiting my mind now, and with just the slightest shift of awareness, I could look through his eyes and see a whole other level of reality all around me. Ordinary people, just walking by, had monstrous creatures crawling all over them, clinging to them, sucking at them, worming under their skins. I could make myself stop seeing these hideous Soul Leeches, but I couldn't make myself stop knowing about them. And just the knowledge that they were there, all around me, on the street and in the cars going past—made me dizzy and nauseous.

Not everything I saw was awful. Now and then, there were beautiful creatures moving among the people too, creatures like that Angel of Innocence I had seen hovering over Favian and his family. Now and then, I saw whole multitudes of gorgeous beings in the air and in the light, at one with the air, at one with the light, so that they were almost invisible even when I caught sight of them in their radiant presence. One old codger I noticed pushing his walker across a mini-mall parking lot, moving from a battered old Chevy to the door of a bodega, was actually melded completely with one of these angelic presences, or maybe he was an angel himself only posing as a man. It was impossible to tell.

But mostly, whichever way I turned, it was a nightmare. The whole sweet city was infested. It stank of fear. It echoed with silent cries of anguish and despair.

All this surrounded me, a revolting blur of sights and smells and strangled voices, as the Priest's black truck barreled over the open lanes of the coastal highway. I pressed the gas pedal down. Sped on, eager—desperate—to get away from it. It was unbearable.

I made my way to Sunset and from there into the hills. The truck went grinding up and up over the city until I came to the gate of Orosgo's house.

I expected trouble here, but the gate just swung open and on I drove, up the dirt path to the ranch mansion. It felt too easy. I wondered if maybe the riflemen were fooled by the fact that I was driving the Priest's truck. Maybe they thought I was my own assassin, coming home.

But that wasn't it. Hillary Baine had phoned my brother from CrazyLand. They knew this was me. In fact, the moment I parked and stepped down from the cab, I was surrounded by aggressive men in black, their rifles couched against their hip bones. I had to blink back the vision of the Soul Leeches perched on their shoulders, wrapped around their necks or plastered over their faces with tentacles reaching down their throats. I had to stop seeing the expressions of agony and despair on their under-faces. But I couldn't stop knowing the truth.

With the circle of killers moving with me like a second self, I went up the path to the front door.

I was received there by Killer Jeeves, the butler with the bulge under his jacket.

"I'm here to see Orosgo," I told him.

He either sneered a murderous sneer at me or cried out for help in pitiable desperation from beneath the giant spiked snake that was slowly forcing its way under his flesh. *God*, I thought. *God, is the whole world a horror show?* There were no angels here on the mountaintop, that was for certain.

I followed the butler-assassin down a hall. We passed a mirror. With a jolt of fear, I turned to see myself. Were these leeches crawling over me as well?

If they were, I couldn't see them, thank God. I couldn't even see my own face clearly. It had somehow become unfocused, blurred, as if I were no longer wholly myself. It was very, very weird.

We passed into the living room. Most of the guests had gone, all those muck-a-mucks and pooh-bahs who had gathered for the death watch. There were only about four or five of them remaining on the patio outside. They were all men. They were all drinking sparkling wine from sparkling flutes. They were all laughing together at some joke one of them had made. And also, at the same time, on that other level only I could see, they were all shrieking in hellish agony as the indescribable succubi sank their claws into them and drew the souls out of their flesh atom by atom.

One of the men was Solomon Vine. After what I witnessed at his party, I did not think I could ever feel pity for such a creature. But seeing him from the emperor's perspective, I did. I could've wept for what was happening to him right in front of the emperor's eyes.

Where was my brother though? Where were my parents? I noticed their little corner with its leather throne was empty. The sight sent a chill through my already-chilly heart. As the gentleman's-gentleman-slash-murderous-goon escorted me out of the living room, led me down the hall toward Orosgo's double doors, I had an intimation of what I was about to see. Again, was it a deduction or an inspiration from my inner Anastasius? Again, I didn't know.

The butler opened the double doors. I moved to the threshold and looked in. What I saw in the bedroom then—it was an epic tableau of horror.

Orosgo was dying. I had arrived just in time for the end. I saw the scene in its multiple realities for only an instant, then I had to make it stop. I couldn't bear it. No one could have.

If I had known when I was being digested into the Serpent of Nothingness . . . if I had known what the creature looked like—really looked like when you saw it straight—I don't believe I would have ever found the will to break away. I think the very hideousness of the creature would have sapped my determination. I think I would have despaired to know reality contained such a thing.

And look—look what it had made of Orosgo, that once mighty man. I couldn't describe it if I wanted to. I don't want to. The puny, shriveled remains of him lay visible in the belly of the beast that pulsed and thrashed in an ecstasy of well-fed satisfaction atop the bedcovers as it consumed the last of him.

My brother stood at the foot of the four-poster, coldly gazing down at the disaster. My father stood muttering to the left of him. My mother stood on his right, straight as a blade. And the thing that had hold of my brother defied imagination. And the things my parents had become . . . my guts curdled at the thought that they had made me. There was almost nothing left of the human beings they must once have been.

There was a doctor there too, a man, and a new nurse, a woman. They were watching Orosgo's life signs on a beeping meter. The nurse was checking the flow of a drip that was running into the billionaire's arm. Both of them were crawling with larva-like leeches. Dreadful.

All of this I saw for a single second, then I made myself stop seeing it. Only the stench of the truth remained in my nostrils. And the nausea remained. And the whispered cries of agony that filled the room until they were indistinguishable from the hum of silence—these too remained in my memory.

My brother turned to me. At first, his large, handsome face with its swept-back golden hair and his golden Viking beard seemed a mask of exultation. Well, no wonder. The whole network of persuasion and control that Orosgo had murdered into being here and all around the world was about to fall completely under his command. But when he looked at me, his expression changed. He narrowed his eyes as if he weren't quite sure what he was seeing. Could he sense the emperor within me? I didn't know.

He stepped away from the foot of the bed, away from the unimaginable horror of Orosgo's demise. He stepped toward me. He peered at me closely.

"What?" he said in a fierce low voice. "Why are you looking at me like that?"

I shook my head. How could I tell him that I could see him being devoured where he stood?

He misinterpreted my silence. "You think you've gotten away with something?"

Our eyes locked. "I got away from your assassin, I know that," I said. "He died screaming, Richard."

"The next one won't. Or the one after that."

"God! You're my brother, you jackass. You're my big brother. Don't you remember who you are?"

His mouth twitched as if the words stung him. "How many times did I warn you? How many chances did I give you, Aus? Did you think this was a game? Did you think you were a hero in a movie?"

I heard my father mutter softly to himself. "Not a game. Oh no. Not a movie either."

My mother hushed him.

For a moment, pity for my family rose up inside me. I gestured toward my brother's neck. The words rose to my lips: *Look at that thing on you, man! Look at what it's doing! Save yourself, you stupid shmuck! Nothing's worth this. Not all the wealth and power in the world.*

But what was the point? He wouldn't have believed me. Even I didn't want to believe me. Even I wanted to believe the things I saw were imaginary. Well, they were, I guess. They were in my imagination, I mean. But the imagination is an organ of perception, like the eye. These horrors were real in some form or other.

I averted my gaze. "Get out of my way," I said. "I need to talk to Orosgo before he's gone."

Richard didn't move at first. But then Orosgo made a noise. Half a whisper, half a moan. The shriveled remnant of him said, "Austin . . ."

Richard blinked. He stepped away. He made a harsh gesture at me with one hand: *Go on.* I moved past him, past my parents, to the far side of the bed. I looked down at what had been Orosgo's face. I forced myself not to see the Serpent devouring him, but the knowledge that it was there turned my guts to ice.

Orosgo stared up at me, his eyes enormous. His voice was a death rattle, a long, gasping sigh. "All real . . ." he whispered in his despair.

I nodded. "Yes."

He gulped in air. "Help me, Austin."

Weirdly, I wanted to. I don't know why, but I did. How many times had this greedy, miserable bastard tried to exterminate me? And yet my hand lifted as if I could pull him from the belly of the nightmare that was digesting him. I couldn't.

I cast a glance down over the bedcovers. The papers that had been there, the drawings of Curtin, were all gone. Then I saw they were stacked up on the bedside table next to me. The one on top was a sketch of Curtin. The wizard's image stared up at me. I could sense his malevolence, as if he were really there.

"The flower. The picture you drew," I said. I pushed the top sketch aside. There was another sketch of Curtin beneath that one and another beneath that, all of them glaring at me. I pushed those aside too, and the rest of the sketches, until I found the one sketch I was after: the sketch of the flower. I pulled it out. Held it up so Orosgo could see it. "This one. It's a carnation, isn't it? I thought it was a rose, but it's a carnation."

The forest is all one tree, the mad girls had told me in the asylum. *Plant the carnation in the earth beneath.*

I still had no idea what that meant. But I knew—or the emperor had told me—that this was the carnation I was looking for.

Orosgo whispered something up at me, but I couldn't make it out. I hated to lean closer to him knowing what was squirming there on the bed, but I forced myself to do it. "What?" I said.

"Amadis," he whispered.

I shook my head. I heard the word this time, but what sense did it make?

"Amadis?" I said. "What does that mean? What does that have to do with the carnation?"

"I thought . . . if I called him . . . if I confessed to him, maybe . . ."

"Confess. To Amadis. It's a person?" I pointed at the scratchings underneath the flower. "And you were going to call him. Is this his phone number? Is that what this is?"

"I couldn't do it . . . I was afraid . . . so many dead . . ."

"Yes," I said. "I understand. You were going to confess to Amadis, but you were afraid of the consequences. You didn't want to face the consequences."

"But now . . . oh God, oh God . . . this . . ."

"Yes," I said.

His body stiffened. He drew a violent breath, wheezing loudly. The doctor came forward eagerly with the eager nurse beside him. As if on cue, the beeping meter that was measuring Orosgo's pulse stopped beeping. It let out a loud tone. This was the end.

I glanced up at my brother. His blue eyes were blazing with triumph. He could barely keep the smile off his lips. My father was muttering rapidly, working his fingers in front of him as if he were some sort of mantis. My mother actually rubbed her hands together with anticipatory glee.

I grimaced. My stomach roiled. What a crappy way to die, even for Orosgo.

The meter kept screaming until the doctor switched it off.

I folded the sketch of the flower in my hand and slipped it into the rear pocket of my jeans. As my family pressed eagerly around the bed, as they waited eagerly for the doctor to pronounce the final word, I shouldered past them. I walked to the bedroom doors.

The butler, Killer Jeeves, was still there. He blocked my way. I saw him glance past me, looking to my brother for instructions. I looked at my brother too. Richard lifted his eager eyes from Orosgo's corpse just long enough to shake his head. Whatever they were going to do to me, they wouldn't do it here.

The butler-slash-assassin stepped aside, and I walked out of the room. Just as I crossed the threshold, I heard a rumbling sound behind me. I caught a rising smell—horrible. I remembered that stench. I remembered it coming off the lake of fire. I remembered it lingering in the air after Littleman, Goodchild, and Hammer had been dragged into the earth.

I hurried out of the room. I did not look back to see what happened next.

26

I BARRELED DOWN THE HALL. I HAD TO GET AWAY FROM that house. It was like being stuck at the bottom of a pit of serpents, drowning in serpents like a rising serpent sea. When I stumbled out the door, I sucked in the fresh spring air as if I'd just fought my way to the surface.

I jogged down the front path to the black truck. Climbed into the cab in blind haste. My vision blurred as my eyes filled with tears. Were they tears for Orosgo? I didn't know. Maybe they were. He had done every evil thing, and yet my heart was heavy for him. No one deserved what had happened to him. Not even he deserved it. If I had had the power, I would have saved him in the end.

I needed to get out of here, go somewhere, sit and gather my thoughts. But when I glanced through the window to the west, I saw the sun descending toward the horizon and remembered: I couldn't rest. Jane's time was running out. I had to get to her.

I hit the ignition with an unsteady hand. Drove down the rough road, the truck bouncing and rocking. I thought someone might stop me for stealing the Priest's vehicle, but the guards were all on their comm devices, spreading the word of Orosgo's passing. No one seemed to care what I did. The gate swung open for me and I barreled through.

I sped away a mile or two before I finally pulled over. Then I sat behind the wheel, panting. I thought I was going to be sick. I thought I was going to go mad. How could I live in this world looking through the emperor's eyes, seeing the hideous things he saw. It was more than a merely human mind could tolerate, more than my mind could tolerate anyway.

But time, time, time was passing. Jane was behind bars, helpless, the killers coming for her. I could not afford to go crazy now.

I pulled the sketch of the flower out of my pocket. Unfolded it. Studied it. I took out my phone.

My hand was shaking so badly now, I could barely read the numbers scribbled beneath the image, barely manage to punch the numbers into the keyboard. I didn't know who I thought I was calling. The ideas running through my mind were lunatic and hysterical. Orosgo had said he had wanted to confess to Amadis, so I had some loopy thought that Amadis was a priest—Father Amadis of the Order of the Carnation, you know, like in some fantasy novel or some video game: a white-bearded sorcerer in a starry cap who would kill all these evil reptilian leeches with a blue cloud of magic . . . something like that. I was losing my mind, in other words. If the things I was seeing were real, it was more reality than I could handle.

The phone rang once. A man answered.

"LAPD. Detective Carnation."

Okay, I wasn't expecting that at all. I didn't know how to reply. I just sat there, holding the phone, blinking. Blinking and thinking: *I know that voice.* It was the voice that had called me to warn me that Jane was in trouble, that she was going to be murdered in her cell. I had recognized the voice when I heard it then, too, but I couldn't remember from where. I still couldn't. How had he known to call me? Why had he called?

"Detective Carnation," I said. "This is Austin Lively."

There was no answer. Not a word. I could hear the detective breathing on the other end of the line, but there was nothing else. I opened my mouth to ask if he was still there. But then I hesitated. Another thought came to me—another deduction-slash-inspiration.

"What I mean is," I said, "this is the Emperor Anastasius."

And still—no answer. Just a long, long pause. Then, finally, the detective spoke again.

"My Emperor," he murmured. "Hail!"

I MET HIM in an alley behind the Hollywood cop shop. It was a grim stretch of pavement, damp with old sewer water, dark as night even now in the spring afternoon. The moment I turned the corner off the sidewalk, I saw Carnation standing at the alley's far end. He was a silhouette among shadows. I could not make out his face.

I walked toward him slowly. I did not think I knew the man. But as I came near, he stepped forward, and a stray patch of sunlight fell across him. I let my breath out. I remembered who he was.

After I had killed Orosgo's first assassin, Sera—after I sent him falling to his death off the construction site near the shopping mall—I had been arrested and hauled into this very police station. Graciano and Lord had been there. They had made a lot of noise about prosecuting me for Sera's death, threatening me, you know, intimidating me, trying to get me to keep my mouth shut about Orosgo. But there was another cop who was different. He was the guy who had arrested me in the first place. He'd put the cuffs on me when it looked like the other cops were itching to shoot me dead on the spot. Essentially, he had saved my life. Then, later, when I walked out of the station, the same cop had been there again. He was a great big guy with a big gut, a hard face, sandy hair, and a bushy mustache. An undercover guy, he seemed like, dressed in a Spartans sweatshirt and torn jeans. He had shepherded me to the door.

And just before I left the station, he had murmured to me, "Go your way." I wasn't sure at the time whether he was speaking the queen's password or simply warning me to blow town.

Now I knew. Because here he was again. Dressed in slacks and a striped shirt this time but still sporting the hard face and the big 'stache.

We came toe to toe in the alley. I examined him closely. I tried to put my mind into Emperor Mode so I could see if there were any evil Soul Leeches crawling on him. None appeared to me. I decided I would trust him. I didn't really have much choice.

He, meanwhile, was looking down at me from his much greater height. He stuck his tongue in his cheek. He looked . . . *skeptical,* I guess is the word.

"You're the emperor?" he asked.

I looked away, embarrassed. "I think so. Sort of."

"What the hell is that supposed to mean?"

I shrugged. "The emperor is living inside me somehow, I think. I think I carried him out of the world of the dead and now—I don't know how to say it exactly—but he seems to be part of me or maybe vice versa."

Carnation sniffed—a big sniff that scrunched up a whole half of his face. Then, to my surprise, he nodded, almost as if I were making sense. "She said something like that might happen."

"She . . .?"

He nodded. I knew what he meant: the queen. "She said it might be you who brought him here to save her," he said.

"How do you know . . . about all this?" I asked him.

He heaved a big breath and put his hands on his hips. Looked over my shoulder with that far-off stare you sometimes see in cops and soldiers, that long stare of a man who's seen too much of what life really is.

"I know the queen. We've met."

"She told you about . . . everything?"

He nodded.

"Are there more like you?" I asked. "More who know?"

"You'd be surprised," he said. "There are not enough of us, but there are more than you'd think. We link up. We find each other. We do what we can for her."

"And did you know about Orosgo? Did you know he was calling you?"

His gaze returned from the distance and lowered to me again. "What do you mean?"

"Orosgo said he called you," I told him. "He was trying to confess. But there were too many murders on his conscience. He couldn't face the consequences."

"Is that who that was?"

"Yeah. Serge Orosgo. The billionaire who . . ."

"Oh, I know who he is, believe me. And he told you this? About calling me? Calling me and hanging up? I was wondering who it was."

"He's dead. He told me just at the end."

"Oh. Dead, huh." He sounded disappointed.

I began to understand what had happened. The whole story began to unfold itself in my mind. "You were investigating him, weren't you?"

Carnation wagged his head. "He was being investigated. By a task force. I was a small part of it."

"I get it. But you questioned him at some point."

"I talked to him on the phone once. It didn't get me very far."

"But that's how he knew who you were. So he started to call you." I gave a little snort at the idea.

"What?" said Carnation. "What's so funny about it?"

"It's just funny, you know. Funny to think about. A guy like Orosgo. A guy so powerful. Who has so much. Calling a cop and trying to confess. It's a strange idea."

"Not really," Carnation said. "A lot of these guys, these big guys. Who run businesses. Who run countries. Who run the world. They're just perps in the end. They're just con men, killers, thieves. They want what all perps want. To beat the system. To control people. To feel like big shots, like they got away with something. And it eats at them, what they are. They want to confess. They want to get it off their chests before it drives them nuts. They got nice clothes. Nice cars. Everything nice. But they're just perps in the end."

"Do you know what Orosgo did? You and the other investigators. Do you know about the 730 Club and all that?"

He cocked an eyebrow at me with real interest. "Why don't you tell me?"

I hesitated a second, but only a second.

"Buy me a cup of coffee," I said.

WE SAT IN a WeHo coffee shop around the corner. Me and the big cop surrounded by frizzy-bearded wannabe screenwriters and shapely aspiring starlets all pounding on their laptops, wasting their afternoons, not to mention their lives. I had to work hard to keep my eyes away from them, to keep my mind from going into Emperor Mode and seeing what, if anything, was crawling on them, sucking out their souls.

I drank coffee and talked. I told Carnation what I knew about the 730 Club, about the powerful people Orosgo had killed and ruined, and about the loyalists he had hired to replace them. Detective Carnation listened without saying a word. Sometimes he jotted a note in a little notebook he had.

Finally, when I was done, he said, "That's a big story."

"And now my brother, Richard, is in charge of it all. Governments, news agencies, movie studios. Police forces too, I think."

"Oh yeah. Definitely some police forces."

"But not everyone, I guess."

"Not everyone, no."

"So there are still good guys. There are more like you. You can still get to them?"

"It's not easy. It's a hard case to prove. You have to prove it down to the ground, so no one can bury it, no one can lie about it. It's a hard case."

"Especially if the police work for the other side," I said. "And the courts are corrupt. And the press cover for them."

Carnation got that far-off look again. He stroked the white foam of a cappuccino off his mustache with one hand. "There are some like that," he said. "Some have gone bad. A lot of them have, yeah. But, no, not all. Not me. Not some others. Like I said: there are more of us than you might think."

"Can you beat them, Carnation? Can you expose them? Get around the ones who are in on it? Get around the journalists who sweep it under the rug? And the politicians and all the rest? Can you ever expose this and make it count?"

Carnation's big shoulders rose and fell. "If you're a cop, you do what you do. You do what you can. You look for the truth. You tell the truth. You take your chances. Every day is a chance. Every day is another day."

I nodded. One corner of my mouth lifted. "All right. That sounds like a plan."

His mustache lifted back at me. "So what do you need? What do you need to save the world? Emperor Austin Lively."

I hid my blush in my coffee cup. "I need Jane, first of all. I need to get her out of the Tower alive. Can you do that? Can you help me?"

It was a long time before he answered. He thought for a while, then he rubbed his eyes for a while, then he sighed for a while. Finally, he said, "Just how powerful are you anyway? Or how powerful is he? The emperor. How powerful is he in you?"

"I don't know." I thought of how I drew my sword and cut off the hand of the Priest of Death. I thought of how I saw the monsters devouring the people all over the city, and the occasional angels too. "I think there's still another level I can get to, but I don't know what it is yet."

"Well, you better find out, my Emperor," Amadis said drily. "I know some people—people who can help us. We might be able to get you inside the Tower before the killers get to your girl. But how you're going to get her out of there . . . that I don't know."

I drew a deep breath. "Me either. But maybe . . . well, like I said, maybe I can level up again."

Another moment and he nodded decisively. "You better get to it, then. Meanwhile, I'll make some calls. Get back to me when you think you might be able to pull this off."

We stood up. We shook hands over the table. Suddenly, all around me, I could sense the red, hungry, lizard-like leeches prowling through the coffee shop, looking for souls to sink their teeth into. I tried not to see them, but I knew they were there. They were everywhere. The city belonged to them. The world belonged to them, for all I knew.

But not the whole world. There were still men like Carnation. Not enough, but more than you'd think.

"Thanks, Detective," I said.

"Amadis," he answered.

"Amadis," I echoed him. "Amadis Carnation. It's a good name."

"I'll be seeing you, Emperor. Soon, I hope. Before midnight."

"Right," I said. "Before midnight."

I turned away and walked to the coffee shop door and pushed through it back into Aona.

27

MOMENTS LATER, I WAS STANDING BEHIND A TABLE
with a canvas map of Galiana and the Eleven Lands spread out on
top of it. Favian was on the other side of the table, still dressed in
his prisoner's ragged brown robe, still grimy and bruised from his
imprisonment.

Maud, though—Maud was radiant, brand new, all new—a
graceful sylph in her whiter-than-white shift, her blond hair spilling
forward over her adorably impish face as she bent to the map and
traced a path to Galiana with her finger. Favian stood close beside
her, leaning over her shoulder, watching.

Outside, I could hear the sound of laughter and music, thousands
of voices raised in joy and song. The people were still celebrating the
emperor's return from the dead.

"I say we go by air," said Favian. "It means a smaller army—only
the flying cavalry—but to travel overland will take too long."

"Agreed," said Maud. Her voice was no longer a rodent voice,
but sweet and musical and mischievously ironic even when she was
being serious as she was now.

Favian and I both looked at her, surprised: a teenaged girl talking
like a general. She glanced up and caught our looks and returned

them defiantly.

"What?" she said. "I was behind enemy lines in Tauratanio's resistance. No one notices a squirrel outside the window. I've spied on the enemy. I know how Curtin operates."

I lifted one eyebrow at Favian. Then I gestured at Maud: *Go on.*

She went on. "The thing is: if we travel by land, we'll be opposed at every pass and castle, our stragglers waylaid in every wood. Curtin will wage a war of attrition—sword and illusion, siege and temptation: every trick he has."

"She's right about that," said Favian. "By the time our infantry reached Galiana, we'd be fewer than we would have been if we'd just flown with the cavalry."

Maud nodded beside him. They both looked up—looked at me. Waiting for my decision.

And I—I returned their gazes, fighting to focus. Mind-wise, I was still in the coffee shop, mulling over what I'd heard from Carnation. But Favian and Maud were waiting for an answer. So I said: "The cavalry goes by air. We'll force Curtin's armies to battle us in the sky. That will leave the overland passage open. Favian, you'll lead the infantry below, and we'll join forces in Galiana to retake the throne."

He straightened, proud of the assignment, ready for it. "My Emperor."

"Now go back to your family," I told him. "They need you. And get some rest."

He bowed once, briskly, and marched out of the pavilion. I watched him go and you know what I was thinking? I was thinking how nice it was to have a brother I admired. What would my life have been like—who would I be now—if my family had not been a gang of villains?

It was another moment before I noticed Maud was still standing there, giving me a look, that look she gave. I knew it meant trouble, but there was no avoiding her forever.

I turned to her. Beautiful Maud—former rodent girl extraordinaire—with her ironic eyes pinned hard on me.

"What is it, Mouse?" I asked her. "Why are you still here? Why are you looking at me like that?"

"My Emperor," she said—and I truly couldn't tell whether she was being sarcastic or not, whether or not she fully understood my bizarre double nature. "I have a request."

"Uh oh."

"I want to fly with you, with the cavalry."

I made a dismissive noise. "Forget it."

She was insulted. She groused at me. "Why? Because I'm a girl?"

"Yes! Exactly! Exactly that. I need men, Maud. This isn't a movie. It's war. I need big men. Soldiers. Centaurs. Ogres. Strong men who can fight other men who are also strong, with big strong arms that can wield swords all day without growing tired."

She scowled angrily. "What *is* a movie?"

"It's a kind of lie in which things are the way people want them to be instead of the way they are. This is not that."

She went on scowling. I was actually kind of hoping she'd storm out in a huff. Never mind the huff—never mind the storm—I was just hoping she'd leave me alone. But she didn't. She didn't move. She just kept that scowl trained on me. She wasn't an annoying rodent girl anymore, but she had retained her near-magical ability to make me feel like crap whenever I disagreed with her.

"I know you," she said finally. "I know who you are."

I lifted my chin. "All right."

"I can see the emperor is inside you now, but I know who you are all the same."

"All right," I said again. "But you're still not flying with the cavalry."

"I've been a good advisor to you, haven't I?"

"I'd have been lost without you, Maud," I answered. Which was only the truth. Without the squirrel girl, I'd have long ago been tortured, executed, or murdered. Or worse, I'd have been back in Hollywood, rich and famous with a greenlit movie and an unseen Soul Leech digging into my bosom and sucking my soul out through my heart.

"Let me go with you and advise you now," she said.

I rolled my eyes. "Would you stop?"

"I'll stay out of harm's way."

"The hell you will."

"You'll protect me, then. But I know more about the evil of the enemy than any other friend you have. I can help you win."

I raised my hand and was about to respond, but the words turned to breath and silence, and my hand went down to my side again.

Maud wasn't always right, but she was right just enough to make a genuine pain in the ass of herself. And this time . . . well, I wasn't sure. The trouble was: deep down, I wanted her with me. It was only my fear for her safety that kept me from allowing her to come. It was true, lithe girl that she was, she'd be useless in a fight. But as an advisor, there was no one like her. From the very beginning, she had been my friend and my support. My guide through the mad hallucination my life had become. Just being with her, right here in the tent, right now, anchored me to the moment. Even quarreling with her was better than being without her. In her presence, my fractured and divided mind began to calm and clear. My focus—the focus she herself had taught me in the sewers of Galiana—was beginning to return.

"Why do you want this so much?" I asked her. And before she could answer, I said, "And don't tell me it's because I need you."

"You do need me," she said. She averted her gaze. "But you're right: it's not that." She took a deep breath and faced me squarely. "The man I love is trapped in Edgimond, cursed by Curtin."

"Ah."

Of course. Natani. He had slipped my mind. He was the magician who had disguised Maud as a squirrel so she could escape Curtin's conquest of their country and the massacre of the women there. In response, Curtin had cursed Natani so that he became the water of a forest lake. Natani had helped me when I was lost in that dark land, and I had promised to return and reunite him with the girl he loved.

Maud spoke as if she had read my thoughts, which, knowing her, she probably had. "You broke Natani's spell on me. You can break Curtin's curse on him."

"Damn it," I murmured. She was probably right.

"My Emperor—he's everything to me: my love, the father of my children . . ."

"You don't have any children."

"Because he's stuck in that damn lake! Get him out and you won't believe how many children I have."

I laughed. I shook my head. "Mouse," I said, "you drive me crazy."

The slender girl flitted around the table to me like some agile phantom. She went down on her knees beside me. She took my left hand in both of hers.

"Don't kneel to me, Maud," I said. "Not you."

She gazed up at me. "Take me with you, my Emperor. Let me help you. Bring me to my love."

"Have I ever told you you're the single most annoying person I have ever met?"

Kneeling there, she kissed my hand. She pressed my hand against her cheek so that her tears dampened my skin. "Thank you," she said. "My Emperor."

"Stop doing that. Please stand up. Please, Mouse."

She climbed to her feet and stood before me, knuckling her eyes dry.

"That Natani is one lucky body of water," I said.

She laughed through her tears.

"Go get some sleep, Mouse," I told her. "We ride at dawn."

SO MUCH HAD been so strange so long that that strange last night before the war seemed hardly strange at all.

And yet—and yet how strange it was, really. I lay awake in my pavilion and drifted as if in sleep between the two worlds. I heard the people celebrating on the cliffs, and I saw my brother Richard in Orosgo's mountain mansion, saw him consolidating his power, contacting his minions around the world to spread the word that Orosgo had been dragged into the fiery nothingness of hell. I worked out my strategy for the reconquest of Galiana, and at the same time, I stood beside Detective Carnation in the cop shop as he spoke into the phone, gathering his allies to help me break into the Tower.

All night, it seemed that way. I seemed to float in space and out of time, like a cloud of consciousness in an endless and ever-changing sky. The two worlds were one inside my mind—the emperor's mind—and everything seemed to be unfolding in both of them at once.

As dawn grew near, I lay on my cot, worn out with worry. I found myself speaking to the emperor inside me. I found myself communing with his will and vision, now mingled with my own. I knew I didn't have the wisdom or the power to do what had to be done, neither here nor back home. But he had them, the wisdom and power both. And I thought if I could only surrender my consciousness to his, if I could only let him take charge within me, this anxiety might lift a little and let me rest.

Maybe it did lift. In any case, just as the sky began to brighten outside the pavilion, I finally drifted off to sleep.

Then—as if a moment later—the trumpets sounded outside on the cliffs. I sat up groggily and looked around me, thinking: *Where? Which land?*

I saw the tent. The table. The map on the table. The emperor's banner—my banner—a sword with a halo—hanging on one wall.

Aona.

A beam of sunlight poured in through the tent flaps.

It was time to go to war.

I groaned and rolled out of bed. I stretched. I yawned. I rubbed my eyes. I went to the pavilion door. I stepped through still wearing the emperor's outfit—but I emerged into the open air fully clothed in Elinda's armor. It flowed over me in a single second, and in a single second, the queen's sword was in the scabbard at my side. Now too, magically, the armor had been transformed. My breastplate sported the emperor's insignia—the haloed sword—and his red cape was secured at my shoulders and fluttered at my back.

A thunderous hurrah greeted me. It shook the air.

There on the plain before me was an amazing sight to behold: my armies in their vast array. The knights in silver armor on their winged horses; the trolls on horseback too, with their long beards and their peaked caps and their crossed belts of throwing daggers; the centaurs with their muscular bodies and their gleaming scimitars; the giant ogres each with a ferocious single eye and a spiked club in his massive, hairy hand; the graceful sprites with their big bows; and rows on rows of infantrymen with shields and spears. The mighty mass of them rolled away before me like the sea itself, glittering like the sea with the sun on their blades and their bright armor. The banners and pennants fluttered like sea waves well into the blue distance. And beyond them, on the walls and scaffolds of the Crystal City, I could see the people with their hands upraised. I could see they were cheering, though they were so far away from us, their voices were lost in the wind between.

As I stood in my armor and gazed at my forces, my heart pounded hard with fear and excitement.

Let me be the emperor, I thought. *Let his mind be mine.*

Favian and Maud stepped up beside me. Favian was dressed and ready to lead the infantry, clothed in mail now, a red-plumed helmet on his head, his sword at his side. Maud was in a studded brown leather vest with a studded brown leather helmet under her arm. The black stallion stood just behind her, and beside him stood a small, elegant gray filly, which would serve as a mount for Maud.

Favian pressed his fist to his chest. "My Emperor," he said.

I nodded with more certainty than I felt—the emperor's certainty, not mine. "Let's do this," I said.

The Battle for the Skies was about to begin.

28

I SWUNG INTO THE STALLION'S SADDLE. MAUD MOUNT-
ed the sleek gray and sat to my right. Favian stood on my left. I
surveyed the ocean of faces rolling away from me, it seemed, into
infinity.

I drew my sword and raised it high. The army cheered again, a
sound like a storm.

I knew I had to speak to them, but I had no idea what to say.
Still, I opened my mouth and began—and the emperor's voice came
out of me, so loud it seemed to reverberate across the heavens.

"Look around you," I said. "What a lovely day. If I could stay
and wile away my hours in the sun, then I would stay. But our backs
are to the sea, and the armies of death are advancing—death and
slavery, which is death-in-life. To live in peace is now no more than
a form of surrender. Every chance of freedom we have lies in victory,
and every chance of victory lies in battle and in blood. I won't tell
you we'll be remembered by name. But if we win, our name will be
'the People's Liberty,' and that will be remembered. If we fail, our
fight will be a secret song in the hearts of the defeated until they find
a way to fight again. Either way, for the sacrifice of this day and even
all our days, we will live forever. Let us fear nothing, then, and do

what we have to do. To Galiana!"

I pointed my sword at the sky. The horses spread their wings. I wish I could have stood on some lofty height and watched as the whole cavalry lifted as one from the earth and rose as one into the bright blue dawn. At Favian's cry of "Advance!" the armies on the ground began their march as well. I looked down as my stallion rose and saw them, metal flashing and flags fluttering and bodies surging forward as if the whole plain had come to rolling life. I looked around me and the sky was full of flying horses. What a sight it was!

Breathless with excitement now, I turned to Maud where she rode beside me on her sleek gray. She let the horse rise up and drop back, expertly maneuvering so that its wings could lift and fall just above the massive body of my stallion. That brought her closer to me, close enough so we could speak to each other over the noise of the rushing wind.

"It was easier to chat when you could ride on my pommel as a squirrel," I called to her. I glanced back to see her smiling a rueful smile. Now that I was the emperor, she couldn't call me names anymore, but I suspected she was thinking them. "Go on," I said. "Go on and speak. That's why I brought you with me."

"All right, then. You remember the red haze we saw as we were coming here?"

"I remember." I had to admit it was good to have her voice in my ear again. It gave me confidence. "You told me it was Curtin's forces unleashed from another world."

"That's right. That will be our first real fight."

"But the form of them . . . How do you do battle with a haze?"

"That haze—from below, it looks like a form of pollution, a miasma, maybe some kind of plague. But when you get above it, you can see it's really Curtin's creatures, the ones you imprisoned after they rebelled against you when you gave Elinda the Galiana throne. To fight them, you have to divide your forces and take them from both below and above, both as a miasma and as a legion of demons. You can't defeat them in only one of their forms."

"How do you fight a haze though?" I asked again.

"The trolls," said Maud. "They are masters of chemistry and the science of war. Their daggers are soaked in potions that can clear the skies of this pollution."

"All right. The knights will follow me and fight the armies from above. The trolls will stay below and fight the haze. Make that my order."

"My Emperor," said Maud—almost as if she meant it. Her filly veered and headed back toward the bulk of the army so she could spread the word.

We didn't have long to wait before the fight began.

When next I surveyed the earth below, I saw we had outstripped the infantry and left them several miles behind. The rolling plains stretched out before us empty, and the White Mountains were growing larger in the distance. As the ground rose under us, the air grew rough around us. The weather began to deteriorate. A thin white mist rushed over us, chilly and damp. As we flew through it, the mist thickened. A heavier, darker system gathered, green-black thunderheads, gravid with lightning. The stallion whinnied as we hit turbulence. The horse lifted and plunged with sickening suddenness and tilted at dangerous angles to keep its wings in the wind. I held on hard and worked the reins to keep the big beast steady under me. The thunder growled in cloud after cloud like a prowling beast circling us. The black haze ignited and flashed here and then there, and the horse bucked and snorted, frightened.

"Here they come." That was Maud, at my shoulder again.

I looked from her into the obscure distance and saw the dark clouds turning the color of blood. The red haze had used the cover of the storm to creep close to us. Another minute and they would be everywhere, on every side.

"Stay below the fight," I commanded Maud. "Go down to the earth and don't return to me until it's over."

"But I can advise you here . . ."

"Go!" I shouted at her. "Now!"

She sighed—but she obeyed. The gray filly dropped down into the gray distance until it was out of sight.

I drew my sword. I raised it high for a signal.

"Take them!" I cried—but my words were washed away by a crash of thunder.

I spurred the stallion. It lifted its wings. Up we rose, straight into the heart of the tempest. All the knights rose while the trolls on their horses dropped down to fight from below.

For a moment—one moment that seemed to go on for hours—we were in the thick of the storm, the horses screaming and rearing as deadly forks of lightning lanced across our paths and the thunder made the air shake violently. The blood-red stain was spreading and surrounding us, turning everything scarlet. I roared at my stallion—"Hah!"—and spurred her on.

Then I—then all the knights on horseback—broke through into the blue-white sky above. And when we looked down, we looked down in horror.

It was as Maud said. What from below had seemed a sort of red fog bleeding into the cloud cover was, when seen from above, a nightmare army. Bloated lizards with thrashing tails and fang-studded jaws. Giant, squirming centipedes with the heads of harpies. Vampire bats the size of airplanes. And gibbering orange imps with flashing eyes and evil grins and flaming tridents gripped in their sharp claws.

The storm clouds flashed and roared and roiled as we charged down toward them through the whirling wind. We met the enemy above the clouds and inside them. They met our attack with their own attack, full force.

It was an ugly fight and desperate from the start. The creatures swarmed us. The lizardy things were the worst. Huge, they were, and they could snap with their jaws and lash with their spiked tails at the same time. The very first one I encountered caught my horse's haunches with a glancing snap of its tail that nearly knocked me from my saddle into its waiting maw. I clapped my legs hard against the stallion's sides as the horse tilted over, its wings flailing. I clung to the reins with one hand and jabbed down at the lizard's eyes with my sword point. The thing was just about to lash again when I skewered it. The blade plunged deep into its brain and out the back of its head. It screeched and died and plummeted, twirling, down into a black thunderhead, where it vanished in a flash of lightning.

An imp leapt at me with frightening agility, and I cut it in half with a single swipe even as it hurled its pitchfork at my head. As the flaming prongs sailed past my helmet, I was assaulted by a centipede that wrapped itself around my sword arm, holding it stiff and helpless as the creature's gray hag face screamed laughter at me. I let go of the reins and grabbed the squirming thing in my open hand just beneath its chin. My fingers sank deep into acid goo as I clawed the centipede's throat open. The still shrieking head dropped sideways, then tore off and went flying as the body gushed black gore. I snapped my arm to get the dead corpse off me, then wheeled my mount to return to the melee.

All around me, it was the same, the knights battling the unimaginable creatures that sailed up out of the black maelstrom as if borne on the wild wind. My men were men of valor, cutting to the left and right of them, each killing more than his share. But some— too many—were overwhelmed. Centipedes wrapped themselves around their bright armor, pinning their arms, while imps leapt for their heads and drove their burning pitchforks into their eyes. Lizards ripped the bellies from their horses and caught the knights in their jaws as they tumbled through space, and swallowed them.

Above the noise of the thunder, I heard the sound of men screaming in terror and agony and the gloating hiss and sting of these creatures out of hell.

Below, though—where we couldn't see at first—the trolls were making headway with the red miasma. Darting beneath the clouds, dodging around the lightning, the little bearded men in their funny caps whiplashed their envenomed daggers up into the haze. Whatever the blades were treated with, it hit the red haze and smoked and sizzled. The haze dissolved and was sucked into the knife, which then went spinning and flashing down to earth. Sometimes, if the troll was quick and battle-tested, he would catch the falling dagger by its handle, give it one short shake that spilled the juice of what had been the haze into the air. Then, with the same motion, he would hurl the same dagger at the haze again and take out another patch of red.

And each one of these fog patches was also—when seen from the higher angle—a demon dying. We knights, as I said, didn't see this at first, but as the trolls worked their way up into the heart of the miasma, as they came into the clouds and rode through the thunder to purge the storm of the red stain, we, the knights above, began to see reptiles and imps and centipedes and even the enormous vampire bats dissolving below us with screams of agony before they dropped down to the earth in a rain of blood.

I gave a cry: "To me! To me!"

And heartened by the sight of the trolls fighting their way up to us, the knights rallied around. I led them charging down into the demon swarm and began fighting through them to meet the trolls.

Curtin's creatures, caught in the vice, could not decide which way to turn their violence, up or down. The lizards tried to lash at the trolls with their tails while lunging upward at the knights with their fanged jaws, but that only divided their efforts and made it easier for us to hack away at their heads and bodies until they lost their strength and fell.

And now, the black storm began to pass over. The thunder and the lightning ceased. The gathered clouds became tendrils of light mist again. I could see the sky battlefield more clearly. The trolls and the flying cavalry were fighting in two lines mere yards from one another. The thrashing demons were caught between us, dropping everywhere as they were cut to pieces by the knights above and dissolved and destroyed by the trolls below.

Soon, I looked around with wonder to see that the hideous things were dying on their own. Everywhere, the beasts were just rolling over in the air, their eyes going white, their bodies turning to blood and evaporating even as they dripped down through the sky.

Breathless, I steadied my foaming stallion in midair and watched the red army collapsing. Maud flew up from below on her gray filly and hovered at my side.

"What's happening to them?" I shouted to her. "Why are they all dying?"

"You've killed the legion. They only seemed like individual creatures. They're really all one thing, the slave of Curtin's will. It's over, my Emperor. You've won."

A feeling like no other I had ever had rose up inside me: a flare of triumph like a roaring flame with, at its heart, a white-hot pang of grief for all the knights who'd fallen. What victory could be worth even one of their lives? But what would their lives have been worth without this victory? The world should not be so sad and impossible, and I wished I'd never learned it was.

With bright, damp, burning eyes, I watched the demon army die. Then, exulting and mourning at the same time, I nodded to Maud and led the way downward. The field of mist below me had parted to make a clear way to the earth, a portal rimmed with golden sunlight. I flew down into it.

And to my absolute shock, a car horn shattered the air around me. Headlights whisked by me, and I only just managed to jump off the street onto the sidewalk and avoid being run over.

Where the hell was I? LA. But not in Hollywood anymore—and not in the afternoon—not at the time or place I'd left. It was night and I was downtown, standing beneath the towering white mausoleum of City Hall.

I glanced at my watch. To my horror, I saw it was nearly nine p.m. My God. Jane. Suddenly, I only had three hours before the assassins came for Jane.

I stood motionless in complete confusion, trying to understand what had happened.

Then I did understand—or at least I thought I might understand—or I thought the emperor understood and was trying to explain it to me.

But I knew there was no time to wait. I had to move. Fast. Now.

I pulled my phone out of my pocket and called Amadis Carnation.

29

HE GAVE ME AN ADDRESS NOT FAR AWAY. I HAD NO IDEA where my Priest of Death truck was, so I used my phone to summon a car. A few moments later, a struggling actor drove up in a white Kia. I hopped in the back seat. The sound system was blaring, and I was immediately surrounded with what I would have called music if I were a savage and deaf. But the semi-handsome fool behind the wheel rode the gas hard, and that was what mattered.

It was late. Traffic was light. We moved fast. My heart beat faster and faster. My emotions were still electric from the Battle for the Skies. I could still feel the giant flying centipede wrapped around my arm as its harpy head snapped at me. But even more electric was my anxiety for Jane—Jane locked in the Tower as her time ticked away.

I looked out the window, trying to think. I could see the Soul Leeches everywhere. Prowling on the pavements in search of food. Gibbering at me through the windows of nearby cars, mocking me before they plunged their fangs back into the throats of the drivers. I saw the Bright Guardians too, a few of them. One gray-white figure of incomparable beauty stood beside a muttering schizophrenic who was pushing her worldly goods along the gutter in a shopping cart.

The angelic figure lifted a hand to me as I went past, wishing me well.

I closed my eyes to all of it, tried to block out the horror and the crap music, tried to clear my thoughts. How had this happened? How had I left LA at one place and come back at another? How had I left at one *time* and come back at another?

I remembered the Battle for the Skies. Curtin's army. A red haze from below but a demon throng when seen from above. It was just like the world, wasn't it? This world I was seeing all around me. From one perspective, it was simply a city of men and women, living, striving, worrying, dying, doing what people do. But from another perspective, from the emperor's perspective, it was Armageddon— Armageddon all day long—a civilization staggering under assault by monsters, an epic struggle between humankind and an evil it could not even see.

Was my actor-driver just a kid with a dream and a god-awful taste in music? Or was he the stuff of angels risking a life of beauty on a whispering delusion? Orosgo—had he died in his bed, a billionaire surrounded by fawning attendants? Or had he been devoured, screaming, by an unthinkable Cosmic Serpent? Which was the reality? Or were both real at once?

I remembered lying in my tent last night before the war, the two worlds mingling in my mind and in my vision. All this long while I had been flashing back and forth between them, passing through doors between Los Angeles and another kingdom. But was it possible I was—we were—all of us were—living in both kingdoms at the same time all the time?

The imagination is an organ of perception, like the eye. It sees as the eye sees.

I thought to myself: What power you would have if you could see—if you could know—if you could live—in the whole truth every minute.

Emperor Mode. That had to be the answer. The last level up. The power to see into—to move into—not just one world or the other but the whole simultaneous fullness of reality. That had to be the power that had let me pass from one place and time to another.

So that had to be the power I could use to free Jane.

I wished I could test it. Try it out. Master it first. But there was no time for that. I had to hurry. Midnight was careening toward me. If I failed or faltered, Jane would die.

I felt the car slow. I opened my eyes. Where were we?

The Kia was rolling down a narrow and deserted lane lined with small shops, all closed for the day. No people in sight here. Just long rows of cars and trucks parked against the curbs. The car came to a stop at the end of the block.

The would-be actor behind the wheel said: "This is it."

I looked out. I saw one lighted storefront window. A striped pole was rotating above it. Gold letters on the glass spelled out the name of the place: *Prince Charming Haircuts.*

I got out of the car and approached the door.

It was an old-fashioned barbershop, a little place from another century. A flickering fluorescent on the ceiling for light. Two old green armchairs against one wall. A long mirror on the wall opposite. One barber chair by the mirror; one customer in the chair. One barber working away at him with scissors, *snip, snip, snip.* The barber was a stooped black man in a white coat. He had pomaded hair and a thin mustache. A living anachronism.

I pushed inside. I stood staring at the uncanny scene.

The customer glanced over at me. "What's the matter, kid? You never saw a man get a haircut before?"

But the barber merely tilted his head. I followed the gesture. There was another door in the back of the room. A blank, brown wooden door. I walked to it, kicking through the hanks of hair that littered the linoleum floor.

I pulled the door open.

My breath caught. I recognized the place right away. It was the place from my dream, if it was a dream. After I had escaped the cemetery in the forest, I had run through the woods, the leeches chasing me. I had seen a doorway in the dark. Four men playing cards in a smoke-filled room.

Here it all was, all real.

I stepped across the threshold. The air was gray and smelly with smoke. The four men were sitting at a round wooden table, just like in the dream. They were playing poker, Texas Hold'em. A stack of chips was piled in the center of the table—red, white, and blue. There was a half-full bottle of whiskey too, and a glass for each man. And two metal ashtrays, because they were all puffing on cigars. The smoke rose from them in swirling lines that traced faint seraphic figures in the foul air. Through the fog of it, I could see a calendar on the wall with a photo of a half-naked woman to decorate the month.

As the door swung shut behind me, Detective Carnation turned a card off the deck and dealt it down onto the tabletop. *Fwip.* The other three men peeled up the cards that lay before them and compared them to the line of cards faceup on the table. They were three thick men, all in their forties. Hard men in shirtsleeves, with their ties pulled loose. Their jackets hung from their seat backs. Their shoulder harnesses were showing, and so were the Glocks holstered under their arms. One of the men was white, bald, with a scruffy gray beard. One man was black, sad-faced. One was Latino with broad, flat features like an ancient Aztec in a stone carving.

All of them seemed relics of another age. The whole scene seemed to float in some imaginary nowhere out of time.

"Bitch!" said the white guy, and he tossed his cards into the center of the table. "I'm out."

Carnation looked up at me. "Where the hell have you been, Mr.

Emperor Man?"

"It's a long story. Is this your army of true believers?"

Carnation glanced at his pals and snorted. "A sad army but my own."

"Have you got a plan to get me into the Tower?"

"We might. Have you got a plan to get out?"

"I might," I said. I didn't think I could explain to him about Emperor Mode. I wasn't sure I could explain it to myself. "What about afterward? You have someplace you can hide Jane?"

Carnation looked around the shabby little room. "This place could use a woman's touch."

The black guy chuckled. "A woman wouldn't touch this place with a ten-foot pole."

The other guys smirked.

Carnation sighed. He dropped the deck onto the table. "Guess this game is over," he said.

"What, we're going?" asked the Aztec guy. He seemed surprised.

But Carnation shrugged and gestured toward me. "Hey. He's the emperor."

IT WAS 9:30 by the time the five of us marched out of the barbershop and piled into the white van parked just in front. We tore away from the curb with a screech of tires. The van jounced on the pitted pavement. The interior quickly filled with cigar smoke. I was afraid it was going to be a nauseating ride.

And oh yes, it was. Carnation drove like a maniac. He sped through the busy streets, running red lights as horns honked all around us. I watched him nervously from the passenger seat. He leaned in hard over the steering wheel, his face close to the windshield. He stared at the road like he could burn holes in the pavement with his eyes. He chomped on the end of his cigar like it was gum. As air blew up through the vents, sparks flew off the lit end of his stogie. When we pulled onto the freeway, he pushed the rickety machine up to eighty.

"What's the matter, Emperor?" said the black guy from the seat behind the driver. "You look a little green."

"You got something against green people?" I muttered.

The bald guy laughed.

"Scotty's with the FBI," said Carnation. He gestured with a thumb over his shoulder, but I couldn't tell which one of the men he was pointing at. "He's got our ID papers. Paulie's from Corrections. He'll pave the way. They'll be expecting us."

"Expecting us?" I had been focused on not puking, but that last statement got my attention. I turned to Carnation. "Why would they be expecting us?" But then I got it. "You mean they'll think we're the assassins."

"Well, they don't know they're assassins, right? They've been told a team from DC is coming to ask Jane questions about a connected federal investigation."

"And that's who they'll think we are."

Carnation nodded. "If we're lucky, yeah. That's how we'll get you in. But how you get out . . . Well, you're on your own."

I blew out a long breath. I swallowed, nauseous. I coughed as the stinking cigar smoke filled my lungs.

"If I don't," I said.

"If you don't what?" said Carnation, chewing his cigar.

"If I don't get out . . ." I said.

"Yeah? What then?"

"Go find my sister. She's in the Orosgo Retreat."

"The crazy house?"

"Yeah."

"What's she doing there?"

"She's crazy."

"Oh," he shrugged. "Well, then."

"But you have to get her out."

"Why's that?"

"They'll kill her once they realize how much she knows. If I don't make it out of the jail, you have to get her."

He eyed me sideways but did not slow the van. It continued to dodge and weave, bump and roll nauseatingly through the traffic.

"How much does she know?" he asked.

"Everything."

"Really?"

"In her crazy way, yeah. She's how I found you. Her and her friends, they told me about . . ."

The van hit a bump and rose and fell in a slow rolling motion at the same time it continued its headlong plunge. I swallowed a throatful of vomit and groaned.

"What?" said Carnation. "What did they tell you?"

I breathed deep, trying to soothe my stomach, but inhaling cigar smoke only made it worse.

"The forest," I said faintly. "They told me about a forest." In fact, I had forgotten about the forest until now. It was the one part of the mad girls' chant I had not yet decoded. "I'm supposed to bring you there," I said.

Handling the steering wheel with one hand, Carnation plucked his stogie from his mouth with the other and spit loose tobacco at the windshield. The gob hung there a moment, then dribbled down the glass.

"Make sense, Emperor Man," he said. "What forest? Where?"

I thought back to what the girls had said. "'The forest is all one tree,' they told me. They told me: 'plant the Carnation in the earth beneath.'"

"What the hell is that supposed to mean? The forest is all one tree?"

My nausea forgotten for a moment, I stared into the clouds of stinky smoke surrounding my head like a cowl. The forest is all one tree, I thought. What *was* it supposed to mean exactly. Then I remembered the Priest of Death, driving me to the killing place. I remembered him saying: *I always prefer it when people disappear.*

Then I and the black poker player in the back seat spoke at the same time.

"Aspens," we said.

I glanced at the black poker player. "What? What about aspens?"

He pointed at me with his cigar. "An aspen forest can be all one tree. Each tree is a clone of the other with one big root system beneath the earth. Pando, they call it. It's latin for 'I spread.'"

"How do you know that?" the bald poker player asked him.

"I read books," the black poker player said. "You should try it."

"It's where I left the Priest of Death—the assassin Richard sent to kill me. I think it's his place, the place where he makes people disappear. That must be what Alexis knew, how she blackmailed Solomon Vine to get the part in my movie. That's why they didn't bury her there. She was too famous to disappear. Someone would have always been looking for her, and they might have found the forest. So they killed her and framed Jane—in case Alexis had told her too. Once Jane hanged herself in her cell, that would wrap up all the loose ends. There'd be no reason to go on investigating. That's what the mad girls were telling me. To plant you—Carnation—in the earth beneath the aspens. To tell you to dig up the forest and find out what Alexis knew."

Carnation shrugged again. "All right. I'll dig the place up. Where is it?"

I gave him directions to the aspen forest where I'd buried the Priest of Death.

Then, to my enormous relief, we came bouncing off the freeway and headed for the jail.

THE TOWER COMPOUND was lit with spotlights now. The beams cut through the drifting tendrils of night mist. The weird lopsided jail looked even more like a gothic ruin in the semidarkness than it had when I visited during the day. I could picture Jane in her cell in the upper stories. Locked away. Waiting for me. Waiting for her assassins. Wondering who would get there first.

"You're sure about the time," I said, looking up at the high, dark windows. "The time when the killers come. You're sure it's midnight?"

"That's what my informants told me," Carnation said. "But no, I'm not sure about anything."

"So we could get there and find her already hanging in her cell."

He didn't answer.

The van bounced over the spiked security barrier and pulled through the compound gate. I was sick and dizzy from the ride, and my chest was so tight with suspense I could barely breathe.

There was a guard in a booth here. Carnation showed him a handful of IDs. The guard was a tall, unfriendly looking Latino guy. He had intelligent eyes, and he studied the IDs carefully for a long time. He shined a flashlight on them, then shined it through the van's windows over each of our faces.

I held my breath. I squinted through the glare at the guard. I caught a glimpse of some slithering something peeking up from the back of his shirt collar. It had a strangely human face. It grinned at me. Then it ducked back into the guard's clothes.

"Kill the stogies," the guard said then. He handed our papers back to Carnation. "This is a no-smoking facility."

He waved us through.

THE JOURNEY INTO the belly of the jail passed in a dream of fear. What if they stopped us before we reached Jane? What if the real assassins arrived and cut us down? What if they had already been and gone? The image of that sweet girl strangled in her cell haunted me every step of the way.

Carnation and the three poker players surrounded me as we came through the metal detector and entered the Tower halls. We stopped at checkpoints. We climbed up stairs. One guard escorted us for a little distance, then another guard took us further on. We strode past tiers of cells above a central courtyard filled with cots. Our footsteps thumped on the concrete walkway.

Aside from us, it was all women here, a purgatory of women. There were the rough, thickset guards with their doughy faces. Their expressions were watchful and combative. Their aggressive figures jutted and bulged. They wore heavy walkie-talkies on their belts and heavy clubs that looked like they could crack an elephant's skull. And then there were the prisoners in their yellow shirts and blue sweatpants, sitting on the edges of their pallets or lying on their backs. Tough, frightened, angry, despairing women dragging their asses through one more shitty moment of their shitty lives.

And then there were the creatures. Oh, it was bad. The Soul Leeches were everywhere. Crawling out of the guards' collars to gnaw their way into the flesh of their necks. Writhing under the prisoners' shirts to latch on to their breasts and suck their spirits like mother's milk. Some were planted in the open on top of the poor women's heads, their claws sunk deep into their scalps and their fanged mouths grinning gorily.

They recognized me now, these demons. Somehow word had traveled between the worlds, and they knew I carried the emperor inside me. They squealed and gabbled at me with indescribable malevolence as I passed by them. They promised me death with their yellow eyes.

You cannot save her, they hissed and whispered. *She's ours.*

We reached the last door, a thick metal door with a thick plexiglass square of a window in the center of it. The guard on our side pressed a buzzer. A guard within looked out at us. As soon as I saw this last guard's face, I knew she was trouble. It was a nasty pie-plate of a pasty white face, with flattened features. No trace of femininity, of kindness or of grace. I think that's what set off the alarm bells in my mind. Not to mention the enormous serpent that had already melded with most of her broad body. I felt the blood drain from my cheeks when I saw it. I must've turned white as paper. She and the serpent were almost one thing, their faces a single human-reptile amalgam.

I turned to Carnation. I saw the tension in my own heart reflected in his expression.

"Go back," I said softly.

He blinked, startled. "Go back?"

"I'll meet you on the northeast corner outside the fence."

He stared at me. I nodded. After a moment, he nodded back. He turned to the others. Made a gesture with his head: *Let's get out of here.*

Just then, the door buzzed so loudly it made me catch my breath. My heart started fluttering. The door swung open. The serpent-guard eyed me across the threshold. I think she could see how rattled I was. One corner of her mouth lifted in an ugly smile. The serpent that was consuming her hissed with glee, its yellow eyes wide.

"What're you looking at?" the guard said to me.

I kept my mouth shut. I glanced back at Carnation.

"We'll be waiting for you," the detective said. "Come on, boys."

The four men turned away and headed back down the corridor with their corrections officer leading the way.

I turned and stepped across the threshold into the final passage. I was alone there with the serpent-guard. She made me show her my ID again. She studied it for what seemed like an hour. All the while, the serpent part of her writhed and glared at me, drooling venom. It knew who I was. The guard part of her sensed something was wrong. I could tell. But she was uncertain. She had been expecting Jane's assassin. She was the inside woman who was going to let him in and look the other way while Jane was strangled to death. So she figured I was the guy. She saw the assassin she was expecting to see, even though the serpent tried to warn her that the emperor had come.

"All right," the guard said finally. "Follow me."

I met her eyes. It wasn't easy since her eyes and the snake's eyes kept blending together and coming apart. I nodded. She turned and led the way down the hall.

We came to the end of the corridor. There was a heavy door there that had no bars or windows. This was solitary. They must have put Jane here to make it easier to murder her in secret. The serpent-guard punched a code into the lock pad by the jamb. The door buzzed; the latch slid back with a loud metallic snap. The serpent-guard hauled the heavy door open.

I saw Jane dangling there from the light fixture, her eyes bulging, her tongue black.

But no, that was just fear. A vision of fear. In fact, she was still there, still alive.

She was standing in the middle of the tiny cell, small and vulnerable-looking in her papery jail outfit. Her little cot was beside her and her pitiful steel toilet and sink behind her to her right. The expression on her face when I first walked in was both calm and ferocious. She wasn't expecting me. She was expecting her killers. She was ready to meet death with serene defiance. She was going to show them how to die invincible.

In the next second, she recognized me. She caught her breath, and only just stopped herself before she cried out in joy and gave the game away.

Behind her—behind and just above her—I saw one of the Bright Guardians hovering in the light from the bare bulb, almost indistinguishable from the light. As I lifted my eyes to it, it blended with the light entirely and was gone.

I turned to the serpent-guard. "Give us a few moments," I said.

The guard hesitated. The serpent was whispering in her ear, but she couldn't quite hear it. Finally she said, "I'll be right outside."

I nodded. The guard left the cell and shut the door. She worked the keypad, and I heard the lock snap back into place.

Jane let out a whispered, "Oh!" and threw herself into my arms. Even then, even full of fear, I reveled in the feel of her body against mine. It filled my heart.

She drew away, her hands on my shoulders. She looked up at me, her eyes brimming.

"What are we going to do?" she whispered.

"We're going to get out of here," I said.

"How? How can we?"

I didn't answer. I just put one arm around her and pressed her against my side. With my other hand, I reached out into the empty air. I remembered how Maud had taught me to suspend my thoughts and rise above my fear. I did that now—and more than that. I suspended myself entirely. I made my own ego shrink into nothing and let that other self inside me take over. As smoothly, as simply as gliding from sleep into awareness, I entered Emperor Mode.

Suddenly, there before me was the secret substance of the air: the movement of matter, the fabric of energy, the weird material of time all dancing in the silence of a living music that even here in this solitary cell left traces on my consciousness of a vast and breathless joy.

I reached into the whirling dance with my extended hand and, pouring all my will into my fingers, carved a doorway out of the nothingness.

A glowing portal opened on the unknown.

Jane gasped. "My God, Austin. What is it?"

"It's just the world, Jane. It's the world as it really is."

"Can we go in?"

"We haven't got a lot of choice. Either we go in there, or we die in this cell."

I glanced from the glowing opening to her. Her gentle face was taut and grim.

"I'm afraid," she said.

"Hold on to me. Don't let go."

I braced myself. I drew breath.

But before we could escape through that glowing portal, the cell door buzzed loudly again and came crashing open. Orosgo's butler-assassin charged into the cell. Two fire-breathing bats were perched upon his shoulder, screeching like demons. He was there to murder Jane. The serpent-guard was right behind him, glaring at me, hissing.

"Get away from her," the butler and the two bats and the serpent-guard all shouted at once.

The butler brandished his weapon: a deadly knife of thick plastic, a killer's blade meant to be smuggled through the metal detectors. He grinned eagerly and stepped toward me. "You're a dead man," he said.

I drew my sword and placed the point beneath his chin. Shocked, he stopped cold. He stopped grinning. He stared as my armor rose to the surface and covered me, my imperial insignia on my breastplate, my red cape draped down over my back.

"What?" he cried out.

"Tell my brother I'm coming for him," I said.

Then—as he and the serpent-guard looked on in shock and wonder—I carried Jane through the glowing portal into the mad depths of reality.

30

JANE LET OUT A FEARFUL CRY.

"Don't look at them!" I shouted. "Look at me!"

The beasts were everywhere, a nightmare sea of creatures seething with red death. We were drowning in their slithering bodies, choking on the green stench of them, deafened by their gibbering and hissing.

I felt Jane's body shudder in my grip. "Oh God, Austin!" she whispered. "Oh God!"

"Don't look!"

"What are they? Oh God, they're awful!"

"It's just the world, Jane! Just look at me!"

I kept my left arm around her. I pressed her hard against my chest. My right arm was raised before us, my sword in my hand. I was fully covered in my armor now, my cape fluttering behind me. But Jane was all exposed, dressed in nothing but her papery jail outfit. Her shuddering grew more intense. Her stuttered breathing shook me to the core.

But how else could she react? Even I, who had seen a million horrors, had never seen anything like this. Who knew such an ocean of evil surged beneath the surface of the everyday? We had entered that space beyond space, that time beyond time, where things are what they are and there are no masks of matter to disguise them. Somewhere, I prayed, there was a heaven as sweet as this was hideous, but not here—not here beneath the jailhouse. This was the undersurface of the worst of the world, and it was all monsters.

No one, no mortal man or woman, could have seen that sight and kept his sanity. But I could. Because back in the shit-filled sewers of Galiana, Maud had taught me how to let myself disappear and I was gone, gone, gone. Only the emperor was in my mind now. Only he—his vision, his perfect imagination—was looking out through my eyes. And only he could bring us through this place alive.

The sea of creatures shrieked and gibbered. They knew me—they knew him, that is, the emperor—on sight. At first, they recoiled from him in fear, opening a narrow space for us to move among the squirming waves of them. I felt them touch us as we passed. They slithered over us, spat at us, and threatened us with dripping fangs and snapping claws. But still, they knew that I—he, the emperor—had slaughtered an army of their kind in the skies above Aona, and they hesitated and drew back.

I kept my sword raised and pushed my way forward. The beasts parted before me, but a filthy slime lingered in the air and clung to us. Their black breath became our only atmosphere, a whole environment of malignant emptiness, a fathomless cancer stinking of despair. Jane held on to me so hard I thought she would become one with my armor. I could feel her trembling violently. I could hear her fighting to draw a breath. I was afraid I was losing her. I was not sure her sanity could survive the sight of this place.

But now, as I edged ahead, as I forced my way step by step through the swelling mass of pulsing forms and malevolent faces, I saw a sight in the distance that gave me hope. Two sentinels of a higher power were posted on the far side of the living darkness. The swelling tide of slithering red degradation broke against them but could not overwhelm them where they stood. Their arms were raised. Their golden-white drapery was blowing in the foul wind. Between them their robes formed a passage into some bright somewhere I could not quite see.

They were far away. God, they were so far. And I sensed the monsters—who, until now, had feared to come at me—were gathering their courage, getting ready to attack. I held the shuddering Jane against me and made my way through the half-parted tide of crawling horror, my eyes trained on that swirling passage between the Guardians. One step. Then another.

Then the beasts surged over us.

One of the braver serpents started the assault. It broke from the impenetrable tangle of the rest. It darted its enormous open mouth at the side of Jane's face where it was bare above my protective arm. It almost plunged its fangs into her—but I plunged my silver sword through its neck first and then tore upward.

The thing's head fell limp, half severed but still snarling. Green, smoky, acid blood gushed out of the writhing body. I threw my sword arm over Jane's head, muffling her scream. The serpent's blood poured over my armor and sizzled and bubbled on the surface of the magic mercury.

The rest of the monsters saw their chance, and the writhing tide closed over us.

Jane and I were both engulfed in the squirming, hissing, hellish wave, unable to move or breathe. The things tried to bite at me, but my armor repelled them. Their teeth shattered on my shoulder and sides, and their heads whipped back and away as they shrieked in agony.

So they went for Jane instead, wriggling under my arm to get at her.

I pressed forward, sucking in their unholy stench. Chopping, stabbing, slashing at anything that got close to Jane's exposed face and neck.

But it was no good. There were just too many of them. A centipede with a hag's face squirmed up from below us and bit into the inside of Jane's thigh before I could stop it. She cried out as if she felt it latch on to her very soul. I stomped on the thing's body with my armored heel—once, twice—then the third time, I crushed it. But even so, I had to flick the head out of Jane's leg with the point of my sword—and by then, a bat had latched on to her neck so that she let out another wail, and I knew it was feeding on her.

I tore the thing off, still pushing forward, every minute pushing forward and fighting to keep myself—my own cringing fear, my own trembling spirit—from rising into my mind and crowding out the emperor. I knew if even for a second I allowed my own ego to see through my own eyes, I'd be lost as Jane was lost and I'd lose Jane too. Both of us would become so much meat and drink to these devils. They would devour us in this nether realm until there was nothing left. I had to let the emperor have all of me—all.

I punched some gibbering demon in the face with the fist that gripped the sword, then jabbed the point of the blade into a hovering serpent who was searching for a spot to strike.

Jane had suddenly gone dreadfully silent. Her clothes were sopping with blood. Her face was smeared with it. I only knew she was still alive because I could feel her trembling. I knew I was losing her though. The snakes were slithering past my defenses. They were wrapping their hideous bodies around her limbs, climbing up her to nose at her face. They were everywhere. I couldn't keep them all away.

But I shouted and struck out with my sword and shouldered deeper into the Monster Ocean. And now, I could see again—just barely see—the draped and lovely Guardians making a space for us before them and holding a portal open between them, a door back into the life we knew.

The portal was closer now. The sight of it so near gave me fresh strength. I roared and somehow yanked my arm free of the tide, free enough to slash to the left and right. Surprised and wounded by the fresh assault, the red waves pulled back from us.

For a moment now, there was a passage up ahead, a free path to where the angels held the exit open. I thought I could almost see the world through the portal, the spotlights of the Tower complex glaring in at us. Four steps across the open space—maybe five—and we'd be through.

I charged the portal.

I didn't make it.

Before I could reach the twin Guardians who stood like columns at the portal's sides, the red tide broke between us. It spilled down into the space before me—serpents and bats and centipedes and goblins all spilled down—and curled up in front of me in the form of a single creature, an immense dragon with leathery wings spread wide as the open sky.

It reared high, snarling. It opened its enormous fanged maw. I saw the flames gather at the back of its throat.

"Jane!" I shouted.

I wrapped both arms around her and turned my back so that my body stood between the dragon and Jane.

The dragon spat a stream of fire. We were bathed in flame. My armor kept us alive—even my cape protected us; it could not be burned—but I could feel the hot death closing in around us. Another moment and we'd be cinders.

I roared in pain. I pressed Jane close to me with one arm. With the other arm, I drove my sword backward, blind. The emperor guided my hand. I felt the blade sink deep into the belly of the beast.

The stream of flame became a coughing spurt, then stopped. I turned, using my full weight to drag my sword as far across the creature as I could, ripping its guts open like cutting through leather.

I tore the sword free, and the beast split open. The creatures that had poured into the making of it started pouring out again, climbing, twisting, falling out of its stomach, the whole tide of red death, the whole black atmosphere of infinite murder, spilling over my feet and rising up my legs to smother me again.

I gave another roar, as loud as the beast had roared. I waded into the center of that surging red-black tide. There, yards away, was the gleaming portal open between the Guardians. I fought toward it. Reached it. And, holding tight to Jane, I hurled myself through.

Then there was only noise, a high, shattering alarm enveloping us. We were outside the Tower, on the street just beyond the compound fence. I was still in my armor. Jane was still in my arms. Someone had set off the jail's alarm. The compound spotlights were sweeping the night territory, looking for the escaped prisoners: me and Jane. The alarm was deafening, and sirens were growing as loud as the alarm as the whirling red-blue of police lights whipped the dark air and a cavalry of LAPD cruisers came speeding down the street to join the hunt for us.

Guards were pouring out of the Tower, guard after guard charging at us in a thick wedge across the compound. They were armed. Some gripped pistols, some rifles. The fence gate was swinging open so they could get at us. As they came closer, I caught sight of the butler-assassin among them. He was running at us too. He was carrying a rifle. His eyes were bright with murder.

Under the sound of the alarm, under the sound of the sirens, there was a wild screech of tires.

"My Emperor!"

It was Carnation—Carnation in the white van. With Jane unconscious and bloody in my arms, I spun to him. The van had pulled up alongside us. The Aztec poker player was holding open the side door.

"Get in!" he screamed.

I swept Jane up into the air. Blood dripped from her onto the macadam. I handed her body through the van door. The Aztec took her. He started to pull her inside.

"Come on!" the bald guy shouted from the van's depths. He reached out for me.

I was about to leap into the van myself when I saw the bald guy and the black poker player both looking over my shoulder. I saw them both go wide-eyed with fear as they stared past me.

I turned around to see what they saw. The army of guards was still charging at us. But the butler-assassin had come to a stop. He was standing on the far side of the open gate. He had lifted his rifle to his eye. He was pointing it straight at the van, straight at Jane where the Aztec was trying to maneuver her inside.

"Go!" I shouted at Carnation.

Carnation didn't hesitate a second. He hit the gas. The van sped away even as the police cars came racing down the street after it.

At the same moment, the butler pulled the rifle's trigger. I wheeled my sword up in front of me in an arc so precise only the emperor within me could have made it. I saw a flash of flame as the bullet ricocheted off the blade.

The assassin looked up from his rifle as if startled. But he wasn't startled. He was stone-cold dead. The emperor's perfect swordsmanship had sent the killer's own bullet bouncing back to hit him in the center of his forehead, smack between the eyes. It was so sudden, the butler's corpse actually stood erect another second before collapsing to the earth.

By then, I was already charging straight at the army of guards all around his body. I rushed through the compound's open gate.

An instant later, I was in a forest full of dead men.

31

I STOOD IN THE FOREST, LOST AMONG THE DEAD. I HAD not thought there could be so many. They lay like discarded dolls beneath the trees, their pudgy bodies slashed and bloody, their strangely samey faces staring up into the lacework of the high branches and the gray-white sky.

They had lost their lives in so many ways. Some had been dismembered, some disfigured, some nearly skinned. Some were mashed together so that they seemed one body made of several. Others had been burned and were still burning. Some had been crushed and others pierced a hundred times and some seemed half devoured. Some were nearly buried in the dirt and some lay sunk in mud and water and some were set atop the surface of the fallen leaves. The trees bowed and whispered above them, moved and swayed while they lay there, still. There must have been thousands of them.

I looked around me dully. I barely understood where I was or what I saw. My battle with the horrors of the reality beneath the Tower had left me shaken. And I could not stop thinking—thinking, wondering, and worrying—about Jane.

Was she all right? Was she even alive? Had Carnation escaped with her in his van, or had the police caught up with them? And even if they had gotten away and even if she was alive, would she ever recover from what she'd seen or would she go mad, knowing what the world was made of? The questions ran through my mind as I stood beneath the trees, gazing over the endless expanse of the dead. I was so disoriented, it was several moments before I realized I was not alone.

All around me, under the forest trees, there were other creatures—living creatures—lots of them. They were moving slowly among the bodies. They looked as exhausted as I felt and as dazed. It was late in the day. The light was failing. Both the living figures and the butchered ones seemed slowly to be blending with the tangled depths of the woods as the woods were slowly blending with the darkening air.

I blinked and squinted to get a better look at who was with me. I saw men and centaurs, trolls and fauns, infantry and knights in armor like me. Like me, I noticed now, they were all covered in blood.

As I began to return to full awareness, I recognized some of them. I saw Favian, the emperor's brother, his stained sword hanging loosely from his hand. I saw the Great Yeti, the fur around his claws dripping with red. I saw soldiers like Spartans gathered around their bearded king, and I saw he was King Cambitus of Menaria, Queen Elinda's father, the Not Altogether Wise.

I began to understand. In Emperor Mode, I could cross dimensions, not only between LA and the Eleven Lands, but through space and time as well. That's how I had gotten Jane out of the Tower. And now, I had returned to the war against Curtin, but not where I had left it.

As I stood with my army in the forest of the dead, I slowly pieced together what had occurred in the time since I had been back in Los Angeles.

After my cavalry had defeated the red army in the Battle for the Skies, we had flown on to the yeti camp to rest. Seeing the emperor return to them, the yetis welcomed us with one of their savage celebrations. And in the hungover aftermath, many of them, including the Great Yeti himself, had asked to join the fight to restore the Galianan throne.

We waited with them for our infantry to catch up with us. Their numbers had grown as well. As they, the infantry, were marching to meet us, the men of the Eleven Lands had left their hearths and families, picked up what weapons they could find, and fell into the ranks alongside them. When we all set off again, we were a mighty force, a sky full of horsemen winging majestically above, a vast sea of infantry spread out over the land below.

We proceeded as one to Menaria. There, we found the people frozen into statuary, waiting for the moonlight to free them from Curtin's daily curse. But I—the emperor—I didn't need the moon. Curtin had worked his will on their corrupted minds. The very presence of the emperor among them set those minds free. They melted into flesh and blood and joined our army. The curse of stone was over.

On we marched and on we flew. When we reached Edgimond, I descended from the sky into the forest to search for Maud's lover, Natani, in the lake. But the Eunuch Zombies were waiting for us, an entire nation of them. They attacked us in the woods. What followed was an awful massacre. Being Eunuchs, they were flabby as pudding, easy for my soldiers to cut down. But being Zombies, they would not stop coming at us even as we sliced them to pieces. Nothing would convince them to drop their weapons and surrender. We were forced against our will to butcher them like cattle before a feast. We turned the forest into a charnel house, and still they kept coming and coming.

So it was I returned from Los Angeles to find myself standing dazed amid the final results of the butchery.

I sighed to see it.

King Cambitus stepped up beside me. He towered over me. He lay his hand on my shoulder.

"Never mind, lad," he said, in his grand authoritative voice. "It's only justice. They slaughtered their own women, remember."

I nodded wearily. "I remember. I saw the bodies. Below the earth in the caves."

"Curtin convinced them that a world without women would make an easier life for the men. No females to defend, no children to feed. A country without consequences."

I nodded again, too tired to answer.

"It wasn't we who killed them, then," said King Cambitus. "They destroyed themselves."

I gave another deep sigh. "I suppose we will have to try to believe that," I said.

My eyes, still moving dully over the carnage, now came upon a little joyful spark of life. Maud. She was standing in the darkening green of the deeper forest, well away from the battlefield, off where I had sent her before the fight began. She was too far away for me to see her expression clearly, but I knew her well enough that I could read her body language. She was all eagerness and impatience, waiting for me to join her. Girlish with anticipation—girlish as she had never been when she was in rodent form.

The sight of her cheered me after all the killing. There were too many men in this forest. Too much death.

"Find a place away from the corpses and make camp," I told Cambitus.

"My Emperor," he replied.

I walked heavily beneath the trees to where Maud waited. She was turned away when I reached her, gazing off into the woods. The light of the falling sun speared through the low branches in brilliant white beams, but shadows were falling from the treetops, and dark-green evening was moving in on every side.

Maud heard my footsteps on the dead leaves. She glanced over her shoulder at me. I noticed again how pretty, impish, and intelligent her face looked now that it was no longer stuck on the head of a squirrel.

"You look weary, my Emperor," she said.

I shook my head heavily. "The things I've seen, Maud. On the earth and under it. So much blood and evil. It's tiring."

She made a sympathetic face and touched my armored shoulder with a small white hand, but she was too much in love to give a damn that life was tragic.

I laughed. "Boo-hoo, right?"

"No. No, I didn't mean that. I'm sorry. It's just . . ."

I silenced her by lifting her hand from my armor and bringing it to my lips. "Let's go find your guy."

She ran ahead of me like a child, a Maud I'd never known. These were her home woods, and she was sure-footed and swift in them, even as the light failed. As I picked my way behind her, I scanned the tangled webwork of the forest depths. Last time I had been here, this was called the Children's Forest. It had been haunted by the ghosts of children the women had not lived to bear. It seemed those ghosts were gone now. At least, I didn't see any.

We went on. Night fell. Maud's white robe seemed to gleam in the darkness up ahead of me. I followed after it. I saw her reach the edge of the lake.

The trees were sparser here around the water. The moon had risen now, a full moon, and the silver light of it streamed down over the crowns of the high pines. As I walked on to catch up with Maud, I saw her kneel down by the lakeside. She began to speak passionately into the moonlit ripples.

I came near. I could see Maud's face, her profile, illumined by the silver glow that filled the clearing. I heard her murmuring. I couldn't make out the words, just the tone of eagerness and affection. It made me smile after all the grim eunuch killing.

She glanced up and saw me approaching. "Here he comes," she whispered to the lake. She was brimming with excitement.

I stood above her. Looked down over her shoulder into the water. And what a shock. I saw myself reflected there, but it was not myself. I saw the haloed sword on my breastplate, the red cape gently fluttering in an evening breeze—but the face. It was not my face.

I gaped in surprise—but before I could get a good look at my reflection, Natani rose up from the depths and became one with the rippling surface, and my own image was gone.

He was a wan, narrow, scholarly young man, his face strained with grief. But there was no mistaking the passion in his eyes, even now when they were made of water.

His voice gurgled up out of the lake. "My Emperor."

"Hello, Natani," I said. "I promised I would bring her back to you. Here she is."

A sequence of emotions rippled over the pale features. He had recognized the emperor, I think, but now he understood that I was also me, Austin, who had sworn to find the woman he loved and return her to him. Some understanding seemed to come to him as I watched, but because he was a scholar, he had to find some explanation for what he understood before he knew how to react to it.

At last he said uncertainly, "You did. You did promise. And you were as good as your word."

"And now I suppose you'd like to come out of that lake. Get yourself a pair of arms to put around your girl and so forth."

A fresh zephyr passed over the lake's surface, and his image dissolved into the water's agitation. Then the lake stilled, and he was there again.

"My Emperor," he said in the mournful tone I remembered

from our last meeting. "I'm afraid that isn't possible. My curse is Curtin's curse, and only Curtin can remove it."

Out of the corner of my eye, I saw Maud smile. I said: "That's how it works, is it?"

"It is," Natani said. "Forgive me, Emperor, but I apprenticed under Lalo, the master magician. I studied the magic arts deeply. I know what I'm talking about."

"I'm sure you do."

"The shape-changing spell I put on Maud to save her from the slaughter of the women, that was only magic. But Curtin—this—me—this is wizardry. Curtin is a wizard, born to power. His curses cannot be reversed but by his own hand. Anything else would defy logic. It would defy science. It would defy all the rules of . . ."

"Does he ever shut up?" I asked Maud.

"No, never," she said. "He's always going on about something. His books and so forth."

"Well, at least it'll be a long marriage, even if it only lasts a day."

"Ha ha," she said. But then she also giggled, a musical sound. I liked her much better as a girl than as a squirrel.

I reached down toward the water. "Give me your hand, magician," I said. "These are my lands now, and I make the rules here. I am what wizards wish they were, and I am not beholden to them. Give me your hand, and we'll defy logic and science both. We'll defy the whole world, for that matter. Believe me, friend. I've seen the world. It's worth defying. Give me your hand."

And still he said to me: "But I've read all the books."

I rolled my eyes. "I love this guy. I'm gonna leave him in the lake."

"Oh, for crying out loud, Natani, give him your hand right this minute," Maud said.

Well, he doubted me, but he loved her, so he would've done anything for her, even defy logic. I saw the tension of effort come into his face at her command. His little portion of the lake surged upward in a curling wave. His hand rose within the rising water and came into mine. And then the wave splashed back into the lake. But the hand remained. The hand and the arm—and I drew him up, and all the rest of him came out of the water and stepped onto the shore.

Maud let out a woman noise that I will keep in my heart forever as a souvenir, something to look back on during my lesser nights among humanity. She rushed into his arms and he embraced her, and I turned away because emperors, you know, must remain above the merely sentimental. But I could see it now—imagine it, I mean. I could imagine the whole affair. The mischievous, adventurous girl and the wan scholar in his study. She with the life of the world inside her and he with the knowledge of the world in his head. It was a nice romance, a good love story. They had my blessing.

"What happened to all the children?" I said after a while, speaking into the dark woods. "All those ghost children you saved from the massacre. Are they gone?"

When there was no answer, I glanced over my shoulder and watched them trying to pry their two faces apart. It looked like it might take a crowbar to get the job done.

"Yes," Natani finally said, pressing his girl tight against him. "I let them go when I heard you were coming. I was afraid before— afraid that Curtin would take them if I released them, but now I know they're free and with their mothers—the mothers who would have borne them if they'd lived."

I nodded. Looked away into the woods again. Thought awhile. Glanced back. "That means this country is empty now. Totally unpopulated. You two have your work cut out for you."

Maud laughed into Natani's chest, and he might have blushed, but it was hard to tell by the light of the moon.

32

WE THREE—MAUD, NATANI, AND I—MADE OUR WAY TO the camp in the town of Newfell. King Cambitus had taken the army there to get them out of the forest and away from the slaughtered Eunuch Zombies.

I recognized the place when we came to it. On my way to Aona, I had been drugged here, kidnapped on Curtin's orders, and lowered into a cave full of dead women as a sacrifice to the great beast down there. It was not a pleasant memory, not at all. I felt no joy returning here, even as a conqueror.

When we came into the town's streets, we found the gutters lined with sleeping soldiers, centaurs mostly, but also ogres and fauns. Cambitus had placed as many men as he could in the empty houses, barns, and shops of the place, but the army had become so large at this point, many were forced to bivouac in the fields around, and some—those most comfortable in the out-of-doors—had simply collapsed where they stood. We had to tiptoe around the snoring bodies to reach the emperor's pavilion.

There were no celebrations tonight. Everyone was too exhausted and depressed by the massacre. We—we three—were exhausted too.

I sent Maud off to join the women and other camp followers and banished Natani to the command post in the tavern. Maud was not happy with this arrangement and let me know it in no uncertain terms, but I held my ground. I didn't want the first new child in Edgimond to be born out of wedlock. It would set a bad precedent.

When they were gone, I went into my pavilion alone. There, at last, my magic armor melted back into my body. My cape and sword vanished. I undressed and crawled onto my cot.

I was so tired, I thought I'd sleep right away. But I lay awake a long time. I thought about what I had seen in the lake: my own reflection, but not my own. My time in these lands, I realized, was coming to an end.

I stared into the moon-made shadows. My mind was buzzing like a beehive, my thoughts swarming like bees. This business of traveling through space and time disturbed me. Not just because of the demon-infested under-territory I had seen beneath the Tower. But also because of the way my life went on without me when I was gone. It was troubling. It meant, for instance, that I couldn't risk going home to check on Jane, to see if she was alive and well. I had to stay here—here in this place and time. I had to stay and see the war to its conclusion. I was the emperor now. I was more the emperor than I was myself.

How had this happened? I wondered. Tired as I was, I tried to reason it out. How had this change come upon me, and what did it mean?

This place, this other kingdom, my story here, had been going on before I arrived. Then—through reading a part of Elinda's book—my consciousness opened to it. I stepped through the door in the Edison Building and entered my own life as it was being lived in Galiana.

That life ended when I fell off the cliffs of Aona and was crushed against the ocean. I had died then. I had descended into the realms of death. I had decayed. I had dissolved in the belly of the Cosmic Serpent. You would have thought that would be the end of me. But death was not always death in the Eleven Lands.

Why not though? Why wasn't it? How had I come back?

The night was silent all around me, and I heard my own deep breathing as I lay on the cot staring into the moonlight.

I hadn't come back, I realized. He had. The emperor. It was I who had descended into the realms of death, but it was he who had returned within me, bringing me with him as he did. The life that I was living in this country was no longer really my life, but his. And slowly, as I allowed him to take me over, I was beginning to vanish. What, then, would happen to me when I was all gone?

I didn't know. I only knew that without him I would already be dead—in the ocean beneath the cliffs or in the shallow grave beneath the aspens. Without him, Jane would be dangling from a rope in her cell. Without him, the demons of the underworld would be feeding on us both, maybe forever.

What, then, could I do but trust him?

It was nearly dawn before I closed my eyes.

A LOW MURMURING outside the pavilion woke me. It was early morning. I stepped out of my tent—clothed magically again in the emperor's armor—and saw a crowd of soldiers—centaurs and ogres, knights and camp followers—gathered at the end of the main street at the edge of town. They parted with bows and curtsies as I walked among them to see what they were staring at. I came to the front of the crowd and stopped beside King Cambitus. My lips parted, and I heard myself give a little gasp of surprise.

The forest beyond the village had turned completely black. I—I, Austin—had never seen anything like it. The leaves, the branches, were draped in sable as for a funeral. Even the ground—the woodland duff—was carpeted with darkness.

I—I, the emperor, I mean—understood what it was a moment before Cambitus spoke.

"It's the Deadbirds," he said. "They've come for the eunuchs."

As if that were their signal to arise, the blackness gave a tremendous flutter, and up the Deadbirds flew. A million of them, it looked like. Wafting from the ground and from the branches and from the leaves, filling the sky like winged night. The morning sun went out, then shone again as they banked and wheeled off deeper into the forest. Birds like vultures. They had come for the feast we had prepared for them.

"The world was made to live and die," Cambitus said, watching them.

I nodded. "It was," I said. "Gather the armies. We march for Galiana."

IT WAS FIVE days' march to Shadow Wood. The winged cavalry flew slowly to let the infantry keep pace with us below. I worried about supplying the now massive force. Edgimond had been in the midst of a false harvest when I came through last time, but now the illusion had been lifted from the land, and it was revealed to be a gothic country, as sere and waste as Galiana itself. I worried we would not be able to find enough food for everyone.

I worried—but the emperor did not. I had underestimated his power.

As we traveled, the dead land came to life beneath us. Spring, then summer, then a rich, ripe autumn seemed to follow one upon the other in mere moments. Orchards sprang out of nothing and bore fruit. The fields turned grassy green, and flocks of animals like sheep arrived to graze in them. Water rushed into the dry ravines, sunlit and crystal clear. From my high perch on the flying stallion, it was a beautiful thing to watch, the green grass and the red fruit and the silver water springing out of the sere and colorless land, instantaneous and amazing, like a special effect in a movie, only real.

And there was still more magic when we reached the wood. It was the evening of the fifth day. The forest was growing mystic with new darkness. As the cavalry landed and rode through the tree line with the great infantry following, music seemed to surge up out of the forest's invisible depths. Creatures detached themselves from the intricate webwork of vines and branches and underbrush so that they seemed almost to manifest out of the empty air. Fauns on their pan pipes. Trolls with drums. Naked nymphs rising like mist from the lakes and rivers, singing a haunting chorus like a living wind. The thickening air was filled with fairies too, their rainbow lights hovering all around us, their naked bodies blurred by the humming shimmer of their gossamer wings.

I ordered Favian to make camp. I dismounted from the black stallion and continued on foot with only Maud, Natani, and King Cambitus beside me. The woodland creatures continued to pour out of the evening, dancing attendance on us. The rainbow clouds of fairies led us through the forest to the court of its king, Tauratanio, and of Magdala, his queen.

They were waiting for us there, seated on their thrones of light by the great oak where I had first found my sword and armor. Tauratanio was a rotund Santa Claus of a monarch with a great beard and red cheeks, a furred robe and a crown of leaves. He rose to greet me and gave his hand to Magdala—a lithe matron made of moonglow, an incredibly grand and lovely being—and she rose too.

"My Emperor," they said, their voices in harmony with each other and with the music all around us. They bowed their heads to me.

What a change it was since the last time I'd been here. It had not been so long ago, but in a strange way, it had been forever. Time did not work the same way in this kingdom as it did back home. The months of forgetfulness I had spent in Hollywood were part of my memory and experience, but time had stood still here and waited for my return. Plus the emperor, who almost second by second was becoming the more dominant presence within me, had been gone from these woods much longer than I had, and I could feel that too.

And there was also this: I had been through so much and was so greatly changed. It felt like years and years since I had stood before the forest king and queen, gormless and afraid. But if they recognized that man, that Austin, within the poised and powerful emperor, they gave no indication of it. I was not sure I recognized him myself anymore.

So I—I, Anastasius—hugged the king with solemn ceremony and kissed the queen's silver hand.

Then the two looked past me at my companions. They bowed to their fellow monarch, Cambitus. Then they turned to the two young lovers. Tauratanio's round and jolly face seemed to narrow for a moment with confusion, but Magdala's glowing white countenance grew brighter with her gentle smile.

"Is it . . . ?" said the king, astounded. He stepped toward the impish girl in her white shift. "Is it Maud?"

Maud fell to her knees before him, took his hand in both of hers, and started weeping.

"Look," the king said in wonder to his queen. "Look how beautiful she is!" He gave a deep laugh—really just like Santa—and beamed down at the crying girl. "What will I do without my squirrel spy?" he said. "My brave and secret soldier!"

Maud only just managed to answer. "I will always serve you, my king."

The moonlight queen moved to stand beside her husband. "We will not need spies and soldiers in this forest anymore," she said.

"These were free and peaceful woods under the good queen, and they will be free and peaceful woods again."

"Yes. Yes, that's right. And who's this?" Tauratanio said, turning to look at Natani.

The magician dropped clumsily to his knees beside Maud, and she lifted her tearstained face to the forest king, smiling and crying at the same time. "This is my Natani," she told him proudly.

"Ah, your Natani! Of course. The great magician who saved the children of Edgimond and sent us our brave squirrel. Look who it is, my queen. Natani the Great."

"No, Your Majesty," Natani mumbled, staring at the ground. "No."

"Edgimond is dead, Your Majesty," I told him. "These two will be the father and mother of a new nation."

"A new nation!" said the king, delighted. "What do you think, Magdala? A whole new nation from just these two."

She took his arm. "It's wonderful, my husband. Fathers and mothers instead of soldiers and spies. The world begins again in front of us."

"The world begins again," said the king, nodding in wonder.

NOW MAGDALA GESTURED toward the great oak, and the moonlight gathered there into a third throne and then a fourth, this last a majestic cathedra larger than the others.

"We should hold council, my lord," she said.

"Yes, yes," said the king. "What was I thinking? I was so distracted by the return of our good friend the squirrel. But here is the emperor. We must hold council. Of course."

The forest king and queen and King Cambitus and I—we all four settled into our thrones of light. I took the cathedra, and Natani and Maud stood behind me to my left and right, each by a finial.

The creatures of the woods gathered in the evening trees around us. The naked nymphs swayed mistily above the moonlit waters. The fluttering fairies graced the air with colored lights. All these together filled the woods with their strange music—a sound that was nearly the same as silence and yet somehow soothed the soul.

"What is the state of the country?" I asked.

Until that moment, you might have thought Tauratanio's face was sculpted into a permanent expression of convivial benevolence. But in the next second, he looked as somber as he had seemed joyful the second before.

"It is grim, my Emperor. Very grim," he said. "All of Curtin's remaining forces have gathered within the walls of Eastrim and are holed up in the castle compound, preparing for the final fight. They keep the citizenry imprisoned within the walls. There is great hunger among them. There are mass deaths. Beloved pets are roasted over trash fires. There is even cannibalism, according to my fairy spies. Some of the citizens murmur against Lord Iron and plot to kill him, hoping thereby to win your favor. But Curtin protects him, and the people are too afraid to act."

"Afraid of Curtin?" I asked.

"Of you, my Emperor," he answered. "They are terrified of your justice."

I nodded. I could understand that. I remembered the streets of Galiana under Lord Iron. The citizens had been reduced to gibbering demons, cheering as innocent men and women were tortured to death for being heretics and traitors. I remembered the sickly smoke of burning bodies hanging in the middle air, the stench of fear and envy and accusation.

"Justice for Galiana would be an ugly business," I said.

Tauratanio inclined his head. "Justice is ugly," he answered. "God keep us all from the fate we deserve."

"Yes. Amen," said the queen.

Cambitus spoke then with his kingly voice. "Perhaps if you were to issue a general pardon," he said. "A pardon to the whole city, the army included. Then there would be no more reason for them to fear you, no more reason for them to remain loyal to Lord Iron and his wizard."

"Curtin and his lord, you mean," said Magdala drily.

"Yes," Cambitus said with a bitter laugh. "Yes, that is what I mean."

I thought a moment, then inclined my chin. "I will consider it," I said. "Mercy for the people and the armies maybe. There can be no pardon for the lord and the wizard. That would not be just."

"No," said Cambitus. "But if you were to forgive the rest—the army, the whole city—they might well surrender, and there would be no more bloodshed."

"But my Emperor . . ." said the moonlight queen. And then to Tauratanio: "May I speak, my lord?"

"Of course," said Tauratanio. "You are my Magdala. Of course."

"Would it be justice to let the people go?" Magdala asked me. "It was they who chose to overthrow the queen. They would have burned her at the stake if my husband had not cast her from this place into another kingdom where she would be safe."

I thought of Queen Elinda—Ellen Evermore—hiding out in the tent city. Safe—more or less safe, I guess—but homeless too, a homeless queen.

"The people followed Iron of their own free will," Magdala continued. "The army most especially was his."

"May I speak, my Emperor?" said Maud at my shoulder.

"Of course," I said. "You are my Maud."

"When we were in Aona, by the sea, we saw the army, your army, how easily they were led. They would have burned a child alive at the command of Littleman, Goodchild, and Hammer. But look at them now. You pardoned them, and they followed you and have freed the nations. Perhaps King Cambitus is right. Perhaps it would be so with the armies of Eastrim too."

"Don't think of what they were but what they could be with your forgiveness," King Cambitus said. "Bring justice where it will do good and mercy where it will do good."

"But that's no rule," Natani blurted out. "Who can follow such a rule? Who has that wisdom?"

Tauratanio and Magdala and Cambitus and Maud and Natani all fell still and watched me, waiting for my decision. The forest around us was full of silent music.

I rose from my cathedra and the others rose.

"I will think it through and do what can be done," I told them. "One way or another, come morning, there will be an end."

33

IF YOU HAD BEEN A SOLDIER ON THE WALLS OF EASTRIM at sunrise, you would have seen the golden morning fill the heavens from horizon to horizon and then spill down over a black and earthly multitude. The emperor's armies—my armies—now blanketed the country, surrounding the city on every side. The ports and fields and forests all were ours.

I sat at the head of the legions, mounted on my stallion outside the main gate. Cambitus was on his charger to the left of me, Natani was on a stolid roan to my right. Favian was nearby on foot, ready to lead the infantry.

I nodded to Cambitus. He spurred his horse. It was he who had suggested that I offer mercy to the people. He had had the courage to insist that it would also be he who took the risk of approaching the city walls himself.

He rode forward slowly, unafraid. His body was relaxed. His kingly crown was glinting in the risen sun. Six archers on the Eastrim ramparts trained their bows on his approaching figure, arrows nocked and hands on the bowstrings, ready to draw. The captain of the guard stood beside them, his hand resting on the hilt of his sword. Even from where I sat, I could feel his tension and anger. There was no chance he would accept our offer. His heart was already at war.

The king's horse came to a stop before the city gates. Cambitus held the reins loosely, and the charger nosed the dust, looking for grass to nibble. The king lifted his eyes to the captain and spoke with quiet authority.

"I am Cambitus, King of Menaria," he said. "I have come to bring you a message from the emperor. All in this city are fully pardoned, the people and the soldiers—all. All except the wizard and his lord—they will face justice. But all others who have transgressed will be forgiven. All who are hungry will be fed. We require nothing but your allegiance to the queen and the old disciplines of freedom: let wisdom reign and each man go his way. Lay down your arms, accept the emperor's mercy, and avoid the destruction of you and your city."

To my right, astride his roan, Natani murmured: "They will not do it. This was a mistake. We should not have listened to Cambitus."

One corner of my mouth lifted. "Yes," I said. "He is not altogether wise. But he was right this far: We had to make the offer. We had to try to avoid war."

"But they will kill him now."

"They'll try," I said.

For a long moment, the captain on the wall did not reply. An almost uncanny silence settled over both the city and my vast army.

Then the captain's face twisted with rage. "Here is Lord Iron's answer," he cried.

He gave a signal, and the archers on the wall drew back their bows, ready to riddle Cambitus with arrows. I heard Natani gasp in fear beside me.

But before the archers could fire, my centaurs, hidden amidst my host by my command with crossbows ready, loosed their bolts. The bodies of the six archers on the Eastrim wall were suddenly bristling with shafts. Their bowstrings twanged. Their bows flew from their hands. Their arrows sailed uselessly into the sky as they tumbled backward and vanished behind the ramparts.

I saw the captain of the guard stiffen with shock. Even at a distance, I saw his eyes go wide with understanding, rage, and fear.

I winked at Natani. "Well, we tried," I said. I lifted my hand. I raised my voice. I shouted the order. "Take the city!"

The army surged forward. We were, by now, so many it was as if the very earth had come to life and thrown itself against the walls. I led the cavalry up into the sky, and we were above the ramparts before the infantry reached the gates. My trolls hurled bombs down on the guards below. Loud explosions and red bursts of flame sent the soldiers on the wall toppling. My knights, meanwhile, landed within the city. Iron's mounted troops were ready for us and met us with a charge. Horses squealed. Swords clashed and rang. Battle cries turned to screams of agony. Blood and dust flew everywhere. The deafening tumult of war surrounded us.

As the horsemen battled for the inner court, my trolls fought their way back toward the city gates, hurling their explosives as they went. Huge blasts erupted. Huge fires climbed up the entranceways. Then all at once, the gates blew inward, and my army flooded the city.

A tide of men, of centaurs, of ogres and fauns and all the rest came pouring into the streets. Iron's forces fell back before the onslaught. We chased them down, slaughtering any who tried to make a stand. As I led the way into the streets, I saw the people, the citizens, cowering in doorways, alleys, and gutters. Through the flying blood-spattered dust, I caught glimpses of their pitiful figures, starved to skeletons. Men, women, and children too. Their ribs pushed through thin draperies of flesh. Their eyes were huge in their sunken faces. I remembered how they had turned on each other under Iron's rule of fear and slander. Now they huddled in despair or ran in panic as their guardians and oppressors fell in a chaos of battle and death.

We fought street to street, littering the ground with corpses, riding our horses over the screaming wounded and the dead. Flames flew up on every side of us as the trolls bombed the buildings, and the buildings burned. Iron's cavalry was already destroyed, and now the foot soldiers were running in disarray as we charged after them and cut them down.

We broke into an open space—a plaza—the very plaza where I had once seen prisoners tortured and killed while the citizens jeered them. The dead had been stacked here like firewood and burned. The ground was still covered with their remains. The air still stank of rot. This was Iron's legacy. Looking for power, he had convinced the people that if they threw off the discipline of the wise queen's reign, the land would become an arcadia of equality. Now I saw the ruins of that promised paradise burning around me. Like every mortal Eden, it was littered with the dead.

I reined my stallion and my stallion reared. Rising above the fight, with the black smoke of the burning city washing over me, I raised my sword and called to the nearest infantry: "Follow me!"

Then I turned and charged out of the plaza and headed up the hill toward the castle compound. The cavalry raced beside me. The infantry, with spears and swords, came storming at my back.

We climbed the hill. The city was in flames beneath us. Above us, the castle compound rose, dark and formidable against the bright morning sky. I led my forces into the old graveyard, a smog-draped field of slanted monuments. As we raced through it, the headstones toppled under our horse's hooves. The roofs of the catacombs collapsed. The under-tunnels opened. The spirits of the imprisoned dead flew out of the black pits. Shadows visible in the mist, they flitted free and vanished in the sunlight.

I took one quick glance around me as we raced on. This was where Betheray had died in my arms, my brave and beautiful revolutionary murdered by the husband who had betrayed her: Iron. Even in the feverish passion of our advance, I felt the talisman that hung around my neck grow hot against my skin. Its heat seeped through me and became the heat of righteous anger. I wished that Beth were here with me now to see her murder avenged, her nation freed, the queen she loved so well restored to her rightful throne. I hoped there was joy in heaven as she watched my armies come.

We charged the compound. The battle grew intense around the castle moat. Iron had posted a large contingent of soldiers there. He was hoping he could stop my forces before we reached him, hoping he could win the day without risking his own life in the fight. He was not a coward, just a devil—he sent others to do the bloodwork for him.

Iron's archers lined the far side of the water and filled the air above it with shafts. My soldiers approached steadfastly under their shields, though many were pierced and went down screaming. My centaurs fired back with crossbows, and the archers went down too. And meanwhile, the infantry fought to build a trio of pontoon bridges across the moat.

At last, as the arrows flew, we breached the water—but the worst was still to come. The infantry charged across the bridges, and I led my cavalry above them in the air. My trolls advanced with me, showering the enemy with incendiaries. The bombs were powerful. The bodies of Iron's soldiers flew out of the blasts in burning pieces.

But then, one of the devices hit the base of a tower. The loud explosion shook the air. The earth erupted, then collapsed. A horrid stench blew up out of the blasted sewers. It covered me even where my stallion winged above.

I heard an unnatural roar. I realized what was coming a moment before it came. I looked down in horror.

The massive Shit Monster that lived in the sewers beneath the dungeon rose up out of the earth and swarmed the fighting armies.

It was a nightmare slaughter. The living shit covered the fighters where they clashed. Without regard to whose men they were, it flowed into their open mouths and filled them like balloons until they burst in a hideous splash of animate excrement. The sewer beast seemed to be everywhere at once, seething beneath the battle, lifting soldiers off the earth as they broke off their sword fights and tried to run for it, screaming. I saw the bodies of men bursting and sinking, dead, into the living tide of dung. For a moment, the abomination froze my brain, and I could not think what to do.

Then with a shout, I drove my stallion down into the thick of the stench.

"Get behind him!" I shouted to my trolls. "Force him into the moat! Infantry, form up in front of him. Lead him on."

The trolls rallied and brought their horses to the shit beast's back. The soldiers lined up before it and retreated in good order over the bridges, drawing the thing toward the edge of the water. The trolls began to harry the flowing brown mass with bombs and fire, driving it forward. As I flew mere feet above the battle, gagging on the sewage miasma, I saw the shit beast flow into the moat and fill the water with the writhing crap of itself.

"Burn it!" I shouted.

The trolls rushed to the moat's edge, throwing incendiaries down at the thing as fast as they could. The shit beast fought to flow free, but the soldiers lining the moat's far side forced it back into the ditch with spears and swords as the bombs exploded on top of it in orange and scarlet flames.

At first, it seemed the fire did no damage. The flames seemed to dance harmlessly on top of the burbling manure as the creature roared. It reached out of the pit and seized another soldier and another. The men screamed and struggled and were filled with shit and burst and died in the creature's clutches.

Then, finally—finally—the flames took hold. With a hollow thump that sent an unbelievable smell up to the very heights of the sky, the shit beast caught fire. Its roar became a high-pitched shriek. Its shriek mingled with the windy clamor of the flames. It burned. Then all in a moment, the beast exploded. Pieces of flaming shit went flying through the air in all directions.

The remnants of the thing sank down into the moat's water. With a cheer of victory, my armies raced across the bridges again and stormed the castle, cutting down Iron's army as they came.

That was the turning point. My host flooded the compound, and Iron's armies fled. Flames flew out of the buildings' windows as the infantry broke down doors and went after the panicking defenders.

I turned my stallion and flew toward the highest tower of the castle, just above the moat. It was there—there in the room at the tower's top—I had first stepped into Galiana. It was there, I knew, I would find Iron waiting, there in his last refuge, the furthest point from the war.

I landed my horse by the moat and dismounted. I made my way to the base of the high tower. The door stood ajar. I entered the stairwell. There were no defenders left here. They had all fled, trying to escape into the castle and the catacombs. I could hear my forces battling them within: the clash of swords, the cries of battle, the shrieks of the wounded and dying.

I headed up the stairs to the room where I had found Lady Kata's body.

I thought back to that day as I took the flight two steps at a time. I thought back on the man I had been then. I could hardly find him in myself anymore. I was almost all emperor now. I wondered again what would become of Austin when the transformation here was complete.

I reached the top of the stairs. I reached the heavy door to the tower room. I pushed against it. It was bolted from within. I could hear a barricade of furniture rattling on the inside.

I raised my foot and felt some fresh energy flow into me. I kicked out once. The bolt shattered. The door flew open. The barricade splintered. The splinters sprayed.

Lord Iron Netherdale was waiting for me in the center of the room. I was surprised to find him there alone. The last time we had fought, he had had Curtin's protection. I could not land a blow against him because the wizard's magic deflected them all. But now he stood before me solitary and erect, his sword in his hand.

He was a tall, broad-shouldered man, a handsome, stately fellow, a political being who knew how to present himself and was always aware of the impression he made. He was dressed now for this final fight not in armor but in the finery of office, gilded clothing with a lining of fur, a purple sash across his chest, a family medallion gleaming on it, a black cape flowing.

When I stepped through the doorway—when he saw me there in my emblazoned armor, my own cape bright red—he took up a dueling stance, ready to do battle. All around him on the walls, torches burned in their sconces, illuminating the tapestries hung between them. The medieval scenes of reapers and hunters and dancing gentlemen and ladies seemed to flicker to life in the flamelight.

Lord Iron glared defiance at me. His voice trembled, but he spoke boldly. "I am not afraid to die, Anastasius."

"Good," I answered. "Because I'm going to kill you."

The color left his cheeks at that, but he still managed a sneer. He angled his sword at my face, and I drew mine.

Then, with cries of fury, we launched ourselves at one another.

I was not prepared for what happened then. I was the emperor and mighty beyond imagination. I thought I would defeat him right away. I was startled by his ferocity and prowess. His eyes gleamed with unnatural intensity. His blade flashed here and there with uncanny speed. Wherever I tried to cut at him, I found him gone.

And when I thought I had an opening, he blocked me and knocked my thrusts and slashes harmlessly away.

He counterattacked with savage blows I could only barely parry. We circled around the circular room, lit by the torchlight and by the pale beams of morning that fell through the windows. The figures on the tapestries seemed to watch us as our blades clashed together, swung back, and clashed again. I leapt toward him and cut at his head with all my might. He caught my blade on his and threw it back and sent me staggering. He rushed in for the kill, and I kicked him at the waistline, shoving him away.

We paused a moment, breathless, sword tips touching in the air between us.

"You think yourself noble because you want to put the people under a monarch's heel again?" he said.

"This isn't a debate. It's a sword fight," I told him. "This is for Betheray. *En garde.*"

"You want to kill me because you slept with my wife?"

"Someone had to."

"You miserable bastard."

"Come on, Iron. Enough talk. I could hand you over to the hounds of hell, but I want to do this myself."

"Well, do it, then!"

He rushed at me again. Again, the little room rang with our two swords clashing. Try as I might, though, I could not find a way into him—and his attacks were getting closer and closer to the mark.

I began to feel the first acid pools of anxiety gathering inside me, deepening into fear. What was going on here? Something was all wrong about this. I was the emperor. He was just a man. I should have been able to defeat him easily. But no. Instead, I could feel myself tiring, while every time we rushed together, he was stronger than before.

If this kept up, the unthinkable was going to happen. It was only a matter of time before he would kill me.

Sure enough—soon enough—the crisis came.

As I struggled to block a flurry of slashes so swift they were almost invisible, Lord Iron drove me against the wall. My back slammed into the tapestry. He pressed in. I caught his blade on mine. The two swords trembled together, edge to edge, flashing with the flamelight from the torch right beside me. Our eyes met across our swords, and I was shocked to see the raging red power in the depths of his glare.

He pushed hard against me. My muscles were beginning to weaken. My arm buckled, and with a swift, circular motion, Iron caught the edge of my weapon with his and flipped the sword out of my hands. The blade twirled through the air and fell, clattering, to the stone floor, right on the spot where Lady Kata had died, right on the bloodstain there.

Triumph flared scarlet in Iron's face. He drew back for the killing blow with me pressed against the wall, defenseless.

"Die, Anastasius!" he said.

He thrust the sword point at my breast.

I wheeled to the side, plucking the torch from the sconce. His blade struck the wall behind me, throwing sparks. I leapt forward and counter-thrust, jabbing the flaming torch into his face.

His flesh sizzled as he fell back, screaming. The stench of his burning skin reached me as his cheek bubbled and turned black. By the time he pivoted to fight off my next attack, one half of his face was melted away to reveal the gray-blue wrinkled countenance beneath, its single eye gleaming with hatred.

"Curtin!" I said.

Of course it was. I remembered how, back in Hollywood, I had seen the demons devour their prey from within. There was hardly anything left of Orosgo when he died. My mother and father were likewise nearly gone, only fragments remaining of the people they'd been born to be.

So it was with Lord Iron Netherdale. There was almost nothing left of him. He was all Curtin now. Curtin lived within him as the emperor lived in me. The wizard had taken him over and he was empty, the hollow image of a human being.

As that realization came to me, I understood why I had not been able to defeat him. Curtin had only one power: the power he stole from other men's minds. He wielded the weakness of their corruption against them. He killed them with the self-consuming fire of their own hate.

And I hated Iron. He had killed my Betheray, my lovely girl. I hated him.

The moment I spoke the wizard's name, he threw off his disguise. It was an awful thing to see. At the last second, I think Lord Iron realized what had happened to him, how he had been used and used up. He was nothing now but a costume to be thrown aside. What was left of his face contorted in a twisted grimace of pain and despair. His howl of agony became a shriek of terror as Curtin seized his body by the chest and tore him asunder like a rag. And still—still—Iron was shrieking as he fell in pieces to the stone floor. His shredded flesh became flame. The flames sank down into the stone and out of sight. But still—still—I could hear him shrieking, those long, long fading screams.

The wizard stood before me unmasked, a shriveled little man with a wizened little face, his beady eyes sunk deep within its folds. His gray tuft of hair quivered on his forehead. His gray tuft of beard trembled on his chin. That robe he always wore, that starry robe of liquid night, flowed out around his shriveled frame. He bared his teeth in fury.

At the sight of him, something went quiet within me. All my hatred ended. I pitied Iron to have had such a creature feeding on him from within. All for what? All for a mere kingdom, here and gone. Nothing.

"Easy for you to say," said Curtin, answering my thoughts as if I'd spoken them aloud. "You, who rule all the Eleven Lands. Why could you not give me just this one?"

I waved my torch between us to hold him back as I crossed to the center of the room to retrieve my sword.

"Because I loved Elinda," I told him. "This country was my bride's by right."

"I wanted it! *I* wanted it!" he said, pounding his chest, as if he thought this were an unanswerable argument.

I swept my sword off the floor and faced him. I held Elinda's blade in one hand and the torch in the other.

"So much misery for just a throne," I said.

"I wanted it!" he screamed.

I shook my head. I sighed. What a dick.

I moved to the wall beside the door. I lifted the torch. I touched the tapestry there with the flame. It caught swiftly and blazed high, the fire roaring.

Curtin watched the fire rise, his beady eyes wild with rage. "You think I'll die here? Did you forget, Anastasius? I set my legion free from the place to which you condemned us. I have the power to open that door now, the same as you have."

"And I have the power to seal it," I said. "Go back and see. Go back where you came from or burn here, Curtin. It makes no difference to me."

The tapestry was now all consumed by fire. Ashes and sparks flew off it and drifted through the room. Another tapestry caught and started burning, then another. In moments, the flames surrounded us. They climbed high. They licked at the wooden rafters beneath the roof. The rafters burned. Black, black smoke coiled through the tower room.

I stepped into the doorway and faced the wizard where he was trapped within. Curtin stood in the midst of the blaze and glared at me. I could tell he was trying to think his way out of this. I could see it in his eyes as they flickered and darkened with the flickering, darkening flames.

"I escaped before," he shouted at me. "I'll escape again. The minds of men will make a passage for me."

"And for me. Wherever you go, Curtin, I'll be there. I'll find you. Count on it."

The walls and the roof were all on fire now. The heat was nearly unbearable, and the smoke so thick it was suffocating. I stepped out the door to the top of the stairs.

"All I wanted was a crown, you bastard!" he screamed after me.

I faced him. I had to lift my voice over the roar of the fire now. "The crown belonged to Elinda," I told him one last time. "It was hers by right."

"*I wanted it!*" he shrieked—and then the flaming roof came crashing down on him. Or nearly on him. At the last second, he vanished, opening a red door in the red fire and flitting away, back into the hell I'd fashioned for him.

I summoned my will and shut the passage, sealing him in there.

Then I walked away, slowly descending the stairs as the tower burned around me.

THE WHOLE CITY burned.

By the time I exited the castle and reached my stallion where it waited beside the moat, the great tower was spouting black smoke at every window. I could hear its wooden supports cracking and splintering. I could hear its big stones grinding and shifting as the mortar that held them in place softened under the heat.

I swept into the saddle and spurred the big beast away. As I rode, my victorious invaders fell into rank behind me. I was leading them across the bridges and down the hill when the high tower collapsed in on itself, the flaming debris crumbling into the core of the structure.

By the time we reached the graveyard again, the entire castle complex had begun to explode behind us. Building after building burst apart where it stood, the debris flying through the air every which way, the heat washing down over us in a billow. My stallion reared and whinnied and spread its wings, but I wrestled it down. I did not want to leave my troops leaderless in the fire. I lifted my sword to rally them behind me. We crossed the cemetery in a hurrying mass. The earth rumbled under us as we went. The last stone monuments shivered and toppled over. Soft explosions hurled dirt in sudden armloads through the air, and snaking tendrils of green gas glowed and then ignited to the right and left of us. Fire rose up from the earth and turned the atmosphere a hellish red.

We rode on. We reached the edge of the castle hill. I looked down and saw fires burning everywhere below me. Great thunderous concussions shook the buildings as the flames licked through their windows and out their doors. I could see patches of gathered gas exploding, pyres of corpses reigniting in the squares. I saw my forces regrouping and moving in a dark tide toward the city's gates. Here and there, I could make out the flesh-hung skeletons of starving citizens emerging from their hiding places to join the exodus. There were no more signs of battle anywhere. The fighting was over. The day was won.

I snapped the stallion's reins and let him spread his wings. We lifted up into the air above Eastrim. The cavalry joined me there. The infantry moved on below. I looked down and watched as my whole host—a huge black mass of humanity—poured over the shattered walls and out into the open country, the city's survivors stumbling after. My stallion's wings beat the air in a slow, majestic rhythm. We rose higher and higher, the sky around us shaking as more and more explosions sounded below us.

I stood watch in the smoke until my armies were clear of Eastrim. Then I and my stallion soared up above the miasma into the heights of the clean, clear morning. I looked down through the mist one last time and saw the buildings tilting—falling—the earth opening—flames spewing up from the exposed tunnels—the whole city sinking, tumbling, crumbling into the ever-widening pit of raging flames.

34

IT WAS NEARLY DUSK AGAIN WHEN WE GATHERED IN Tauratanio's clearing. I and Cambitus, Favian, Maud, and Natani stood together by the oak and waited for night to fall. My weary armies were spread all through the forest. I could see the lights of their campfires flickering among the trees, melding with the last bright rays of the setting sun. I could hear the people singing hymns of celebration.

A strange sorrow had come over me now, a strange mingling of sorrow and of joy. Victory was ours, but the city had fallen. The quest was successful, but the journey was coming to an end.

As the sun began to disappear beneath the horizon, as the rays of its light receded over the forest floor, drawn back toward the edge of gathering twilight, I moved away from my companions. I went and stood beside the river, alone. I looked across the water into the darkening trees. I thought about where I had left myself back in Los Angeles. Outside the Tower, unarmed, surrounded by onrushing guards. What would become of me, I wondered.

I heard a light footstep on the leaves behind me. I smiled to myself. I knew it was Maud.

"My Emperor," she murmured softly.

I turned to face her. In the last of the light, I let my eyes linger on her elfin beauty. How happy she looked. How much in love.

"You don't have to call me that," I told her.

"But it's who you are."

I let out a broken sigh. "It's who I am for now while I'm here, but I can already feel myself leaving."

Her lips quivered. She frowned. "Yes. I know."

"I'm going away from here, aren't I?"

She nodded again, her eyes glistening.

"I will miss you very much," I told her.

She reached out impulsively and rested her cool, unsteady hand on my elbow. She said nothing.

I tried to smile at her. "I'm afraid, you know," I said. "I'm afraid of what I'll become when I'm gone. I don't know what I'll do without you to annoy me and advise me. Without the emperor inside me. I'm afraid to be alone."

Maud gave a little puff of laughter through her tears. "You will never be alone, Austin," she said. Still holding my elbow, she moved closer to me. She looked up at me. Her damp cheeks reflected the gloaming. "I've been a good friend to you, haven't I?"

"Always," I said. "An incredibly irritating, incredibly good friend."

"And a good advisor."

"Likewise irritating, but yes, the best."

"Then let me advise you now, before you go."

I drew a deep breath. I nodded.

Maud went on. "Nothing you have seen here vanishes. Nothing you have won is ever lost. You know the place to which you are returning. It is a place of flickering shadows masquerading as the real. You know there will be trouble there, and worse than trouble, and pain and worse than pain. You will be surrounded by corruption always and evil sometimes, and you will be tempted to despair."

"So far, not encouraged," I told her.

"Then remember this," said Maud. "This, which your good friend tells you: Despair is a delusion. The battle is over, Austin. You have already conquered. Victory is yours."

"Ah, Maud!" I said, my voice breaking.

"Can you remember that?"

I bit my lip. I shook my head. "I don't know."

"Try. Try to remember," Maud said. "Then all will be well."

With that, the sun went down. The woods went dark except for the campfires visible in the distance all around us. Maud took my hand and led me to rejoin our friends beside the oak.

We waited there together. And barely had the evening spread beneath the trees when the weird sights and sounds of the forest gathered around us. The wings of fairies humming, their colored lights. The white of misty nymphs rising from the river and their sweet songs. The drums of trolls, the trumpets of the centaurs, the pan pipes of fauns all blending into a sweet silence of pervasive music as the creatures assembled under the branches to await their king and queen.

Tauratanio and Magdala came as they always came, on chariots of starlight. They descended among us and sat on their moonlight thrones.

I approached the king alone. I inclined my head first to his noble queen, then to him.

"Your Highness," I said.

He rose, taking his wife's hand, and she rose, and they stepped forward to greet me.

"My Emperor," they answered together.

Tauratanio, crowned with leaves and wreathed in smiles, lifted his voice so all his creatures could hear him, but he spoke to me. "These lands belong to you now, Emperor, sea to sea."

I bowed my head and answered: "And because you saved Elinda's life, Your Highness, I grant this forest to you and your queen forever."

"We will rule here as you and your queen rule everywhere. Let wisdom reign and each man go his way."

The strange company of the woods let out a sound that was something like a cheer and something like a choir singing.

I waited for them to grow quiet, then I raised my voice and said, "But how, then, shall I reign without my wisdom, Tauratanio? The danger is finally over, my friend. Bring the queen home."

With that, the whole moonlit forest came to a silent hesitation. We waited. Tauratanio took one step toward the oak and lifted up his hands. The great tree glowed and creaked and began to open at the center. From far away came the jarring noise of traffic and confusion. As we all stood watching, a doorway opened into another kingdom: LA.

A moment later, Ellen Evermore stepped from the broken city into Shadow Wood, transforming into Queen Elinda as she came. Her blouse and skirt became a golden robe that dazzled even in the forest evening. Her golden hair acquired a sun-bright crown that haloed her with light.

Behind her, in the blurred and fading city, I could see the mad, addicted homeless gathering shoulder to shoulder, dumbstruck, dazed, raising their hands to her in farewell. I imagined they'd tell the world what they had seen until the doctors gave them enough medication to make them forget.

The portal closed, but the great oak went on glowing. As Queen Elinda stepped clear, King Cambitus, the not altogether wise, cried out in happiness. His daughter smiled and wept at once as she came into his arms and he embraced her. He held her a long time and then Magdala held her. Then the king took her by the hand and led her to the emperor, to me.

The last time I saw them—the last time I saw any of them— they were all gathered around the King of Shadow Wood as he performed the double wedding ceremony with due solemnity. The fairies flashed their rainbow lights, the misty nymphs sang, and all the creatures played their instruments as King Cambitus presented Elinda to Anastasius, and Magdala stood by Maud and Natani, playing mother of the bride. The king pronounced the rites over both beaming couples simultaneously.

I could never be quite sure when I detached from the emperor and became only myself again. I think it was when the queen reached out to me—to him—and took his hand. Some shock of completion seemed to dislodge me from his body then. I felt myself reeling gently away into the night, back and away from him toward the glowing oak as it opened once again into a portal so that I could drift through it, a free spirit, alone.

The magic wood grew small and distant, then faded to darkness like the end of a movie.

35

THE NEXT SECOND, EVERYTHING WAS BRAIN-SHATTER-
ing noise and blinding lights. I was standing, goggle-eyed, within
the fence of the Tower compound, an army of guards rushing at
me, their weapons drawn as they screamed curses and threats. I saw
at least a dozen pistols and rifles pointed at my face. I stood there,
frozen with confusion, shock, and fear, too dazed and stupid to fight
or run.

"Hold it right there!" the guards screamed.

"Hands up!"

"Move and I'll blow your head off!"

Their shouts were nearly swallowed by the screaming sirens.
But I understood them well enough. I raised my hands as they
surrounded me. It was a hell of an end to a double wedding in a
magic wood.

One man—a guard—a captain—stepped from the crowd and
strolled casually toward me, holstering his pistol as he came. He
was taller than I was and stared down at me with eyes narrowed in
disdain. Slowly, deliberately, he drew a club from his belt and tapped
it against his thigh. He fixed his eyes on me, silently daring me to
make a move.

The sirens screamed. The searchlights flashed around us, crossing the night-shadowed compound fence to fence. *Tap, tap, tap* went the captain's billy.

A long time passed that way. My hands still raised, I looked around me. I tried to enter Emperor Mode, to see the Soul Leeches that fed on the corrupt, to try to open a passage into the hell beneath reality so that I could fight my way through the devils there and escape from this place.

But it was no good. I couldn't do it. I couldn't see the real-beneath-the-real. I couldn't make a portal in the surface of the world. I couldn't locate that level of consciousness within myself. It was no longer available. I felt like a character at the end of a video game who has acquired all sorts of weapons and powers and now has to start the sequel stripped of them all, with nothing left to fight with but his fists and the ability to jump up and down like some kind of idiot.

My heart sank, and a pall of sorrow draped me head to toe. Where was my sword? My armor? Where were my armies and the voices shouting "Hail!" Where were even my magic friends to encourage me? I felt lost and abandoned on the hostile planet of everyday existence.

The sirens stopped, all of them together. Silence—a city silence full of the whisper and rumble of traffic—settled over us as the sweeping lights came to rest on the gates where we all were gathered.

The captain went on looking down at me, went on tapping his club against his thigh. He was a formidable figure with skin the color of dark chocolate and with a thin patina of black hair on his narrow skull. He was tall and fit and wide and straight as a ramrod.

In the sudden quiet after the alarms, a woman's rough voice called to him.

"He's dead, Cap."

The captain glanced over his shoulder—and I glanced. I saw

Orosgo's butler-assassin lying spread-eagle on the asphalt, felled by his own bullet, dead in a pool of his own blood.

The captain looked back at me and scowled darkly. I wondered what sort of demon had its teeth sunk into the core of him, but I couldn't see.

"You son of a bitch," he growled at me.

His club stopped tapping. I saw his fist tighten on the shaft. He deked me with a sidelong glance, and instinctively, I dropped my hands and reached across my body for my sword.

My hand closed on useless nothing. No weapon at my side. No armor surrounding me. Of course not.

My powers—all my powers—they're all gone. That was my last thought before the captain's club smacked into the side of my head.

I felt the world career away from me. My eyes rolled up. My legs wobbled. My body crumpled to the ground. My mind was drowned in darkness.

VAGUELY, I REMEMBER being hauled semiconscious on wobbly legs to the nearby Men's Facility. I gazed stupidly at one hostile face after another as they processed me through fingerprinting and mug shots and a humiliating cavity search. I fought to regain my senses, muttering drunken nothings at one guard after another. Bloody drool rolled down my chin as two guards shackled me, seized me by the arms, and marched me into the core of the jail.

We crossed a common area of open cots surrounded by yellow cell doors with plexiglass windows. We headed toward a metal stairway in one corner.

I started to come around, look around. What a nightmare place this was, full of men weeping on their cots, rocking on them with their heads in their hands. Voices screaming from the cells. Shadowy figures pounding on the windows with both fists.

These weren't criminals. Not all of them anyway. Many were simply madmen. Left on the streets until they snapped and did violence, then locked up here.

The guards marched me up to the next tier, then marched me down the tier past one yellow door after another. Prisoners pressed their faces to the windows and watched me go. I heard them shouting, their voices muffled by the thick steel of the doors. Hard to make out the words—but I thought one of them called out to me, "My Emperor. Free us!" Or maybe I just wished for that in my heartbroken solitude.

We came to rest before the last door on the tier. The latch buzzed loudly, and one guard worked the door open. The other guard took off my shackles and hurled me, staggering, over the threshold.

Then the door slammed shut behind me.

I reeled, my head throbbing. I blinked at the walls, at the steel toilet, at the cramped bunk bed. To my still-foggy mind, the cell seemed about the size of a shoebox. And if that didn't make me claustrophobic enough, add to it the fact there was a humongous three-hundred-pound beast of a lunatic evildoer sitting on the bottom bunk, his gigantic feet taking up most of the open floor space.

The monster was studying the floor and muttering when I first saw him. Then suddenly, he raised his face. Even with him sitting down, his face was level with mine: a pale-brown countenance of pure crazy. He only had one eye. The other socket was empty and wrinkled and gray. He stared at me with his single pulsing orb. He growled like an animal.

"Easy, dude," I muttered at him.

Apparently, that was exactly the wrong thing to say. Maybe there was no right thing. In any case, the moment I spoke, he leapt to his feet, enormous, roaring. In that cramped space, there was only half an inch between his great belly and my nose. His eye glared down at me from an unimaginable height.

He lifted a great brown fist like a wrecking ball—raised it all the way up to the ceiling, ready to drop it on top of my head.

I jabbed my hand between his legs and made a fist.

His roar changed to a breathless howl. He doubled over, clutching himself. I braced my feet in what little floor space remained to me, dropped my fist low, and swung as hard as I could at his head. I heard the hinge of his jaw crack as I connected. He smashed into the bunk, then tumbled to the floor so hard the whole cell trembled.

"That probably wasn't as much fun as you thought it was going to be," I said.

I stepped over the mound of his body to the door. I pounded on the window.

"Man down!" I shouted.

I heard footsteps clanging on the tier outside. The door buzzed again and opened. The captain of the guard was standing there, glaring at me. It was as if he'd been waiting for a call.

I glared back at him. "If you want something done right," I told him, "do it yourself, you son of a bitch."

For a second I thought he *would* do it, right then and there. He went on glaring, and if eyes could shoot death rays, I'd have been cinders. But after a long moment, he turned away and gestured down the tier. One of the guards who'd brought me here stepped back into the cell, grabbed the fallen giant by his giant wrists, and dragged him out.

The captain of the guard remained where he was in the doorway. I remained where I was in the cell. We looked at each other in silence. The shouts and moans and wailings of the jail surrounded us.

He smiled with one corner of his mouth. "Just wait," he said. "We have all the time in the world. You're not going anywhere."

He slammed the door in my face, and I heard the bolt shoot home.

Breathing hard, I returned to the bed, one hand massaging the bruise on my head where the captain's billy had smacked me. I climbed up onto the top bunk and lay down on my back. The bare bulb in the ceiling was inches from my face. It burned hot and bright. I flung my arm across my eyes to shield them.

In that near darkness, with the madhouse cries crawling over the cell walls like ants and spiders, I thought back to the wedding in Shadow Wood—I reached back for it with my whole soul. I tried to hear the music of the creatures in the forest. I tried to see the rainbow fairy lights under the evening branches. I tried to see, in the red-blackness behind my eyelids, the emperor and his queen, their hands linked together, Maud and her magician lover, gazing into one another's eyes. I tried to remember the benevolent faces of the forest king and queen as the king pronounced the words of the ceremony that would transform the two couples before him into husbands and wives . . .

But no. How gone it was. So gone. The woods, the creatures, Galiana, and all the Eleven Lands—gone utterly. A whole world of wonders—a whole life of adventure, heroism, and love lost to me forever. Was it ever real, or was it all imagination?

Because here—here in this cell—there was no music, no light, no love. My Jane—where was she? Was she still alive? Was she hurt? Was she free—had Carnation and the three poker players escaped with her—or had the police run them down? Had the sight of the world beneath the world driven her mad? And even if she was sane, would she ever be able to prove her innocence? Would I ever be with her again?

And what about my sister? That poor drugged child locked helpless in that hellhole with Hillary Baine for an overseer . . .

Lying on the bunk with my arm across my eyes, I let out a

trembling sigh. I could feel the walls of the cell pressing close around me. I could hear the cries of the mad and evil and imprisoned men. The captain of the guard was right. I wasn't going anywhere. I was trapped here, helpless. What could I do but wait—wait until one of my brother's minions came to put an end to me?

Hiding my eyes behind my arm, I let out a long, broken breath.

Be a man, I told myself, trying to imitate that squirrelly voice I remembered, that Maud I loved.

Then I shuddered where I lay and I began to cry.

THOSE HOURS—THOSE long night hours in that cell—those were the darkest hours of my life. I thought they were the end of my life, the end of my story. What was left for me but the moment when Richard's killers came through the yellow door, when his ubiquitous forces hunted down Carnation and Jane, when some nurse with a tender smile injected Riley with poison and sent her into a final oblivion?

I had no other expectations. I had no hope at all, lying there. In Shadow Wood—if there even was such a place—I was a conqueror. I had completed my quest. I had crossed the Eleven Lands. I had brought the talisman to the emperor. We had returned together to destroy Curtin's forces and bring down his corrupted city. We had freed the people and the creatures from sea to sea, restored the queen to the throne of Galiana, and brought together the emperor and his love.

But that was there—and as always, now that I had returned, it seemed unreal, a mere fantasy. Maybe my triumphs in that other country were hallucinated make-believe, a dream to distract me from the utter disaster of my actual life. Because here—here, in this cell, in this material moment—the world was all Orosgo, all Richard. I was alone. The battle was lost.

That's what I thought anyway. That's what I believed in those imprisoned, suicidal hours.

But the truth was different. The truth was: everything I thought—everything I believed—every little bit of it—was completely wrong.

The truth was, even here, even in this undeniably real and tragic place, the battle was over—and I had won. Outside my cell, the forces of the emperor—my forces—were everywhere on the march, and Orosgo's forces, my brother's forces, were collapsing into defeat and disarray.

Even as I lay there in despair and tears, my armies were taking back the planet.

Despair, as it turned out, was a delusion. Victory—as it turned out—was mine.

36

JANE HAD ESCAPED ALIVE—THAT WAS THE FIRST THING. Carnation, crazy driver that he was, had pushed his old white van beyond the limits of its power, and for ten whole minutes after streaking away from the Tower, he had outstripped the entire screaming cavalry of patrol cars on his tail. As he rocketed through the city, more cop cars raced to join the chase, and helicopters took to the sky to track him. A few moments more and Carnation and his crew and his sweet cargo—Jane—would all have been caught in an inescapable web of expert pursuit.

But just then, the van careened around a downtown corner onto a dark block of abandoned warehouses and sped into the deep shadows of an empty lane on which all the streetlamps had gone strangely dark. Only one cruiser was close enough to see the turn and follow. That cruiser was driven by a young Latino so handsome he looked like an actor playing a cop on some TV show. His partner—the husky, red-haired oaf in the passenger seat—radioed their location to the cars behind them—then whooped with glee as the scream of their siren was joined by the scream of their smoking tires taking the corner in the van's wake.

But the next second, the patrol car seemed to fly out of control. It skidded, the body rocking, and turned sideways. The handsome young Latino wrestled the wheel and hit the brake until the cruiser jolted to a stop sidelong, blocking the street. The next three cruisers came around the corner fast and had to swerve to miss the first car where it sat still, its flashers making the night go bright and dark. One cop car hopped a sidewalk, smacked into a fire hydrant, and stalled as a jet of water shot up into its engine. Another cruiser turned full around so that its headlights blinded the driver of the next. That driver was forced to swerve right, and the two cruisers scraped metal before both came to rest at angles, fully stopped.

Carnation's white van disappeared down the dark street as more and more cruisers piled up behind it.

In the lead patrol car—the car that had caused the jam-up in the first place—the handsome Latino driver watched Carnation vanish, then turned to his partner and shook his head ruefully.

"I guess he'll go his way," he said.

The red-haired oaf nodded solemnly. "Let wisdom reign," he answered.

MINUTES LATER, CARNATION'S van parked beside an idling Escalade. The Escalade's driver threw open the door and the Aztec poker player, with the bloody, unconscious Jane in his arms, hurried from one vehicle to the other. Carnation, the bald poker player, and the black poker player followed after quickly—and off the Escalade raced.

When Jane awoke, she was in the cigar-stinky little poker room behind the barbershop downtown. The barber had set up a cot for her against the paneled wall under the girlie calendar. He had called in two women—a doctor and a nurse. They cared for Jane's wounds and dressed her in fresh clothes while the men waited in the shop outside.

When the doctor allowed the men to come in, they found Jane sitting up on the cot and looking around her, faintly mystified.

The nurse, who objected to the calendar, was in the process of pulling it down and tossing it into the waste bin.

"Hey," said Carnation, annoyed.

She gave him a look over her shoulder. She had creamy caramel-colored skin and just the sort of compact, busty figure Carnation always fancied. He decided to stow his objections for now in the hopes he could make a play for her later.

The doctor, meanwhile, explained that Jane's wounds were mostly just scratches, though there were a couple of ugly gouges on one of her thighs.

"It looks like an animal attacked me," Jane said, peeking under one blood-stained bandage. "But I can't imagine how something like that could have happened." She fell silent and her gaze grew distant as she tried to reason it out. The men and women in the room hovered over her with concern.

Then she came back to herself. She smiled up at them, a bright, angelic smile. They were all surprised at how beautiful she actually was when she wasn't trying to hide it.

"Austin came to rescue me," she said. "That's the last thing I remember."

THAT SAME NIGHT, almost that same hour, Death—Death, its mighty self—Death, that unwitting servant of creation—also became my ally.

The news had reached the media: Orosgo was gone. And my brother, Richard, was discovering that taking over his global enterprise was not going to be as simple as he'd hoped. The people the old Russian had put in place around the world—the company heads and media moguls and politicians and investors—were, after all, wealthy and powerful creatures in their own rights. They did not see why the apparatus of communication and control should fall into the hands of an upstart intellectual like my brother just because the old man had taken a liking to him. The old man was dead. That was the whole point. Death had erased him and all his influence. He no longer had anything to say about what happened here in the land of the living.

Richard had spent every moment since his patron's passing contacting the leaders of his organization around the world, trying to bring them into line with his new regime. Some of these calls went unanswered, and that alone made Richard suspicious. But then—ah, then—the story exploded on every media: Jane Janeway, the killer of Alexis Merriwether, had escaped from prison. And who had helped her get away? Reportedly, it was Richard's annoying brother—namely me.

Now this was unhappy news for Orosgo's minions around the world. Hadn't they been promised Jane would be taken care of? And wasn't Richard's brother supposed to be dead by now—like, dead three times over? The minute he heard about this, Richard knew he was in trouble. It made him look incompetent and weak. And that, in the current crisis, was dangerous.

Sure enough, as midnight passed into moonless morning, four of the gunmen who had served as Orosgo's bodyguards, now secretly in the employ of the motherly tech mogul Susan Roth, moved quietly through the hallways of Orosgo's mountain mansion. Two of them entered the guest room where my mother and father were sleeping. The two others crept down the hall toward the small study where my brother was pacing the floor. If the gunmen who went after my parents had not fired their weapons a few seconds early, Richard would have been caught off guard and assassinated where he stood. But even through the suppressors, the gunshots that killed Mom and Dad were loud enough to be heard through the house. In a panic of sudden fear, Richard escaped through a window and managed to gather the remaining loyal bodyguards around him for protection.

At least he thought they were loyal. He hoped they were.

BY THE TIME the sun rose, everything had changed. My parents had been found dead in their bed. Richard had vanished. Gerald Hannity was said to have handed in his resignation at the cable news company he ran and gone on indefinite vacation to Venezuela. A United States senator had overdosed on sleeping pills. It was said he might suffer brain damage, though it was uncertain whether he would lose his job.

Hillary Baine left home for the Orosgo Retreat that morning a full hour early. As her BMW sped up the road to the forbidding mansion, she saw the police cruisers gathered in the lot outside. She brought her car to a jolting stop. She stepped out and looked over the rise. Grim-faced law officers were leading her patients—gaping and stupid with drugs—out of the mansion into the bright new day. Hillary Baine jumped back in her Beamer, turned the car around, and sped away; no one knew where.

By the next day, even at the media outlets where Orosgo had handpicked the leadership, journalists were beginning to ask questions. Editors and publishers were trying to distract them by calling for more stories about Jane, more stories about Alexis. *Get me more on the big Hollywood murder!* they were saying. *Bring me more on the trial of the century!* But the reporters couldn't help noticing that that story was beginning to seem part of a bigger story, much bigger. CEOs who had been members of the 730 Club were resigning or issuing statements through their PR departments full of vague apologies and excuses. Law officers in big cities around the country were suddenly calling press conferences to demand investigations into the systemic corruption within their own departments. Heads of news operations and even heads of whole TV networks were being accused of financial and sexual malfeasance that had been hidden for decades. What the hell was going on? some journalists were wondering.

Then, a day later, in a whispering aspen grove in the mountainous wastelands just outside of Los Angeles, the morning quiet was disturbed by the grind of engines and the thunking of vehicle doors being swung shut. After a long moment of breeze-blown stillness beneath the trees, a small army of federal and local law officers came marching up the hill toward the woods. They were carrying shovels over their shoulders. Two backhoes followed after them like pet dinosaurs.

These, it soon became known, were members of a task force that had originally been formed two years before to investigate the trade in sex slaves out of Mexico. Apparently that investigation had changed direction. No one knew who had given them the order to start digging in the aspen woods, though later, many of their bosses would take credit for the decision.

No one knew, either, who sent the four policemen to waylay Solomon Vine's private jet as it tried to take off from the airport in Burbank. Vine's lawyers were on the phone to the police chief almost immediately, demanding to know why their client had been led away in handcuffs. What was the meaning of it? Who was this Detective Amadis Carnation? What the hell did he think he was up to? Was he unaware of who Solomon Vine was and how many buildings had been named after him? The chief of police said he would check it out and get back to them. He never did get back to them.

Not long after, the endless stories about Alexis's murder and Jane's escape quite suddenly ended. They were replaced first by rumors and then reports and finally official announcements that Solomon Vine had been charged with multiple counts of murder, and that he was negotiating a plea deal and naming names.

The nation's business seemed to stop for a moment as people gathered around their devices and watched the videos of the little bodies being carried on stretchers down the hill from the aspen grove to the ambulances waiting on the road below. It was shocking how few of these show-biz children had been reported missing, shocking how many of their parents, while disappointed to have fallen short of the grand prize of celebrity, had settled for the consolation prize of cold, hard cash. It was shocking, too, how many of Orosgo's most influential associates had used their money and power to indulge this one particular sexual predilection—and shocking, finally, how many of them had been willing to have their victims killed to keep that predilection a secret.

Try as they might, even Orosgo's news media could not hide this story forever. The whole internet had it now, and the truth came out.

Over the following days, the aspen grove came to be known as the Children's Forest.

ALL THIS TIME, I lay in my cell, despairing. Day after day—two whole weeks. The guards would not let me out, even to exercise. They would not let me communicate with the other prisoners. No visitors came. No news reached me. I heard nothing about Jane, nothing about Riley. I did not know if they were dead or alive. I feared the worst. The fear ate at me.

When the guards brought me food, I demanded a lawyer. When

the lights went out at night, I waited for an assassin. No lawyer arrived and no assassin either. Even the captain of the guard was gone. I never saw him again.

I had no idea what was happening or what would happen next.

Then, on the fourteenth day, at dawn, I was awakened by the jarring buzz of the cell unlocking. I rolled off my bunk and landed on my feet as the door swung open. I saw a single guard standing outside on the tier.

At first, I just stared at him, gormless, and he stared at me. Then it occurred to me he was waiting for me to step out of the cell.

I stepped out. He shut the door and walked ahead of me. After a moment of hesitation, I followed.

Jail—as I had noticed over the last two weeks—was a remarkably noisy place. It was like the city itself, never really silent. Voices, ventilation, metallic bangs, and buzzing locks were always filling the air with discord. Guards shouted commands. Prisoners shouted curses. Worst of all were the madmen in their misery who cried out against the demons no sane man could see.

But now—now as I followed the guard down the stairs into the common area—there was a strange quiet in the place. There was a man standing at every cell window, peering out. The men on the open cots were sitting up. Even the madmen seemed to have paused in their tormented soliloquies. No one was saying anything. All of them were watching me—watching me go.

More doors unlocked, and I was led out into the processing area—and there stood a tall, gangly, and goofy-looking fellow, blinking behind his large glasses and clutching a battered briefcase in his two hands.

"Feltz!" I cried in amazement.

For so it was. Jane's lawyer, Roland Feltz.

A guard stationed in the cubbyhole in the wall handed me a plastic bag. Feltz gestured at it.

"Your street clothes," he said. "Put them on."

As I dressed, he brought me up to date: the arrests, the discoveries, the suicides, the escapes. The corporate news media—the core of Orosgo's enterprise—was doing everything it could to keep the public from connecting all these incidents together. Elected officials were appearing on TV to make mocking, dismissive comments about "conspiracy theories," and the social media sites were quick to ban anyone who tried to link numerous disparate events to the death of Serge Orosgo. "We will not allow the voices of hate to speak on our platforms," said one social media CEO.

But the independent websites were beginning to put the picture together. Obscure legal blogs were filing Freedom of Information Act requests with reluctant law enforcement agencies. Angry citizens were calling talk radio. The kooks and cranks were ranting on their podcasts. On one block in Manhattan, an anonymous street artist papered a construction barrier with images of my face, and the blood-red words splashed across it: *Free Austin Lively!*

I tried to take all this information in as Feltz escorted me out through the security gates. By then, he was explaining how he had gone before a judge to demand I be arraigned immediately or released. The district attorney had tried to oppose him, but her office was, it seemed, in a chaos of confusion. First, they accused me of murdering Orosgo's butler-assassin. But that charge was mysteriously dropped after it turned out the butler-assassin had been employed by Orosgo and had no business being on the scene in the first place. On top of that, he had been killed by a bullet from his own gun, and how had that happened? Reports that I had deflected the slug with some kind of high-tech weapon were dismissed with ridicule, especially after the security tape—albeit weirdly digitalized and blurred—showed nothing of the kind.

The DA then tried to hit me with aiding and abetting an escape, but those charges, too, fell away after a closed-door conference between the prosecutor and the chief of police. The chief was a much-celebrated local character who had enjoyed the glamorous perks of his job, like photo ops with movie stars and consultations on television shows and parties with Hollywood luminaries such as Solomon Vine. Lately, however, he had begun to complain to friends that he'd been lying awake at nights. He said his conscience was eating at him. It felt, he said, as if a gigantic leech were sitting on his chest, sucking out his soul. He was ready to make a change.

In any case, the escape charges against me were also dropped. In fact, the new official line was that Jane hadn't escaped at all. She had been released after her innocence was established by conscientious police work. The confusion arose because our heroic DA had had to act quickly to save Jane from a conspiracy to do her harm in jail.

Feltz rattled all this off with such breathless rapidity I could barely take any of it in. But as we began walking together toward the glass doors that led out of the jail and into the open air, I turned to him, blinking stupidly in my confusion. I said, "You mean I'm free?"

He held the door open for me. "You're free, Austin," he said—and he smiled broadly. "Go your way."

I stepped through the door—and if ever there was a portal that transitioned me from one world into another, it was that one.

Because there was Jane waiting for me—Jane, surrounded by Carnation and the other poker players. And before I could even comprehend the reality of it, she was in my arms, my own most girly of girls, and I was pressing her against me as if I could meld her body wholly with my own.

I rested my cheek against her silken hair and turned my face up to the sky. I was still trying to understand what Feltz had told me, what was happening here on the outside, happening everywhere, what it all meant. But I couldn't. I was too dazzled by the rapid flow of events. I couldn't make any sense of it. It would be a long time—a long time—before I would begin to comprehend the reality: that, with the information I had gotten about Orosgo's obsessions, with the names and histories I had gathered from the 730 Club, with the things I had seen at Solomon Vine's party, and with the things I had deduced about what lay beneath the aspen trees, I had all but single-handedly unraveled a vast conspiracy to lead the world into blithe, unwitting slavery, and I had given the forces that opposed that conspiracy the upper hand—at least, for now.

But while I didn't fully grasp all that until much later, even then, in that moment, standing there outside the jail, holding Jane so close and loving her so much, I did have my first small intimation of the truth: this fight might well go on forever, but the day was mine.

I pressed my face against Jane's and touched her ear with my lips.

"Well, then," I whispered to her softly. "Let wisdom reign."

Epilogue

SO WHAT NOW? Well, here's what I can tell you.

There is a house on a cliff above the ocean, a rambling old cabin battered by the wind. I bought it outright with the last of my movie money, and I live there quite comfortably off the advance from a book contract plus a surprisingly large inheritance that Riley and I split between us, with a portion set aside for Richard, should he ever show up to make a claim.

The house has three large bedrooms, one for my wife and me, one for Riley, and one we're preparing for the baby. Eventually I guess we'll need a bigger place with more bedrooms for the rest of the babies. Because there are going to be a lot of babies. A lot, a lot of babies.

Riley spends her days by the seaside. She walks along the sand and sings sad songs into the wind. Sometimes she returns to the house and goes into her bedroom and records one of her videos. She explains how the Illuminati and the space aliens have been dispersed but not defeated, that they are regrouping even as the authorities pretend they were never there. She doesn't post the videos online. Which is just as well. Because I suspect she's right in her own crazy way, and it's best her enemies don't find out how much she knows.

I don't know whether Richard is alive or dead, but a lot of Orosgo's other disciples are plenty alive and even thriving. Their news outlets and entertainment studios and experts and politicians have done a marvelous job convincing the public that—as an editorial in the *New York Times* put it—the "exposure of isolated areas of corruption should not be allowed to undermine our faith in our institutions." It's only the usual cranks and crazies who keep insisting those areas aren't isolated, that the arrests and murders and suicides and disappearances are all one story, and that corruption is the very soul of the machine.

So the time goes by and it will be as it will be. The world belongs to the people in it. You can't force them to accept the truth. You can't chain them to their freedom.

Riley is healthy and even happy sometimes, and that's the important thing. And Jane is happy—happier than I've ever seen anyone be happy in fact. Taking care of her house—her house instead of some movie star's mansion—taking care of Riley, taking care of me, feeding the life inside her: all this gives her enormous joy. Plus she spends a lot of time reading books about babies. I guess she will have to know a lot about babies. We are going to have a lot of babies. Have I mentioned that already? Well, we are.

As for me, I write my book in the morning. How I exposed Orosgo's enterprise. The philosophy he tried to sell through my brother and his other minions. The threat to our freedom he created, and how that threat can be opposed and maybe even destroyed. In the afternoon, I do research and interviews. And I travel occasionally to make speeches to anyone who will listen. In the evenings, I relax on the deck outside. Jane brings me a glass of wine, and we sit together and watch the sun set gloriously behind the red waters.

And when we fall silent, just before twilight, I sometimes think back over what happened—what really happened, I mean. I remember Betheray, her rose and ivory body beautiful in my arms. I remember the squirrel-girl Maud coming to my cell to rescue me, and the young woman Maud and that heart-wrenching sound she made when her lover stepped out of the lake. I remember the monster in the nightmare mansion. I remember Curtin vanishing amidst the flames. And I remember the Emperor Anastasius in a forest full of glittering music in that moment he took the hand of Queen Elinda and made his wisdom his bride.

I often remember something else too, when dusk settles over the ocean. I remember myself—myself as a child. Playing with plastic figures against a backdrop made to look like starry space. Moving my little knights and alien monsters into battle against each other. Creating tableaux. Whispering dialogue. Making movies of the mind.

I remember the stillness that was in me then—a perfect stillness of creation and delight. And I feel that stillness come upon me again as I turn and see Jane in the last glimmer of sunset, her hand resting on her belly.

And sure, I have to admit: there are times I miss the excitement of Hollywood. I always loved the movies and wanted so much to be part of the business, and now I don't think I ever will. There are a lot of people in that town—a lot of powerful people—who used to love to attend Solomon Vine's glamorous Malibu parties. These days, they give interviews about how much they hate him for the terrible things he did. But the truth is, as much as they say they hate him, they know I helped expose him for what he was, and for that, they hate me more.

As I said, it will be as it will be. I don't really know what will happen next. But I am confident—confident all will be well. I hope for the best because I know despair is a delusion. Victory is already mine.

For now, I am content in my house on the cliff above the ocean. Writing my book in the daytime. Drinking wine with Jane as evening falls. It's a good life. A beautiful life. My sister walks by the sea and sings. My wife keeps house and grows our baby. The glorious darkness comes and then the glorious morning.

And I? I have no sword. I have no shield, no armor, no magic power left to me. I continue the fight with the only weapon that remains:

I tell my story.

THE END